Praise for Elin Hilderbrand's

28 Summers

"In her twenty-fifth novel, Elin Hilderbrand gets everything right and leaves her ardent fans hungry for number twenty-six. Hilderbrand sets the gold standard in escapist fiction." —*Kirkus Reviews*

"Summer on Hilderbrand's Nantucket is never dull. This time she focuses on former lovers who now lead separate lives but share an island idyll once a year. Captivating and bittersweet." —*People*

"This sweeping love story is Hilderbrand's best ever...Her stories are relatable in an aspirational way, but her attention to detail is what makes her characters feel like living, breathing people you want to know. They would never skimp on citronella candles; they would save the least creaky rocking chair for you."
—Elisabeth Egan, *New York Times Book Review*

"Hilderbrand steers this tightly written novel with ease and skill...Less a story about a secretive affair and more a tale of sweet nostalgia and fate, *28 Summers* will be popular with a wide audience."
—*Library Journal*

"An unabashedly romantic read."
—Christina Ianzito, AARP

28 Summers

ALSO BY ELIN HILDERBRAND

28 Summers

A Novel

Elin Hilderbrand

Little, Brown and Company
New York   Boston   London

Copyright © 2020 by Elin Hilderbrand
Excerpt from *Golden Girl* copyright © 2021 by Elin Hilderbrand

Hachette Book Group supports the right to free expression and the value of copyright. The purpose of copyright is to encourage writers and artists to produce the creative works that enrich our culture.

The scanning, uploading, and distribution of this book without permission is a theft of the author's intellectual property. If you would like permission to use material from the book (other than for review purposes), please contact permissions@hbgusa.com. Thank you for your support of the author's rights.

Little, Brown and Company
Hachette Book Group
1290 Avenue of the Americas, New York, NY 10104
littlebrown.com

Little, Brown and Company is a division of Hachette Book Group, Inc. The Little, Brown name and logo are trademarks of Hachette Book Group, Inc.

The publisher is not responsible for websites (or their content) that are not owned by the publisher.

Printed in the United States of America

Originally published in hardcover by Little, Brown and Company, June 2020
First Little, Brown and Company mass market edition, June 2021

10 9 8 7 6 5 4 3 2 1

In memory of
Dorothea Benton Frank
(1951–2019)

I love you, Dottie. And I miss you.

Prologue

Fifties

Summer #28: 2020

What are we talking about in 2020? Kobe Bryant, Covid-19, social distancing, Zoom, TikTok, Navarro cheerleading, George Floyd, Ahmaud Arbery, and Breonna Taylor, and… The presidential election. A country divided. Opinions on both sides. It's everywhere: on the news, on the late-night shows, in the papers, online, online, online, in cocktail-party conversations, on college campuses, in airports, in line at Starbucks, around the bar at Margaritaville, at the gym (the guy who uses the treadmill at six a.m. sets TV number four to Fox News; the woman who comes in at seven a.m. immediately switches it to MSNBC). Kids stop speaking to parents over it; couples divorce; neighbors feud; consumers boycott; employees quit. Some feel fortunate to be alive at such an exciting time; they turn up the volume, become junkies. Others are sick of it; they press the mute button, they disengage. If one more person asks if they're registered to vote…

Turns out, there's a story this year that no one has heard yet. It's a story that started twenty-eight summers earlier and that only now—in the summer of 2020, on an island thirty miles off the coast—is coming to an end.

The end. Under the circumstances, this feels like the only place to start.

Mallory Blessing tells her son, Link: *There's an envelope in the third drawer of the desk. On the left. The one that sticks.* They all stick, Link thinks. His mother's cottage sits on a strip of land between ocean and pond; that's the good news. The bad news is...humidity. This is a home where doors don't close properly and towels never dry and if you open a bag of chips, you better eat them all in one sitting because they'll be stale within the hour. Link struggles with the drawer. He has to lift it up and wiggle it side to side in order to get it open.

He sees the envelope alone in the drawer. Written on the front: *Please call.*

Link is confused. This isn't what he expected. What he expected was his mother's will or a sappy letter filled with sage advice or instructions for her memorial service.

Link opens the envelope. Inside is one thin strip of paper. No name, just a number.

What am I supposed to do with this? he wonders.

Please call.

Okay, Link thinks. But who will answer? And what is Link supposed to say?

He would ask his mother, but her eyes are closed. She has fallen back to sleep.

Link walks out the back door of the cottage and along the sandy road that runs beside Miacomet Pond. It's June on Nantucket—sunny and sixty-seven degrees, so the nights and early mornings are still chilly, although the irises are blooming among the reeds and there's a pair of swans on the flat blue mirror of the pond.

Swans mate for life, Link thinks. This has always made them seem morally superior to other birds, although somewhere he read that swans cheat. He hopes that was an internet hoax.

Like most kids who were born and raised on this island, he's guilty of taking the scenery for granted. Link has also been guilty of taking his mother for granted, and now she's dying at the age of fifty-one. The melanoma has metastasized to her brain; she's blind in one eye. Her hospice care will start in the morning.

Link broke down crying when Dr. Symon talked to him, then again when he called Nantucket Hospice.

The RN case manager, Sabina, had a soothing manner. She encouraged Link to be present in each moment with his mother "through her transition." This was in response to Link confessing that he didn't know what he was going to do without her.

"I'm only nineteen," he said.

"Worry about later, later," Sabina said. "Your job now is to be with your mother. Let her feel your love. She'll take it with her where she's going."

Link punches the number on the strip of paper into his phone. It's an unfamiliar area code—notably *not* 206, Seattle, where his father lives. He can't imagine who this is. Link's grandparents are dead, and his uncle Cooper lives in DC. Coop and his wife, Amy, are splitting; it's his uncle's fifth divorce. Last week, when Mallory still had moments of clarity and humor, she said, *Coop gets married and divorced the way most people eat Triscuits.* Coop has offered to come up when it gets to be too much for Link to handle alone. This will be soon, maybe even tomorrow.

Does his mother have any other friends off-island? She stopped speaking to Leland when Link was in high school. *She's dead to me.*

Maybe this is Leland's new number. That would make sense; they should make peace before the end.

But a man answers the phone.

"Jake McCloud," he says.

It takes Link a second to process this. *Jake McCloud?* He hangs up.

He's so startled that he laughs, then glances at the back door of their cottage. Is this a *joke?* His mother has a sense of humor, certainly, but she's witty, not prone to pranks. Asking Link to call *Jake McCloud* on her deathbed just isn't something Mallory would do.

There must be an explanation. Link checks the number on the piece of paper against the number in his phone, then he looks up the area code, 574. It's Indiana—Mishawaka, Elkhart, South Bend.

South Bend!

Link cackles. He sounds crazy. What is going *on* here?

Just then, his phone rings. It's the 574 number, calling back. Link is tempted to let the call go to voice-mail. There has been a tremendous mistake. In all of his interviews, Jake McCloud seems like an extremely decent guy. Link could just explain the situation: His mother is dying and somehow Jake McCloud's number ended up in his mother's desk drawer.

"Hello?" Link says.

"Hello, this is Jake McCloud. Someone from this number called me?"

"Yes," Link says, trying to sound professional. Who knows; maybe Link can use this weird misunder-standing to get an internship with Jake McCloud—or with *Ursula de Gournsey!* "Sorry about that, I think it was a mistake. My mother, Mallory Blessing—"

"Mallory?" Jake McCloud says. "What is it? Is everything okay?"

Link focuses on the swans gliding along, regal in their bearing, king and queen of the pond. "I'm sorry," Link says. "This is Jake McCloud, right? *The* Jake McCloud, the one whose wife…"

"Yes."

Link shakes his head. "Do you *know* my mother? Mallory Blessing? She's an English teacher on Nantucket Island?"

"Is everything okay?" Jake McCloud asks again. "There must be a reason you're calling."

"There is a reason," Link says. "She left me your number in an envelope and asked me to contact you." Link pauses. "She's dying."

"She…"

"She has cancer, melanoma that metastasized to her brain. I've called hospice." These words are painful to say, and Link can't help but feel he's throwing them away. Why would Jake McCloud care?

There's silence on the other end, and all Link can imagine is Jake McCloud realizing that he has taken a call meant for someone else and wondering how to gracefully extricate himself.

"Please tell Mal…" Jake McCloud says.

Mal? Link thinks. Does Jake McCloud, who has a better than decent chance of becoming the First Gentleman of the United States, somehow *know* Link's mother?

"Tell her…that I'll be there as soon as I can," Jake says. "Tell her to hold on." He clears his throat. "Please. Tell her I'm coming."

Part One

Twenties

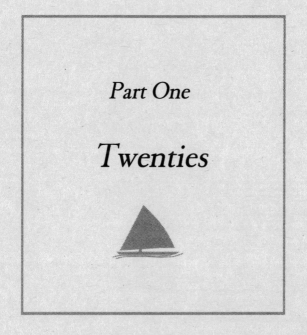

Summer #1: 1993

What are we talking about in 1993? Waco, Texas; the World Trade Center bombing; Arthur Ashe; R.E.M.; Lorena Bobbitt; Robert Redford, Woody Harrelson, and Demi Moore; NAFTA; River Phoenix; the EU; Got Milk?; NordicTrack; Rabin and Arafat; Monica Seles; Sleepless in Seattle; the World Wide Web; the Buffalo Bills losing the Super Bowl for the third straight time; Jerry, Elaine, George, and Kramer; Whitney Houston singing "I Will Always Love You."

When we first meet our girl Mallory Blessing (and make no mistake, Mallory *is* our girl; we're with her here through the good, the bad, and the damn-near hopeless), she's twenty-four years old, living on the Upper East Side of New York with her very best friend in the whole world, Leland Gladstone, whom she's starting to despise a little more each day. They're renting a fifth-floor walk-up in a building with a French restaurant on the ground level, and during the week, the line cooks give Leland the duck confit and lamb shank they have left over at the end of service. Leland never offers to share her culinary windfall with Mallory; she accepts it as her due because *she* found the apartment, *she* negotiated the lease, and *she* made seventeen visits to ABC Home for furniture. The only reason Mallory is living in New York at all is that Leland made an offhand comment (while drunk) that she might want a roommate, and Mallory was so desperate to get out of her parents' house in Baltimore that she misconstrued this as a full-blown invitation. Mallory pays one-third of the rent (even that amount is so astronomical that Mallory's parents are footing the bill), and in exchange, Mallory sleeps on a futon in a corner of the living room. Leland bought a faux-Chinese screen that Mallory can put up for privacy, though she rarely bothers. This sparks the first argument. Turns out, Leland bought the screen not so Mallory can have privacy but so Leland doesn't have to see Mallory reading novels while all wrapped up in the hideous calico-print comforter from her childhood bedroom.

It's…unseemly, Leland says. *How about some self-respect?*

The issue of the screen causes only minor friction compared to the issue of the job. Leland moved to New York to work in fashion—her dream was to "do creative" at *Harper's Bazaar*—and when Leland told Mallory about an opening for an editorial assistant at *Bard and Scribe,* the hottest literary magazine in the city, Mallory immediately applied. The mere prospect of such a job transformed Mallory's idea of what New York might be like for her. If she became an editorial assistant at *Bard and Scribe,* she would make new, artsy, bohemian friends and embark on a fascinating life. Little did Mallory know that Leland had already applied for the job herself. Leland was granted an interview, then a second interview, and then she was offered the job, which she snapped up while Mallory looked on, silently aghast and yet not at all surprised. If New York were a dress, it would fit Leland better, whereas Mallory would always be tugging and adjusting in an attempt to become more comfortable.

Now, every morning, Leland heads to the *Bard and Scribe* office, which is housed in an airy loft in SoHo complete with a rooftop garden where they throw chic soirées for people like Carolyn Heilbrun, Ellen Gilchrist, Dorothy Allison. Mallory, meanwhile, works as a receptionist at a headhunting firm, a job she was offered because her own "career consultant" felt sorry for her.

However, on May 16, 1993, Mallory receives the phone call that changes her life.

It's a Sunday, eleven thirty in the morning. Mallory went for a run in Central Park, then stopped for a coffee and a sesame bagel with scallion cream cheese, and she is ecstatic to come home and find the apartment empty. This happens only in small bites—on the rare occasion when Mallory gets home from work before Leland or leaves after her—and the sense of freedom is mind-altering. Mallory can pretend that she's the lady of the manor instead of a 1990s-Manhattan version of Sara Crewe, living in the garret without coal for a fire. On the morning of May 16, Leland is at Elephant and Castle, having brunch with her new *Bard and Scribe* friends. She faux-generously extended an invitation to Mallory, knowing Mallory would decline because she couldn't afford it.

The phone rings, and before answering it, Mallory goes to the stereo to turn down "Everybody Hurts," by R.E.M., which she has on repeat. It's her favorite song that year, though she's forbidden to play it when

Leland is home because, for Leland, Michael Stipe's keening is nails on a chalkboard.

"Hello?"

"Honey?"

Mallory drops into one of the chic but uncomfortable café chairs that Leland purchased at ABC Home. It's Mallory's father. Realistically, it was only going to be one of a handful of people: her parents; her brother, Cooper; her ex-boyfriend Willis, who is teaching English on the island of Borneo (he calls Mallory on Sundays, when international rates are lowest, to brag about his exotic new life); or Leland, saying she forgot her ATM card and would Mallory please get on the subway and bring it to her?

"Hi, Dad," Mallory says, her voice barely concealing how underwhelmed she is. Even hearing Willis talk about Komodo dragons would have been better.

"Honey?" her father says. He sounds so dejected that Mallory perks up in response. Mallory's father, Cooper Blessing Sr.—referred to by Mallory and her brother as simply "Senior"—is a CPA who owns four H&R Block franchises in greater Baltimore. As one might expect from such a man, his manner is reserved. He may be the only person in the history of the world born without emotions. But now his tone is heavy with something. Has someone died? Her *mother*? Her *brother*?

No, she decides. If something had happened to her mother, her brother would have called. If something had happened to her brother, her mother would have called.

Still, Mallory has a strange feeling. "Did someone die?" she asks. "Dad?"

"Yes," Senior says. "Your aunt Greta. Greta died

on…Friday, apparently. I found out only an hour ago. Greta's attorney called. I guess she left you something."

Do things like this happen in real life? Obviously they do. Mallory's aunt Greta had had a massive coronary. She was at home in Cambridge on Friday evening making pasta puttanesca from *The Silver Palate Good Times Cookbook* with her "housemate," Ruthie. (*Housemate* is Senior's word, as though Greta and Ruthie were two Gen Xers on *The Real World.*) The detail about the puttanesca is one that Mallory supplies from her own imagination because she has visited Greta and Ruthie at the house in Cambridge for weekends often and knows that Friday evenings they cook at home, Saturdays are for museums followed by dinner out and sometimes the theater, and Sundays are for bagels and the *Times,* then Chinese food for dinner while watching an old movie on TV. Ruthie called the paramedics, but there was nothing they could do. Greta was gone.

Ruthie arranged for Greta to be cremated and contacted their attorney, a woman named Eileen Beers. It was Eileen Beers who called Senior. Senior and Greta had been estranged for ten years, which was how long it had been since Uncle Bo passed and Aunt Greta moved in with a Radcliffe colleague, Dr. Ruth Harlowe, who was more than just a housemate. Eileen Beers informed Senior that Greta had bequeathed to Mallory the startling sum of a hundred thousand dollars and her cottage on Nantucket.

Mallory starts to cry. Mallory alone in the family had maintained a relationship with Greta after Uncle Bo died. She wrote letters each month and secretly called every Christmas; she invited Greta to her college graduation over her parents' objections; she had ridden four hours on the bus to spend those perfect weekends in Cambridge.

"Is this real?" Mallory asks Senior. "Greta is dead? She left me money and the cottage? The money and the cottage are mine? Like, *mine*-mine?" Mallory doesn't want to sound like she cares more about the money and the cottage than about her aunt's passing. But she also can't ignore what might be a life-changing reversal of fortune.

"Yes," Senior says.

When Leland returns from brunch, she has a Bellini glow; her skin actually appears peachy beneath the asymmetrical bangs of her new haircut. It takes Leland a moment to process what Mallory is telling her: After Mallory gives proper notice to the headhunting firm, she's moving out. She's going to Nantucket.

"I still don't understand why you would leave the center of the civilized world to live on an island thirty miles off the coast," Leland says.

It's now two weeks later, Sunday, May 30. Leland is treating Mallory to a bon voyage brunch at the Coconut Grill on Seventy-Seventh Street. They're sitting at an outdoor table on the sidewalk in the broiling sun so that they can be properly observed by the boys with popped collars and Ray-Ban aviators who are on their way to J. G. Melon's for burgers and Bloody Marys. One such specimen—in a mint-green Lacoste—lowers his shades an inch so he can check out Leland. He looks like the Preppy Killer.

Leland sounds perplexed and also sad. The

announcement of Mallory's imminent departure promptly restored love and affection between the two friends. Over the past two weeks, Leland has been sweet. She not only tolerates the sight of Mallory's messy bedding, she sits on the edge of the futon for long, gossipy conversations. And Mallory can absorb the changes taking place in her friend—the edgy haircut for starters, the leather jacket purchased for a whopping nine hundred dollars at Trash and Vaudeville, the switch from Bartles and Jaymes wine coolers to proper bottles of Russian River chardonnay—without feeling resentful or left behind.

Mallory and Leland will miss each other. They've been friends since before memory, having grown up three houses apart on Deepdene Road in the Roland Park neighborhood of Baltimore. Their childhood years had been idyllic: they biked to Eddie's Market for jawbreakers; they listened to the *Grease* soundtrack on Leland's turntable, stuffing their training bras with rolled-up socks and singing into hairbrushes; they sat in the Gladstones' hot tub on snowy nights; they watched *General Hospital* after school in Leland's rec room, playing hands of spit on the shag rug during commercials. They had been perfect angels until high school, when their shenanigans started. Leland's father, Steve Gladstone, bought a convertible Saab when the girls were seniors. Leland had taken it without permission, swung over to Mallory's house in the middle of the night, and thrown pebbles at Mallory's bedroom window until Mallory agreed to go for a joyride. They'd put the top down and driven all the way to the Inner Harbor with the cassette player blasting Yaz's *Upstairs at Eric's*. They were caught, of course. When they arrived back to Deepdene Road, their hair blown crazy from the wind, all four of their parents were standing in the Gladstones' driveway.

We're not angry, they said. (This must have been Steve Gladstone's influence; he was the most lenient of the four.) *We're disappointed.*

Mallory had been grounded for two weeks, she remembers. Leland had been grounded too, but she got out of it after three days.

"I need to try something different," Mallory says now as she dunks a sweet potato fry into the maple dipping sauce. "Set out on my own." Besides, the center of the civilized world is already a cauldron, and it's not even June; the concrete is baking, the trash can on the corner stinks, and there's no place less hospitable than the platform of the 6 train. Who wouldn't want to be headed to Nantucket for the summer? Or for forever?

Six weeks later when Mallory's brother, Cooper, calls to say that he has proposed to Krystel Bethune, his girlfriend of three months, and they will be getting married at Christmas, Mallory is so intoxicated with her new island life that she forgets to be properly shocked.

"That's great!" Mallory says.

"Aren't you going to ask if I knocked her up?" Cooper says.

"Did you knock her up?"

"No," Cooper says. "I'm just madly in love and I know I want to spend the rest of my life with Krystel, so I figure, why wait? Let's get married as soon as we can. Within reason. I mean, I don't want to elope. Senior and Kitty would kill me. As it is, they aren't too happy."

"Right," Mallory says. "How'd you two meet again?"

"Krystel was my waitress," Cooper says. "At the Old Ebbitt Grill."

"Nothing wrong with being a waitress," Mallory says. Mallory is waitressing herself at the Summer House pool out in Sconset three days a week. "Did she go to college? Like, at all?"

"She went to UMBC for a while," Cooper says.

That's vague, Mallory thinks. *A while* meaning a few semesters or a few weeks? It doesn't matter. Mallory won't judge; they have their mother for that. Kitty Blessing is downright obsessed with education, breeding, social standing.

"You're getting married at Christmas," Mallory says. This is a phenomenon she has never understood— Christmas is already so busy, frantic, and filled with angst; why make it worse?—but again, she won't judge. "Where will it be?"

"In Baltimore," Cooper says. "Krystel's mother has no money and her father isn't in the picture."

Mallory tries to imagine her mother's reaction to this news. Kitty has lost the war but won a crucial battle. Krystel's family is a disappointment, so there will be no dynasty-building. However, that means Kitty will have no competition in planning the wedding. She'll insist on tasteful Christmas (white lights, burgundy velvet bows, Handel's *Messiah*) rather than tacky Christmas (elves, candy canes, "Jingle Bells").

"I'm happy for you, Coop," Mallory says. For what might be the first time in her life, she's telling the truth about this. For all of her twenty-four years, Mallory has suffered from a chronic case of sibling envy. Cooper is the golden child to Mallory's silver.

He's the chocolate chip cookie to her oatmeal-raisin, which people like, just never quite as much.

"So now's the part where I ask you a favor," Cooper says.

"Oh," Mallory says. He wants a favor from *her*? This is new. Cooper is a policy wonk for the Brookings Institution, a think tank in DC. His job is important, prestigious even (though Mallory's not going to pretend she understands what he actually does). What could he possibly need from her? "Anything for you, you know that."

"I'd like to have a bachelor…well, not a *party* per se, but a weekend. Nothing crazy, just me, Fray, obviously, and Jake McCloud."

Fray, *obviously,* Mallory thinks, and she rolls her eyes. And Jake McCloud, the mysterious Jake McCloud, Cooper's big brother in his fraternity, Phi Gamma Delta—Fiji—whom Mallory has never actually met. She's had some intriguing phone conversations with him, however.

"Oh yeah?" she says.

"And I was thinking maybe I could do it there on Nantucket over Labor Day weekend?" He pauses. "If you don't mind three guys crashing on the sofa…or the floor…wherever."

"I have two spare bedrooms," Mallory says.

"You *do*?" Cooper says. "So it's, like, a real house? I always got the impression it was more like, I don't know, a shack?"

"It's not a *house*-house but it's better than a shack," Mallory says. "You'll see when you get here."

"So it's okay, then?" Cooper says. "Labor Day weekend?"

"Sure," she says. Labor Day weekend, she thinks, is

when Leland said she might come, but those plans are tentative at best. *"Mi casa es su casa."*

"Thanks, Mal!" Cooper says. He sounds excited and grateful, and after she hangs up, Mallory runs her hands over the worn-smooth boards of the deck and thinks about how good it feels to finally have something worth sharing.

On the day this conversation takes place, our girl is so tan that her skin looks like polished wood, and her mousy-brown hair is getting lighter. From certain angles, it looks nearly blond. She has lost eight pounds—that's a guesstimate; the cottage doesn't have a bathroom scale—but she is definitely more fit thanks to the fact that her only form of transportation is a ten-speed bike that she found listed in the classifieds of the *Inquirer and Mirror.*

Aunt Greta's cottage is now Mallory's cottage. Greta's attorney, Eileen Beers, takes care of transferring the deed and changing the name on the tax bill and insurance. Signed, sealed, delivered. But something nags at Mallory, a question she wasn't brave enough to ask Senior but she does ask Eileen.

"Shouldn't the cottage rightly go to Ruthie? They were"—she isn't going to use the word *housemates,* but a more suitable term eludes her. *Girlfriends? Lovers?*—"partners."

"Ruthie got the Cambridge house," Eileen says. "She prefers city life. And your aunt was very clear that she wanted you to have the Nantucket cottage. When she wrote the will, she said it was a magical place for you."

Magical.

Mallory used to visit Nantucket during the

summers when she was in grade school and then middle school—right up until Uncle Bo died. She'd felt awkward the first summer, she remembers, because Aunt Greta and Uncle Bo didn't have children and, according to Mallory's mother, wouldn't have the foggiest idea how to deal with one.

"They were smart to ask for you and not your brother," Kitty said. "All you do is read!"

One entire side of Mallory's suitcase that summer was packed with books—Nancy Drew, Louisa May Alcott, a contraband copy of *Are You There, God? It's Me, Margaret.* In subsequent years, Mallory didn't pack any books because she'd discovered that the length and breadth of one wall in the cottage's great room was a library. In the summer, her aunt and uncle abandoned their work reading for pleasure reading. Over the course of six summers, Mallory was introduced to Judith Krantz, Herman Wouk, Danielle Steel, James Clavell, Barbara Taylor Bradford, and Erich Segal. Nothing was off-limits, nothing was deemed "too adult," and nothing took precedence over reading; it was considered the holiest activity a person could engage in.

Mallory loved her aunt and uncle's cottage. The common area was one giant room with wood beams and chestnut-brown paneling. There was a dusty brick fireplace, a rock-hard green tweed sofa, two armchairs that swiveled, an ancient TV with rabbit-ear antennas, and a kidney-shaped writing desk under one of the pond-facing windows where Aunt Greta wrote postcards and letters to people back in Cambridge. A long narrow harvest table marked the boundary between the living room and the kitchen. The kitchen had vanilla-speckled Formica counters and fudge-brown appliances; a black lobster pot sat on the stove at all times. There was one bathroom, with tiny square tiles that sparkled like mica, and Mallory's room had twin beds, one with a mattress that felt like a marble slab, where she kept her books, and one a little bit softer, where she slept. She sometimes ventured into the third bedroom, but that room had only one window, and it faced the side yard, whereas Mallory's bedroom had two windows, one that faced the side yard and one that fronted the ocean. She fell asleep each night listening to the waves, and the breeze was so reliable that Mallory slept without a fan all summer.

This island chooses people, Aunt Greta said. *It chose Bo and me, and I think it's chosen you as well.*

Mallory remembered feeling...*ordained* by that comment, as though she were being invited into an exclusive club. *Yes,* she thought. *I'm a Nantucket person.* She loved the sun, the beach, the waves of the south shore. *Next stop, Portugal!* Uncle Bo would cry out, hands raised over his head, as he charged into the ocean. She loved the pond, the swans, the red-winged blackbirds, the dragonflies, the reeds and cattails. She loved surf-casting and kayaking with her uncle and taking long beach walks with her aunt, who carried a stainless-steel kitchen bowl to hold the treasures they found—quahog shells, whelks, slippers and scallops, the occasional horseshoe carapace, pieces of satiny driftwood, interesting rocks, beach glass. As the days passed, they became more discerning, throwing away shells that were chipped and rocks that wouldn't be as pretty once they dried.

She loved the stormy days when the waves pummeled the shore and the screen door rattled in its frame. Uncle Bo would light a fire and Aunt Greta would make lobster stew. They played Parcheesi and read their books and listened to the classical station out of Boston on the transistor radio.

There is still one photograph in the cottage of Aunt Greta and Uncle Bo together, and Mallory had studied it when she'd first moved in. It's a picture of them on the beach in their woven plastic chairs, their hair wet and their feet sandy. After looking at it a few seconds, Mallory realized it was a picture she herself had taken with her uncle's camera. Aunt Greta was wearing a red floral one-piece bathing suit with a tissue tucked into her bosom so her chest wouldn't burn. Her dark hair, cut short like a man's, was standing on end. She was beaming—and one could sense in her expression the carefree exuberance of summer. Uncle Bo was wearing sunglasses and had a copy of James Michener's *Chesapeake* opened across his hairy chest.

They look happy in that picture, Mallory thought. And yet, if she wasn't mistaken, this was taken the summer before Uncle Bo died, so a scant year before Aunt Greta got together with Ruthie and thereby fractured her relations with Mallory's family.

Mallory has of course wondered if her aunt was a lesbian all along and if her uncle was, perhaps, gay. Maybe theirs was a marriage of convenience or a marriage of deep, intense friendship, a meeting of minds if not bodies.

Mallory doesn't care. She misses her aunt and uncle, but she suspects some spiritual shreds of them remain here, because although Mallory was often lonely in New York, she has not felt lonely in Nantucket even once.

Mallory works Tuesdays, Wednesdays, and Thursdays as a lunch waitress at the Summer House pool.

Her favorite coworker is a young African-American woman named Apple who also happens to be the guidance counselor at Nantucket High School. Mallory asks Apple if there are any openings at the high school for teachers or even substitute teachers.

"I majored in English," Mallory says.

"You might get lucky," Apple says. "Mr. Falco currently teaches honors and AP English but he just turned seventy and he's deaf in one ear, so we're thinking maybe he'll retire? In which case, in September, I'll put your résumé right in front of Dr. Major, our principal. We could use some new blood."

Mallory is grateful, though she doesn't want to wish her summer away. The Summer House pool has jaw-dropping views of Sconset Beach and the Atlantic Ocean. Guests can enjoy lunch on the chaises or sit at one of the patio tables under an umbrella. The food isn't bad—Mallory steers people toward the burgers, the grilled chicken sandwiches, the salads topped with crab cakes—but most of Mallory's business is drinks. The bar's specialty is something called the Hokey Pokey, which has four kinds of liquor in it; the drink costs ten dollars and most people have two or more of them. Mallory makes nearly two hundred dollars a day in tips. She works with either Apple or a girl named Isolde, who is kind of a bitch but who knows her stuff. The bartender's name is Oliver. He's cute and has an Australian accent, making him a key contributor to the Summer House pool's success. Oliver brings in the young ladies ("Ollie's dollies," Isolde calls them). And the crowd of young ladies at the bar lures in the men with money.

It's the best job Mallory has ever had. Working three days a week is enough because she has the nest egg from Aunt Greta tucked away in the bank. With a part-time job, Mallory still has time to read, to swim and sun, to explore the island on her bike, to go out with Apple after their shifts.

Every night before Mallory falls asleep, she silently thanks her aunt Greta. What a gift. What an opportunity.

Everybody hurts; she knows this. But not Mallory this summer.

The last Friday in August, the phone rings late at night. Mallory lets the answering machine pick up— but when she hears Leland's voice, she stumbles out of bed. She has barely talked to her friend all summer. Mallory sent her one letter early on describing her cottage, her new job, and her ongoing flirtation with Oliver the bartender. (This ended in an ill-advised one-night stand that Mallory's mind now swerves around as though it's emotional roadkill.) In response, Mallory received a long and descriptive letter about summer in the city—an Indigo Girls concert in Central Park; a work lunch at the Cupping Room in SoHo, where Leland was seated at a table next to Matt Dillon; the bounty at the Greenmarket in Union Square. Leland's writing was so lush and powerful that Mallory saved the letter in case Leland became famous and the Smithsonian came calling.

Mallory snatches up the phone in the dark. "Hello? Leland?"

"Mal." Hearing just this one syllable, Mallory can tell that Leland is drunk. Martinis at Chumley's, perhaps, or maybe she joined the throngs at Isabella's, where Jerry Seinfeld was known to hang out. God, Mallory doesn't miss New York at all.

"Hi," Mallory says. "It's late, you know. Everything okay?" There's a part of Mallory that fears she will one day get a phone call that takes away her new life as swiftly as it was granted.

"So, listen…," Leland says. *Listen* comes out as "lishen." "I called and booked my flights. I land Friday at eight p.m. and I'm sorry but I have to leave Sunday instead of Monday because my friend Harrison is having this rooftop thing—"

"Wait, wait," Mallory says. Her thoughts feel like a tangled skein of yarn. "Which Friday are we talking about?"

"Next Friday," Leland says. "Labor Day weekend. Like we planned."

Planned is an overstatement. What Mallory knows for sure is that when she and Leland hugged good-bye, Leland had said, "I hope to come visit you. Maybe Labor Day weekend?" To which Mallory said, "You're welcome anytime, Lee. Obviously. You're my best friend."

And then in the letter, Leland had closed with *Labor Day is still on my radar!*

Certainly it has been on Mallory's radar too, though it feels like Leland missed an intermediary step, the step where she called to make sure Labor Day weekend still worked for Mallory, at which point Mallory had intended to tell her that Cooper, Frazier Dooley, and Jake McCloud were coming for Cooper's bachelor-party weekend and Leland should pick a different weekend. But that step was skipped too, which is a little irritating. They are no longer the little girls who ran indiscriminately between each other's houses; they're grown-ups.

Leland has bought plane tickets. She lands Friday at eight.

"I have something to tell you," Mallory says. She isn't sure how her news will be received. "Labor Day weekend, when you're here..."

"Yeah?" Leland says.

"Cooper will also be here!" Mallory adds a handful of verbal confetti to the announcement to make it sound like a wonderful surprise: "I haven't had a chance to write to you about this, but he's getting married at Christmas to a waitress named Krystel." Mallory pauses to let this sink in before she zaps Leland with the rest of it.

"I know," Leland says. "My mother told me."

"She did?" Mallory says, then she thinks, *Of course she did.* Kitty and Leland's mother, Geri Gladstone, are best friends and play tennis together every single day from May through September at the country club. "Okay, good—so Coop asked if I could host a little bachelor weekend here over Labor Day and since I wasn't a hundred percent sure you were coming, I said okay."

"Bachelor weekend?" Leland says. "Does that mean what I think it means?"

"Yes," Mallory says. "Fray is coming."

Mallory had thought that for Leland, the prospect of seeing Frazier Dooley would be twenty nails in the coffin as far as her visit was concerned, but all Mallory hears is heavy breathing followed by a string of slurred declarations in a tone that sounds like Leland is trying to convince Mallory—or maybe herself—of something.

"It'll be fine, it'll have to be fine, it's over, it was so long ago, he has another girlfriend now, Sheena or Sheba, but I heard they broke up, and I have dates every weekend, nobody special yet, but it's only a matter of time, I've been picky because being with Fray, frankly, taught me how easy it is to settle into something second rate." Leland stops, catches her breath. "Does he know I'm coming?"

"No," Mallory says.

"Well, don't tell him," Leland says. "Let it be a surprise."

Mallory recognizes a recipe for disaster when she sees one. Leland is coming for the weekend and so is Frazier Dooley, Leland's high-school boyfriend, the one she went to the prom with, the one she lost her virginity to. They officially broke up when Fray went to college, but Mallory knows they never really broke up. For example, there was a high-school-reunion gathering at Bohager's the year Mallory and Leland turned twenty-one. Fray had been in attendance and at the end of the night, Leland left with him.

Maybe Leland coming this weekend is a good thing? Maybe she and Fray will sleep together for old times' sake and it will be the closure they both need?

This might be Pollyanna thinking. What's more likely is that Leland coming will create unwanted drama for Coop during what's supposed to be his carefree bachelor weekend. But what can Mallory do?

Cooper calls Mallory a few days later and Mallory thinks, *I have to tell him.* It can be a surprise, *maybe,* for Fray, but it *cannot* be a surprise for her brother.

Turns out, Coop has a surprise of his own. "Bachelor weekend isn't happening," he says.

"It's not?" Mallory says. On the one hand, this is a

relief. Apple has put Mallory's name at the top of the substitute-teacher list at the high school, and she told Mallory she would likely be called on the very first day. But on the other hand, Mallory feels a piercing disappointment. "How come?"

"Krystel doesn't want me to have a bachelor party," Coop says. "She thinks they're gross."

"They are gross," Mallory says. "Please tell Krystel this isn't a bachelor party. This is a weekend with the guys. There won't be strippers or beer bongs or sex-on-the-beach shots." She pauses. "Will there?"

"Not now," Cooper says glumly.

"Surely she'll understand if it's just you and two friends staying with your *sister*?" Mallory says. "Although, honestly, maybe it's better if you do cancel because…Leland is also coming this weekend."

"She *is*?" Cooper says. "You're kidding, that's *awesome!* Now we *have* to come. If we don't, Fray will never forgive me."

"It's supposed to be a surprise for Fray, I guess," Mallory says. She feels her spirits rising; her brother's enthusiasm is unexpected. "At least that's what Leland wants."

Cooper chuckles. "That is so *great!*" he says. "Forget what I said before. We're coming, and I'll tell Krystel she'll just have to deal with it. Fray, Jake, and I will be on the ferry that gets in at three o'clock on Friday afternoon."

"I'll be there," Mallory says. "Bells on."

A couple of positive consequences have come out of Mallory's one-night stand with bartender Oliver. One, it ended a long romantic drought. Mallory hadn't been with anyone since Willis left for Borneo the previous

August. Two, Oliver put Mallory in touch with his buddy Scotty, who was trying to sell his 1977 convertible K5 Blazer before getting married and going to business school.

Early Friday afternoon, she goes to look at the Blazer, which is so *beachy* that Mallory falls in love with it immediately and doesn't even blink when she realizes that it's a standard and the gearshift is as long as her thighbone. *New tires,* Scotty says. *Indestructible*. He shows her how to take the top off and put it back on clean and tight, but it's summer, so Mallory is going to keep the top off, off, off. Mallory hands Scotty three thousand dollars in cash and takes the title.

(Scotty, meanwhile, feels the same way about selling the Blazer that he did about putting his yellow Lab, Radar, to sleep. He loves the car; he's selling it under duress. His fiancée, Lisa, thinks he should buy a "city car" for Wharton, a Jetta. He can't even say the word *Jetta* without grimacing. *Part of growing up is letting go,* his parents told him back when they all hugged Radar for the last time. Scotty is comforted by the fact that the chick who's buying the K5 is not only cute behind the wheel, but happy. He can't remember the last time he saw a girl that happy.)

Mallory owns a convertible! A K5! It's sleek black with a white racing stripe—Scotty spared no expense on the paint job—and any trepidation that Mallory feels about the upcoming weekend falls away. She turns up the radio and drives to the ferry.

She's standing on Straight Wharf when the boys come off the boat. Her brother's in a tomato-red polo, collar up, and Frazier, whose blond hair is longer and shaggier than Mallory has ever seen it, has something on his lip that Mallory realizes is a mustache. Behind them is a person Mallory knows is Jake McCloud. She has seen pictures of him. The one that comes to mind was taken at a fraternity formal, his head tipped back and his mouth open (laughing? singing?), but Mallory is unprepared for how seeing him in person affects her.

He's…

Maybe he's not classically handsome. Or maybe he is. Jake is tall, strapping, clean-cut. He has dark hair, dark brown eyes, so nothing too remarkable, except his face is put together properly, and when he smiles…*gah!* He has the smile of a cute little boy, the cutest little boy, except this infectious smile is on his classically handsome face, so, wow, yeah. Mallory is…she is…well, initially, she's self-conscious. She should have done something with her hair. It's gathered in a scrunchie on top of her head. She's wearing Wayfarers and no makeup. She has on cutoffs and a white tank and a pair of tan suede flip-flops that show her chipped nail polish and her silver toe rings.

Why did she not give herself a pedicure? Or dress up? Her mother would be aghast.

"Hey, guys!" Mallory says. She hugs her brother, hugs Fray, and offers Jake her hand. "Mallory Blessing," she says. "Nice to finally meet you in person."

"It's crazy, right?" Jake says. "That we've never met? I remember when Coop first showed me your picture. I said—"

"'Coop, I have to tell you, man, I'm in love with your little sister,'" Coop supplies.

Mallory presses the soles of her flip-flops into the

dock. He's just teasing her. "Oh, really?" she dead-pans. "You said that?"

The previous night before falling asleep, Mallory went through the conversations she'd had with Jake McCloud while Cooper was in college. Three separate times during Mallory's freshman year at Gettysburg, she had called Coop at the Fiji house at Johns Hopkins and Jake McCloud answered.

The first time Mallory talked to Jake, he'd immediately started peppering her with questions about life at Gettysburg: What was her major? (English.) Did she like her roommate? (Indifferent.) Had she been to any parties? (Some, yes.) Did she have a boyfriend? (No.)

"That's good," Jake said. "Save yourself for me."

Mallory had laughed. "Okay, I'll do that. Will you please tell Coop I called?" She'd been so flustered that she hung up just as she heard Jake say, "You're hanging up on me so soon?" She chastised herself and considered calling back, but in the end she had the good sense to return to reading Stephen Crane.

The second time she spoke to Jake was a few months later, close to Christmas break. It was a Saturday night and Mallory was studying for her American lit final. She decided to call Coop while she was waiting for her popcorn to pop in the microwave in the common area; she'd set the timer for two minutes and ten seconds. If the popcorn burned even a little, the smell lingered for days and everyone in the dorm dreamed up creative ways to retaliate against you.

"Good evening, Cooper Blessing's room," a voice said.

Mallory smiled; she knew it was Jake. Every time she called Coop, she halfway hoped (okay, all the way hoped) that Jake would answer again. Now he had. Mallory heard laughter and music in the background. A party? It *was* Saturday night.

"It's Mallory," she said. "Cooper's sister. Is he... around?"

"Mallory!" Jake said. "It's Jake!" His voice was so loud, it was like he was calling out to her across a canyon.

"Hey!" She thought, *Be witty!* Should she tell him she was babysitting her popcorn? Definitely not. She was *such* a nerd! "Is Coop around, Jake?"

"Nah," Jake said. "I mean, yeah, he's here somewhere, but it's our Christmas cocktail party so he and Stacey are probably making out on the dance floor in the basement."

"I'm sorry, I didn't realize," Mallory said. "I'm studying for finals and I just needed a break."

"Oh yeah?" Jake said. "What final?"

"Am lit," Mallory said.

"That's me right now," Jake said. "I. Am. Lit." He laughed. "That was bad, sorry. American literature?"

"Yeah," Mallory said. "I don't want to keep you from the party. I'll call Coop tomorrow."

"You're not keeping me from anything," Jake said. "My date drank a bottle of wine by herself while she was getting ready and she started puking at the pre-party and didn't make it over here. Good news is I got to take off this damn tartan bow tie."

This damn tartan bow tie. He was talking as though she could see him lying back on Cooper's bed with the top of his tuxedo shirt unbuttoned and a red and green MacGregor bow tie hanging around his neck. Jake must be cute, she thought. He sounded cute.

"Who are you reading in Am lit?" Jake asked.

"Um…" Mallory said. She couldn't believe he wanted to know. She was just a freshman and hadn't been invited to any Christmas cocktail parties, though if she *were* at one, even without a date, the last thing she'd want to talk about would be school—even worse, someone else's school. "The usual? Hawthorne, Emerson, Thoreau, Crane, Twain, and automobiles…"

Jake laughed. "You're funny!"

"Maybe just because you're lit?" she said.

He laughed again and then she heard him take a gulp of something. "You know, I've had to take all these pre-med bio and chem classes, and it's only this year that I've been able to take something for fun. So I'm in this English class called Art of the Novella, and it's so great! We're reading Jim Harrison and Tolstoy and Ethan Canin and Andre Dubus and Philip Roth…"

"Wow," Mallory said. She didn't admit that the only two writers she'd heard of were Tolstoy and Roth and she hadn't read anything by either one.

"You know what I'm going to do the second I graduate? I'm going to start reading. I want to become a bookish person. I should have majored in English but my parents insisted on biology so I could get in all the pre-med requirements. My father's a burn specialist and my mother's a surgeon."

"Are you going to med school, then?"

"Not next year, maybe not ever. It's just…my parents were always working when I was growing up and I want a job where I can come home at night and spend time with my kids."

He was thinking so far ahead that he seemed like a different category of person from Mallory. She was just trying to read the basic English literature canon (all white males, as her roommate, Bisma, had pointed out, a fact Mallory hadn't even *noticed,* which was completely pathetic); she wasn't in a position to think about a career, much less kids. "So what will you do?"

"Probably work for a lobbyist in Washington—one of the good guys, though. I'm one of the good guys, Mallory."

"I can tell," Mallory said, then she worried her tone was too earnest. Time to wrap it up, she thought. The microwave was beeping its reminder. "Well, have fun tonight. I'll call Cooper back tomorrow."

"I'll tell him," Jake said. "And hey, good talking to you. You saved my night."

The third conversation was months later, at the tail end of the spring semester. Mallory had just hung up with her mother, who'd told her that Cooper had gotten an internship in DC and that he'd be renting a room in a house in Chevy Chase that summer. Mallory was calling to beg him to come home instead. Mallory couldn't bear the thought of spending an entire summer alone with their parents and being the sole recipient of her mother's irritating attention.

Jake picked up on the first ring. "Blessing residence."

Mallory grinned. "Jake?" she said. It was now the end of freshman year and she had acquired some moxie. "It's Mal."

"*Mal* means 'bad' in French," Jake said. "But you must be the good kind of bad."

Mallory couldn't believe that talking to someone

she'd never met could feel so *seductive*. "How are you?" she said. "Are you…getting ready to graduate?"

"Yes, thank you for asking," Jake said. "But I have zilch in the way of job offers, so I'm sitting on the end of your brother's bed teaching myself Cat Stevens songs on the guitar so I can support myself as a subway performer."

"I love Cat Stevens," Mallory said.

"All the best people do," Jake said.

"I have every album. My favorite is *Tea for the Tillerman*." Mallory tried to tamp down her enthusiasm. She hadn't thought her crush on Jake McCloud could get any worse, but now that she knew he liked Cat Stevens, she was a *complete goner*. "Put the phone down next to you and let me listen while you play."

"Tell me if I'm any good," Jake said. "And if the answer is no, please lie to spare my ego. Okay, something from *Tea for the Tillerman*, here we go." He set the phone down and then she heard him strumming the first chords of "Hard Headed Woman." He started to sing: *"I'm looking for a hard headed woman, one who will take me for myself…"*

His voice was *great*. It had strength and it was on key and controlled. It was sexy. He sang to the bridge and then he picked up the phone.

"What do you think?" he said. "Should I quit and apply at Long John Silver's?"

"Woo-hoo!" Mallory cried. "You sounded terrific! You're going to be a very rich and successful subway performer."

"Aw," Jake said. "Thank you, that's sweet." He cleared his throat. "Hey, did you call to talk to Coop?"

"Coop?" she said.

* * *

Mallory doesn't know if Jake remembers the content of their repartee or even that they *had* a repartee—it was so long ago, over five years. As she leads the boys to the car, she thinks it might have been better if Jake had turned out to be not her type because then she could just be her normal self instead of being sick with infatuation.

The boys *love* the car! Cooper whistles and calls shotgun; Fray and Jake climb in the back, and Mallory cranks up the radio.

Fray says, "Should we swing by the package store? I have money."

"For once," Coop says.

"I have two cases of beer at the house," Mallory says. "And a fresh fifth of Jim Beam. I know my audience."

"I love you, Mal," Fray says.

"Hey," Jake says, smacking Frazier's shoulder. "She's mine."

"She's mine"? Mallory thinks. *Is it going to be this easy?*

She wants to believe that. Everything this summer has been charmed except for the fact that she hasn't fallen in love. Could that be next? Could that be *now*?

When they get to the house, Mallory shows them their rooms—Cooper says he'll stay in a room with Jake so that Fray can have a room to himself. (He gives Mallory a wink, meaning *Leland*.) The boys change into their board shorts and run down the slope of the beach into the ocean. Mallory watches them from the porch for a minute. Jake has strong, sculpted shoulders; he's a powerful swimmer. He dives under a breaking wave, then surfaces and whips his wet hair out of his face. He notices Mallory checking him out, and he grins.

Complete goner, she thinks, and she heads inside to fix some snacks.

Seven hours later, Mallory and Jake will be standing alone together in the cold sand and Mallory will scream until her throat is on fire and Jake will tell her to call 911 and Mallory will flash back to the moment she stood on the porch grinning as she admired Jake's shoulders and she will wonder how everything went so horribly wrong. She will suspect it's her fault.

Mallory puts out Brie, water crackers, and a little dish of chutney. She's channeling her mother, who believes that life begins with hors d'oeuvres. Mallory has been chilling the beer all day in a galvanized tub that her aunt and uncle used as a footbath. She sets up the Jim Beam, a trio of cold Cokes, a bucket of clean ice. The boys come up from the beach. When Cooper sees the cutting board loaded with cheese and crackers, he gives Mallory a look.

"Against all odds, you've turned into Kitty."

Mallory shrugs as Jake and Fray dig in. No one has ever been unhappy about seeing hors d'oeuvres.

Mallory is tempted to put on some Cat Stevens but she doesn't want to be obvious—and what if Jake doesn't remember? She puts on R.E.M., "It's the End of the World as We Know It."

Fray pours himself a Beam and Coke. "And I feel fine," he says.

During the golden hour, the sun's rays hit the front porch in a way that feels sacred. Mallory is two beers in; she's being careful because she has to drive to the airport to get Leland. Mallory has set the harvest table for four people but she leaves room for a fifth. She has prepared burger patties; she has shucked corn, sliced tomatoes. She cuts the last bloom off her sole hydrangea bush by the pond-side door and sticks it in a mason jar for a centerpiece. The boys take showers. *Make them quick,* Mallory has warned them. This fall, she's going to hire someone to build an outdoor shower off the side of the house. Every time she gets home from work or comes up off the beach, all she wants is to shower outside—sun or stars and moon above, pond stage right, ocean stage left.

Jake walks into the great room in just a towel. "This place is a slice of heaven."

Cooper is sprawled across the green tweed sofa. "I should have been nicer to Aunt Greta."

Yes, you should have, Mallory thinks, but she doesn't want to quarrel.

Jake looks at Mallory's CDs. He says, "I'll DJ." Next thing Mallory knows, Cat Stevens is playing— "Hard Headed Woman."

"Hey!" she says.

"This is our song," Jake says. "Remember?"

Fray steps out of the bedroom, also wearing only a towel. "What is this crap?" he asks, waving his drink at the stereo. "It's terrible." Then he snaps his fingers. "I forgot, Mal, I brought you something." He disappears into the bedroom and emerges holding a large wrapped gift that he hands to Mallory. "House-warming present. Thank you for having me."

Mallory nearly has to pick herself up off the floor. Has Frazier Dooley grown *up*? "Thank you," she says. "That's so thoughtful. But you didn't have to. You're family, you know that."

He shrugs. "Open it."

It's a French press and a pound of coffee from Vermont. "Wow," Mallory says. "It's almost like you knew I've been living with that dinosaur." She points to the Mr. Coffee machine on the counter; it was here back in 1978 when Mallory first visited the cottage.

"Stop making the rest of us look bad," Jake says to Fray.

"Sorry," he says. "It comes naturally."

Mallory tears her attention off Jake for a second so that she can take fresh stock of Frazier. He has been Cooper's best friend since forever; when Mallory said he was family, she meant it. Frazier lived with his grandparents around the corner from the Blessings, on Edgevale Road. Like the Blessings and the Gladstones, Frazier's grandparents belonged to the country club. His mother, Sloane, would sporadically appear—she was a professional disco dancer (she was also a cocaine addict—Mallory had learned this from eavesdropping on her parents). Frazier's father was never even *referred* to, and now that Mallory is older, she suspects that Sloane didn't know who the father was. Walt and Inga, Fray's grandparents, were lovely people; Walt served as president of the board of trustees at the country club, and Inga did the flowers each week for Roland Park Presbyterian. Despite this, Fray had always been troubled. He was smart but didn't apply himself. He was a good athlete but a poor sport—he yelled at the refs in basketball, started fistfights on the lacrosse field. He got into UVM on a partial scholarship and intended to walk on to the lacrosse team, but he tore his ACL during tryouts, and that was that. His freshman-year grades were so bad that Walt and Inga made him earn the money he would have gotten from his scholarship, so he got a job as a barista at a coffee shop in downtown Burlington. After he graduated, he stayed on to manage the place. Mallory knows that he'd suggested improvements—an expanded menu, proper coffeehouse evenings with local musicians. Mallory feels proud of him for getting out of Baltimore and for becoming the kind of person who thought to bring a hostess gift without his grandparents' prodding.

Mallory pulls Coop aside. "When the coals turn gray and ashy, throw the burgers on," she says. "I'll be back in fifteen minutes."

Leland is standing in front of the airport terminal wearing a red gingham sundress that clashes with her bangs, which she has dyed neon pink. She squeals when she sees the Blazer; it's a proper *jalopy,* she proclaims. She leans her head back against the seat and looks up at the night sky. "The air here is delicious. I needed to get out of the city."

"I hope you're hungry," Mallory says. "The boys are grilling burgers. They should be ready when we get back."

"Fray's there?" Leland asks.

"Fray's there."

"He doesn't know I'm coming?"

"Nope," Mallory says. Is this cruel or funny? Mallory isn't sure. She has a sickening vision of Fray losing his temper when he sees Leland and feeling so tricked, so *betrayed,* that he smashes the French press against the wall.

When Mallory and Leland walk into the cottage, Cooper has just pulled the burgers off the grill. Jake is manning the stereo, and Fray has his head in the fridge.

"Look who *I* found!" Mallory says, ushering Leland forward.

"Leland!" Cooper says. "Hey, sweetie, love the hair! How are you? Welcome, welcome!"

Mallory holds her breath as she watches Frazier take in the sight of Leland Gladstone, there on Nantucket, there in the living room.

"Lee?" he says. He seems dazed—but it's a happy daze, not an angry daze.

"Hey, Fray," she says.

It's fine, it's fine. They set a place for Leland, and Mallory pulls out a bottle of Russian River chardonnay. Her hands are shaking and when she gives Leland the glass, she sees that Leland's hands are shaking too. But no matter, they're all grown-ups now, sitting down to dinner at the narrow harvest table that Aunt Greta always said was meant to inspire conversation. They raise their drinks and toast the next chapter for Cooper. He's getting married. When they clink one another's glasses, Mallory notices that Leland's and Fray's arms cross, which Kitty always claimed was bad luck.

"No crossing!" Mallory says, but nobody hears her.

Lenny Kravitz is on the stereo, "Are You Gonna Go My Way."

After dinner, things are still okay. Leland wants to change before they go out. Frazier goes into the bathroom holding a razor—seeing Leland has clearly inspired him to shave that thing off his lip— and Cooper picks up the phone and takes it into his bedroom. Mallory washes the dishes; Jake offers to dry.

Jake says, "I feel like I'm out of the loop."

"Leland and Fray were an item in high school."

"Ah," Jake says.

"They've always had a thing," Mallory says. "A thing that refuses to die."

"I can relate," Jake says.

"Can you?" Mallory says. She's seized by jealousy. Obviously, Jake is too terrific not to have a girlfriend, or many girlfriends. But she'd hoped she'd caught him on the in-between. "Where did you grow up? I don't think you told me."

"South Bend," Jake says. "Indiana."

She knows nothing about the place except that Notre Dame is there. "Are you still hung up on a girl from South Bend?"

"*Hung up* is too strong a phrase," he says. "We just…I'm not sure. It's been one of those things. Complicated."

"What's her name?" Mallory asks. She can't believe she's being so bold.

"Ursula," he says. "Ursula de Gournsey."

"She sounds like a supermodel," Mallory says.

He laughs. "Yeah…no. She's not. She's…"

"Back in Indiana?" Mallory asks hopefully.

"In DC," he says. "She graduated from Georgetown Law and now she's an attorney with the SEC. She goes after insider trading and corporations who aren't following the rules, that kind of thing. She got recruited right out of law school."

"Slacker," Mallory says. She grins at him, which is heroic of her because the night has turned into a puddle of mud at her feet. Jake has a complicated relationship with a legal eagle named Ursula de Gournsey. Mallory is a lunch waitress. Jake's flirtation with her is a distraction for him, a game. She's the little sister. He doesn't take her seriously. She isn't…substantial enough. She is a line drawing of a woman that has been only partially colored in.

Mallory grabs the bottle of Jim Beam—it's nearly half gone already—and takes a swig, then she hands it to Jake and *he* takes a swig, and she says, "Let's gather the troops. We're going out."

Everything is fine, everyone is game. Leland has changed into white jeans; Fray, now clean-shaven, has put on a Nirvana T-shirt, and they're all piling into the Blazer when they hear the phone ringing inside.

"Let it go," Mallory says to Cooper. "It's probably Kitty making sure you arrived safely."

"No, it's…" Cooper races back inside, leaving the four of them to sit in the idling truck.

"The wife," Fray says.

"Well, I'm taking shotgun, then," Jake says, and he moves up next to Mallory.

They sit in silence waiting for Cooper to reappear. Then Mallory hears the faintest noise behind her and checks her rearview mirror to see Leland and Frazier making out.

Well, this *is awkward,* she thinks. She closes her eyes and waits for them to stop, but of course they don't and Mallory is afraid to look at Jake, but Cooper is taking so long that finally she says, "Will you check on him?"

"Yep," Jake says. He seems grateful for a reason to escape the car. He runs into the cottage and Mallory turns up the radio. Counting Crows, "Mr. Jones." She wishes for a blizzard or a plague of locusts—anything that will make Leland and Frazier stop.

Ursula de Gournsey. Working for the SEC in Washington, which is where Jake lives too. He ended up taking a job as a lobbyist for Big Pharma, a company called PharmX, he told them at dinner. They aren't exactly the good guys, he said, but it was too much money to turn down and he gets to use his pre-med background.

Jake comes jogging back out. "Coop's not coming."

"What?" Mallory says.

"He said we should go without him."

"But it's *his* bachelor weekend," Mallory says.

"Just go, Mal," Fray says from the back seat. "The ball and chain is heavy and it is tight."

The Chicken Box is jam-packed. This weekend is the last hurrah for every summer kid on the island. Mallory is proud of how grungy the Box is. It's a real dive bar, with pool tables and a beer-sticky floor and live music every night, people of all ages waving Coronas in the air while belting out the lyrics to "I Want You to Want Me."

Jake slips through the mob at the bar and emerges victorious with beers for everyone. He and Mallory get up close to the stage, and Mallory grabs the lead singer and requests "Ball and Chain" by Social Distortion. They launch right into the song, and while Mallory is happy about this—it's a hilarious bust on Cooper— she's also bummed that her brother isn't here. People have always called Cooper an old soul. He radiates peace, wisdom, an effortlessness that says, *Yeah, I've been here before, I've got this, don't worry about it.* When they were kids doing jigsaw puzzles, he knew where a piece went the instant he picked it up; when Kitty found a knot in the chain of a necklace, she would bring it to Cooper and he would methodically untangle it. Mallory, however, is a brand-new soul, squeaky clean, fresh out of the box, like a pair of penny loafers that needs, desperately, to be broken in. She has always had a difficult time seeing the big picture.

Except for right now. Because right now, Mallory knows Cooper is taking the fool's path. He's letting Krystel ruin their weekend. If Kitty knew that Cooper had declined to join a celebration that was being thrown in his honor, she would be dismayed. Nothing irks their mother more than bad manners.

Mallory turns around. Leland and Fray are nowhere to be seen, and she'll never find them in this crowd. Jake is right behind her and suddenly his hand lands on her hip, then lifts. Mallory isn't sure what to do. Should she turn around and raise her face to his, or is that too obvious? She decides to act natural. She dances like no one is watching.

Everything is still okay. After last call, the lights come up and the crowd spills out of the bar onto Dave Street.

"Are you all right to drive home?" Jake asks.

She's fine. She had two Coronas and half of a third, but she's sweated most of it out.

When they reach the Blazer, they find Fray sitting in the back seat polishing off a beer.

"Where's Leland?" Mallory asks. She has known Frazier so long that she can tell just by the set of his jaw that something is wrong.

"She left."

"What?" Mallory says. "Where did she go? Did you two have a fight?"

"She bumped into a group of people she knew from New York," he says. "They invited her to go to a bar downtown and she said yes. She didn't want to stay here, it was too crowded, they don't have chardonnay or whatever she drinks now."

True, Mallory thinks. *No chardonnay at the Chicken Box. That's kind of the point.*

"Didn't they invite you?" Mallory asks.

"They did, reluctantly, but these weren't our type of people, Mal. These were New York people, Bret Easton Ellis people."

"Ah," Mallory says. "Okay. Well, she's a big girl. She'll find her way home."

Everything is still okay, sort of. Mallory drives safely back to the cottage. She hopes that Leland has the phone number with her, otherwise…well, big girl or not, she's going to have a difficult time finding the cottage on the no-name road.

Mallory pulls into the driveway; Frazier jumps out while the car is still moving and storms into the house. By the time Mallory and Jake get inside, Frazier has the bottle of Jim Beam by the neck.

"She's not here," he says. "I'm going for a walk." He leaves; the screen door bangs shut behind him. Mallory watches Fray drop onto the beach and head right. The darkness swallows him up.

"He probably shouldn't be by himself," Mallory says. "I'll get Coop."

"I can go after him," Jake says.

"No, let's get Coop," Mallory says. "He's known Fray forever, he'll talk some sense into him."

(Later, she'll hate herself for not letting Jake go after Frazier. But in that moment, all she wants is to be alone with Jake.)

Cooper's bedroom is dark; the door is open a crack. Mallory pokes her head in. "Coop?"

No answer. Mallory turns on the light. The room is empty.

Empty? Mallory notices his duffel bag is gone and then sees the note on his pillow.

Sorry, Mal, I took the last ferry back. It's not worth doing this to Krystel. She threatened to call off the wedding if I didn't come home.

"*What?*" Mallory shouts.

Jake steps out of the bathroom. "Something wrong?"

Mallory shows him the note.

It's not worth doing this to Krystel.

It's not worth doing this to *Krystel?* They aren't doing *anything* to Krystel! They're enjoying a weekend at the beach. Krystel threatened to *call off the wedding* if Cooper didn't go home? Krystel is holding Cooper at emotional *gunpoint?*

"I don't know Krystel," Mallory says to Jake. "And now I don't want to."

"I've met her." Jake sighs. "I don't normally comment on other people's relationships, but…"

"Say it."

"It probably won't last," Jake says. "She's very pretty—blond hair, dark eyes, amazing body…but that's all there is. Once you get past the shiny wrapping paper and the fancy bow, the box is empty."

"Ouch," Mallory says. "Should I…what should I do?"

Jake sweeps Mallory's hair out of her eyes. "Kiss me," he says.

* * *

It's rapture—Jake's mouth, his lips, his tongue, his face, his arms. He falls back onto the sofa and pulls Mallory on top of him. She stretches out each kiss like it's taffy. But there's something else tugging at her. What is it?

"Wait," Mallory says, surfacing. She blinks, looks around the room. "We have to check on Fray."

On the beach, Mallory calls Frazier's name and Jake jogs along the waterline. The waves slam the shore with uncharacteristic force, or maybe it just seems that way because it's so late and so dark. There are some stars, but clouds cover the moon, and there are no other homes on this stretch of beach, no homes until Cisco, nearly a mile away. Mallory has never realized how isolated her cottage is.

Jake calls her; he's picking something up. It's Frazier's clothes—jeans, the Nirvana shirt.

"Did he?" Mallory looks at the water. "Did he go *in*?"

Jake drops the clothes and strips down to his boxers. "You're not."

He charges into the water.

Mallory starts to shiver. The night has suddenly turned sinister. She thinks back to the moment they were all sitting around the dining table toasting Cooper. Everyone was comfortable, safe, together.

But then Leland and Fray had crossed arms. Bad luck, if you believed her mother.

Mallory keeps Jake in sight, his dark head, the sleek curve of his back when he dives into an on-coming wave. She scans the water to the right and the left. She screams down the beach, "Fray! Fray! *Fray!*"

Her voice sounds like something broken or ripped. *"Frazier Dooley!"*

Jake staggers onto the beach, out of breath. "Leave his clothes where we found them," he says. "Go call 911."

Mallory tells the dispatcher that she lives in the cottage on Miacomet Pond and she has lost a friend in the water. An eternity—four and a half minutes—passes before she hears sirens, and another minute passes before she sees lights. One ambulance pulls up; it's followed by a truck towing a trailer with an ATV. Jake leads the rescue team—one uniformed officer and two divers in wetsuits—down to Frazier's clothes. The team members have lights; they have boards and rings and buoys.

One officer stays at the house. He's beefy, with reddish hair and freckles. He's...familiar-looking?

"I'm JD," he says. "You were my server last week at the Summer House."

"I was?" Mallory says. She's too panicked to go back and search her memory.

"How long ago did he leave?" JD asks. He has a clipboard. He's the information man.

"I'm not sure," Mallory says. How long were she and Jake kissing? "Half an hour?"

"Had he been drinking?"

"Yes," Mallory says. "Beer and...Jim Beam."

"Why didn't you try to stop him?"

"I didn't know he was going swimming," Mallory says. "He told us he was taking a walk. I thought he wanted to be alone." She drops her face into her hands. Why did Fray go *swimming* in the middle of the night? Why did he drink so much? Why did

Leland go to town with her friends from New York? She could have seen them Sunday when she got home for her friend Harrison's rooftop thing or whatever. Why did Cooper leave? His best friends were here! The weekend was for him!

JD is looking at Mallory sympathetically, but she knows what he's thinking: She shouldn't have let Frazier wander off by himself. Whatever the consequences are, she deserves them. "I watched him leave. I should have gone after him."

JD sighs. "I've seen situations like this go both ways."

This doesn't make her feel any better.

"Let's start with his name and date of birth. Just tell me what you can."

The divers search the water for ten minutes, fifteen, twenty. When Mallory is finished with JD, she goes down to the scene. JD has lent Mallory his jacket, but still, she's freezing. Jake is in his wet boxers and T-shirt; they won't let him go back in the water because the risk of losing him is too great.

"He's not out there," Jake says to Mallory. "They would have found him by now."

"They have to keep looking," Mallory says. To stop looking is to…what? Give up? Switch from a rescue mission to a recovery mission? It's too heinous to even contemplate. If something bad has happened to Fray, Mallory will never forgive herself. She wants to blame Cooper or Leland, but she was the last person to see Fray. She watched him head into the dark mouth of the night holding the bottle of Jim Beam by the neck. She knew his volatile history, the shadow of tragedy that followed him everywhere

because of the gaping hole where his parents should
have been.

Fray! she thinks.

There's shouting. The ATV is barreling down the
beach toward them. They found Fray. Mallory hears
the officer on the beach calling in the divers.

Alive? she thinks. *Or dead?*

Alive. The officer on the ATV found Fray all the way
down at Fat Ladies Beach, passed out in the sand. He
was unresponsive at first, the officer said, but just as
they were moving him onto the backboard, he came
to and puked in the sand.

The rescue mission takes some time to reel in and
pack up. Once the paramedic checks Fray's vitals, asks
him a few questions, and determines he doesn't need
a trip to the hospital, Jake helps Fray into the cottage.
Mallory thanks JD and the beach officer and the ATV
officer and the two divers a hundred times apiece. She
pulls twenty dollars out of her shorts pocket and tries
to press it into JD's hands.

He laughs. "Keep it. This was your tax dollars
at work."

"Well, then, I'll bake you some cookies and drop
them at the station."

"Cookies work," JD says. He smiles at Mallory and
she shuffles back through her mind to last week at the
Summer House. Yes! This guy had come in with a
white-haired gentleman, his father, who had engaged
in some harmless flirting with Mallory and then left
her a huge tip.

"I remember you," Mallory says. "Your dad was
terrific."

"He told me I should ask you out," JD says. "Are you here year-round or just the season?"

"Year-round," Mallory says. "I'm hoping to be working at the high school this fall."

"Cool," Officer JD says. "Would you want to…or is that guy, or the other guy…I mean, do you have a boyfriend?"

"I don't," she says. "But…" She shakes her head. "I think I'll need a few days before I can think straight. You have the number here. Maybe give me a call next week?"

"Yeah, I will, I'll do that. Hey, I'm glad things turned out okay."

"I'm sorry," Mallory says. "Thank you, sorry, thank you."

JD waves as he climbs into the cruiser. "That's why we're here."

Mallory and Jake fall asleep in her bed on top of the covers and with their clothes on, but when Mallory wakes up, Jake's arm is draped over her waist and his breath is warm on her neck. She opens her eyes, and before everything comes flooding back, she savors the weight of his arm, the steadiness of his breathing.

Is he her boyfriend?

No. But lying beside him feels incredible. She doesn't want to move. She could die right here, she thinks, with no regrets.

When Fray rises, he drinks a quart of orange juice, then sets the empty carton on the table and says, "I'm going home."

While Frazier is in the shower, Jake cracks eggs and drops slices of Portuguese bread in the toaster.

Mallory looks out the window and sees a cloud of dust heading for the cottage. A boxy white Jeep Cherokee with a rainbow stripe of Great Point beach stickers across the bumper pulls up out front. Leland hops out and runs inside.

Mallory closes her eyes. She hopes Fray disobeys her "quick-shower" mandate; she doesn't have the energy for a scene. She says to Jake, "Tell Leland to come into my room, please."

A few moments later, Leland knocks on Mallory's bedroom door. "Hey."

Out the window, she sees the Cherokee is idling.

"They're waiting for you?" Mallory says. Her voice is hoarse from all the screaming on the beach. "You're not staying?"

"They've invited me sailing," Leland says. "Kip's friend's dad has a huge yacht, I guess."

"Who's Kip?" Mallory asks. "You know what, never mind, I don't care who Kip is. Just pack your stuff and leave before Fray gets out of the shower, okay?"

"I could come back tonight," Leland says. "Or, I mean, these guys have a reservation at Straight Wharf at eight, so maybe you could join us?"

Mallory wonders if maybe the run-in with these New York friends wasn't random. Maybe Leland had planned this. But either way, Mallory can't compete with yachts and an impossible-to-get reservation at Straight Wharf. "I'm all set," she says. "But please go now. Frazier is pissed off."

"Fray needs to grow up," Leland says. "He needs to move on."

Mallory decides not to say anything to her about the events of the previous night. Leland quickly changes into a bikini and a cover-up, runs a brush through her chic haircut, fluffs her pink bangs. She turns to Mallory. "Are you angry?"

Yes, I'm angry! Mallory thinks. Leland wanted to surprise Fray, and she thought nothing of making out with him in the back of the Blazer; that was all fine. But walking off with her new fancy friends was rude—and, Mallory has to admit, utterly typical of Leland. She plays with people's feelings. Mallory wouldn't put it past Leland to have dreamed up this whole scheme—lure Fray back in, then abandon him so that she could be the one who was finally walking away from their relationship, in complete control.

Mallory sighs. She dislikes arguing with anyone, especially Leland. "Disappointed," Mallory says, and she lets half a smile slip. It's their old joke from high school. Their parents.

Leland kisses Mallory on the cheek. "I'll see you when you come back to the city."

Mallory isn't going back to the city, ever.

"Okay," she says.

No sooner does the white Cherokee pull away than there's another knock on Mallory's bedroom door. It's Frazier. His blond hair is wet and combed and he smells okay, but he's pale and his eyes are puffy. His duffel is slung over one slumped shoulder.

"I'm catching the ten o'clock ferry," he says.

"Okay." Mallory checks her bedside clock. "I'll drive you. We should leave in twenty minutes."

"I'm going to walk," Frazier says.

"You can't walk," Mallory says. "It's too far."

"I need to clear my head, Mal," he says. "I'll see you later, and thanks for having me and all that. You have a nice setup here. I'm happy for you."

"Fray."

"Mal, please."

Fine. If that's the way he wants it, fine! Through her bedroom window, Mallory watches him head down the no-name road, which is still dusty from Leland's departure. Mallory knew there was a chance the weekend would blow up this way, but even so, she feels stung: her brother and her best friend both failed her.

When she steps into the great room, she smells browned butter and coffee. Jake has used her new French press. "I made omelets with the leftover tomatoes and the Brie," Jake says. "Come eat."

Tears fill Mallory's eyes as she sits at the table. "Are you leaving too?" she asks.

"No," Jake says. "If it's okay with you, I think I'll stay."

Summer #2: 1994

What are we talking about in 1994? O. J. Simpson, Al Cowlings, LAPD chasing a white Bronco down the 405, the bloody glove, Mark Fuhrman, Marcia Clark, Johnnie Cochran, Robert Kardashian, Kato Kaelin, Judge Ito; Tonya Harding; Kurt Cobain; Lillehammer; Jackie Onassis; the World Series canceled; Newt Gingrich; the internet; Rwanda; the IRA; Pulp Fiction; Nelson Mandela; the

Channel Tunnel; Ace of Base; Rachel, Monica, Chandler, Ross, Joey, and Phoebe; Richard Nixon; The Shawshank Redemption.

Whether or not our boy Jake (and he is our boy, we're with him here through the good, the bad, and the incredibly stressful) wants to admit it, his life has been changed by spending Labor Day weekend with Mallory.

He would like the record to show that he went to Nantucket as a free and single man. A week before Jake headed to the island, he and Ursula had a category 5 breakup that destroyed everything in its path—Jake's self-esteem, Ursula's promises, both of their hearts.

He hadn't been looking for another romantic entanglement, not even an easy rebound. But by Saturday, after first Cooper, then Leland, then Frazier had left—bringing to mind the children's song about the dog that chased the cat that chased the rat— he realized this was what he'd been hoping for since the moment he saw Mallory waiting on the dock of Straight Wharf.

Mallory's eyes, he'd noticed, were bluish green or greenish blue; they changed, like the color of the ocean.

They were green when she stared at him across the harvest table with her empty breakfast plate in front of her. She had devoured every bit of her omelet, making little sandwich bites with her toast. Jake couldn't believe how at ease he felt with her, almost as if she were *his* younger sister.

Nope, Jake thought. *Scratch that.* His feelings were *not* brotherly. When he came around to clear Mallory's plate, he saw a golden toast crumb on the pale pink skin of her upper lip. He brushed the crumb away with the pad of his thumb, gently, so gently, and then he kissed her and he experienced the most intense desire he had ever known. He wanted her so badly, it scared him. *Go slowly,* he'd thought. Jake had been with only a handful of women other than Ursula, most of them casual dates or one-night stands in college. He spent a long time kissing Mallory's lips before he moved down to her throat and the tops of her shoulders. Her skin was salty, sweet, her mouth and tongue buttery. She made cooing noises and finally said, *Please. I can't stand it.* This was how Jake felt as well; the want in him was building like a great wall of water against a dam, but he savored the nearly painful sensation of holding himself in check. Slowly, he moved his mouth over the innocent parts of her body. And then, finally, she cried out and led him by the hand to the bedroom. Somehow, he'd known that the experience would change his life, that he would never be the same again.

Mallory's eyes were still green when she propped herself up on her elbow after they'd made love.

"Put your bathing suit on," she said. "I want to show off my island."

They headed out the back door and down a nearly hidden sandy path that led through the reeds and tall grass to Miacomet Pond. On the shore was a two-person kayak painted Big Bird yellow that Mallory dragged out to knee-deep water. She held it steady as Jake climbed on—he wanted to appear confident, though he hadn't been in a kayak since he was twelve years old, back when his sister was still healthy enough to spend the day on Lake Michigan. Mallory handed Jake his paddle and effortlessly hopped up front.

Away they went, gliding over the mirror-flat surface of the water. Jake let Mallory set the pace for their paddling and he matched her strokes. She didn't talk and although there were questions he wanted to ask her, he allowed himself to enjoy the silence. There was some birdsong, the music of their paddles dipping and skimming, and the occasional airplane overhead— people lucky enough to be arriving or, more likely, poor souls headed back to their real lives after an idyllic week or month or summer on Nantucket.

Jake tried to absorb the natural beauty of the pond—what an escape from the Metro stations and throngs of monument-seeking tourists in DC—but he was distracted by the stalk of Mallory's neck, the silky peach strings of her bikini top tied in lopsided bows, the faint tan lines on her back left by other bathing suits. Her hair was swept up in a topknot and the color was darker underneath, sun-bleached on the ends. He examined her earlobes, pierced twice on the left, a tiny silver hoop in the second hole.

Suddenly, she leaned back, her paddle resting against her lap, her face to the sun, eyes closed beneath her Wayfarers.

"You paddle," she said. "I'm going to lie here like Cleopatra."

Yes, fine, he would paddle her for as long as she wanted. In twenty-four hours, she had become his queen.

Mallory's eyes were blue when she gazed into the lobster tank at Sousa's fish market later that afternoon. She was wearing cutoff jeans and a gray Gettysburg

College T-shirt over her bikini. Her hair was in a ponytail; little wisps of hair framed her face. She had freckles on her nose and cheeks from the sun that afternoon. There was a tiny gap between her two bottom front teeth. Had she ever had braces? Jake knew every single thing about Ursula—they had been together since the eighth grade—but Mallory was a whole new person, undiscovered. Jake would get to know her *better* than he knew Ursula, he decided then and there. He would pay attention. He would learn her. He would treasure her. He would make a study of her eye color, the tendrils of her hair, the shape of her tanned legs, and the gap between her teeth.

When Mallory picked out two lobsters, her eyes misted up. The blue in her eyes then was sadness, maybe, or sympathy.

"You're going to have to cook those buggers by yourself," Mallory said. "I don't have the heart."

That night was their first date. Mallory melted two sticks of butter and quartered three lemons. She opened a bottle of champagne that had been in the cottage when she moved in, left by a long-ago house-guest of her aunt and uncle. They ate cross-legged out on the porch while the sun bathed them in a thick honeyed light. Once it was dark, they laid a blanket down in the sand and held hands, faces to the sky. Jake tried to identify the constellations and explain the corresponding mythology. Mallory corrected him.

She told Jake that her aunt Greta had moved in with a woman after Mallory's uncle died. This had scandalized everyone in the Blessing family except Mallory.

How could it possibly matter if Aunt Greta chose

to be with a man or a woman? Mallory said. *Why wouldn't everyone who cared about Greta just want her to be happy?*

Jake had responded by telling Mallory about Jessica. *I had a twin sister,* he said. *Jessica. She died of cystic fibrosis when we were thirteen.*

That must have been so difficult for you, Mallory said.

It was, Jake said. *Survivor's guilt and all that. Cystic fibrosis is genetic. Jessica inherited the genes and I didn't.* He swallowed. *She never got angry or made me feel bad about it. She just sort of…accepted it as her albatross.*

I've never lost anyone close to me like that, Mallory said. *I can't imagine life without…Cooper. How do you ever recover from something like that?*

Well, the answer was that you didn't recover. Losing Jessica was the central fact of Jake's life, and yet he almost never talked about it. Everyone he grew up with in South Bend already knew, but once Jake got to Johns Hopkins, it became something like a secret. He remembered being at a fraternity event, beer and oysters, and mentioning his sister to Cooper without thinking. Cooper said, "I didn't know you had a sister, man—how come you never told me?" Jake froze, unsure of what to say, then blurted out, "She's dead." It felt like the party stopped and everyone turned to stare at him; he was that uncomfortable. Cooper said, "Hey, man, I'm sorry." Jake said, "Nah, man, it's fine." It wasn't fine, it would never be fine, but Jake learned to keep Jessica out of casual conversation. He couldn't believe he'd told Mallory about Jessica after knowing her for little more than twenty-four hours. But there was something about Mallory that made him feel safe. He could turn himself inside out and show her his wounds, and it would be okay.

* * *

Sunday morning, Jake woke early and again made omelets, this time using sautéed onions and leftover lobster meat. Mallory wandered out of the bedroom wearing only Jake's shirt from the night before. Her hair hung in her face, and one eye was still half shut.

"You're beautiful," he said, then he nearly apologized because Ursula had found those very same words demeaning. *Women are more than just objects to be looked at,* she'd said. *We're people. You want to give me a compliment? Tell me I'm smart. Tell me I'm strong.*

"And also," he said, "you're smart and you seem very strong."

Mallory tilted her head and grinned. "You feeling okay?" she said.

After breakfast, they climbed into the Blazer and Mallory drove down a long and winding road—the Polpis Road, she called it—to a gatehouse, where she hopped out of the car and let some air out of the tires using the point of her car key. Then they bounced over a slender crooked arm of sand where the landscape emptied—houses disappeared, trees disappeared, the road disappeared—until it was just beach, water, grassy dunes, and, in the distance, a white lighthouse with a black top hat. Mallory pulled into a private little "room" created by the natural curve of the dunes that she had discovered on another trip. Had she been with someone else there? He couldn't help but wonder as they fell asleep in the sun.

When Jake opened his eyes, Mallory was holding a metal mixing bowl. "Come on," she said. "Treasure hunt."

They walked along the shore, eyes trained a few

feet in front of them. Mallory showed him slipper shells, quahogs, and mermaid purses. She picked up a sand dollar.

"Perfectly intact," she said. She held it up to the sun so that Jake could see the faint star pattern. "You should take this back to Washington to remember me by."

"Do I need something to remember you by?" Jake asked. "I mean, I'm going to see you again, right?" He was half thinking that he might never leave Nantucket at all.

"Sure," she said, but her tone was too casual for his liking.

They strolled all the way down to Great Point Light, collecting pieces of frosted beach glass, scallop shells, and driftwood until the bowl was filled, then they turned around.

"Why can't this work?" Jake asked. "We like each other."

"A lot," Mallory said, and she squeezed his hand. "I haven't been this happy with a guy in a long time. Maybe ever."

"Okay, so…"

"So…you're going back to Washington and I'm staying here."

"Couldn't we figure something out?" he said. "You visit me, I visit you, we meet someplace in the middle—Connecticut, maybe, or New York City? We rack up massive long-distance bills."

Mallory shook her head. "I did the long-distance thing with my last boyfriend and it was agonizing," she said. "Of course, he was in Borneo."

Jake laughed. "DC is closer than Borneo."

"The basic problem is the same," Mallory said.

"You have a job and a life in Washington and my life is here. I lived in New York for nearly two years and every single day I wished I were someplace else. I'm not doing that again." She paused. "And in the spirit of full disclosure, the officer who was up at the house the other night asked me out."

Jealousy, strong and swift, caused Jake to stutter-step. "What did you tell him?"

"I was vague," Mallory said. "I said he should maybe call me next week."

Jake didn't like this answer, nope, not one bit. "Can't we just pretend that we're the only two people in the world and that this weekend is going to last forever?"

Mallory stopped in her tracks and turned to face him. The lighthouse floated over her right shoulder. She stood on her tiptoes and kissed him. "We're the only two people in the world and this weekend is going to last forever."

"Are you humoring me?" he said.

"Yes," she said, and she grinned.

Back at the cottage, Mallory took the first shower. Jake was studying the books on the shelves of the great room when the phone rang. Jake's first instinct was to answer it. He liked answering other people's phones. He used to answer Coop's phone all the time—which was how he'd gotten to know Mallory in the first place. But of course he shouldn't answer Mallory's phone—what was he thinking? It might be Cooper apologizing for his exit, and how would Coop feel about Jake staying to shack up with his sister? Then again, what if this was that officer calling to ask Mallory on a date? Maybe Jake should scare the guy off.

Mallory raced out of the bathroom, naked and dripping wet, to snatch up the phone before the machine picked up. Jake wondered if she, too, thought it might be the officer from the other night. Jake's neck and shoulders tensed. His emotions were spiraling out of control. He was *gobsmacked* by this girl.

"Hello?" Mallory said. "Yes, this is she. Oh, yes. Yes!" There was a pause, and Jake imagined the officer asking if she was free the following night. Would he see her tan lines; would he have a chance to appreciate the shallow dip in her lower back? Would he cook eggs for her? Would he wipe the crumbs from Mallory's lips?

"I'm so sorry to hear that," Mallory said. "Yes, yes, of course I'd be willing. Oh my, thank you so much. Seven thirty. Okay, I'll see you Tuesday." She hung up and said, "The English teacher at the high school is at Mass General in Boston getting some tests done and he won't be in for the first week of school, so they've asked me to cover for him."

The relief Jake felt made him light-headed. "That's great!" he said. "That's what you wanted, right?"

"I wanted someone to *retire*," Mallory said. "I didn't want anyone to get sick."

Jake gathered Mallory up and kissed the top of her head. He was happy for her, but he didn't want to think about Tuesday.

"It's Sunday night," she said. "When my aunt was alive, that meant Chinese food and an old movie on TV."

They ordered from a place called Chin's—egg rolls, wonton soup, spare ribs, moo shu pork, fried rice, Singapore noodles, beef with broccoli.

"And dumplings!" Mallory cried into the phone. "Two orders! One steamed and one fried."

It was too much food, but that was part of the fun. Whenever Jake and Ursula ordered Chinese, Ursula ate only plain white rice and she refused to eat fortune cookies; she wouldn't even read the fortunes. The fortune cookie, she claimed, was a cheap gimmick that diminished the complexity of Chinese culture.

Jake watched Mallory dip one of her golden-brown dumplings into soy sauce, then deliver it deftly to her mouth with her chopsticks. She loaded a pancake with moo shu pork until it was dripping and messy and took a lusty bite. Jake was so stunned by the vision of a woman enjoying her food rather than battling it that he wondered if he might be falling in love with her.

Mallory handed Jake a fortune cookie. He was about to inform her that the purpose of the fortune cookie was to dupe a gullible public and distort the wise sayings of Confucius, but before he could share Ursula's skepticism, Mallory said, "Whatever it says, you have to add the words 'between the sheets' to the end."

Jake laughed. "Are you serious?"

"My house, my rules," Mallory said.

Jake played along. "'A fresh start will put you on your way'"—he paused—"between the sheets."

Mallory gazed at him. Her eyes were green tonight. "Damn. Was I right or what?"

"Read yours," he said, handing her a cookie.

"'Be careful or you could fall for some tricks today,'" she said, "between the sheets!"

He gathered up both fortunes. He would take them home, he decided. Along with his sand dollar. Things to remember her by.

They turned on the TV and found a movie that was just starting: *Same Time, Next Year* with Alan Alda and Ellen Burstyn. It was about a couple who meet at a seaside hotel in 1951 and decide to return together on the same weekend every year, even though they're both married to other people.

"Now, *that* is something we could do," Mallory said. She was lying between Jake's legs on the couch, her head resting on his chest. "You could come back to Nantucket every Labor Day, no matter what happens. We could do all the stuff we did this weekend. Make it a tradition."

A year? he thought. He had to wait an entire year?

On Monday, pregnant, pewter-colored clouds hung on the horizon, and when Jake stepped onto the porch, there was a chill in the air. It felt like an ending—not only of the weekend and the summer, but something bigger.

Jake made omelets while Mallory pulled a Joyce Carol Oates novel off the shelf that she wanted him to read.

"One thing I like about you," she said, "is that you're secure enough in your masculinity to read female novelists. Who are, in case you're wondering, superior to male novelists." She winked. "Between the sheets."

She was keeping things light, which made sense. She was excited about her substitute-teaching opportunity, and she got to stay here, in her beachfront cottage on Nantucket. The cottage had grown on Jake nearly as much as Mallory's company. The wood paneling made it feel like the cabin of a boat and Jake liked that the cottage smelled like summer—a little salty, a little marshy, a little damp. He loved the single deep blue hydrangea blossom in the mason jar on the harvest table; he loved the table itself, how unusually long and narrow it was. He loved the wall of swollen paperback books and he loved the sound of crashing waves in the background. He imagined being back in Washington with the traffic and the sirens and thought of how his heart would ache when he thought about the sound of the ocean.

The end of summer was the saddest time of year.

Jake gave Mallory a long, deep kiss goodbye. "I'm happy the dog chased the cat that chased the rat."

"Excuse me?"

"I'm happy it ended up being just you and me this weekend. And I'm coming back next year. Same time next year."

"No matter what?" Mallory said.

"No matter what," Jake said, and it did make leaving a little bit easier.

It isn't until the invitation to Cooper's wedding arrives in the mail—on expensive ivory stock, printed in a script so fancy, it's nearly unreadable—that Jake realizes he won't have to wait a year to see Mallory.

But there's a complication that our boy had not foreseen. He and Ursula have decided to give their relationship one last try.

"If we break up again," Ursula says, "we break up for good."

Jake thought they already *had* broken up for good. In their last breakup, the one that took place before Jake left for Nantucket, they had been point-of-no-return honest. Ursula admitted that she valued her career *above everything else*. It was more important than her health (she'd lost twelve pounds since starting at the SEC and now looked severely malnourished— passing supermodel stage, heading for famine victim), more important than her family (her parents were back in South Bend; her father was an esteemed professor at the university, her mother a housewife, Ursula rarely visited them and she discouraged them from visiting her because it would require sightseeing trips to the Air and Space Museum and the National Archives), more important than her faith (at Notre Dame, Ursula had been vice president of the campus ministry, but now she didn't go to Mass, not even on Christmas Eve or Easter. There simply wasn't time). Finally, she said, her career was more important to her than Jake was.

"Really?" he said.

"Yes, really," she said, leaving no room for interpretation.

Jake had wanted to say something back that was equally cruel—but what?

Jake had met Ursula in sixth grade at Jefferson Middle School. He knew her from his "smart kid" classes—pre-algebra, Spanish, accelerated English— and also because she was friends with his twin sister, Jessica. Ursula was the only one of Jess's friends who remained steadfast once Jess's health started to decline. When Jessica's blood-oxygen level was too low for her to go to school, Ursula swung by with Jessica's homework assignments, and she didn't just drop and run, the way any other twelve-year-old would have. Ursula used to sit in Jess's room, undeterred by the fact that Jess was hooked up to an oxygen tank, unfazed by the terrible coughing fits or the thick, gray mucus that Jess used to spit into a purple kidney-shaped basin, unbothered by their mother, Liz McCloud, who had taken a sabbatical from Rush Hospital in Chicago, where she was a gynecologist, so that she could care for Jess herself.

Jess was happiest when Ursula was around. Jess called her Sully, a nickname that Ursula didn't tolerate from anyone else. Jess liked to listen to music, so Ursula would put on Jess's favorite record, which she had ordered from a TV commercial. It was a compilation of novelty hits—"The Monster Mash," "Itsy-Bitsy, Teeny-Weeny Yellow Polka Dot Bikini," "The Purple People Eater"—and the two of them would sing along. Jake wasn't in the room but he suspected that Sully was also dancing, because he could hear Jess laughing.

Jake was always home when Ursula came over, stationed at the kitchen table, dutifully finishing his homework. Once Liz McCloud determined that Jess had had enough, and it was time for Sully to go, Ursula would pop into the kitchen to say hello and goodbye to Jake and their housekeeper, Helene, who was usually making Jake an omelet for his afternoon snack. Once, Helene offered to make an omelet for Ursula, and Jake could remember thinking, *Yes, please sit, please stay*—but Ursula said no, thank you, she had to get home, she had the same homework as Jake. As soon as Ursula left the house, Helene made a comment that had stayed with Jake all these many years.

"Sully is pretty girl, Jake. But more important, Sully is *kind* girl."

Ursula had been an altar server at Jessica's funeral. If Jake closed his eyes, he could still see Ursula in her white vestments that morning, her heavy, dark hair hanging in a braid down her back, her expression stoic in front of the coffin that held her friend.

* * *

Jake and Ursula had shared every single memory since that tragic year—right up until Jake went to Johns Hopkins and Ursula stayed in the Bend and attended Notre Dame. Over eight semesters of college, they had been broken up for only three, and as soon as Jake graduated, he moved to Washington so they could be together. He had taken the job lobbying for Big Pharma—possibly the most nefarious industry in America—because he wanted to impress her. Jake *hated* working for PharmX. The best thing about breaking up, he told Ursula, was that he could quit his job.

She'd laughed. "And do *what*?"

Maybe he'd teach chemistry at Sidwell Friends, he said, or maybe he'd go into fund-raising. He was good with people.

"Fund-raising?" she said.

"The great thing about breaking up," Jake said, "is that it doesn't matter what you think." This landed; he saw her flinch. "I don't fault you for putting your career first. I know how badly you want to…achieve." Ursula had been without peer academically at John Adams High School. She'd gotten into Harvard, Yale, and Stanford, but Notre Dame was free because her father taught there, so she stayed. She had been resentful about this, but she continued to soar. She was valedictorian at Notre Dame and got a perfect score on her LSAT. She was editor of the *Georgetown Law Review* and aced the bar exam. She was recruited by the trading and markets division of the SEC at the start of her final year of law school. In another year or two, she could move into private practice, write her own ticket, name her own salary. But what did it matter? She didn't enjoy the things money could buy; she never relaxed, never took a vacation, didn't have girlfriends to meet for drinks. "Just be aware that what you achieve doesn't matter as much as what kind of person you are," Jake said in his final blow. "You know, I sometimes think back to the girl I met in sixth grade. But that girl is gone." What he meant was that Ursula was no longer the kind of person who would spend even one hour with a sick friend. She was no longer the girl who would move the arm of the record player back to the start of a song again and again and again to bring someone else joy. She was no longer Sully and hadn't been for a long time. "Your own parents"—here, Jake was venturing into dangerous territory, but if the gloves were off, they were off—"apologized to me over how gruesomely self-centered you've become."

Ursula shrugged. "I don't care what my parents think of me, Jake. And I care what you think even less."

Those had been her last words to him—forever, he'd thought.

After Jake returned to DC from his weekend in Nantucket, he avoided any place he might run into Ursula; he even changed his usual Metro stop. But then, when Jake was home in South Bend over Thanksgiving, he bumped into her at Barnaby's. They were both picking up pizzas.

"You're here," he said. "You came home."

"Yeah," Ursula said, her tone uncharacteristically sheepish. "I thought about what you said about my parents. And then Mom told me Dad has heart issues and is putting in for early retirement and Clint wasn't coming home..." Clint, Ursula's brother, five years older, was a rafting guide in Argentina. "So, yeah, I'm home for a few days."

Jake hadn't responded right away. Quite frankly, he was startled by Ursula's presence *there,* in the place they'd grown up. If he'd seen her running along the Potomac or at Clyde's in Georgetown, he would have ignored her. But this was where they'd first kissed (at the ice-skating rink) and where they'd lost their virginity to each other (in Ursula's bedroom their junior year in high school while Mr. and Mrs. de Gournsey were away on a research trip in Kuala Lumpur). After Ursula graduated from Notre Dame, it was as though she had graduated from South Bend, from the state of Indiana, from the Midwest. Jake couldn't believe she'd come back of her own volition, without him prompting/urging/forcing her to.

It seemed notable.

Before he spoke, he noted how *thin* Ursula was— way thinner than she'd been when they parted at the end of August. Her cheekbones jutted out, her wrists were as skinny as sticks, and her chest, beneath her sweater and parka, seemed concave. She was holding a pizza but Jake knew how Ursula ate pizza—she pulled off the cheese and the toppings until it was just sauce and bread and then she took one bite.

If he mentioned her weight, she'd get defensive.

"Do you want to get a drink later?" he asked. "At the Linebacker?"

"Sure," she said.

One hour and four Leinenkugel's between them was all it took before they were making out in the front seat of Jake's old Datsun like the teenagers they had once been.

They ended up flying back east together and sharing

a taxi from Dulles to Dupont Circle. Ursula debated staying with Jake that night but opted to return to her own apartment. It was as she got out of the cab in front of the Sedgewick that she said it. "If we break up again, we break up for good."

Jake lived every day as though it might be his last day with Ursula. It felt a little bit like he was cheating death; he knew the end was coming, but when? It would have been a terrible way to live, except that Ursula was trying. She picked up the invitation to Cooper's wedding from Jake's desk and said, "Have you already RSVP'd to this?"

"Uh," Jake said, "no, but I mean, yeah. I'm standing up. I'm a groomsman."

Ursula tilted her head. In the two weeks since they'd been back together, she'd started looking better. Not any heavier, but she did have slightly more color. Ursula's paternal grandmother was from a town in the French Pyrenees close to the Spanish border, and Ursula had inherited her looks—hair like sable and a touch of olive to her skin. When she was outside in the sun, she turned bronze in a matter of minutes, but since she lived almost exclusively indoors, her skin tended to look jaundiced. Now, however, there was pink in her cheeks.

"I want to go to this," she said. "I like Cooper."

"Ah," Jake said. "Well…"

"You don't want to bring me?" Ursula said. She studied the invitation. "Cooper hates me now? He thinks I've been jerking you around? He thinks we're toxic together?"

"It's not that," Jake said. "I don't talk about…I've never said anything bad about you." This was mostly true, but Jake must have drunkenly slandered Ursula at some point in front of Coop. Every single one of Jake's friends knew that Ursula was his kryptonite.

"Who is Krystel Bethune?" Ursula said. "I haven't met a Krystel. I would have remembered."

Right. Ursula was particular about names. Her litmus test had always been, Is your name suitable for a Supreme Court justice? Safe to say, in Ursula's opinion, there would never be a Supreme Court justice named Krystel. This was a perfect example of why people disliked Ursula.

"He met her back in the spring," Jake said. "At the Old Ebbitt Grill." Jake didn't bother mentioning that Krystel had been Cooper's waitress; Ursula would have had a field day with that.

"This country club is nice, I've heard," Ursula said. "Old railroad money. Tell them I'll be your plus-one, will you?"

"Um…" Jake said. He didn't want to take Ursula to Cooper's wedding. He hadn't thought it would be an issue. Ursula was always working and she didn't like to leave the District for any reason. It was like she was umbilically connected to SEC headquarters. "I already said I was going solo. It's pretty fancy and the wedding is next week. I don't want to spring this on them."

"They'll understand," Ursula said. "I may take a lunch today and go buy a dress."

"Or you could take a lunch and eat lunch," Jake suggested.

Ursula slapped the invitation down. "I'm excited about this. A wedding! Maybe we'll be next."

Jake put off asking Cooper to add Ursula to the guest list because Jake was certain she would cancel.

Work emergency. The wedding was on December 18, and Ursula was hip-deep in an investigation that she couldn't talk about. Jake was *hoping* Ursula would cancel. He wanted to see Mallory alone.

Mallory. Mallory. Mallory.

When, by December 15, Ursula still hadn't changed her mind—she had, in fact, bought a black velvet off-the-shoulder gown—Jake called Cooper and told him he was bringing a plus-one. Coop checked with his mother, Kitty, who said that was a stroke of phenomenal luck because they'd had one last-minute cancellation.

"Way to go," Cooper said. "You managed to add a guest without pissing off Kitty."

"Great," Jake said half-heartedly. Kitty wasn't the person he was worried about.

The ceremony was to start at five. Ursula and Jake pulled into the church parking lot at ten past four because there would be a quick run-through for the groomsmen and bridesmaids—and also some Jim Beam, Cooper said.

"What am I supposed to do while you rehearse?" Ursula asked snippily, sounding very much like her pre-back-together self. "I don't want to sit in the church alone."

"Work in the car?" Jake said. At her feet, Ursula had an attaché case filled with depositions. He was relieved she didn't want to come into the church early. Mallory was a bridesmaid and although she was eventually going to find out Ursula was in attendance—it was possible Coop or Kitty had already told her—at least they would have the rehearsal hour together. Jake could talk to her, warn her, explain.

He'd brought Mallory a gift camouflaged in white wrapping paper with silver bells that he'd told Ursula was a private-joke-groomsman-thing for Coop. He wasn't sure he'd have the courage to slip it to Mallory, although now was his best chance. He plucked the gift from the back seat, where it rested next to the KitchenAid stand mixer that they'd gotten for Coop and Krystel, and tucked it under his arm.

The sanctuary of Roland Park Presbyterian was lit by hundreds of ivory pillar candles, the altar blanketed with white poinsettias. The other groomsmen and Cooper were all in white tie and tails. Jake set Mallory's gift in an empty pew and rushed up the aisle; he was the last to arrive. He saw five bridesmaids lined up in the first pew; they were listening to the pastor's instructions. Jake tried to pick out Mallory from the back of her head, but then he saw Coop urging him to hurry up and take his place in the formation.

"Sorry," Jake whispered. "Traffic on the Beltway."

Coop slipped Jake a leather flask, and Jake stood next to Frazier, who was the best man.

"Good to see you upright," Jake said.

Fray smirked. He looked far better than he had that summer; he had a good haircut and was clean-shaven. "At least *I* was on time."

Jake turned his head toward the cross while he took a slug off the flask; he had never needed a drink as badly as he did right that second. He tapped Frazier. "You want some, man?"

"Nah," Frazier said. "I'm on the wagon for a little while."

That probably wasn't a bad idea, Jake thought, considering what had happened the previous summer. Jake took a second swig and, thus fortified, he looked over at Mallory. She was wearing a long ivory dress with lace cap sleeves. Her hair was swept up in a style that had a name Jake couldn't remember. She was wearing full makeup and although Jake had grown attached to his unvarnished memories of Mallory, he thought, *Wow. Drop-dead.* Her eyes looked bigger; her cherry-red lips were incredibly sexy. She had on a pearl choker and pearl earrings and there was baby's breath woven into her hair.

When she saw him, she grinned and waved like a little kid. The sheer earnestness of her excitement made Jake want to pull her up to the altar and marry her right there and then. Also, it made him hate himself. It was obvious she didn't know he'd brought Ursula.

They ran through the wedding choreography, minus Krystel and the maid of honor, who were off-site getting ready. Jake had not been partnered with Mallory, which crushed him so badly that he nearly offered Cooper's colleague, Brian from the Brookings Institution, a hundred bucks to switch. Jake was insanely jealous when he saw Brian and Mallory with their arms linked. He was such a hypocrite! Ursula was waiting in the car. He and Ursula were back together, all the way back.

The run-through took ten minutes. They did it twice and then the bridesmaids were supposed to retreat to an anteroom to wait, but Mallory hurried right over to Jake. The expression on her face made it look like she wanted to tackle him in wild passion, but when she was a couple feet away, she stopped, probably just then reminding herself that they were in a church and that no one on earth knew what had transpired between them on Labor Day weekend.

"Hey," she said. "Good to see you."

Her restraint was adorable. "You look beautiful," he said. "Take-my-breath-away beautiful."

She dipped her chin. "You look beautiful too. The tails."

"Listen," he said. "There's something I have to tell you."

She raised her face. She was as luminous as one of the ivory pillar candles. "That you've thought about me each and every day for the past three and a half months?"

"I have," he said honestly. "Of course I have. But...at the last minute, I brought a guest to this thing."

"Guest?"

"Ursula."

Mallory's eyes searched his face and he saw her swallow. It was excruciating, watching her be brave. She bobbed her head and Jake wanted to march out to the car and tell Ursula to drive home, there'd been a mistake, she wasn't welcome. This, of course, was impossible, and Jake did love Ursula, or at any rate, he found himself unable to live without her.

Mallory said, "I know I don't have any claim on you."

You do, though, he thought. "Listen, I brought you something." He retrieved the gift from the pew and handed it to Mallory.

"A book?" she said. She tore off the paper, crushed it into a ball in her fist, and, without missing a beat, slid it into Jake's pants pocket. Her fingers brushing his leg made him weak for a moment. "*The Virgin Suicides.* Jeffrey Eugenides."

"It's by a man," Jake said. "But it's good anyway. Merry Christmas, Mal."

A tall, frosted-blond woman in an elegant long-sleeved ivory knit dress appeared at the head of the aisle. "Mallory, darling, chop-chop."

Mallory gave Jake a wobbly smile. "That's Kitty," she said. "I have to go. Save me a dance." She stood on her tiptoes to kiss Jake's cheek, then scurried away, hitching up the hem of her dress so she wouldn't trip.

Jake was distracted during the ceremony. He'd been the one who led Ursula to her seat on the groom's side, and she'd clutched his arm and whispered, "I shouldn't have come. I don't know a soul." He then stood at the altar practically incandescent with anger. Why had he allowed Ursula to come as his date? The answer was hardly rocket science. She had said she wanted to—and Ursula always got what she wanted. Jake was so angry he couldn't even look at her, so instead he sneaked peeks at Mallory, who seemed genuinely absorbed by her brother and Krystel exchanging vows. *For richer, for poorer, in sickness and in health.*

Maybe we'll be next, Ursula had said.

Ha! Jake thought. If he were to lose his job, go bankrupt, get hit by a bus, or be diagnosed with terminal cancer while he was married to Ursula, he'd be on his own.

He would never, ever marry Ursula.

Mallory wiped away a tear. Cooper kissed the bride. The organist played "Ode to Joy." Everyone clapped. Jake sought out Ursula. She was looking into her lap. Reading…the program? No. She'd brought *work* into the church. She folded her papers in half, tucked them into her purse, then looked up to see that Jake had caught her. She blew him a kiss.

* * *

In the car on the way to the country club, Ursula said, "Bride was pretty. But wearing a white fur stole at the altar? Wearing a white fur stole, period? T-a-c-k-y."

"Please," Jake said. "Don't be a bitch."

This was a standard start to one of their arguments: Ursula said something unkind, Jake called her on it, Ursula objected, the thing escalated. But tonight, Ursula stared at her hands. "You're right," she said. "I'm sorry."

The ballroom at the country club had been transformed into a winter wonderland, and even in his agitated state, Jake found it hard not to be impressed. Everything was done in shades of white. Each round table had a small tree with white leaves in the center. From the branches hung glowing white ornaments. There was a wooden bramble arch decorated with white fairy lights and what must have been every white rose in the state of Maryland in creamy round bouquets. The orchestra was onstage in white suits; the waitstaff wore white dinner jackets. The cake was seven stepped layers iced with white fondant and topped with coconut meant to look like snow.

Jake and Ursula were seated at table 2. Mallory was seated at the far side of table 1 with the bride and groom, her parents, and Brian from Brookings. Mallory already had champagne and her head was tilted toward Brian as he told her something that made her laugh.

"Do you want champagne?" Ursula asked. "I'm having some."

"I need something stronger," Jake said.

* * *

Weddings were tricky, Jake decided after his third bourbon. They were either terrific or downright awful. This one was, technically, terrific—a lot of time, effort, and money had been invested—but because Jake had to babysit Ursula while at the same time pining for Mallory, it was also awful. He auto-piloted through dinner and the toasts, noting only that Frazier's toast was touching and appropriate, probably because he was stone-cold sober. Ursula was chatting with the guest to her left, Cooper's cousin Randy, who was the in-house counsel for Constellation Energy in downtown Baltimore. They were talking shop, leaving Jake free to watch Mallory. She seemed *very* into Brian from Brookings—either that or she was trying to make Jake jealous.

The first dances came and went, then the band launched into "Holly Jolly Christmas," and Brian pulled Mallory onto the dance floor. Jake watched them for a few seconds; Brian had the nerve to undo his bow tie and pop his top shirt button. Jake flashed back to the night at the Chicken Box. Mallory had danced with such gleeful abandon. Jake had been so close behind her that he could smell the strawberry scent of her shampoo.

That tiny gap in her front lower teeth. The soft skin of her throat. The sand that gathered in the whorls of her ears. The crumb on her lip. It was agonizing to think about.

He turned to Ursula. The right thing, he supposed, was to ask her to dance. But she had pulled out whatever document she'd shoved into her purse and was reviewing it.

Jake shook his head and went to the bar.

Krystel threw the bouquet; Cooper slipped off her

garter. Ursula made no secret about finding both rituals distasteful, so she and Jake remained seated throughout. Meanwhile, Brian from Brookings was getting a little handsy with Mallory, and at one point, he kissed the top of Mallory's head. Jake wanted to punch him. Could he reasonably cut in? The night was slipping away. *Save me a dance*.

"You look miserable," Ursula said. She stuffed the brief back into her handbag. "I shouldn't have come."

Jake didn't respond.

"Let's dance," Ursula said. The song was "Build Me Up Buttercup" and everyone else was out on the dance floor, so Jake offered Ursula his hand. They stayed in the back corner. Ursula was a terrible dancer, but Jake was used to it. He knew she felt self-conscious, so it was a major concession for her to even be out there.

Just as the song was ending, one of the white-jacketed waiters tapped Ursula on the shoulder. She had a phone call, apparently.

"Is everything okay?" Jake asked. He thought immediately of Ursula's father, his heart trouble.

"It's work," Ursula said. "I gave them the number here—sorry. It's that thing I've been looking over...due Monday."

"Go," Jake said. This was so predictable that he didn't even pretend to be surprised or indignant. "Take your time."

Ursula swept off the dance floor in a flurry of self-importance and the band segued into "At Last." Jake marched right up to where Brian and Mallory were dancing, tapped Brian on the shoulder, and said, "May I?"

"Really, dude?" Brian said.

Mallory said, "This is my old friend Jake and he promised me a dance. I'll find you later." She stepped into Jake's arms and Brian skulked off.

"Hi," Jake said.

"Hi," Mallory said.

They fit their hands together. Jake took firm hold of Mallory's back and they began to sway. "I didn't want to bring her," Jake said. "She invited herself at the last minute."

"She's very pretty."

"*You're* very pretty," he said.

"It's not a contest," Mallory said. "She's your girlfriend."

"Yes," he said miserably.

"Thank you for the book," she said. "That was very sweet. You didn't have to get me anything."

"Every book I've read since I left Nantucket has reminded me of your cottage," he said. "I was just waiting until I read something good enough to share with you."

"Jake." Her tone was almost chiding. Was it wrong of him to make such a romantic gesture when he'd brought Ursula to the wedding?

Mallory rested her head against Jake's chest for one brief second, then murmured, "I know where there's a quiet spot. Want to sneak off for sixty seconds and kiss me?"

"Yes," he said.

She left first and he followed at what he hoped was a discreet distance. She strode down one hallway and turned into a second hallway that was definitely staff only. She opened a door and closed it. A second later, he followed. It was a supply closet. She locked the door behind him and turned the light off.

He got lost in her. He could not stop kissing her. He wanted to memorize how her face felt in his hands and the pressure of her lips on his.

She was the one who pulled away. "You'll come to Nantucket Labor Day weekend?"

"No matter what," he said.

When they were back in the car, Ursula—now in the driver's seat—turned to him and said, "Who was the bridesmaid you were dancing with?"

Jake was ready for this. Ursula could be drowning in depositions, but if an attractive female came within five feet of Jake, she would notice. She didn't want to spend time with him but neither did she want to share him.

"Cooper's sister," Jake said. "Mallory Blessing." It was a relief, a joy, even, to say her name out loud to Ursula. "I've known her for years."

"She seemed to have quite a crush on you," Ursula said. "It was actually kind of cute."

Labor Day is eight months away, then seven, then six. Still six months away. Then the spring arrives, cherry-blossom season in Washington, when the paths of the National Mall look like pink carpets, and time moves a little faster. Jake plays for the PharmX softball team and spends his spare time scheduling practices and games. Then June arrives; it's officially summer and Washington is so beastly hot that even Ursula agrees they should get out of town on the weekends. They go to Rehoboth Beach twice and then Ursula does the unthinkable and takes a week's vacation so that they can go to Paris.

"It would be such a romantic place to get engaged," she says.

It is, in fact, romantic. They go at the beginning of August, when the Parisians are on vacation, so they have the city to themselves. Ursula splurges on a room at Le Meurice, which is the nicest hotel either of them has ever stayed in. Jake blanches at the prices on the room-service menu, then rationalizes that Ursula works so hard, they deserve a little luxury. They order breakfast in the room each morning. The coffee is rich and fragrant; Jake enjoys hearing his spoon chime against the sides of the bone-china cup. It sounds like privilege. He feels the same way about the French butter, which he paints across the flaky insides of the croissants. As doctors, Jake's parents make plenty of money, but they're too busy to spend it. Ursula is exactly like them, so Jake figures he should enjoy the luxuries while they're on offer.

They stroll in Le Marais, holding hands, admiring the shops on the charming narrow streets. Ursula is drawn to the florists and wanders in to inhale the scent of the freesias and chat with the owners in her impeccable French. The women compliment Ursula's scarf, her dress, her bag; they think she's a Parisienne. Jake watches, amazed, feeling very much like a big dumb American; he stops wearing his Hopkins Lacrosse hat on the second day.

Ursula has picked the best brasseries in the city, where they sit in plush banquettes and feast on *moules et frites, frisée aux lardons, entrecôte avec béarnaise.* Ursula's abstemious eating habits seem to be on vacation as well. One evening she polishes off her Dover sole, though she scrapes off the butter sauce; the next night she treats herself to six of Jake's *frites.* She counts them out.

She has intentionally saved Montmartre and Sacré-

Coeur for their final evening. She wants to see the church all lit up and the view over the city. They buy an outrageously expensive bottle of Montrachet to drink from plastic goblets in the grassy park at the base of the church.

Ursula sighs. "I want to get married."

"Right now?" Jake asks.

"No, but, you know...I want you to propose. Soon."

Jake feels his throat constrict. He knows that Ursula has been expecting a proposal, or hoping for one, on this trip. There were a couple times in the past few weeks when Jake thought, *I should just go buy a ring.* But something stopped him. He wasn't *inspired.* If he bought an engagement ring now, it would be because Ursula wanted him to. And he'll be damned if he's going to let her railroad him into a decision that he's not ready to make. "Will you just let me handle it? Please, Ursula?"

"*Will* you handle it?"

"That's not letting me handle it."

"What are we *doing,* Jake?"

"I don't know what you're doing," Jake says. "But I'm putting in the time. I'm trying to grow up. I'm trying to build a relationship that's going to last for the long haul. And we're just not there yet, Ursula. I'm sorry, but we're not."

When she stands up, her wine spills.

"You're holding back to be cruel," she says. "Or to show me how powerful you are." She looms over him, blocking out the moon, and he feels all the Parisian magic drain away as though someone has pulled a plug. Of course this is how their week away will end.

"Don't ruin this," Jake says. "Let's go to dinner."

"You're the one who's ruining it," she says, and she storms off.

When Jake gets back to Washington, he has a pile of work on his desk, and mixed up in his in-box are not one, not two, not three, but *four* phone messages from Cooper Blessing.

He calls Cooper at Brookings and is told that Cooper is out on personal leave.

What?

He calls Cooper at home. Cooper answers in a broken, hoarse voice and says, "Krystel left me."

Jake has to work late that night in order to catch up, but the moment he's finished, he goes to Georgetown to meet Cooper at the Tombs.

Krystel, it turns out, is a drug addict and has been all along. Cooper knew she occasionally did cocaine with the other servers at work but he chalked it up to the restaurant business, the late nights, the double shifts. Then he found out that Krystel had been venturing over to Fourteenth and U to buy crack.

"She was smoking *crack!*" Cooper says. "Like a…like a…"

"Oh, man," Jake says.

"I tried to get her in rehab," Cooper says. "But she won't go. She doesn't *want* to quit. She moved back to her mother's house in Rising Sun, she *says*— but honestly, I think she's living in a flophouse some-where."

"Is she crazy?" Jake says. "You're the best thing that ever happened to her."

"She loves the drugs more," Cooper says.

Jake nearly says he understands. Substitute the

word *work* for the word *crack* and that's Ursula. But it's not the same, Jake knows it's not the same. Krystel is addicted to crack; Krystel has walked out on a marriage after less than nine months. It's a problem so big that Jake is at a loss.

"What can I do, man?" Jake asks. "How can I help?"

Cooper says he needs to get away. He *has* to get out of DC, if only for a long weekend.

"Mallory wants us to come back up to Nantucket," Cooper says. "She says we need a do-over."

"Oh," Jake says. "Really?"

Mallory picks them up at the airport. She's tan and fit; her hair is sun-bleached to the color of golden wheat. She's wearing her jean shorts and a T-shirt from someplace called the Rope Walk as well as her Wayfarers, her suede flip-flops, and half an arm's length of rainbow-colored friendship bracelets. There's a thin tattoo of a vine around her ankle.

Jake is smitten. He loves everything that's familiar and everything that's different.

Mallory hugs her brother first, long and hard, eyeing Jake over Cooper's shoulder. Her expression is partially obscured and therefore hard to read. Here it is, one year later, and they're together—though not under the circumstances they might have hoped for.

When Mallory and Cooper separate, she turns to Jake. "Hey, stranger," she says. "Welcome back." She stands on her tiptoes to hug him, grabs a hank of hair at the back of his head, and tugs.

His heart crests like a wave.

Jake is so deliriously happy when he climbs into the back seat of the Blazer that he feels like he could levitate—and he didn't even have to lie to Ursula. He's on Nantucket to console his brokenhearted friend. But brokenhearted Cooper is in good spirits. He flirted with the flight attendant and walked off the plane with her phone number. She, too, will be on Nantucket all weekend and they've made plans to meet up at the Chicken Box.

When Mallory drives them down the no-name road, dirt, dust, and sand fly up in a cloud. When the air clears, the cottage is before them, perched on the lip of the beach. The ocean is a blue satin sheet beyond. They're here. They're back.

The cottage looks the same; it smells the same. This year, Jake and Cooper get their own bedrooms. Jake quickly claims the one next to Mallory's.

"Swim?" Cooper says.

"Hell yes," Jake says, though he's eager to talk to Mallory. He wants to know how her year has been, he wants to look at the new books on her shelf, he wants to paw through her CDs and play some music. This cottage, this stretch of beach, this island, has imprinted itself on his consciousness, like a watermark on fine paper.

"You guys swim," Mallory says. "I'll get the hors d'oeuvres ready, and in a little while we can light the charcoal. I made burger patties."

"That's funny," Cooper says. "It's just like last year."

Rewind, repeat; it's just like last year.

There *is* something different this year, however: an outdoor shower. Mallory shows it off, calling it "the mansion." It is roomy and beautifully crafted, made of pressure-treated lumber that has only just started to weather to gray. It has a changing area with a bench and towel hooks that look like anchors. Jake is just tall enough that he can peer over the top—ocean to one side, pond to the other. The water is hot and plentiful. It's the greatest shower in the world.

Then he notices a pair of men's board shorts hanging from one of the anchor hooks.

He scrambles for a second. He was the first person in the shower; Cooper is in the kitchen, talking to Mallory. So these belong to…

Someone else.

Cooper grills the burgers while Mallory tends to the corn and tomatoes. Jake plays music—Dave Matthews, Hootie and the Blowfish, and then "Hard Headed Woman." This gets Mallory's attention; he can see her looking at him through the billow of steam from the pot of corn. Whatever they had is still there. Ursula doesn't matter, and whoever the other guy is doesn't matter.

Cooper comes in, holding the platter of burgers and grilled buns. "What is it with you and this song?" he says.

Over dinner, Mallory is direct. "Do you want to talk about Krystel or not talk about Krystel?"

"Not talk about Krystel," Cooper says. He piles pickles on top of his burger, and Jake notices Mallory doing the same. Without warning, Jake thinks about Jessica—the diving contests they used to have at Potawatomi pool, the way she would flip her wet hair over so that she looked like Dolley Madison. He misses having a sister.

Mallory raises her wineglass. "Here's to not talking about Krystel."

They touch glasses and drink.

"I don't understand love," Cooper says. "How many times have I eaten out in my adult life? Hundreds. Which means I've had hundreds of servers, and half of them were female. Why did I fall in love with Krystel Bethune at the Old Ebbitt Grill? It doesn't make any sense."

"She's beautiful," Mallory says. "Was that it? Did you succumb to surfaces?"

"She wasn't the most beautiful girlfriend I've ever had," Cooper says. "Tiffany Coffey in high school was prettier. And Stacey Patterson from Goucher..."

"Yeah," Jake says. "Stacey was hot."

Mallory kicks Jake under the table and suddenly the night comes alive. She's jealous!

"It was timing," Jake says. "You were ready to meet someone and she was there."

"I was wearing my Hopkins Lacrosse T-shirt," Cooper says. "She mentioned that she knew a bunch of players from the '87 championship team. I was impressed, I guess. But that's the kind of thing that keeps me up at night. What if Krystel hadn't mentioned Petro and Wilkie? Or what if I'd worn a different shirt? We wouldn't have started talking, I wouldn't have asked for her number, and I would not be sitting here on Nantucket a broken man."

Mallory kicks Jake again, only this time the kick is more of a nudge, her bare foot on his shin. If she gets any more intimate, he's going to pick her up and carry her to the bedroom, Cooper be damned.

"What about you, Jake? Do you understand love?" Mallory asks.

Jake sets about buttering his corn. "No."

"You do, though," Cooper says. "You love Ursula.

You've always loved Ursula." He looks at Mallory. "They've been dating since the eighth grade."

"On and off," Jake says. "There's been a lot of off, actually."

"But you're together now?" Mallory asks. The light is fading. There's only a single votive candle on the table, but even so, Jake sees the question in her eyes, which are green tonight. He prefers them green.

"We are."

Mallory cuts her burger in half in a way that seems aggressive. "Will you marry her?"

"I can't believe you haven't asked her already," Cooper says.

Jake has reached a crossroads. He isn't sure what to disclose under these circumstances. Should he spill his guts as though Mallory has no stake in the answer? There's a way in which they're both playacting for Cooper and for each other. "We went to Paris last month," he says. "She demanded a proposal and I told her I wasn't ready."

"Ouch!" Cooper says.

Mallory throws her brother an exasperated look. "At least *he's* not rushing into anything."

"Hey," Cooper says. "You're supposed to treat me with kid gloves."

Jake looks down at his burger, then up at Mallory. "What about you, Mal? Have you ever been in love?"

"Coop, may I have the ketchup, please?" Mallory says.

"Answer the man's question first," Cooper says.

"Just please pass the ketchup."

"Come on, Mal. We're having a heart-to-heart here. Have you ever been in love? And Mr. Peebles doesn't count."

"Who's Mr. Peebles?" Jake asks, already hating Mr. Peebles and hoping he's long dead.

"Her ninth-grade English teacher," Cooper says. "Mal was in love with him. It was well documented in the diary that I stole from her room and read to my friends—"

"Thereby scarring me for life," Mallory says.

"But that doesn't count because Mr. Peebles was married and very devoted to his wife."

"All the more reason to love him," Mallory declares. "Plus, he introduced me to J. D. Salinger. That year, I dressed up as Franny Glass for Halloween, remember? I wore a white nightgown and carried a chicken sandwich and the only person who got it was Mr. Peebles."

"You're trying to change the subject," Jake says.

"Yeah," Cooper says. "Just tell the truth for the sake of honest, good-faith conversation. Have you ever been in love?"

"Yes," Mallory says.

"Yes?" Cooper says. He sounds surprised. Jake is holding his breath.

"Yes," Mallory says again. "I'm in love right now, as a matter of fact. So…would you please hand me the ketchup? My burger is getting cold."

She's in love with me, Jake thinks. Or she's in love with the owner of the board shorts. It's agony not knowing. He'll ask her when they're alone.

No, he won't. Why ruin the weekend?

At ten o'clock, they pile into the Blazer to go to the Chicken Box. Cooper sits shotgun, Jake is in the rear, mesmerized by the back of Mallory's neck, her earlobe, the tiny silver hoop.

"Your first time to the Chicken Box!" Mallory says to Coop.

"I should have known Krystel was bad news when she told me to come home last year," Cooper says.

"We're not talking about Krystel," Mallory says.

"We're talking about Alison!" Jake says.

"Who's Alison?" Mallory asks.

"The stewardess whose number I got today," Cooper says. "She's meeting us at the bar."

Jake isn't sure the flight attendant will show up, but there's a woman waiting out front when they arrive, and that woman is indeed Alison from USAir.

"Cooper!" she says. "Hey!"

Cooper pulls Jake and Mallory aside. "Don't be pissed, but if this goes well, and I'm going to make sure it does, then I probably won't be back tonight. Or maybe tomorrow either, who knows."

Will he and Mallory be that lucky? Jake wonders. "Mal and I will be fine," he says. "We're old friends."

"Mal?" Cooper says. "Is it okay with you? I need this."

Mallory swats her brother away. "Go have fun. Don't worry about us. Just be a gentleman, please."

As Cooper and Alison disappear into the bar, Jake thinks about lobsters and stargazing tomorrow night, Great Point on Sunday, then home to play music and talk about books and maybe shower together in the mansion before they order Chinese food and watch an old movie. Maybe the networks play *Same Time, Next Year* the same time every year, to be clever.

Mallory is about to follow Cooper inside, but Jake grabs her hand. "Can I talk to you for a second?"

She bounces on her toes. "He sure was easy to get rid of."

"Mal, seriously."

"Seriously what?"

"I noticed the board shorts hanging in the outdoor shower, and I want to make sure there won't be some guy in there waiting to kick the shit out of me."

"Ah," she says. "Those belong to JD."

Jake waits.

"The rescue officer, from last year."

Jake was afraid of that.

"We're dating," Mallory says. "Casually."

"But not *too* casually—because he showers at your house and leaves his clothes behind."

"Well, we're not engaged or planning to get engaged," Mallory says. "And...he's away this weekend, at my suggestion, mountain-biking with his buddies." She grins. "So you're safe."

"We're the only two people on earth," Jake says.

"And this weekend is going to last forever," Mallory says. "Let's go dance."

Summer #3: 1995

What are we talking about in 1995? The Oklahoma City bombing; Bosnia, Serbia; molten chocolate cake; the Macarena; Windows 95; Des'ree; the Unabomber;

Yitzhak Rabin; Toy Story; *Selena; Bye, Felicia; Steve Young; Eight-Minute Abs; Yahoo!; Jerry Garcia; Frasier, Niles, Lilith, Daphne, and Roz;* The Bridges of Madison County; *O. J. Simpson found innocent by a jury of his peers.*

When we check in with our girl at the beginning of 1995, we are cheered to see how well things are going for her.

Mallory is now—after Mr. Falco's retirement and four months of traveling to the Cape twice a week for her certification classes—a real teacher. She joined the union and attends faculty meetings; she overprepares the night before the principal, Dr. Major, comes to observe her class. On Tuesdays and Thursdays, she's the cafeteria monitor, and she accepts bribes from the kids in the form of Cheetos and Hostess cupcakes. She stands over anyone with pizza and sings "Ain't Too Proud to Beg" until the student offers up the crispiest piece of pepperoni. At the end of each school day, Mallory swings by the guidance office to debrief with Apple; sometimes they gossip, sometimes they vent, sometimes they have constructive conversations about how to better reach the kids. On Friday afternoons, Mallory and Apple go to happy hour at the Pines. They order beers and mozzarella sticks and toast to another week survived as though they are living in a combat zone—life with 112 teenagers—and Apple will say, "Only twenty-seven [or "nineteen" or "twelve"] weeks until summer vacation."

Mallory is almost embarrassed to admit it, but she doesn't want the school year to end. She starts off each class by reading a poem and asking the kids to react to it. She chooses Nikki Giovanni, Gwendolyn Brooks, William Carlos Williams, Audre Lorde, Linda Pastan, Eldridge Cleaver, Robert Bly, and everyone's absolute favorite, Langston Hughes. Mallory photocopies short stories by Joyce Carol Oates, Maxine Hong Kingston, John Updike. They discuss editorials in the *New York Times*. They read *The Member of the Wedding* by Carson McCullers, which only a few of the kids warm to, and then they read *The Handmaid's Tale,* which is a crowd favorite. Dystopia, Mallory thinks. Teenagers love dystopia, the world as they know it falling apart at the seams. Her students keep journals in which they relate passages of what they've read to their own lives. They write short stories, sonnets, personal essays, persuasive essays, haiku (which they like because they're short), and one research paper, mandated by the state, which makes the kids stressed and peevish, and the unit falls in the middle of March, when everyone on Nantucket hates everyone else anyway.

Mallory is popular because she's young, because she's "cool," because she wears long blazers and leggings and friendship bracelets that the ninth-grade girls weave for her, because she's friends with Apple ("Miss Davis"), who is also young and cool, because she talks to her students like they're people, because she takes an interest in their lives. She knows who just started dating whom and who just broke up. She knows to pack an extra sandwich and invite Maggie Sohn, whose parents are divorcing, to spend lunch in her classroom so they can talk. She knows where the parties are, who goes, who doesn't, who throws up, who hooks up. Some of this she gleans from reading the kids' journals; some she overhears as they're coming in and out of her classroom; some she hears from the kids who confide in her. Mallory locks it all in the vault, and opens the vault for Apple only—she never says a word to the principal, Dr. Major, to the parents, or even to JD.

And then, when it seems like things can't get any better, they don't. They get worse. Much worse.

Mallory was warned by Apple and the other teachers: Once the kids return from spring break, they're impossible to control. And after the first seventy-degree day, forget about it.

Spring fever, Apple says. *Everyone gets it.*

Over April break, Mallory and JD go to Vieques, a tiny island off the coast of Puerto Rico. Mallory chooses it because it's undiscovered, relatively undeveloped, and cheap. She books seven nights in a one-story beachfront motel in a tiny village called Esperanza. Their room is dim and the bedding iffy, but they aren't picky. Mallory is cheered because the motel sits on a strip of white-sand beach on a turquoise bay. JD is cheered because the motel has a happening bar and restaurant out front.

On the first full day, JD plants himself on a barstool and starts drinking Modelos; after lunch, he switches to margaritas. Mallory is indulgent at first—she knows that JD is used to all-inclusive resorts where the point is to drink as much as possible in order to get your money's worth, but after two days, she loses patience and begins to worry about their bill, which they've agreed to split. Mallory wants to explore the island. She wants to snorkel; she wants to tour Mosquito Bay and see the bioluminescence; she wants to visit the plaza in Isabel Segunda. There's a nearby island called Culebra that has a famous Chinese restaurant. Mallory wants to hire someone to take them over by boat.

JD says, *Sure, sure, whatever you want, baby*. But getting him off his barstool is another matter. Mallory rents a mask and fins from the surf shop down the street and snorkels in the bay out front. She buys two tickets for the New Moon tour of Mosquito Bay, but JD is passed out cold at eight o'clock, so Mallory goes alone. It's as she's floating around and the water lights up around her—the dinoflagellates in the bay glow a brilliant blue when they come in contact with other creatures—that she finally acknowledges that she and JD just aren't compatible.

They've been dating for eighteen months—though, as Mallory told Jake, it has been very casual. Or casual for Mallory, at least. JD is far more passionate about the relationship; he's always asking for more. He likes Mallory to come watch him play darts at the Muse on Wednesday nights, which she does only when she doesn't have too much grading. On Friday evenings after her standing happy-hour date with Apple, Mallory will join JD at the Anglers Club for their weekly appetizer party. This means clams casino and pigs in a blanket with a collection of longtime Nantucketers in the funky, weather-beaten clubhouse on Old South Wharf. JD invites Mallory to his parents' house and introduces her as "my girl," which makes her feel queasy. But it's been nice, too, to have someone on the island day in and day out who cares about her. JD is in excellent physical condition but the sex is reminiscent of Mallory's college years, with him humping and grunting in the dark; he's intent on pleasing only himself. And JD is explosively jealous of every single man Mallory comes in contact with. He's jealous of Dr. Major; he's jealous of Mallory's male students, especially the seniors.

Twice this past winter, JD mentioned *moving in to-gether,* and the phrase nearly sent Mallory into shock. *Moving in together* can only mean JD moving into Mallory's cottage—and no, sorry, that's never going to happen. Mallory doesn't even let JD do work around the cottage. Small jobs—fixing the bathroom fan, replacing the screen in the back door—Mallory has learned to do herself. Anything bigger—building the outdoor shower, having the cottage winterized, clean-ing the chimney—she hires other people to do, and JD is jealous of all of them.

When Mallory gets back to the motel after the tour of Mosquito Bay and gazes upon JD snoring in bed, she decides to make a clean break once they're back in Nantucket.

JD feels awful about missing the bioluminescence trip, so the next day, he arranges for a taxi to take them to Isabel Segunda. Once there, they wander the plaza holding hands and they stumble across a cute open-air bistro that is suffused with the heady scent of basil. Sure enough, the proprietress has just made pesto, which she tells them she's going to drizzle over a tomato, peach, and fresh mozzarella salad. Yes, please, one for Mallory. JD orders the whole grilled fish. They sit at a table on the edge of a balcony over-looking the Caribbean. The proprietress fusses over them, calling them lovebirds, and two hours pass in such an enchanted way that Mallory wonders if she overreacted the night before.

JD pays for lunch and they wander out into the white-hot afternoon in a daze. They stroll a little more, poking into galleries and gift shops. JD wants to buy Mallory something, a souvenir that she can take home, and Mallory (tactlessly?) repeats her mother's decree that anything one buys on vacation always looks like hell once you get it home. JD flinches. Has she ruined the mood? No, or at least not completely. He picks a red hibiscus blossom off a bush and tucks it behind Mallory's ear. "Thank you for planning this trip," he says. "I'm lucky to have you."

They try to find a taxi back to Esperanza but have no luck. It's hot, neither of them speaks much Spanish, and when they go back to the bistro to ask the proprietress for help, they find it shuttered, closed for the afternoon. JD starts to huff and puff. He prides himself on being a problem solver and doesn't like feeling helpless. He flags down a white pickup and offers the driver twenty bucks to take them to Esperanza. The driver is a young, handsome Latino in a white polo. He smiles at Mallory—the flower in her hair—and accepts the money. Mallory and JD climb into the truck.

Problem solved! Mallory squeezes JD's thigh. She leans back against the headrest and closes her eyes. The window is open but the air is hot and syrupy. She is bobbing along the edge of consciousness when suddenly she hears the driver speak.

"So, where are you guys from?"

Mallory opens her eyes. She is surprised by his perfect, unaccented English.

"Nantucket Island," she says.

"Ever heard of it?" JD asks. "It's an island in Massachusetts, off the coast of Cape Cod. South of Boston."

"Yeah," the driver says. "I spent a few summers on Nantucket growing up."

JD laughs like the guy has told a joke. "Oh, really?" he says. "Were you a Fresh Air Fund kid?"

There is a moment of noxious silence during which Mallory wants to vaporize and float away through the open window.

"Sorry, man," JD says. "I was only kidding."

The driver reaches a stop sign and stomps on the brake harder than he needs to. "I can't get you all the way to Esperanza. You'll have to walk from here. Follow the road to the sea, then take a right." He hands JD the twenty. "Here's your money back."

Later, nothing JD says will change Mallory's mind. Their relationship is over, and all Mallory feels is an overwhelming sense of relief.

Mallory tries not to play favorites with her students but she has become very close with Maggie Sohn, who is struggling with her parents' divorce, and she has a soft spot for one other student, Jeremiah Freehold. Jeremiah is a sweet, bright kid. His father is a scalloper, his mother a seamstress. They live in an antique home on lower Orange Street. Jeremiah is the oldest of five children. None of this is particularly remarkable. What is remarkable is that, at eighteen years old, Jeremiah has never been to the mainland. Mallory thinks of the Freehold family as a throwback to Nantucket in the 1800s. They're Quaker; they live a quiet, sustainable island life. In his journal for class, Jeremiah keeps a list of things he's never actually seen: a traffic light, a McDonald's, an escalator, a shopping mall, a cineplex, an arcade, a river, a skyscraper, an amusement park.

Talk about sheltered, Mallory thinks. But his life has a purity that she can't help admiring.

Back in the fall, Mallory asked Jeremiah what his

plans were for college. He told her he wasn't going to college; he would become a scalloper like his father. Mallory asked how he felt about this. He was bright, an enthusiastic reader; it seemed a shame for him not to continue his education.

"I'll be continuing my education on the water," he said. "And when I want books, I'll borrow them from the Atheneum."

Right after spring break, Jeremiah starts stopping by Mallory's classroom after school. He asks her to read his poetry. He asks her to recommend books. Mallory is enthralled with Michael Ondaatje's novel *The English Patient,* which Jake had sent her at Christmas. The inscription: *Again, by a man. Again, good. XO, Jake.* Mallory isn't willing to lend Jeremiah her own personal copy—it's too precious with Jake's handwriting inside—but she makes a special trip to Mitchell's Book Corner and buys a copy for Jeremiah.

He reads it in two days, then comes by to discuss it with Mallory. Jeremiah is a tall, lanky kid with a high forehead and a pronounced Adam's apple; Mallory thinks he looks like a young Abe Lincoln. Most days, he wears a flannel shirt, jeans, and sturdy boots. However, today he's wearing a new shirt, white linen, and there's a brightness to his eyes, a flush to his cheeks. He speaks so quickly about how much he loved the book that he trips over his words: *Hana, Caravaggio, the Bedouin with their tinkling bottles of ointment, Kip the sapper, the North African desert, the Italian villa with holes blown through the walls.*

Jeremiah has a crush on her, she thinks. Or maybe she's just flattering herself.

The next few days, she shoos Jeremiah away after

school, claiming she has meetings, a dentist appointment, she's taking the Blazer in for a tune-up—and this works. Jeremiah stops coming by.

A couple of weeks later, however, he reappears. He's visibly upset, hot-cheeked, perspiring. All the seniors are going on the annual three-day senior-class trip to Boston (Apple is a chaperone every year, and she hates it—a Best Western in Braintree with forty horny teenagers who think it's party time—but the honorarium is too attractive to turn down), and Jeremiah's parents aren't letting him go.

"We had a family meeting and discussed it," Jeremiah says. "I made my points and they made theirs but it came down to this: I live under their roof so they are in charge of me until I move out. And they don't want me to go."

"Oh," Mallory says. "Wow." She's at a loss. She, like just about everyone else she knows, had wished for different parents growing up. Kitty would cook elaborate family dinners every single weeknight, and it was Mallory's responsibility to do the dishes. Mallory's tendency—every teenager's tendency?—was to try to find shortcuts, but it was as if Kitty had second sight.

"Properly," Kitty would call from the other room if she heard the plates landing in the dishwasher at too brisk a pace for them to have been thoroughly rinsed. "Do them properly."

Mallory had learned to tune out her mother; the endless stream of whatever was coming from Kitty's mouth became an unintelligible *Wah-wah-wah,* like the teachers in the *Peanuts* TV specials.

Senior was a man of few words unless the topic was traffic on 83 or the Orioles. He was frugal—the heat in their house on Deepdene Road was turned on and set to sixty-seven degrees on December 15 and not a day before; it was turned off on March 15 and not a day later. "If you're cold, put on a sweater," he would say. And Senior's political views were pulled right out of the Eisenhower administration—for starters, his attitude about his very own sister, Greta.

But as exasperating as Kitty and Senior could be, they fell within the parameters of "normal parents" for twentieth-century America. They would never have kept Mallory or Cooper from an experience that could expand their horizons. Mallory tries to understand why the elder Freeholds would not want Jeremiah to go to Boston on a supervised trip with his peers, children he has known his entire life.

"Is it a matter of money?" Mallory asks. The trip fee, she knows, is a hundred and ten dollars per student, but the kids have been selling candy bars all winter to fund-raise, and some of that money is earmarked for families in need. Mallory could put in a word with Dr. Major.

"No," Jeremiah says. "It's a matter of principle. They see the mainland as needlessly complicated." He shakes his head. "I love this island. But as soon as I have enough money saved, I'm leaving. I'm going to North Africa."

Mallory brings up Jeremiah the next day at the faculty meeting. She's hoping someone—Apple or even Dr. Major—will offer to call the Freeholds and persuade them to let Jeremiah go on the trip. But Dr. Major, who is normally very progressive and involved, shuts Mallory down. "There is no persuasion powerful enough when it comes to that family," he says. "Let it be."

Apple follows up with her later, in the hallway. "And don't you go knocking on their door, Mal, please. I know you—you feel for the kid, he's a little different, he doesn't have many friends, you want to save him, but do not get involved. He'll be fine. You want to feel sympathy for someone, feel sympathy for me—I'll be confiscating cigarettes and trying to prevent teenage pregnancy for seventy-two hours."

The seniors leave early Monday morning and are due back on the late ferry Wednesday night. The school is eerily quiet without them. Mallory teaches two seniors-only classes, so her days are baggy with time. On Monday, she catches up on her end-of-the-year progress reports. Tuesday, it rains and she holes up in her room and reads the new Anne Tyler novel. Wednesday dawns sunny and warm. It's a terrific day to play hooky. What's to stop Mallory from calling in sick or taking a personal day and getting some sun on her front porch? A sense of responsibility, that's what. When she gets to school, she realizes her sophomores have a field trip to Jetties Beach, leaving Mallory with even more free time.

Mallory walks past the library and sees Jeremiah sitting at a table alone, his journal open in front of him. Her heart lurches. She can't let him just sit there.

"Want to go get some lunch?" she asks him. "My treat?"

"In the cafeteria?" he asks. Mallory notices his steel lunchbox with the domed lid, the kind construction workers used to carry. She knows that Mrs. Freehold packs Jeremiah a lunch each and every day; he doesn't even buy milk.

"No, let's go on an adventure," Mallory says

impulsively. Jeremiah is a senior and therefore has off-property lunch privileges, though she doubts he's exercised them even once this year. Which is all the more reason for him to go today. The rest of his class is watching street theater outside Faneuil Hall or farting in the elevators on their way to the Top of the Hub in the Prudential Center, so what harm will it do if Jeremiah goes to the beach? Or… "Maybe you can show me someplace I've never been?" Mallory has lived on Nantucket just shy of two years and there are still whole swaths of the island she hasn't explored.

Jeremiah cocks his head. She can tell he's wondering if she's serious.

"Come on," she says. "My car is out front."

Jeremiah says he wants to show her Gibbs Pond, which is in the middle of the island, because that's where his father first taught him to fish. Mallory's interest is piqued because she knows from reading the kids' journals that Gibbs Pond is where most of the high-school parties are held.

"We have fifty minutes," Mallory says. "Can we get there and back in fifty minutes?"

"Yes," Jeremiah says. He grabs his journal, his books, and his lunch with purpose, and for a moment, Mallory feels like *that* teacher—the one who thinks outside the box, the one who goes the extra mile, the one who saves a kid's life, at least figuratively.

They head out the Milestone Road in the Blazer. The top is on but it's warm enough for them to open the windows and let the sweet spring air rush in. Mallory turns up the radio. It's "Crazy" by Aerosmith, and Jeremiah throws his head back and campily sings along.

"So you have a radio at home, then?" Mallory asks.

"Yes," Jeremiah says. "And a TV. *Cable* TV." He grins.

Jeremiah directs Mallory to turn left down a dirt road, and they wind through thick, scrubby woods. It was a pretty tough winter, lots of snow, rain, and wind, and the road is in bad shape with dramatic whoop-de-dos and rogue branches sticking out that etch Nantucket pinstripes along the sides of the Blazer. Mallory begins to wonder about the wisdom of this adventure. The road is one-lane—three-quarters of a lane, really—so there's no possibility of turning around until they get to a clearing. "You're sure this is the right road?" she says.

"Yes," Jeremiah says. He's got one elbow hanging out his open window and he's so tall, his head nearly grazes the roof. "Just keep going and we'll drive right into it."

Mallory tries to relax. The adventure is in the journey. And she'd rather be here than in the cafeteria eating chicken potpie, right?

The woods start to thin out and there's light ahead as though they're coming out of a tunnel. A moment later, the landscape opens up and a large silvery-blue pond lies before them. There's a formation of ducks paddling their way across the surface.

"It's…it's…" Mallory lives on a pond, Miacomet Pond, but Gibbs is different. It's surrounded by open space and yet it's hidden from the main roads; it's like it's been dropped in here, a secret. Mallory can't believe she has been living on Nantucket this whole time without knowing this spot existed.

"My dad has a canoe," Jeremiah says. "The first time he brought me out here, I was six or seven and we caught a bunch of yellow perch that we took home for dinner. The pond is named for John Gibbs. He was this Native American preacher who got into trouble with his tribe and came here to hide from them. The white settlers liked Gibbs's preaching so much that *they* paid the penalty he owed—eleven pounds. It's weird, right? This happened hundreds of years ago...but the pond is still here." Jeremiah swallows. "My parents believe that this is our island, we're its stewards, and this is our time to care for it, so why would we go anywhere else?"

Mallory drives closer to the pond's edge, wishing she'd brought her camera. She turns off the engine and opens her door. She wants to see the pond up close; they've come all the way out here, they might as well. No one will notice if they're five or ten minutes late getting back. Mallory doesn't have another class until eighth period and Jeremiah is in independent study all day.

When Mallory puts one foot out of the car, she steps in mud. She not only steps in mud, she *sinks* in mud, all the way to the top of her shoe. Then she sees her front tire is mired in mud as well. "Uh-oh," she says. Jeremiah is already out of the car, standing a few feet away; his boots are caked with mud. "Jeremiah, get back in, please. I want to make sure we aren't stuck."

She pulls her foot back in, starts the Blazer, and gently shifts it into reverse. When she hits the gas, the front wheels spin. Mud sprays everywhere.

"No," Mallory says. She is such an *idiot!* She puts the car into four-wheel drive. That will do it, she thinks. This is, after all, a Blazer, the toughest of all off-road vehicles, or so she likes to believe.

Again, the wheels spin. Mud sprays everywhere; flecks hit Mallory's face through her open window.

Jeremiah says, "You'd better stop. You're digging in deeper. I'll get out and push."

Mallory tries not to panic. Everything is going to be fine. They will get the car unstuck. They will drive back down the horrible dirt road over the whoop-de-dos, and then they will be back on familiar turf, Milestone Road. They'll get to school by the start of seventh period, at the latest. Mallory will wash the car by hand this weekend. She'll buff out the pinstripes. She has never felt protective about this car anyway. It's a road warrior. It's supposed to take a beating.

Jeremiah crouches in front of the car and pushes. The water is at his ankles; his boots must be flooded. Mallory can see the tendons in his neck strain; his cheeks turn red, the veins in his forehead pop. Mallory steps on the gas, praying, praying, *Come on, baby, easy does it, here we go...*

The wheels spin. They take a deeper bite of the muddy earth.

Mallory takes her foot off the gas.

Jeremiah says, "Do you have any boards we could put under the tires?"

She blinks. "Do I have any *boards?*"

It's a Wednesday morning. There is no one else at Gibbs Pond—no cars, no people, nothing but birds and the cloudless sky above. They'll have to go for help. What choice do they have? Mallory tries to decide if she should send Jeremiah out to find help or leave him here with the car. Well, it's her car and he has longer legs. She sends him out to Milestone Road.

"Just flag down the first person you see and explain what happened," she says. "We need someone to tow us out."

Jeremiah heads out on his own while Mallory gets out of the car and assesses the situation. She's stuck. Stuck! She sits on the hood with her face in her hands and tries not to cry. She only wanted to help—but what does Kitty always say? No good deed goes unpunished. Mallory hopes that Dr. Major will understand. He already knows that Mallory feels awful about Jeremiah being left behind, so naturally she would offer to do something nice for him. A little fresh air. It's such a gorgeous day, and everyone gets spring fever. Even Mallory.

What our girl doesn't predict (though the canny among us might) is that the person who drives Jeremiah back to the pond is none other than JD. He's in the Nantucket Fire Department's Suburban.

Mallory can't *believe* this. This is…so awkward. Mallory wonders if maybe it's no coincidence that JD was the first person Jeremiah was able to flag down. Mallory has noticed JD driving the Suburban on the roads between the school and her house pretty frequently since they broke up. She hadn't considered that JD was following her or checking up on her…until now.

JD pulls up behind the Blazer and hops out. He's in his black uniform. Mallory used to joke about how sexy he looked in that uniform, but now she finds him intimidating.

He inspects the front of the Blazer and lets out a low whistle. "You're stuck, all right."

Mallory yearns to keep things professional. "Do you have a tow rope?"

"I do," JD says. "Mind telling me what you and young Mr. Freehold were doing out here at Gibbs by yourselves in the middle of the school day?"

Mallory stares at JD, her cheeks aflame. She will not let him poison this situation with his pathological jealousy.

But then again, how will she stop him?

"I told you, Miss Blessing and I were having an adventure," Jeremiah says.

Mallory closes her eyes. She feels JD's imagination moving as swiftly as a duck's webbed feet beneath the calm surface of the pond.

"An adventure," JD says. "How about that."

When the seniors arrive back at school the next morning, Mallory learns that Christy Belk and, yes, Maggie Sohn sneaked out of their hotel room, crossed a highway to get to a liquor store, bought a bottle of Wild Turkey with Christy's fake ID, smuggled it into the hotel, and shared it with their roommates, both of whom spent the early-morning hours puking their guts up.

This, however, is not the talk of the school. The talk of the school is Jeremiah Freehold and Miss Blessing caught alone out at Gibbs Pond.

Apple stops by to see Mallory between classes. "Please tell me it's not true," she says. "Please tell me you listened to my advice and left that boy alone."

"How did you find out?" Mallory asks.

"How did I find *out*?" Apple says. "There's been a lot of whispering, baby. A *lot*."

Oh, for God's sake! Mallory thinks. People can't possibly believe that anything *funny* was going on, can they? Mallory is stung, and worried, and crestfallen—

not only because she and Jeremiah have become an object of curiosity (best-case scenario) or potential lascivious rumors (worst-case) but because in every class, she notices that her students avoid eye contact with her while simultaneously watching her every move. One of the boys slaps Jeremiah on the back.

At the end of the school day, Mallory is called down to Dr. Major's office. She'd expected this, even welcomed it, because she wanted a chance to explain herself. But now, after talking to Apple, she figures she's about to get fired. She wonders if Mr. and Mrs. Freehold will be there to complain about Mallory Blessing corrupting their son.

As soon as Dr. Major closes the door to his office, Mallory says, "I exercised horrible judgment, sir. I thought it would be okay to go for a ride during lunch. I felt so sorry for him. But I know how it looks and I understand why you have to let me go." Only in the last few hours has it occurred to her how *bad* the situation might appear to others. She and Jeremiah went to Gibbs Pond alone. A female teacher and a male student. He is eighteen—but still. What were Leland's words back in New York? *It's unseemly. How about some self-respect?* Has Mallory learned *nothing* in the past two years? Has she not grown up at *all*? That's what it feels like. She's back at square one.

"Let you go?" Dr. Major says. "I'm not giving up on my most promising teacher. Are you kidding me?"

Mallory keeps her job, but the incident with Jeremiah Freehold casts a pall over her summer. It feels like everywhere Mallory goes, people are avoiding her, whispering about her. She lives in mortal fear of bumping into Jeremiah or his parents; she wishes she knew what they drove so she could scan the parking lot at the Stop and Shop before venturing inside.

She decided earlier in the spring that she would not return to work at the Summer House pool; she wanted to enjoy a real teacher's summer off. But a week into vacation, this feels like an unwise choice. Apple is away—she took a job as head counselor at a camp for disadvantaged girls in North Carolina—and without her friend, Mallory finds herself feeling lonely.

She wants to call Jake but she can't. When they parted the last time, they agreed they would call for only four reasons: engagement, marriage, pregnancy, or death.

How will I know if you're coming back next year? Mallory asked.

I'm coming back every year, Jake said. *No matter what.*

Mallory accepted that answer, but a year is a long time and a lot can happen. Last summer, Jake had the convenient excuse of Cooper to bring him back up to Nantucket. But what about this year? What is he going to tell Ursula?

Maybe he and Ursula broke up, she thinks. It's not impossible.

Mallory is desperate for company. She calls Cooper and invites him to come for the weekend.

"The rest of my summer is booked," Cooper says. "Alison and I are in Vegas this weekend, then we have tickets to see Mary Chapin Carpenter at Wolf Trap the next weekend with Jake and Ursula, then we're going to Denver, then to Nashville."

"Ah," Mallory says. It feels like she's been hit in the forehead with a poison dart. Jake and Ursula have *not* broken up. They're a couple, doing couple things with other couples. "So, you and Alison…I guess it's more than just a rebound?"

"Definitely more than a rebound, Mal," Coop says in his overly patient old-soul voice. "Why would you even suggest that?"

Oh, I don't know, Mallory thinks. *Maybe because you started up with Alison less than a month after your wife left?* "I'm happy for you," Mallory says. "Have fun."

She plays "Everybody Hurts" umpteen times in a row one night and drinks a bottle of wine by herself. This is a low point. The lowest, she hopes. The next day, she calls Leland, but the phone at Leland's apartment has been disconnected. What? Has Leland moved? Tracking Leland down requires a phone call home to Kitty, who can get Leland's new number from Geri Gladstone. A call with Kitty is never a simple thing; Mallory limits her communications with her parents to once every two weeks. It's always the same; her mother talks about tennis, what's happening at the country club, and her perennials bed, which is (apparently) the envy of Deepdene Road. Then she'll ask about Mallory's love life. Kitty didn't approve of JD (no surprise there) and so she was relieved to hear about the breakup, but her pestering has grown tiresome. ("There *are* wealthy men on Nantucket, Mallory, out on those big yachts. You might meet one if you ever got out of your cutoffs and put on a dress.") Kitty will then ask when Mallory plans to leave Nantucket and "rejoin civilization."

On this call, as on every call, Mallory says, "I'm here for the foreseeable future, Mom."

To which Kitty replies, "Oh, darling." Heavy sigh. "Your father wants to say hello."

"Leland's number, Mom!" Mallory calls out as a reminder.

But it's Senior who responds. "She's already on her way over to Geri's. She'll be gone an hour, so thank you. The Orioles are playing."

Turns out, Leland has moved from Eighty-Second Street to Greenwich Village.

"Apparently her block is quite gentrified," Kitty says.

Mallory rolls her eyes. Kitty's idea of New York City is frozen in 1978; she thinks everyone who lives in the Village looks like Sid and Nancy. "It's all gentrified now, Mom."

"Well," Kitty says. "I'm surprised you didn't know Leland moved."

"I haven't talked to Leland since the holidays," Mallory confesses. The day after Christmas, Mallory and Leland had lunch in Baltimore at Louie's Bookstore Café; Leland was leaving the next day to go back to New York. Their conversation was stilted because their lives were so different. Leland had been promoted to the features editor of *Bard and Scribe*. She boasted about her upcoming interview with Fiella Roget, the twenty-four-year-old Haitian woman whose novel *Shimmy Shimmy* was "all anyone in the city is talking about." In turn, Mallory had bored Leland to tears by describing her life at the high school and how she hung out with JD while he played darts at the Muse.

Mallory feels guilty that she hasn't called Leland before now, but the longer she waited, the more oner-ous catching up seemed. This will be good, though—calling for a concrete reason, to invite Leland for the weekend.

An unfamiliar female voice answers at Leland's new number. *"Allô?"*

"Hello?" Mallory says. "I'm looking for Leland Gladstone?"

"One moment, plisss," the voice says.

There's whispering. Or maybe Mallory is imagining that? She's lying on her porch in the sun because that's where she feels the safest, gazing at the ocean in her front yard.

I am lucky, Mallory thinks. *I am blessed.*

I am so, so lonely, she thinks. She's not sure what she'll do if Leland turns her down.

"Hello?"

"Lee?" Mallory says.

"Mal?" Leland says. "Is that you?"

"Yes, hi, how are you? Kitty got your number from Geri, I didn't realize you'd moved, and I was busy with the end of the school year, and anyway, I'd love for you to come visit this weekend, or next weekend…" Mallory is talking too fast. She's nervous. She can't imagine why—for years, she and Leland were as close as Siamese twins. But that's the issue, she supposes. They were once so close that now it feels awkward to be not as close, though Mallory knows this is what happens when you grow up: paths diverge, people lose touch. Mallory didn't know that Leland had moved. She doesn't know who just answered the phone. Leland's new roommate, presumably.

There's a sigh from Leland—annoyed? regretful?

"I wish I could," she says. "But I'm leaving tomorrow for Bread Loaf."

"Bread Loaf," Mallory says. It takes her a second to understand because at first she thinks *Sugarloaf,* which was where the Blessings and the Gladstones used to take their family ski trips. But Bread Loaf is something else, a writer thing.

"At Middlebury, in Vermont," Leland says. "I'll be there for three and a half weeks, so…"

"As a student?" Mallory asks. "Are you…writing a novel?"

"Me?" Leland says. "No!" She starts laughing and Mallory laughs right along with her, even though she feels miserable because Leland won't be coming to Nantucket. Mallory wants to hang up but that, of course, would be rude and will make the chasm between them even wider and deeper. "I'm going with Fifi."

"Fifi?" Mallory says.

"Fiella," Leland says.

"Fiella Roget?" Mallory asks. Surely she's missing something. Just last week, Fiella Roget appeared on the cover of the *New York Times Magazine*. She's famous, a bona fide literary phenomenon.

"Yes, Fiella Roget," Leland says, and in the background Mallory hears the same voice that answered the phone. Leland did the interview with Fiella and they became friends; is that it? They're such good friends that she calls Fiella "Fifi"? They're such good friends that Fifi answers Leland's phone and has invited her to Bread Loaf for three weeks? "She agreed to teach last year, before the book came out and she became so in demand. She decided to honor the commitment."

"Okay," Mallory says. She wonders why she's supposed to care about any of this. "And what will you do while she's honoring the commitment?"

"Network, obviously," Leland says, and Mallory relaxes because this, at least, is a Leland she recognizes.

"The waiters and waitresses are the promising writers, you know, because they're the ones on scholarship. Everyone else pays to go. So I thought I'd sit in on Fifi's workshops, see if I can identify budding talent, and maybe get a scoop for the magazine."

"I guess that makes sense," Mallory says.

"Besides, I need to fend off her admirers," Leland says. "You do know they call it 'Bed Loaf.'"

Fend off her admirers? Mallory thinks. An outrageous notion enters her mind. "So...you moved to the Village, right?"

"Charles and Bleecker," Leland says. "Fifi has the greatest apartment, and things moved so fast that...yeah, she asked me to move in with her in March."

Things moved so fast?

"Are you..." Mallory doesn't even know how to ask the question. She's afraid if she does, Leland will laugh or be angry. Leland is heterosexual—all those years with Fray, her hunt for the perfect square-jawed, lacrosse-playing Princeton-educated investment banker, Kip or whoever. "Are you *dating* Fiella Roget? Are you two *together?*"

"Dating, together, head over heels in love," Leland says. "Can you believe it?"

Wow. No, really—wow!

That's great, so happy for you, enjoy Bread Loaf, hopefully you and Fifi can come see me another time, Christmas Stroll or next summer! When Mallory hangs up, she thinks: *I have to call someone!* But who? Apple is away, Cooper is busy crisscrossing the country with Alison. Mallory could bike out to the Summer House and tell Isolde and Oliver, but they've never met Leland and they don't read so they wouldn't even know the name Fiella Roget. Mallory supposes she could call Kitty, but she's not desperate enough for that. She wonders about the Gladstones. Do they know their daughter is now dating a successful female novelist? Do they find it as startling as Mallory does?

After a little while, the novelty of the news wears off, and by the time Mallory wakes up the next day, she feels only left out and lonely. Cooper has Alison, Leland has Fifi…and Jake has Ursula.

August drags on. Mallory's days, which were so frenetic during the school year, gape with unfilled hours. She should go out to the bars at night—21 Federal, the Boarding House, the Club Car—and try to find someone of her own. But instead, she reads and writes lesson plans for the upcoming school year. She runs and lies in the sun. She buys Sarah Leah Chase's *Nantucket Open-House Cookbook* and makes the baba ghanouj, roasting fresh eggplants from Bartlett's Farm and fat cloves of garlic until they're soft and golden brown. The result is so delicious, Mallory can't scoop it into her mouth fast enough.

It's a tiny victory.

Finally, the last week of August arrives. Mallory is both relieved and anxious. She has awakened at three a.m. the past five or six nights, imagining Jake arriving by pirate ship or hot-air balloon.

No matter what.

Does this mean the same thing to both of them: *No. Matter. What?*

Mallory waits for the phone to ring. She waits for a telegram. How are those delivered? By hand? She lives on a road with no name. She peers out the back windows, searching for a lost telegram-delivery guy.

No matter what.

It's Monday; Labor Day is a week away.

It's Tuesday.

On Wednesday, finally, she goes to the post office to check her box. Jake has her address; this is where he mailed her the book last Christmas. When Mallory finds only the usual assortment of bills and back-to-school catalogs, her eyes burn with tears. As if that isn't bad enough, she bumps into two people coming into the post office as she's leaving, physically bumps into them, because her sight is blurred.

"Mal. How's it going?"

Mallory looks up, blinks. "JD," she says.

JD is with a woman. She's older, but attractive, with long copper-colored hair, hair that is so beautiful, it nearly demands a compliment. Mallory knows this woman. It's…

"Miss Blessing, hi," the woman says. "I'm Tonya Sohn, Maggie's mother."

JD is dating Tonya Sohn, Maggie's newly divorced mother. Mallory sits behind the wheel of the Blazer for a second, wondering if she should scream or laugh.

Laugh, she decides. She wants JD to be happy so he'll leave her alone.

Mallory tosses her mail onto the passenger seat, and a plain white postcard flutters out of one of the catalogs to the floor. Mallory sees her name printed on the front. She snaps it up, flips it over.

It says: *I'm flying in on Friday the first at 4:45 p.m. If you're not waiting at the airport, I'll take a taxi to the cottage.*

The postcard is unsigned, though obviously Mallory knows who it's from.

She sits a second, wondering if she should cry or laugh from utter relief.

Laugh, she decides. She has so much to tell him!

Summer #4: 1996

What are we talking about in 1996? Leap year; Bob Dole; Braveheart; Chechnya; cloning; a bomb at the Atlanta Olympics; Princess Diana divorcing Prince Charles; Tickle Me Elmo; JonBenét Ramsey; Whitewater; Kofi Annan; Ask Jeeves; the Menendez brothers; Tupac Shakur; mad-cow disease; the Spice Girls; jihad; Dr. Ross and Nurse Hathaway; Alan Greenspan; "Show me the money, Jerry."

The year 1996 is uneventful for our boy.

So, he thinks, let's skip to the good stuff.

On the Friday of Labor Day weekend, Mallory is waiting for Jake on the ferry dock. Her hair is longer and blonder; she's wearing it in braids. She's wearing her usual cutoff shorts. He would like to rip them off her. Contrary to their established protocol, which allows no displays of affection until they're safely at home, he takes her face in his hands and lays a kiss on her that leaves them both breathless.

When she breaks away, she grins. A year is too long

to live without that smile, he thinks. He wishes he'd brought a camera; he wants to take her picture.

While Mallory fixes the appetizers, Jake goes for a swim, then takes an outdoor shower. There are no men's board shorts hanging up. That's two years in a row, which is good news, although he doesn't like thinking of Mallory alone.

Yes, he does. It's completely unfair because Jake and Ursula are now living together—meaning that Jake is living in the same apartment that Ursula uses to take a shower and change her clothes before going back to work—but Jake prefers to think of Mallory spending her evenings lying by the fire with only Cat Stevens, a book, and the howling wind for company.

Jake walks into the cottage, towel wrapped around his lower half. Mallory hands him a cold Stella and a cracker slathered with smoked bluefish pâté from Straight Wharf Fish. It is one of the most delicious things Jake has ever tasted.

"If you like it so much," Mallory says, "we can get you some to take home. It freezes."

"Or it can be just one of those things I enjoy once a year," he says.

"Like me," she says, and she beams. "I'm going to shuck corn and you can play some music. Did I tell you I got a five-CD changer?"

Jake scoops her up and carries her to the bedroom.

"Again?" she shrieks.

Again, again, again; it's their fourth Labor Day weekend together, and this year, for whatever reason, Jake can't get enough of her. It would make Mallory uncomfortable, probably, if he told her how often he thinks of her the other 362 days of the year. Some days occasionally, some days frequently, some days constantly.

Once the corn is shucked and the tomatoes sliced and drizzled with olive oil and balsamic, once the burgers are grilled and they each have a drink and are listening to Sheryl Crow and gazing at each other over the light of one votive candle—it's romantic, Mallory claims, so romantic that Jake can't see his food—she says, "So, how's Ursula?"

"Fine," Jake says. "I don't know what happened, but she kind of gave up on the engagement talk."

"She *did*?" Mallory says.

"No," Jake admits. "But I bought myself some time by agreeing that we should move in together."

"Oh," Mallory says. She stops layering pickles on top of her burger and gives him a direct look. "Did you move into her place or did she move in with you?"

"We got a new place," Jake says. "That was what she wanted. Fresh start, place of our own. We split the rent."

"And you can just stay there once you get married," Mallory says.

Every year, there comes a moment when he wonders if Mallory is going to kick him out. This year, that moment is now.

"I guess that's the idea," he says. He swigs some of his beer. He doesn't like talking about Ursula, though he understands why it's necessary for Mallory. She likes to do it on Friday night, get it out of the way, get caught up on Jake's romantic life at home so that it isn't looming over her head like a thundercloud.

Better to know than to wonder, she says.

Jake isn't sure he agrees.

"Where does she think you are?" Mallory asks.

"Nantucket," he says.

"With Coop?"

"I'm not sure I specifically said 'with Coop.' I just told her I was coming up to Nantucket for the weekend because I barely got away this summer at all, and also, she thinks it's a tradition now."

"It *is* a tradition now," Mallory says. And they both sit for a second, Jake fending off guilt because it's obviously not the kind of tradition that Ursula is imagining. "Does she know it's *my* cottage?"

"She's never asked. I would guess if she was pressed, she would say it was your family's cottage."

"But she knows I exist, right?" Mallory says. "She remembers me from the wedding?"

"She might," Jake says. "I mean, yes, she noticed us dancing at the wedding and she asked about you but she hasn't mentioned you since then. She hasn't mentioned you in connection with the cottage."

Mallory takes a bite of her burger, then butters an ear of corn. She seems put out by this statement, but why?

"It seems so unfair," Mallory says. "I spend so much time being jealous of her and she doesn't even know enough to be jealous of me."

"Well," Jake says, "if she knew how I felt about you, she'd be very jealous indeed. Does that make you feel better?"

"Yes," Mallory says, and she blows him a kiss across the dark table.

Jake wakes up alone in the low, wide platform bed. The crisp white sheets have light blue piping; Mallory admitted that she splurged on them at the Lion's Paw in honor of his visit. There's a stripe of sunshine peeking through the wooden blinds (also new) that lands directly across Jake's eyes. He inhales Mallory's scent from her pillow and stretches.

Jake makes coffee in Mallory's French press and takes a mug out onto the front porch. He watches the waves fold over themselves again and again and again. It's hypnotic. There isn't a soul on the beach in either direction. What's to stop Jake from running into the ocean naked for the first swim of the day?

Nothing, he supposes. He does it.

As he's bobbing around in the water, he sees Mallory, home from her run. No braids; her hair is in a ponytail. She pries off each sneaker with the toe of her other foot, peels off her socks, stops to drink some ice water, and bends over to touch her toes. She goes back into the cottage and he hears her voice. She must be calling his name. Is she worried? Does she think he left? No, surely she sees all his things still there.

A second later, she appears back out on the porch. She takes a bite of a peach, sees him swimming, waves.

He waves back.

She lifts her arms over her head and places her right foot alongside her left knee. It's her yoga tree pose, the one she showed him last night and made him try. (He failed.) He sees her green vine tattoo standing out against the golden skin of her ankle. It feels like he has vines wrapped around his heart.

He's in love with her, he thinks.

If they count the Fridays and the Mondays, then today is the start of their fourteenth day together, the end of their second week. Is that how long it takes to fall in love?

He swims in and Mallory hoots at his nakedness.

She holds out a striped beach towel, which he wraps around his waist. He takes the peach out of her hand, sets it on the little outdoor table, and kisses her, long and deep. When they finally separate, Mallory grins at him. "Good *morning!*" she says.

"I'm…"—should he tell her? He wants to, but he's afraid—"…crazy about you."

"Or just crazy," she says, and she kisses him again.

He cooks bacon and chops up onion and tomatoes for the omelets. He finds a wedge of Brie and holds the cheese up for Mallory to see. "Okay if I use this?"

"I'm crazy about you too," she says.

"Is that a yes on the Brie?" he asks.

She shrugs. "Sure."

Jake sets about beating the eggs and heating the butter in the pan. He turns to the stove and he hears her over by the stereo, the *click-click-click* of her looking for CDs. She has changed into a sunny yellow bikini and her cutoff shorts. They're planning on kayaking on the pond and then provisioning for their lobster dinner, as usual. They skipped the Chicken Box last night. Mallory was disappointed by this, he knows, because the Box is part of the tradition. They almost had an argument about it. She accused him of being afraid of bumping into someone from Washington. While it's true this always lurks in the back of his mind—how would he explain dancing and kissing Mallory if he saw one of Ursula's coworkers?—the real reason he wanted to stay home was that he didn't want to share Mallory. He wanted to play with her hair, trace her ribs, listen to her breathe. If that's not the definition of love, he doesn't know what is.

Jake folds the omelet over. He gives Mallory the

one that is a little superior—with more gooey cheese and more golden-brown onions—and that's another demonstration of his love. At home, he always takes the better portion because giving it to Ursula would be a waste.

They eat at the table, Mallory moaning over every bite, which drives him mad with desire, although she's not doing it for effect. She is genuine, and that's what he appreciates most about her. There is no artifice, no manipulation, no games. Every woman in Jake's office is reading *The Rules,* which is, as far as Jake can tell, a guide to ignoring men in order to get them to pursue you. Jake happens to know this strategy works; it's one reason why he's still with Ursula.

He can't love Mallory…because he loves Ursula, though that often feels less like love and more like succumbing to some kind of witchcraft. Jake and Ursula are connected in ten thousand ways: the shared memories, the inside jokes, the secret language, the references that only they understand. Ursula is a connection to his sister; she made Jess smile, made her laugh, made her feel like a normal eleven- or twelve- or thirteen-year-old girl the way no one else could. Jake's emotions about these memories venture into territory that has no language. He can picture Ursula standing before Jessica's coffin in her white vestments; her nobility in that moment is something Jake will never forget.

A life without Ursula is impossible to imagine. And yet, what Jake feels for Mallory isn't merely infatuation. It's something bigger.

They're crazy about each other. *Crazy about* is where they are this year. They'll leave it at that. For now.

The song changes to "Sunshine," by World Party.

Sunshine, I just can't get enough of you. Sometimes you just blow my mind. Everything about the moment feels holy: the choice of song, the summer light flooding the room, the harmony of the flavors in the omelets, the deep periwinkle blue of the last hydrangea blooms of the summer, which Mallory placed in the mason jar as she always does. And Mallory herself, across the table, still glowing from her run.

Everything at this moment is so sublime that Jake thinks, *Freeze! I want to stay right here forever.*

But of course, life doesn't work that way. The waves fold over themselves again and again and again, and nothing can stop them.

On Sunday, it rains. It's the first day of rain that Jake has experienced on Nantucket in four years. Mallory goes running anyway and when she comes home, she's soaked through and her teeth are chattering. Jake wraps her up in a fluffy white bath towel and brings her a mug of the delicious coffee, light and sweet.

"Should I light a fire?" he asks. "Run you a bath?"

"I'm going to climb back into bed," she says. "You coming?"

It's raining too hard to drive to Great Point. They lie in bed and read—Mallory insisted he try something called *Bridget Jones's Diary* (it's not bad). When Jake has had enough of Bridget and Daniel and Mark ("It's a reinterpretation of *Pride and Prejudice*," Mallory says. "Right, I know that, obviously," Jake says, though he hadn't a clue), he throws the book down and spoons up against Mallory's warm back, hooks his chin over her shoulder, breathes in the scent of her hair. When he met her, she smelled fruity, but now she smells herby, like clover and sage.

After they make love, Mallory suggests they head into town, to the Camera Shop, to rent the video of *Same Time, Next Year*. They can pick up the Chinese food on the way home.

Jake's spirits are leaden. How have they already reached the Sunday-night Chinese food and movie stage? This weekend seems to have moved at double speed. They should have gone to the Chicken Box, maybe. If they'd jammed more activities in, would it have seemed longer?

Mallory misreads his hesitation. "I can go alone if you just want to stay here."

"No!" he says. He doesn't want to be without her for even half an hour.

They brazenly hold hands as they walk up the stairs to the Camera Shop. The front of the store is the developing center, and there are greeting cards and picture frames for sale, and as soon as they step inside, they bump into an older gentleman whose face lights up when he sees Mallory.

"Miss Blessing!" he says. "What a pleasant surprise."

"Dr. Major," Mallory says. She gives the gentleman a hug and Jake tries to read her face. Who is this? Is it her actual *doctor*? "This is my friend Jake McCloud. Jake, this is Dr. Major, the high-school principal."

Handshake. *Hello, nice to meet you, do you live on the island? No, I'm just visiting. Oh, from where? Washington, DC. Wonderful, enjoy, I'd better be off, Mrs. Major is eagerly waiting at home, we'll be watching* Braveheart *for the third time, I think she's carrying a torch for Mel Gibson, take care, bye-bye, see you Tuesday, Mallory.*

Mallory heads to the back room where Jake can see video boxes lined up on the shelves; he loiters in the front room, looking at disposable cameras. He feels a hand on his arm and turns to see Dr. Major, who bows his head and says in a low voice, "Mallory is a very special young woman and she's one hell of a teacher." (Dr. Major wants to add, *Treat her right, she deserves the best*. Dr. Major has always felt protective of Mallory and this guy should know what a treasure he has.) "You're one lucky fella."

"Oh." Jake swallows. "Yes, I know."

Mallory appears a few minutes later with a cassette in a white plastic bag. "I didn't rent it," she says.

"You didn't?"

"I bought it!" Mallory says. She notices the bag in his hand. "What did you get?"

As they enter the cottage, they hear the phone ringing.

Mallory says, "That's probably Apple. I won't answer. I can worry about school after you leave." The machine's message is Mallory's voice: *This is Mallory, I'm either not home or not answering! Leave a message, please, or don't.* Jake brings the disposable camera up to his eye and centers the lens on Mallory standing by the phone. He clicks. He took four pictures of her in profile driving the Blazer and she swatted at him, telling him he needed to let her properly pose. But he doesn't want her to pose, he wants to capture her in the ordinary moments. He snaps one of her looking down at the answering machine, waiting. But whoever it is hangs up and there's a loud dial tone.

"Good," Mallory says. She grins at him. He clicks.

* * *

White takeout boxes, fragrant steam, soy sauce, chopsticks—then Mallory presses Play on the VCR and settles next to him on the couch and they're back at the Sea Shadows Inn in Santa Barbara with George and Doris, who notice each other eating alone in the inn's restaurant. They raise their glasses to each other and eventually end up sitting side by side in front of the fire. They're talking, laughing, building the foundation for a relationship that will last one weekend per year for the rest of their lives.

"Fortune cookies!" Mallory says when the movie is over. She throws one at him. He snaps her picture.

Mallory's fortune: *Competence like yours is underrated.*

"Between the sheets," she says.

Jake's is *Go for the gold! You are set to be a champion.*

"Between the sheets," he says.

Mallory gets up. "Let's go, champ." She's standing before him in her cutoffs and an Espresso Café T-shirt, her hair flattened on the side where she was lying on his chest during the movie.

What if he called Ursula and told her he wasn't coming home? What if he quit his soul-sucking job with PharmX? What if he opts out of the lease for their new apartment on Twenty-Second and L? What if he stays here and finds a job, even if that job is playing guitar at the Brotherhood of Thieves?

"Are you okay?" Mallory asks. "It looks like you're a thousand miles away."

"Actually," he says, "I'm right here."

They're kissing on the bed when the phone rings again.

"Apple," Mallory murmurs. "Ignore it."

He can feel her tense a little as the message plays. It's followed by the beep.

"Uh, hi?" a voice says. "I'm looking for Jake Mc-Cloud? This is Ursula"—"What the hell?" Jake says. Mallory sits up—"de Gournsey, his girlfriend, and I need to get a hold of him. It's urgent."

Ursula's father has died. He suffered a heart attack in the middle of an orientation event for Notre Dame freshmen, a picnic at the lakes. He was taken by ambulance to St. Joe's but was pronounced dead on arrival. Ursula tells Jake she's going to fly to South Bend in the morning and Jake says he'll meet her there. They hang up, then Jake spends over an hour on the phone with the airline, switching his flight, while Mallory sits on the couch with her face in her hands.

When Jake finally leads her to bed, they lie side by side in the dark. Mallory says, "I'm sure this is the last place you want to be right now. It's one thing for us to be together when Ursula is happy and preoccupied with work. But it's another thing for us to be together when she's dealing with this kind of life-changing loss. You shouldn't be with me. You should be with her."

Mallory is right. Dr. de Gournsey—Ralph, or "Ralphie," as Jake and Ursula had jokingly referred to him since they were thirteen—is dead. Dr. de Gournsey was bald with a slight build, but he had a deep, powerful voice, which made him intimidating. That, and his formidable intelligence. Dr. de Gournsey was an expert on Southeast Asian culture; in the de Gournseys' living room was a curio cabinet filled with jade and coral figurines that he and Mrs. de Gournsey had collected in their travels to Thailand, Singapore, the Philippines. Over the years, Ralphie had been an ally of Jake's; both he and Mrs. de Gournsey (Lynette; she insists that Jake call her Lynette) had. The three of them bonded in order to deal with the force that is Ursula.

"Ralph loved model trains," Jake says. He thinks of Ralph inviting him down to the basement to see the trains for the first time, Christmas of ninth grade. The setup was elaborate, a serpentine track on a custom-made platform with hills and curves and a meticulously detailed Christmas village. Ursula's brother, Clint, had no interest in the trains, Jake knew, so Jake, hoping to win over Ralph de Gournsey, had been an enthusiastic admirer of his model trains. He wants to explain this to Mallory, but would she care or understand?

She might understand better than he thinks because she says, "Do you want me to sleep in the guest room so you have some space to grapple with this? I feel like such an interloper. I didn't know him."

"No, stay here," Jake says. Part of what he's feeling is anger and resentment that the timing is so bad—if only this had happened next week, or even tomorrow. But it had happened today, when all he'd wanted was to make love to Mallory one last time—and now the waters are muddy, indeed.

Jake flies to South Bend through Boston and Detroit and he lands there on Monday at four o'clock in the afternoon. He plans on taking a taxi to the de Gournsey house but when he steps off the plane, he sees his father. Alec McCloud opens his arms and Jake steps into them.

"You're no stranger to grief," Alec says. "You'll help her get through this."

* * *

When Jake and his father climb into the car, Alec says, "So Ursula told us you were...on Nantucket? With your friend from Hopkins? What's his name again?"

"Cooper," Jake says. "Cooper Blessing."

"Right," Alec says. "Ursula said it's become quite the tradition."

Jake's heart feels like it's being feasted on by jackals. After Jessica died, Jake made a vow to be good for his parents' sake. They had been through so much; he didn't want to add to their burden. He would meet or exceed his potential; he would stay out of trouble; he would not lie to them. Jake imagines telling Alec about his relationship with Mallory. *Every Labor Day weekend, no matter what.* It would be such a relief to tell someone. What would Alec say? What would Jake's *mother* say? He's too ashamed to even venture a guess. He can't confide in his parents. He can't confide in anyone.

"Yes," Jake says. "I go every year. Labor Day."

Ursula isn't doing well. When Jake gets to the de Gournsey house, she's lying facedown on her childhood bed.

"Hey," Jake says as he eases down next to her. "I'm here."

She starts sobbing into her pillow, eventually lifting her face to the side like a swimmer taking a breath. Then the words come, making sense but no sense: She's a terrible daughter, the worst, she's bossy, ungrateful, domineering, cold, harsh, superior. Both her parents feared her and they should because she's held them in contempt all her life...until now.

"My father loved me but he didn't like me," Ursula says, whimpering. "You told me yourself they said I was gruesomely self-centered. And I was! I am! I am this very instant!"

Jake rubs her back. She'd sounded much stronger over the phone and Jake imagined that when he showed up, she'd be organizing the reception at the University Club, picking hymns for the service, writing an obituary for the *South Bend Tribune*. A part of Jake suspected that she might even be *working*.

But now Jake sees he was wrong. Ursula's armor has been pierced.

They make it through Tuesday in a daze. Friends and neighbors stop by to visit with casseroles, flowers, banana bread, boxes of Chocolate Charlie, books about dealing with grief, and bottles of Jameson, which was Ralph's favorite, though no one else in the house touches the stuff. Everyone says a variation of the following to Jake and Ursula: *You two are so lucky to have each other.* Also: *When are you getting married?*

Wednesday, at the funeral, Jake and his parents sit in the front pew with Ursula, Lynette, and Ursula's brother, Clint, who has arrived from Argentina in the nick of time with one hell of a beard. Half the faculty of Notre Dame is there; President Malloy gives the eulogy, a soloist from the university choir sings the "Ave Maria." The Mass is beautiful. Ursula cries through the whole thing. Jake had thought she might speak, but it's clear that's just not possible. Ursula is lost and sinking. Jake wonders if this is what he's been waiting for all these many years: a chance to serve as Ursula's buoy, a chance to swoop in like Superman and catch her as she plummets.

* * *

They both have to get back to work, so they fly to Washington together first thing Thursday morning. It's only after they take their seats in first class—the gate agent looked at Ursula and gave them a free upgrade—that Ursula turns to Jake and says, "How was Nantucket?"

"Oh," he says. "It was fine, I guess. With all that happened, I can barely remember."

"There was a young woman's voice on the answering machine," Ursula says. "Who was that?"

"That?" Jake says. "I'm not sure." He plucks the in-flight magazine out of the seat pocket in front of him in an attempt to seem unconcerned. "Coop's sister, maybe? It's a family cottage."

"Coop's sister?" Ursula says. "That's the bridesmaid you danced with at his wedding, right?"

Jake lowers the magazine in mock frustration. "Honestly, Ursula, I don't remember."

"Well, was she there?" Ursula asks. "The sister?"

Jake has spent four weekends with Mallory. He's lucky, he supposes, that he only now has to lie about it. "No, Ursula, like I told you, it's a guys' weekend." He'd told Mallory before he left that he had given Ursula the number for the cottage in case of emergency. *Obviously I never thought she'd use it,* he said. *I've known Ursula since she was thirteen and there has never been an emergency she couldn't handle by herself.*

Ursula nods—but does she look wholly convinced? "Okay," she says.

When Jake unpacks that evening after work, he comes across the disposable camera. The close call on the plane is fresh in his mind and so his first instinct is to throw the damn thing away. He can't risk doing so here in the apartment, however—even if he buries it in the kitchen trash, there's a chance Ursula will find it. She's a bloodhound about certain things. Jake slips it into his briefcase and tells himself he'll toss it on his way to the office. But the next morning, he passes one trash can, then another, then a dozen more. He can't throw it away. On his lunch break, he walks ten blocks to a film-developing center on the sketchy edge of Southeast and drops it off. It'll be ready in three days, the clerk tells him.

He waits a whole week to pick it up, pays eight dollars in cash. Then he takes the packet of pictures to a bar on Thirteenth Street where he'll see no one he knows and he flips through them; it feels as illicit as looking at pornography, though they're all just innocent pictures of Mallory. Mallory with her head back, dangling lo mein noodles over her mouth with a pair of chopsticks, Mallory driving the Blazer, Mallory asleep in the moment before he woke her up to take him to the airport.

His intention is to look at the photos, then throw them away—but no, he can't bring himself to throw them away. He places them back in the envelope and stashes the envelope inside the code-of-conduct pamphlet for employees of PharmX in his bottom desk drawer. The world could end and no one would find them there.

Jake survives one week, then another week—but it is only just that, making it through each day without any major incidents, crises, or upheavals. Technically, it's still summer, the sidewalks are still hot as a griddle, but kids have gone back to school, and khaki suits and sundresses have been moved to the back of the closet;

it's on to the serious business of autumn. There's Halloween candy at the Giant and everyone has high hopes for the Redskins.

Ursula seems different. She's softer, quieter; she snuggles in bed with him now rather than presenting him with her cold back. She speaks to her mother on the phone every few days, just to check in. She comes home from work by eight o'clock, and sometimes even seven thirty. Jake's only complaint is that she eats even less than she used to. Her suits, which used to make her look trim and sharp, now hang on her like she's a cardboard form. She's disappearing.

One day, Cooper calls Jake at the office at a quarter to five, which means he wants to meet for drinks. "Hey, buddy, what's up? Haven't heard from you in a while."

When Jake hears Cooper's voice, he pulls out the one picture of Mallory that he's moved from the envelope to his center desk drawer. It's the one of her dangling the lo mein noodles over her mouth. Mallory is a little awkward in the world, it's part of her charm, but he loves the way she handles chopsticks, and when he looks at this picture, it feels like the chopsticks are skewering his heart.

"Hit a rough patch," Jake says. "Ursula's father died."

"Oh, man, I'm sorry," Cooper says. "I was calling to see if you wanted to grab a drink after work, but if you're not up to it…"

"I'm up to it," Jake says, surprising himself.

They meet at the Tombs, get a pitcher of beer, a couple shots of Jim Beam, and an order of wings. The normalcy feels good. Alanis Morissette is doing her wailing thing in the background and the usual preppy, well-heeled, after-work crowd drinks, talks, laughs, drinks as though it's just another day, because for them, it is just another day. Jake studies Cooper across the table. The word that always comes to mind when he thinks of Cooper is *sweetheart*. He's more than just a guy's guy who wants to talk Tiger Woods and Norv Turner; he has depth—and intelligence, compassion, thoughtful opinions. He admits when he's wrong; he admits when he doesn't know. This is why their friendship has lasted while so many others have fallen away.

Cooper asks how Ursula is handling things and Jake, who has given his spiel over and over again, goes off script. "Harder than I expected, man. And you know what? It's kind of restored my faith in her…basic humanity."

Cooper sips his beer. "I can see what you mean," he says. "Ursula scares the shit out of me."

Jake asks about Alison. Are they still together? (Jake knows the answer is no. Mallory told him that Cooper and Alison broke up.)

"No," Cooper says. "The distance was too much. She was fun, though, and a great rebound after Krystel. And then, just a couple days after Alison and I had the talk, I met Nanette."

"Nanette?" Jake says. Mallory didn't mention anything about a Nanette.

"I went to Clyde's to drown my sorrows," Cooper says. "And Nanette was my bartender."

"I thought you said you were staying away from women in the service industry," Jake says.

"Nanette is different," Cooper says. "She's a bartender and a slam poet. Besides, we can't all meet our soul mates in the eighth grade."

"Well," Jake says.

"Seriously," Cooper says. "Why are you making Ursula wait so long? Just marry her already."

Jake laughs. "I think we need more shots."

Jake is drunk when he leaves the Tombs. The Jim Beam in his system acts like steam from the shower that reveals a word written on the bathroom mirror: *Propose*.

The saleswoman at Market Street Diamonds, Lonnie, wears a lot of makeup—sparkling eye shadow, glistening red lipstick that reminds Jake of a cherry lollipop—and she has a huge head of permed hair that is iridescent with hair spray under the lights. The shop is empty and probably about to close for the day, but Lonnie welcomes Jake in. He's sure she sees an easy mark: a young guy on a bourbon-fueled mission.

"What kind of engagement ring are you looking for, handsome?" Lonnie asks.

"The kind that looks more expensive than it is," he says, and she laughs. She asks about his budget and he says five thousand dollars because it sounds like a reasonable round number, and she says she can work with that. She produces one ring after another, from the minuscule to the absurd, displaying them on a black felt cloth. He can't decide. She asks rapid-fire questions about "the lucky girl," a term that would surely make Ursula shudder. Jake says, "She's been my girlfriend for the past fourteen years, on and off, but we've both been with other people."

This ratchets up Lonnie's enthusiasm. "You were each with other people but you've found your way back," Lonnie says. "Now *that* is true love."

It's a lot more complicated than this, but he won't get into it with Lonnie.

"She's an attorney for the SEC." Jake waits a beat to see if Lonnie is impressed, but she might not know the SEC from the FCC or the EPA. Washington is a town of acronyms. "She's a serious person. I don't want anything flashy."

"Simple," Lonnie says. "Classic, tasteful. Does she wear other jewelry?"

Well, he says, she's fond of a gold cross she received from her parents for her confirmation in ninth grade, and she wears the slim gold watch they gave her when she graduated from law school. She has a strand of pearls, Jake says, but her ears aren't even pierced. He feels like he's slurring his words, but if Lonnie notices this or the smell of cigarette smoke and cooking grease that followed him out of the Tombs, she doesn't mention it.

"This," she says, "is the ring I would recommend. You'd be a fool not to get it. It's a bit out of your price range—sixty-four hundred—but it's head and shoulders above the rest of these rings. A carat and a half, clarity at the top of the charts, in a setting of white gold." She holds the ring out on her outstretched palm.

"Okay," Jake says, looking at it. "Let's go with that one, I guess."

"Don't sound so excited," Lonnie says with an exaggerated wink. "Trust me, handsome—Mallory is going to be thrilled with this ring."

Jake's head snaps up. "Mallory?"

Lonnie's eyes grow wide and a bit of glitter under her eye shines like a tear. "Did I get the name wrong? You said Mallory, I thought." She lays her hand on his arm. "I'm so sorry."

"It's Ursula," he says. He's drunk! He told Lonnie

his girlfriend's name was Mallory! Why did he do that? Probably because he was thinking that when this was all over, he would have to call Mallory, and as soon as she answered the phone, she'd know. She knew before he even left Nantucket, he's pretty sure. She was silent when she drove him to the airport in the early morning on Monday. When he'd said, "Same time next year?" she'd shrugged.

"No matter what, Mallory Blessing," he'd said. He kissed her, climbed out of the Blazer, then turned back. "No matter what."

Jake makes himself focus on Lonnie—eye shadow, hair spray, and all. "My girlfriend's name is Ursula. Her name. Is Ursula."

Lonnie doesn't miss a beat. She snaps the box closed, rings up the purchase, and accepts his credit card. "Ursula is going to be very happy," she says.

He wonders how to propose. Over a romantic dinner? He can't imagine Ursula agreeing to go out to dinner when she's still so sad, and she wouldn't eat anything anyway. He could take her to one of the monuments tonight—the Lincoln Memorial or the Jefferson. He could lure her on a jog tomorrow and get down on one knee in front of the Reflecting Pool just as the sun is rising and the wavering image of the Washington Monument appears on the surface of the water.

Paris was a missed opportunity, he thinks.

He considers waiting for Thanksgiving, when they'll be back in South Bend. He can take Ursula to the skating rink on Jefferson, the place where he screwed up his courage to ask her to skate couples. He was so nervous back then that his hand had been sweating inside his glove.

He holds the vision of thirteen-year-old Ursula—still in braces, wearing a turtleneck printed with bicycles under her navy-blue Fair Isle sweater under her navy pea coat, the striped hat with earflaps and strings that ended in pom-poms on her head—as he enters the new apartment. The apartment is so big that if Ursula is in the bedroom, she can't hear him enter.

The foyer is dark and Jake thinks she must still be at work until he sees her attaché case at the foot of the mail table.

Jake heads down the hall to the bedroom. He's a man on a mission. He taps on the door, cracks it open. Ursula is lying on the bed in a sleeveless navy dress, the belt of which is pulled to its last hole. She has a washcloth over her eyes.

Jake eases down onto the bed next to her. "You okay?"

She reaches up to remove the washcloth. "Headache."

Jake holds out the box. "I got you something."

She blinks, accepts the box, opens it. Her expression reveals nothing—not surprise, not joy, not *Well, it's about time*. She takes the ring out and slips it on the fourth finger of her left hand. It's too big, he can see that, but they can go back to the store and have it sized.

"It's lovely," she says. "Thank you."

"Will you marry me?" Jake asks.

Ursula sinks back onto the pillow and closes her eyes. "Yes," she says, and all Jake can think is how devastated Lonnie would be if she could see Ursula in this moment.

Summer #5: 1997

What are we talking about in 1997? Princess Diana; Harry Potter; Madeleine Albright; the Hale-Bopp comet; Lima, Peru; Tony Blair; Google; Gianni Versace; "I'm the king of the world!"; Garuda airlines; Brett Favre; Hong Kong; Notorious B.I.G.; "Candle in the Wind"; the Heaven's Gate cult; Louise Woodward; John Denver; Promise Keepers; Mulder and Scully; Chris Farley; Evander Holyfield and Mike Tyson.

On the third weekend of June 1997, Jake McCloud and Ursula de Gournsey are to be married in South Bend. The ceremony will be held at the Log Chapel on the campus of Notre Dame, and a small wedding dinner will follow at Tippecanoe Place. Mallory has learned these particulars because Cooper is serving as Jake's best man. Mallory asked Coop for details in a casual way. *Are there groomsmen?* Only one, apparently, Ursula's brother, Clint. *And who is Ursula's maid of honor?*

Cooper has no idea. "Her mother, maybe?"

Her *mother? How bizarre, how bizarre,* Mallory thinks. (This was her students' favorite song this past year and the lyrics are an unwelcome earworm.) Or maybe what's bizarre is that Mallory would never in a million years ask Kitty to be her matron of honor.

"Is Jake excited?" Mallory asks. Her voice is tense, but Cooper won't notice.

"Excited?" Cooper says. "I don't know. Do you get excited about marrying someone you've been dating for sixteen years?"

Mallory can't tell if it's a good thing or a bad thing that Jake's wedding weekend is the only weekend of the summer—of the past four summers—that Leland is able to come to Nantucket for a visit. She and Fiella arrive at six o'clock on Friday. Mallory drives down to Steamboat Wharf to pick them up from the ferry.

"That took for*ever*," Leland says. "Five hours on the highway and two on the boat."

"Why didn't you just fly?" Mallory asks. She checks behind Leland for Fiella. She's nervous to meet her, not just because Fiella is her best friend's lover and she wants to make a good impression but also because she's famous, a real famous writer. Fiella's first novel, *Shimmy Shimmy,* is being made into a movie starring Angela Bassett and John Malkovich, and her second novel, *Cold Ashes of the Heart,* was picked for Oprah's Book Club and has been sitting at the top of the *New York Times* bestseller list for twenty-seven weeks.

Mallory spots Fiella halfway up the gangplank, surrounded by college-age girls who are asking for her autograph. It's not surprising that she's been recognized because her looks are so distinctive. She has deep copper-colored skin and corkscrew curls that start dark brown at her part before turning golden at the ends. She's wearing a bright orange halter dress that puts her breasts on perfect display. Honestly,

Fiella Roget is even more breathtaking in person than she is in photographs or on TV (Mallory has seen her on both Oprah's and Jay Leno's shows).

"Fifi didn't want to fly," Leland says irritably. "She wanted to 'experience the journey over water.'"

"I can see that, I guess," Mallory says. No sooner does Fiella sign an autograph for one person than another girl appears in her place and Mallory wonders if Leland has to deal with this everywhere they go and also if they're ever going to make it off the dock and back to the Blazer.

Eventually Leland has to wedge herself into the crowd and yank Fiella free, causing a bit of a scuffle.

"Personal space!" Leland shouts at a perky blond girl in a Tarheels T-shirt who's holding a paperback copy of *Shimmy Shimmy*. "We're on vacation!"

Still the girl thrusts the book at Fiella, and still Fiella seems happy to sign it. Then she eases out of the crowd like she's slipping off a silk robe and offers her hand and a radiant smile to Mallory. "Sorry about that," she says. "I'm Fifi and you're Mallory. I know because I've seen all the photographs of you and Lee from growing up. I couldn't be happier to meet you." Her voice makes Mallory shiver. Fiella—Fifi— has the slightest French Creole accent. The woman is majestic; she is royalty. Mallory can see why Leland fell in love with her.

"Honestly, I'm *sick* of it," Leland says on their way through the parking lot. "They sat on the boat ogling you for two hours but they only screwed up the courage to approach you as we were *disembarking*?"

"They're harmless," Fifi says, waving away Leland's complaints. "Plus they pay the bills. Anyway, look at this charming place! Aren't we just the luckiest creatures on earth. Thank you, Mallory, for inviting us." They come upon the Blazer, freshly washed and waxed and vacuumed for their arrival. "Oh, is this our chariot?"

"Please," Leland says. "Talk like a normal person."

It's fun entertaining houseguests when one of them is as enthusiastic as Fiella Roget. Fifi sits in the front of the Blazer while Leland rides in back with the luggage; when Mallory peers in the rearview mirror, she sees Lee glowering, a look Mallory knows only too well. Still, she assumes it must be humbling, and maybe even demoralizing, to have a famous girlfriend—especially for someone like Leland, who is used to being the center of attention. But surely Leland has grown accustomed to her role. She and Fiella have been together for over two years.

Fifi pulls a clothbound journal out of her leather satchel and starts scribbling things down even as the Blazer bounces over the ruts in the no-name road.

"Stop!" Fifi cries. Mallory hits the brakes, thinking Fifi is uncomfortable or she's forgotten something back on the wharf, but Fifi jumps out of the car, runs to the banks of the pond, picks a fuchsia blossom off a rugosa bush, and inhales the scent.

"Look at this, Lee!" Fifi cries out, holding her hands over her head. She seems to be hugging the entirety of the landscape—the flat blue mirror of the pond, the electric green of the surrounding reeds, the pink and white explosion of the rugosa rose.

"It's called nature," Leland says. She does not look amused.

*   *   *

At the cottage, Fifi spends a long moment taking in the vista of the beach and ocean, then she turns her attention to every detail inside. Mallory has done a proper spring cleaning. She bought a new duvet and sheets for the bigger guest room. There's a crystal pitcher and glasses on one nightstand and a bouquet of wild irises on the other. Over the winter, Mallory had her sole bathroom renovated; now there's clean white subway tile, a new vanity instead of the pedestal sink with the rust stain that was impossible to get out, and a new toilet with a slow-closing lid—such a luxury! Mallory kept the porcelain claw-foot tub because her contractor Bob (who has such a thick New England accent that Mallory thinks of him as "Bawb") said that it was in good shape and would be hell to replace. Mallory got some new throw pillows to soften up the unyielding green tweed sofa and she placed a jar of shells and beach glass on the coffee table next to Cary Hazlegrove's book of Nantucket photographs. She bought Russian River chardonnay for Leland and a bottle of Bombay Sapphire for Fiella, who drinks only gin over ice. Mallory made a layered fruit salad and baked Sarah Chase's orange-rosemary muffins, which she'll serve for breakfast with homemade honey butter.

Fifi exclaims over the cottage, the shells, the narrow harvest table, the bowl of peaches, plums, nectarines, and apricots—and then the wall of books.

"My God," she says. "I'm never leaving."

Leland emerges from the bathroom. Mallory gives her friend a hug and whispers, "I'm glad you're here. I'm happy to see you."

Leland pulls away, and her expression says it all: Leland is suffering. Fiella takes up all the oxygen in every room.

"Tim Winton, *The Riders*?" Fifi says, pulling the book off the shelf. "I've been *desperate* to read this!"

Mallory nearly snatches the book from Fifi's hand. It was Jake's Christmas present to her this past year. *This is by a man too. But it's good anyway. XO, Jake.*

"You're welcome to borrow any books but the four on that shelf," Mallory says.

"Why?" Leland says. "Are those sacred?"

Fifi replaces *The Riders*. "I feel the same way about certain books," she says. "*Song of Solomon. The Bone People*. All of my Jamaica Kincaid." She plucks a book from the shelf below. "The new Mona Simpson! Okay if I borrow this?"

"Yes!" Mallory says. "I loved it."

"Wine, please," Leland murmurs.

Mallory mentions that she has tuna steaks marinating and a fresh baguette and fixings for salad. "Or we can go out," she says. "I'm friends with the bartender at the Blue Bistro and he has a table for us at eight o'clock if we want it. But I didn't want to assume..." Mallory looks at Leland. "Did you two make other plans?"

"Other *plans*?" Fifi says. "Don't be ridiculous, Mal-lorita, we came to Nantucket to spend time with *you*. So that I can get to know you. Of course we'll stay in; we'll eat the beautiful meal you prepared and we'll talk all night and share our deepest secrets." Fifi takes Mallory's hand in both of hers and Mallory looks down to see their fingers, dark and lighter, wound together. Mallory is mesmerized, but when she looks over Fifi's shoulder, she sees Leland rolling her eyes.

They pour wine, snack on the salt-and-pepper cashews that Mallory made earlier in the week.

"When did you learn to cook?" Leland asks. "If memory serves, you couldn't even operate your Easy-Bake Oven."

"Stop it, darling," Fifi says. "You sound like a petulant witch."

"I taught myself," Mallory says. "It's quiet here in the winter."

They toss a salad, heat the bread, grill the tuna, shake up a vinaigrette. Mallory lights the sole votive candle. They raise their glasses.

"Thank you both for coming," Mallory says. "I'm so happy you're here." As they touch glasses, Mallory realizes this is true. She has barely thought of Jake and Ursula's rehearsal dinner—which is being held at a pizza parlor called Barnaby's—at all.

During dinner, Mallory tries to keep the conversation focused on Leland.

"So," she says. "How are your parents?" What she really wants to know is: How do the Gladstones feel about Leland and Fifi together?

"They're getting a divorce," Leland says.

Mallory sets down her fork. "What?"

"My father is sleeping with Sloane Dooley," Leland says.

It takes Mallory a minute. Sloane *Dooley?* Fray's *mother,* the disco dancer and maybe cocaine addict? "You have got to be kidding me."

"Not kidding," Leland says. "My mother seems to think it's been on again, off again for a long time. Like maybe even since Fray and I were together."

"I can't believe this," Mallory says. She *cannot,* in fact, believe this. Steve Gladstone and Sloane Dooley *sleeping* together? Maybe even way back when Mallory and Fray and Leland and Cooper were all in *high school*? "When did you find this out?" What Mallory means is why didn't Leland *call* her when she found out? And why didn't Kitty call her? But then Mallory remembers that Kitty *has* called, three times in the past few weeks, and left messages begging Mallory to call her back, messages that Mallory ignored.

"End of May," Leland says. "Geri went to the Preakness with the Ladies Auxiliary and she came home to find my dad and Sloane in the hot tub together."

"Geri is a wreck," Fifi says. "We almost brought her up here with us."

"That was Fifi's idea," Leland says. "I didn't entertain it for a second."

"So you and Geri…" Mallory says. "You're close?"

"Best friends," Fifi says. She holds up two crossed fingers. "But then, I love Steve too. I think his involvement with Sloane is such a betrayal."

Mallory is stopped by that. Fiella Roget considers Steve's affair with Sloane Dooley a betrayal? This statement sounds grandiose and self-important. Fifi doesn't even *know* them! She didn't grow up on the same street with them!

"Steve is crap," Leland says morosely. "Sloane is worse crap. They're moving into a place in Fells Point."

"Whoa," Mallory says. She tries to summon the memories she has of Sloane. Their school bus stop was in front of Fray's grandparents' house and Mallory vividly recalls that one frigid morning, a taxi pulled up and Sloane emerged, wearing only a purple lace bra and jeans under a loosely belted leather coat. She remembers Sloane going away to St. Michael's for the weekend with a man who worked for Alex Brown,

Senior wondering aloud if she was being paid for her time. Sloane smoked hand-rolled cigarettes and liked KC and the Sunshine Band. *That's the way (uh-huh, uh-huh) I like it!* Sloane Dooley hovered around the edges of their lives, acting scandalously, then disappearing.

The Gladstones, meanwhile, had been like second parents to Mallory. She remembers the day Steve came home with the convertible Saab and asked Leland and Mallory if they wanted to go for a ride. He'd bought the car on a whim, without telling either Geri or Leland, and Mallory had been startled by that. (Senior and Kitty didn't even bring a pizza home on the spur of the moment.) Geri had called it Steve's midlife crisis, and now Mallory wonders if maybe Steve bought the car to impress Sloane Dooley.

Mallory feels a deep sorrow. She had assumed that the Gladstones would stay together season after season, year after year, in their house on Deepdene Road. The life they'd created seemed normal, happy, and, above all, permanent. Whenever Mallory thought of Leland's parents, she pictured Steve setting out the recycling bins as Geri climbed into her Honda Odyssey dressed in her tennis whites. The Gladstones hung Christmas lights; they had a house account at Eddie's. They skied and went on European river cruises. When they went to visit Leland in New York, they took her to a Broadway show and then out to dinner at one of Larry Forgione's restaurants. Apparently, news of Leland's relationship with Fiella Roget hadn't bothered them in the slightest. They both embraced Fiella—and how wonderful is that? Mallory is horrified that slatternly, slothful Sloane Dooley has managed to pry the Gladstones apart. Maybe there was a loose seam or a fault line—or maybe the problem is marriage itself. Marriage is a gamble with even odds; half the time it works, half the time it doesn't.

Mallory throws back what's left of her wine and goes to the fridge for another bottle. She's glad she's not the one who's getting married this weekend.

The talk turns to Fiella, which feels inevitable. Fiella Roget learned the "art of storytelling," as she puts it, at her grandmother's feet. Fiella grew up in Petit-Goâve, Haiti, with one new cotton dress and one new pair of sandals per year. She had a rag doll named Camille that she dragged everywhere and a picture Bible. Her favorite story was Daniel in the lions' den.

"If you think about it," she says, "*Shimmy Shimmy* is just a postmodern retelling of that story from the perspective of a young woman of color."

Leland's eyelids flutter closed—clearly she has heard this a few thousand times—and although Mallory could listen to Fifi all night, she knows she should gracefully end the evening.

"I'll clear the dishes," she says. "You've had a long day. Sleep as late as you want tomorrow. I go running early, but I'll set out things for breakfast."

"Leland will go to bed," Fifi says. "But I'm a natural night owl. I'll help you clean up. One more glass of wine and I'll spill the salty stories—losing my virginity to Mr. Bobo the loan shark, then stealing money from his wallet in the night. He was a heavy sleeper and I never got caught, though I shudder to think what would have happened if—"

Leland clears her throat. "Fifi, stop."

"I can handle the dishes," Mallory says. "But thank you."

"Don't be ridiculous, Mallorita," Fifi says, picking up the breadbasket. "Let me help you."

"Mallorita" seems to be her new nickname, which is fine, though Mallory is sensing some pretty heavy static coming from Leland. Mallory and Fifi start washing the dishes and wrapping up the leftovers. It's nearly eleven, and Mallory wonders if the rehearsal dinner in South Bend is over. Are Jake and Ursula spending the night separately? Do people who have been together for so long follow the usual traditions? Mallory guesses yes. Ursula will stay at her mother's house and Jake and Cooper will stay with Jake's parents. The wedding is at five o'clock the next evening. Mallory isn't sure how she's going to feel tomorrow at six o'clock, when Jake is officially married. Will all of her love, longing, guilt, joy, misery, and confusion condense inside her? Will her heart become a black hole? Or maybe she'll feel exactly the way she does now—numb. Jake isn't hers; he has never been hers. Their time together is something she borrows. Or, okay, steals.

The bedroom door slams, startling Mallory so badly that she cuts her finger on the serrated bread knife. A line of blood rises. It's not bad, but still—what the hell? Mallory spins around, sucking her finger. Fifi is standing at the head of the harvest table, the last of the dirty silverware clutched in her hand like a postmodern bouquet of flowers.

"Please excuse her," Fifi says. "She's throwing a tantrum."

Mallory doesn't need to ask why; she knows why: Leland is jealous. Fifi paid too much attention to Mallory, and Mallory was unsuccessful in reflecting that light back onto Leland. Mallory wonders if this happens often, maybe even every time they're out with someone else.

"I cut myself," Mallory says.

"Let me see."

"No, it's fine. I just need a Band-Aid."

"She's insecure," Fifi says. "I have to admit, I'm starting to find it tiresome." The statement is an invitation for Mallory to join Fifi in some Leland-bashing. There's no denying it's tempting. Leland has real flaws—but then, so does everyone. And Leland must be traumatized about her parents' split and her father's relationship with Sloane Dooley, of all people. Can anyone blame Leland if she feels sensitive, even suspicious?

"I'm going to bed," Mallory says. "I'll see you in the morning."

"Mallorita."

The nickname instantly becomes cloying. Fiella Roget hasn't known Mallory long enough to bestow a nickname on her. But this is how she draws people in, how she wins them over, makes them feel special.

"My finger," Mallory says. "I'll see you in the morning. Stay up as late as you want, but please don't go walking on the beach."

"Is it not safe?" Fifi asks.

"It's safe, but…"

"You'll worry?" Fifi says. "That's sweet." Before Mallory knows what's happening, Fifi takes Mallory's wounded finger into her mouth and sucks on it gently. Maybe it's the effect of the wine, but Mallory has the sensation of stepping out of her body and watching this interaction from a few feet away. She sees herself with her finger in Fiella Roget's mouth. Her first thought is *How bizarre, how bizarre,* which makes her want to laugh because, guess what, kids, this really *is* bizarre. Mallory's finger instantly feels better, held tight by Fifi's lips and tongue.

The bedroom door opens and Fifi quickly but gently removes Mallory's finger from her mouth and pretends to study the cut.

"What's going on out here?" Leland asks.

"Nothing, *mon chou*," Fifi says. (The whole history of the world, Fiella has come to realize, is a matter of timing. Five more minutes and she might have been able to kiss adorable, straight-as-a-pin Mallorita. There's no denying that, for Fiella, there is still a deep thrill to be found in such conquests.) "I'm coming to bed."

The next morning, when Mallory gets home from her run, she hears Leland and Fifi screaming at each other. They're in the kitchen; Mallory can see them through the screen of the back door. Leland is wearing white silk pajama shorts and a matching camisole. Fifi is naked. She's standing in a shaft of sunlight that makes her skin look like molten gold. Fifi's breasts are firm and upturned; her stomach is a smooth, flat plane with a dark oval divot for a navel. Fifi's lower half is blocked from view by the counter.

"You're trying to seduce her!" Leland says. "Not because you're *attracted* to her, not because you find her *interesting*...you're doing it to make me *angry!*"

Mallory's eyebrows shoot up. Wow.

"She's your friend," Fifi says. "I want to know her."

"Oh, right," Leland says. "Like you wanted to know Pilar."

"Pilar was a mistake," Fifi says. "Anyway, Mallory is straight."

"*I* was straight until I met you!" Leland says. "Every woman is straight until she meets you. And Mallory is particularly suggestible. Easily swayed. I told you that before we got here. She's a follower—"

"I think you might be wrong about that. She has spunk. She's uncomplicated, maybe, but she's hardly a doormat. She reads—"

"She reads what people tell her to read," Leland says. "The entire time we lived in New York, she borrowed a book as soon as I was finished with it."

"The point is, she's harmless," Fifi says. "And she's nice. You should try being nice sometime—"

"Ha!" Leland says. "If I were nice one day, you'd leave me the next—"

"Oh, do shut up, *Leland,*" Fifi says. The name on Fifi's tongue sounds like a taunt, probably conveying Fifi's disdain for her lover's WASPy-ness.

"*You* shut up!" Leland says.

Suddenly they start kissing, and then Leland's mouth travels down to Fifi's breast. Mallory is trembling with rage and humiliation and other feelings she's probably too *uncomplicated* and *nice* to identify.

"Hey, is anyone awake?" Mallory yells through the screen. She stamps her sandy sneakers against the welcome mat to give them a moment to compose themselves, and by the time she steps inside, Leland is standing at the counter pretending to inspect the platter of muffins. Fifi has disappeared into the bedroom.

"Hey," Leland says, her voice wavering ever so slightly. "How was the run?"

"It was…*nice,*" Mallory says, hitting the word with a sledgehammer. "So, listen, I've had a change of plans. You guys are on your own today and probably tonight as well."

"Change of plans?"

"Yes," Mallory says. "And unfortunately, I'm taking the car, but there are two bikes, or you can call a taxi. The numbers are listed in the phone book."

"Mal," Leland says. She knows, or suspects, that Mallory overheard, and now she'll backpedal, apologize, or, worst of all, downplay what she said and try to persuade Mallory that she meant something else.

"Forget that," Mallory says. "I'll bike. You two can take the Blazer."

"Mallory."

But Mallory is having none of it. She goes into the bathroom, grabs a towel, and heads for the outdoor shower.

An hour later, Mallory is sitting at the bar at the Summer House pool drinking a Hokey Pokey, which was purchased for her by the man sitting next to her, Bayer Burkhart. The name Bayer, he tells her, is spelled like the aspirin, but he pronounces it like the animal that he sort of resembles. He's a burly guy with a dark beard. He asked Mallory if he could buy her a drink and she said yes, a Hokey Pokey, because her sole intention was to get drunk. She wondered if this counted as being suggestible. What she was...was easy to get along with. Unlike some people.

"I'm easy to get along with," Mallory says once she has sucked down her Hokey Pokey. "Unlike some people."

"Cheers to that," Bayer says. "Looks like someone needs another drink."

Isolde and Oliver don't work at the Summer House

anymore and neither does Apple—she's back at the camp for girls in North Carolina this summer—so Mallory is anonymous, which feels wonderful. Bayer seems to have the exact same goal as Mallory: To drink the afternoon away and tell the complete stranger on the next stool all his troubles because he doesn't know her and she doesn't know him but we are all human and therefore can offer empathy and an unbiased opinion.

"So," Bayer says. "Who are you?"

Mallory, she says, though she doesn't reveal her last name in case Bayer is a serial killer. She's the daughter of an accountant and a housewife; she grew up in Baltimore, lived in New York City briefly until her aunt Greta died and left Mallory her cottage on the south shore and a modest sum of money, at which point Mallory moved to the island permanently and now she's an English teacher at Nantucket High School.

"Now for the real question," Bayer says. "Why are you drinking all alone in the middle of the day?"

"Two reasons," Mallory says. "One is I have house-guests. My best friend from growing up and her lover, also a woman, who is famous. I can't tell you who she is…" Mallory pauses and studies Bayer more closely. Does he look like a person who reads? He has intelligent-seeming brown eyes and he's wearing a polo shirt and a Breitling watch with a blue face (expensive, she knows). "Do you read?"

"Mostly nonfiction," Bayer says. "And biographies. My favorite book of all time is *October 1964* by David Halberstam."

Mallory mentally adds this book to her list, then chastises herself for being suggestible. "Anyway, my friend Leland and her girlfriend had a fight, a loud fight, during which they said insulting things about me and I overheard them."

"Ouch," Bayer says. "What were the insulting things?"

"Not important," Mallory says.

Bayer tips his glass. "To me, you're flawless."

"Because you just met me," Mallory says. "I haven't had a chance to disappoint you yet."

"Amen," Bayer says. "What's the other reason?"

Mallory is still coherent enough to stop and ask herself just how honest she wants to be with her new-friend-but-maybe-serial-killer Bayer. "My ex-boyfriend is getting married today."

"That," Bayer says, "is quite the double whammy."

"Tell me about it," Mallory says.

Bayer suggests food for both of them, says he's buying, she should get whatever she wants, and she confesses that she used to work at the Summer House and she knows the best thing on the menu is the bacon cheeseburger. She'll take hers medium rare with extra pickles and she'd like her fries seasoned and crispy.

"I love a woman who knows how to order," Bayer says. "I'll have the same."

"Now you talk and I'll listen," Mallory says. "Why are you drinking all alone at the Summer House pool today?"

Bayer just arrived on Nantucket on Wednesday, he says. He sailed in, he's living on his boat, and he's rented the slip for the entire summer, though he's not sure how long he'll stay. He has a larger boat in Newport—that one has a crew—but he needs time away from them and them from him so he set off on his own for a while.

The Hokey Pokeys have done their job; Mallory has no inhibitions. "What do you do for a living?" she asks. "You sound rich."

Bayer throws his head back and howls with laughter, and it's this laugh—and *not* the fact that Bayer Burkhart owns two sailboats, one with a crew—that makes Mallory see him differently. While laughing, Bayer becomes instantly desirable, even sexy.

"I invented a bar-code scanner," he says. "The one used in most retail stores across the country."

"Oh," Mallory says. She grapples with this a minute. He's not a lawyer or a doctor or an investment banker. He's an inventor. He invented a bar-code scanner. "How old are you?"

This makes him laugh again and he says, "How old do you think I am?"

Mallory fears the answer is forty or maybe even forty-five, which would be too old. Mallory can date someone ten years older, maybe. "Thirty-seven?" she asks hopefully.

"Bingo!" he says.

They eat and have more drinks, though how many more, Mallory can't say. At some point, however, she realizes she is too drunk to bike home. Bayer says no problem, he'll call her a taxi that will deliver her and her bike safely back to her cottage. This is very kind, but Mallory won't deny that she's disappointed.

"Don't you want to invite me to see your sailboat?" she says.

"If you're too drunk to bike home, then you're too drunk to see my sailboat," Bayer says. "I'm not like that."

Mallory frowns and Bayer lifts her chin with one

finger. "I will take your number, though, if you're willing to give it to me."

Mallory arrives back at the cottage around sunset. The Blazer is gone; Leland and Fifi are out. Mallory gets herself a glass of ice water and passes out facedown on her bed. She feels like she's forgotten something. The oven? No. The iron? No. Well, if she can't think of it, then it must not be that important.

When Mallory wakes up the next morning, she has a headache and her heart feels like one of the mermaid purses she finds washed up onshore, brittle and empty.

She instantly remembers the thing she had forgotten the night before: Jake is married to Ursula.

Mallory, meanwhile, is single and the reasons why have been cataloged by her very best friend in the world: She is neither interesting nor original. She's suggestible, a follower. She's "nice," like a jelly jar filled with daisies or a pony that trots in a circle.

Jake is married to Ursula.

Through the walls, Mallory hears a woman's voice moaning in ecstasy.

No, Mallory thinks, *this is not happening.*

The phone rings. Mallory checks her clock radio. It's early but not that early—eight thirty. Maybe this is Cooper calling to tell her that Jake left Ursula at the altar.

"Hello?" Mallory says. Her voice sounds like pea gravel in a blender.

"Mallory, it's Bayer. Feel like a sail?"

*   *   *

How bizarre, how bizarre—Leland and Fifi's disastrous visit leads Mallory right into a romance with Bayer Burkhart.

Bayer takes Mallory sailing that first Sunday and she falls in love—not with Bayer but with life on the water. His sailboat is a seventy-foot racer-cruiser called *Dee Dee*. Mallory asks if Dee Dee is an ex-girlfriend, the one who got away, and he says no, he named the boat after Dee Dee Ramone. Does Mallory approve? She answers in the affirmative, even though she knows only three songs by the Ramones. *Dee Dee* has a finely appointed cabin. There's a galley kitchen with an espresso machine, a sitting area with satellite TV, a round dining table, a master suite in the bow with a low, wide bed and a head that has a hot shower, and a second, smaller suite that Bayer uses as an office. All of the doors are heavily varnished and have hook-and-eye closures so they don't fly open in rough seas.

They sail every day the wind is good—to Tuckernuck and then farther on to tiny Muskeget. They sail past Martha's Vineyard to Cuttyhunk. They sail around Monomoy up to Chatham.

For the first few trips, Mallory lies on the foredeck in her bikini, reading, but after a while she starts to take note of what Bayer is doing—when he trims the headsail and lets out the mainsail, how he tacks, how he handles the ropes. She loves the focus on Bayer's face when he's sailing. He seems interested only in getting them from one place to another in this most ancient and storied of ways.

When they're lying in the low, wide bed looking out the open hatch above them at the towering mast and the stars, Bayer is very, very interested in Mallory's body. He's such a skilled lover that she finds herself counting the hours until night falls, when *Dee Dee* is secure in its slip and they make it rock.

Bayer says he wants to turn Mallory into a proper mate. He shows her how to tie up the boat; turns out, she's a natural with knots. She loves standing on the bow in bare feet and tossing the rope over the bollards like she's a cowgirl lassoing a calf. She misses every once in a while but Bayer is patient. There hasn't been one cross word between them. Why would there be? Their days are filled with sunshine, water, wind. They swim, Mallory reads, Bayer casts a few lines and nearly always catches something big enough to keep, a striper or a bluefish. He grills the striper on his hibachi; he soaks the bluefish in milk.

They spend a week like this, two weeks. She calls him Skipper; he calls her Mary Ann. On days when there's no wind, Bayer works on the boat and Mallory returns to her cottage, goes running or biking, and waits for him to call her. She never appears at the dock without being invited, though she wants to surprise him, just once, because at some point, she gets the feeling he's hiding something. She can't say what it is or even what makes her feel that way. Kitty calls and, as usual, asks Mallory about her love life. Finally, Mallory has something to tell her mother— she's found a wealthy man with a yacht!—but when Mallory thinks about it, she realizes she barely knows the first thing about Bayer.

She makes a list: He invented the bar-code scanner. He lives in Newport, where he keeps a boat even bigger than *Dee Dee*. His favorite book is *October 1964,* and recently she has seen him reading something called *The Perfect Storm*. He likes the Ramones as well as the Violent Femmes, the Clash, AC/DC, and INXS; he has encyclopedic knowledge of the band members' names. He talks about Joe Strummer and Michael Hutchence like they're his friends. Maybe they *are* his friends?

Mallory once asked him what he did with his time when it wasn't summer and he wasn't sailing.

He said, "I dabble in politics."

Mallory pressed him. What did that *mean*? "Do you go door to door handing out flyers for your favorite candidates?" she asked. "Do you work the phone banks?"

He laughed. "I pull the puppet strings."

Bayer is a master artisan when it comes to crafting vague comments like this one. He'd told her just enough that first afternoon to make her think he was opening up. But now, weeks later, he remains a mystery.

Sometimes, Bayer will tell Mallory stories of the high jinks of his past—his buddy Icarus, his buddy Dennis; Havana, Islamorada, Hamilton, Nassau; sailfish, storms, sharks; this guy who owned a boat called *Beautiful Day,* great boat; another boat, *Silver Girl,* that Bayer tried to buy but the guy refused and then, months later, he went bankrupt. *Did you buy the boat then?* Mallory asked. *No. Turns out I wanted it only when I couldn't have it,* Bayer said. Mallory wonders if this is a hint that she should try to play hard to get. But why would she do that when they're so happy and the summer is so short?

Bayer gives her hundreds of dollars when he sends her to the grocery store or the liquor store. He hates running errands himself so she's doing him a favor, he says. He protests when she tries to give him the change. *Keep it,* he says. *It's just money. What's mine is yours.*

He smokes one cigarette at the end of each day and if Mallory has been drinking, she'll take a drag, though most times she just watches Bayer's figure against the darkening sky, the ember glowing, the smoke releasing from his mouth.

"Will you take me to Newport?" she asks one night. It dawns on her that they rarely spend any time ashore—in Chatham, it rained, so they'd gone for lunch at the Squire, and they had spent a blissful afternoon on the beach on Cuttyhunk, but they hadn't seen another soul.

"I left Newport this summer because I wanted to get away," Bayer says.

"Let's go out to dinner here, then," Mallory says. "We haven't been anywhere since that day at the Summer House." Bayer hasn't even been to Mallory's cottage. When she invited him, he said, *Trying to make a landlubber out of me?* She understands his point: her cottage isn't a boat, and life is just flat-out superior on the water. "How about dinner tomorrow night? My friends work at the Blue Bistro." She swallows because she's afraid he's going to say no. She's breaking a rule of some sort, or she's revealing herself to be the kind of person who needs society to be happy, whereas Bayer is quite obviously content with her company alone. "I'll pay."

He laughs. It's a real laugh; she at least knows him well enough to tell that. "You will not pay. I'll pay. Do I have to wear shoes?"

Mallory wears a Janet Russo sundress and Bayer wears shorts, flip-flops, and a button-down shirt in peach gingham, and he wets his hair and trims his beard and looks more than presentable when they walk into the Blue Bistro, which is beachfront fine dining, tucked between Jetties and Cliffside. The restaurant smells delicious and it's buzzing with conversation and laughter, and there's a piano player doing an easy-listening version of "I Fought the Law," which actually elicits a smile from Bayer. Isolde has set them up at a two-top out in the sand, so close to the lapping waves of Nantucket Sound that it's almost as if they're eating on the boat. Isolde brings menus and the wine list but Bayer waves them both away and orders a bottle of Sancerre and the seafood fondue for two.

"Very *good,*" Isolde says, and she awards Bayer one of her rare smiles. "How did Mallory get so lucky?"

Bayer takes Mallory's hand across the table. "I'm the lucky one."

Oh my God, Isolde mouths to Mallory over Bayer's shoulder.

The wine comes; they drink. The kitchen sends out a basket of savory rosemary-and-onion-flecked yeast doughnuts. These doughnuts are famous across the island, but Mallory had assumed they would fall short of expectations. But…wow…they are, without doubt, the most delicious thing she has ever tasted. To Bayer, she knows, the most delicious thing is something far more simple—a cold, ripe plum—but she sees his eyes pop.

"God *damn,*" he says.

He's happy. The date is going well, then? She's not sure why but she feels there's something at stake here.

They take their glasses of wine to the water's edge and get their feet wet. The sun is setting; there are stripes of magenta flaring across the sky. A gull soars low, just skimming the surface of the water; the ferry glides across the horizon, heading for the mainland. Mallory has lived on Nantucket for four years and still she finds the summertime here so beautiful that it hurts. Probably because the summer is fleeting, evanescent. It always ends. Mallory doesn't want it to end. She yearns for something that will stay, something permanent. Is she talking about Bayer? Is she talking about Jake?

She's getting drunk. She leads Bayer back to the table.

A second bottle of wine. The seafood fondue appears. Mallory spears a shrimp with her fondue fork, plunges it into the hot oil, and then, when it's plump and pink, she dunks it into one of the three delectable sauces.

This dinner is perfect; this restaurant, the entire evening, couldn't be any better. Right?

Before dessert, Oliver sends over shots of sambuca in tiny frosted glasses. Mallory holds hers aloft. "To you, Skipper," she says.

Bayer grins. "To you, Mary Ann."

A woman materializes out of nowhere. She's in a red floral wrap dress with a matching headscarf. She has dark hair and wears red lipstick. She's pretty enough. Older. Bayer's age.

"Bayer?" she says. "Is that you?"

Bayer stands up. "Caroline, hello, yes." Air kiss, hand on Caroline's back, and a sweeping arm to introduce Mallory. "Please meet my friend Mary Ann."

Mallory has been raised by Kitty; she knows to stand up when meeting someone. But she doesn't account for the sand or the proximity of her chair behind her or her drunkenness or her confusion because Bayer has chosen not to use her real name. Mallory's chair falls backward at the same time that she lurches forward, and she practically watches herself fall face-first into all the glassware and the candle's flame, but at the last minute, she catches herself and nothing breaks or spills.

"Pleasure to meet you, Caroline." Mallory's words, while not slurred, are not exactly crisp either.

Caroline's hand is smooth, her grip firm, her eyes assessing. She takes Mallory in and must draw the conclusion that further conversation is unnecessary because she turns back to Bayer. "I heard you were here," Caroline says. "From Dee Dee."

From Dee Dee. Mallory reaches for her wineglass and, finding it empty, picks up Bayer's and throws back what's left. Is this rude? She doesn't care.

Bayer says nothing. His face is still; his eyes are those of a man facing his own execution.

"How are the children?" Caroline asks. "Enjoying camp?"

"Not if you believe their letters," Bayer says. His lips turn up ever so slightly at the corners. "Good to see you, Caroline."

"Oh," Caroline says. "Well, okay, then. Good to see you too." She nods at Mallory. "Enjoy your evening."

Caroline's visit brings the evening to a premature end. Mallory says she doesn't want dessert. She goes to the ladies' room, trying to tell herself that there's an explanation, that the only lie is who he named the boat for, which is minor. *Dee Dee Ramone.* He was making a joke and she didn't know any better. When she returns to the table, Bayer is leaving a pile of hundreds for the check, and it's this that lets Mallory know he's guilty. Just throw money at the people you're wronging and their friends, and they'll forgive you. Isolde sees the pile of bills as she brings a to-go box with complimentary desserts from the kitchen and she murmurs in Mallory's ear, "Everything okay?"

"Yes, yes," Mallory says—though actually, she has no idea.

Back on the boat, Bayer lights a cigarette, sits in the stern, and pats the cushion next to him.

Mallory shakes her head. She feels she should remain standing. Where does she even start? "You have children?" she says.

"Guinevere, age ten. Gus, age nine. They're at camp in Maine this summer."

Guinevere, ten. Gus, nine. Why is this the first she's heard of his children? Well, there can be only one reason, right? "And Dee Dee?"

He clears his throat. "My wife."

"Your wife."

"Yes," Bayer says. "When I told you I had a bigger boat at home, with a crew, and I needed time away from them…"

"You meant you had a family."

"It was a euphemism."

"It was a lie. A *lie,* Bayer."

"I do have a second boat," he says.

"I don't care about your second boat," Mallory says. "I care about your wife. By not telling me, you made me complicit. What must Caroline think?"

"Who cares what she thinks? Do you care? You don't even know her."

"Well, then, what about what *I* think? You lied to me. Now, of course, all the things that have been bothering me about our relationship make perfect sense."

He turns on her. "Are there things about our relationship that bother you? Because, frankly, you've seemed pretty damn content."

Well, she *was* content—when she'd thought that she had landed a rich, eligible bachelor with time and money to lavish on her. She supposes now that it was no accident she got involved with Bayer directly after hearing Leland say all those unkind things about her. Leland was right; Mallory *is* suggestible. And she's gullible. A more clever person would have realized she was being duped.

"This whole thing was a sham. I feel so…stupid. So used. I'm a nice person, Bayer! I'm a *good person*."

(Bayer stubs out his cigarette. He considers Mallory. She looks beautiful tonight, but then, she always looks beautiful. She's young, maybe too young to understand. She told him during their first meeting at the Summer House that she wondered if he was a serial killer. No, he's not a serial killer, and honestly, he's not even a garden-variety philanderer, though he's aware it must appear otherwise to Mallory. He and Dee Dee agreed to spend the summer apart. The kids were at camp; it seemed like the right time.

Do what you want, Dee Dee said. *But go elsewhere. I don't want to hear about it.*

Where Dee Dee is concerned, all is fair—though she'll likely be hearing from Caroline Stengel in the morning, if not tonight. But Bayer admits to himself that all this probably hasn't been fair to Mallory. He should have come right out and told her he was married. He's curious why she never asked. This has made him wonder about her as well. There were times when he would have described her as not-there. Meaning somewhere else, with someone else.)

"You are a nice person and a good person, Mary Ann. Yes, you are. But even nice, good people aren't perfect. Everybody has weaknesses. I suspect there's a secret you're keeping as well. Maybe even something big?"

Mallory feels like she's in a hot-air balloon that's about to crash into a cornfield. Either she'll be killed in a fiery wreck or she'll walk away unscathed.

The latter, she thinks. It's her choice and she chooses the latter.

And Bayer is right. She is keeping a secret. Something big.

"I'm in love," she says.

He looks genuinely surprised. "With me?"

"No," she says. "I'm in love with Jake McCloud."

(*Ah,* he thinks. His instincts were correct.) "Is Jake McCloud the boyfriend who got married the day we met?"

"He's the one who got married," Mallory says. She hesitates and thinks, *How bizarre, how bizarre, that Bayer Burkhart is the person I finally tell.* "But he was never my boyfriend. He's my...my Same Time Next Year. Like in that movie. He comes to Nantucket to see me every summer for one weekend, no matter what."

Bayer nods. "Interesting arrangement." (He can't believe it, but he feels *jealous.* It's something about Mallory's expression. Jake McCloud is one lucky bastard. Frankly, Bayer would like to strangle him.) "That sounds nice."

She shrugs. "It has its ups and downs."

Summer #6: 1998

What are we talking about in 1998? Monica Lewinsky, the blue dress, Linda Tripp, Kenneth Starr, "I did not have sexual relations with that woman"; El Niño; Nagano; Linda McCartney; MMR vaccines; Mark McGwire; the Elliptical; Hurricane Mitch; Babbo; Phil Hartman; Windows 98; Viagra; Matthew Shepard; There's Something About Mary; Jesse Ventura; "Chickity China, the Chinese chicken"; Eric, Kyle, Stan, and Kenny.

Mallory spends Thanksgiving with Apple and ten members of Apple's family—her parents, her two brothers and two sisters, and their significant others—who are visiting Nantucket from all across the country. They reserve one of the private, tucked-away rooms at the Woodbox Inn, a place that feels like it's been around since the original Thanksgiving. The Woodbox has low ceilings and creaky, wide-plank wood floors and a fireplace in every room. It's the first Thanksgiving of Mallory's life that feels relaxing. At home in Baltimore, Kitty frets if she can't find the twelfth Tiffany dessert fork or if Senior doesn't carve the turkey at the correct angle or if Cooper comes home drunk from the Gilman–Calvert Hall alumni touch-football game, which he always does.

This year, Mallory doesn't even eat turkey. She orders the beef Wellington, because she can.

Skipping Thanksgiving means that Mallory *must* go home to Baltimore for Christmas. On Christmas Eve, the Blessings normally go over to the Gladstones' house to drink Steve Gladstone's wassail and eat Geri's famous hot crab dip, then they all dance in the living room to songs like "Rockin' Around the Christmas Tree." On Christmas morning, Kitty will wonder just what Steve Gladstone puts in the wassail.

For the second year in a row, there will be no Christmas Eve frivolity at the Gladstone house. The year before, the Blessings had tried to take over the tradition but it felt stiff and forced and Geri had spent most of the evening crying on the couch. This year, Leland and Fifi have whisked Geri away to Jackson Hole to ski, leaving the Blessings to fend for themselves. Kitty suggests the party at the country club but that involves Santa and screaming children so both Mallory and Cooper veto it. They want to get pizza from Angelo's and watch *The Year Without a Santa Claus.*

"Sounds good to me," Senior says, handing Cooper a hundred-dollar bill. "Christmas falls at the end of the year and so do taxes. I'll be in my study. Let me know when the pizza is here."

Kitty scowls, but only for a second. "Fine," she says. "I have cooking to do anyway. We're having a surprise guest tomorrow."

"Who's the surprise guest?" Mallory says. It's now late—the pizza has been devoured (along with a bottle of Dom Pérignon that Mallory bought with Senior's hundred—why not, it's Christmas!), Heat Miser and Snow Miser have performed their soft-shoe, and Mallory and Coop are lying on the floor of the living room, the only light coming from the Christmas tree and the dying fire. It's nice—but Mallory feels sad about their lost tradition. When Steve Gladstone started sleeping with Sloane Dooley, did he realize he was sabotaging not only his marriage but Christmas Eve for the family across the street?

"I have no idea," Cooper says.

"Not a new girlfriend?"

"Nooooo," he says. "I'm staying away from women for a while. Alison was fun, Nanette was fun but a hypochondriac, and Brooke was a card-carrying psycho. Like a Glenn Close–type psycho."

"Let's not forget Krystel," Mallory says. "You *married* her!"

"I'm attracted to head cases," Cooper says. "Alison was an anomaly. She was normal. We broke up because of the distance but also because I felt like there was something missing…and what was missing was the crazy."

Mallory closes her eyes. She thinks about how, when she was growing up, Cooper was her superstar big brother, and in many ways she resented him for that. Now he's her friend and life is so much better.

"I must have been a real jerk in my past lives," Cooper says.

"Don't worry, you'll find someone," Mallory says. "There are plenty of crazies out there."

At five o'clock the next afternoon, right before Christmas dinner, the doorbell rings.

"Mallory," Kitty calls out, "would you answer that, please?"

Mallory's expectations are low. She suspects it's going to be the new tennis instructor from the country club. Kitty has been talking about setting Mallory up with him.

Mallory opens the door to find a woman—plump, nervous smile, a long shiny curtain of silver hair, funky teal cat's-eye glasses bedazzled with rhinestones.

"Mallory," the woman says. "My God, look at you."

Mallory blinks. The voice—she recognizes the voice. The hair, the glasses, that smile. She knows this woman, but who is it?

Then Mallory gasps. "Ruthie!" It's Aunt Greta's Ruthie, Dr. Ruth Harlowe.

Ruthie opens her arms and Mallory steps right into them. Tears leak from the corners of Mallory's eyes, not only because she's gobsmacked by seeing Ruthie but also because, along with the pile of sweaters and CDs, this is a gift from her parents. This is the best gift Mallory can imagine.

The Gladstones may have owned Christmas Eve, but Christmas dinner belongs to Kitty. The instant that Ruthie steps inside, a cork pops. There are champagne cocktails and hors d'oeuvres in the library—clams casino and Kitty's famous gooey Brie with pecans and sour-cherry chutney. Everyone greets Ruthie like she's an esteemed personage, which she is, but also like she's a complete stranger, which she is to everyone except Mallory.

Ruthie is gracious in the face of what must be a very awkward situation. She still lives in "the house in Cambridge," she says, though she's in the Baltimore area over the holidays visiting her nephew, his wife, and their new baby.

Ruthie isn't afraid to suck down a couple of champagne cocktails and neither is anyone in the Blessing family. Johnny Mathis sings "Sleigh Ride"; the fire crackles. Mallory tells Ruthie about her job at the high school on Nantucket and how the gift of that cottage has changed her life. "I can't thank Aunt Greta," Mallory says. "But now I can thank you."

"Greta was so fond of you," Ruthie says. "She thought of you as her own."

Mallory is saved the embarrassment of crying by her mother, who calls everyone into the dining room.

Standing rib roast, Kitty's incredible creamed spinach, homemade popovers with sweet butter—and for dessert, as always, there will be a sticky date pudding with warm toffee sauce and pillows of freshly whipped cream.

Senior says grace and then Kitty raises her glass of Ponzi pinot noir. "There's something I'd like to say."

Oh no, Mallory thinks. All she can imagine is Kitty ruining the evening by trying to demonstrate how evolved she is now. *We know other lesbians* (by which she would mean Leland and Fifi) *and have found them quite agreeable.*

Mallory locks eyes with Cooper. If she were close enough, she would squeeze his hand until Kitty finishes blurting out whatever cringe-worthy remarks she's prepared.

Kitty says, "Ruthie, I want to thank you for sharing in Christmas dinner with our family. We owe you an apology for all the years we weren't as accepting as we might have been. But now, in our advanced years, Senior and I have come to the realization that love is love." Kitty hoists her wineglass higher. "And really, there's no explaining it."

"Hear, hear," Coop says, and they all touch glasses without crossing.

Mallory watches her father take a sip of his wine and then fumble for the carving knife. She isn't at all surprised that he let Kitty do the heavy lifting here, but neither is Mallory willing to let him off the hook.

"Is that how you feel, Dad?" she says. "Love is love and there's no explaining it?"

Senior levels a direct gaze at Mallory. Her father's face is so familiar to her, but in this moment she sees something new in his eyes. It's as though tiny doors are opening to reveal...an actual person.

"Yes," he says. "I do feel that way." And then something even more extraordinary happens: her father smiles. "Thank you for coming, Ruthie. You've honored us with your presence. We don't deserve your forgiveness but we are grateful for it."

"Merry Christmas," Ruthie says.

Cooper is more than ready to leave Baltimore the day after Christmas, but Mallory is staying until the twenty-seventh and she has begged him not to abandon her. Can he eke out one more day, please?

Sure.

"The Bellos are hosting a cookie exchange tonight," Kitty says. "Why don't you two come with me?"

"Absolutely not," Mallory says.

"What's the point of a cookie exchange *now*?" Cooper asks. "Christmas is over."

"I think the answer to that is obvious," Mallory

says. "People want to pawn their stale cookies off on the unsuspecting."

"Well, if you don't have anything better to do," Kitty says, "Regina and Bill and the rest of the neighborhood would love to see you."

Coop's rescue arrives when Jake McCloud calls the house to ask if Coop will meet him at PJ's, their old Hopkins hangout, for beer and wings.

"You didn't go to South Bend for Christmas?" Coop asks.

"Nah. Ursula's mom came to DC. And those two are going to *The Nutcracker* tonight, so I'm flying solo."

"Perfect," Coop says. Ursula makes him nervous.

"And hey, invite your sister if she's free," Jake says.

"Oh, she's free," Coop says.

Cooper knocks on Mallory's bedroom door. He can hear her playing "I've Done Everything for You," by Rick Springfield, on her stereo and singing out, *"You've done nothing for me!"* at the refrain.

"Come in," she says.

Coop cracks the door open. Mallory is reading in her purple shag beanbag chair, the one the whole family calls Grover. "Intervention," he says. "Rick Springfield? Grover? You're regressing. So you're going out with me tonight. We're meeting Jake Mc-Cloud at PJ's at eight."

Mallory sits straight up. "What?"

"I got you out of the cookie exchange—you're welcome. We're meeting Jake."

Mallory says, "Is this you inviting me because you feel sorry for me? Because I don't want to infringe on your male bonding. Or…I mean, is Ursula going to be there?"

"Ursula has *The Nutcracker* with her mother. Jake is taking the train up by himself."

"To meet you."

"To meet *us*," Coop says. "He asked for you specifically."

Her eyebrows shoot up. "He did? He said 'Bring Mallory' without your prompting?"

"Yes. Can you stop being such a weirdo? I'm going to break the news to Kitty."

At quarter to eight, Mallory enters the kitchen wearing jeans, a black turtleneck, and a pair of Chucks—that's normal—but also the new silver hoops that she got for Christmas and makeup—mascara and lipstick.

Jewelry? Coop thinks. *Makeup?*

"You didn't have to get all dolled up," he says. "It's just PJ's."

"Your sister looks lovely," Kitty says. She has decided to forgo the cookie exchange as well. She and Senior are fixing leftover roast beef sandwiches to enjoy in front of the fire. Apparently, romance in the Blessing household isn't dead. "You never know, your sister might meet a doctor tonight!"

PJ's Pub is a dive bar beloved of all Johns Hopkins students, and Cooper Blessing and Jake McCloud are no exceptions. The bar is right across from the library and down the street from the Fiji house, so they used to go all the time—after studying, after chapter meetings, before and after lacrosse games. There were dollar imports on Wednesday nights and fifty-cent pizza slices on Sundays. Just saying these prices out loud makes Cooper feel a hundred years old, but the second he and Mallory descend the steps from street level and smell the old beer and cooking grease, Coop is twenty-one again.

Jake is sitting at their usual table next to the juke-box under the Stella Artois mirror where Jerry, the owner, writes the specials. When Jake sees them, he jumps to his feet.

"Oh, boy," Mallory says.

The Hopkins kids are away on break, so the crowd is local and a little older. Jerry comes over to shake hands; he still remembers Coop and Jake by name even though they graduated nine and ten years earlier, respectively. They order one pitcher of beer, then another, and Mallory is keeping up, her face is *glowing,* and Coop understands; it does feel good to be out of the house. Mallory tells Jake the story about Ruthie showing up for Christmas dinner and Jake looks interested—though why would he care? Jake says that their Christmas was mellow. Ursula and her mother, Lynette, are still mourning the loss of Ursula's father two and a half years earlier. Christmas isn't the same without him and never will be.

"I'm happy to have some time away from them, honestly," Jake says. "They don't get along. Ursula had work to do yesterday—"

"On Christmas?" Mallory says.

"Sounds like Senior," Coop says.

"And Lynette asked her to please put the work away and enjoy her family time." Jake finishes off his beer. "You can imagine how that went over."

"Well," Mallory says. "I've about had it with family time myself."

"Cheers to that," Coop says.

* * *

Another pitcher, an order of wings, an order of mozzarella sticks. Coop gets up to take a leak and make a quick phone call. When he gets back, Mallory and Jake are leaning toward each other across the table, deep in conversation. Cooper remembers what a pain-in-the-ass little sister Mallory was when they were growing up, her and Leland always spying on Coop and Fray and his other friends and giggling and asking to tag along. Coop is psyched that Mallory has turned out to be such a cool person who can hang out with his friends like this.

"You got the book?" Coop hears Jake say.

"I did. I read it in two days. Thank you," Mallory says.

"You know it's a retelling of *Mrs. Dalloway*?" Jake says.

She swats his arm. "I knew that, yes—but did *you* know that?"

Cooper reclaims his seat and Mallory and Jake look up—startled? He's interrupting their little tête-à-tête? "What book are you guys talking about?"

Mallory stands up. "I'm going to pick some songs."

Jake clears his throat. "It's called *The Hours,* by Michael Cunningham. Have you read it?"

"No, I haven't *read* it," Coop says. "I don't read anything for pleasure. I do too much reading for work. So, what, you sent the book to Mal? You two have…a little book group?" Coop laughs at his own joke— but maybe it's not funny. Maybe Coop should start reading and join a book group. What a great way to meet smart women.

"What do you guys want to hear?" Mallory asks.

She's standing at the jukebox. "They don't have any Cat Stevens."

"Thank God," Coop says.

"No Rick Springfield either."

"Even better," Coop says.

"Surprise us," Jake says.

"Yeah," Coop says. "If you pick something I don't hate, I'll be surprised."

Mallory drops in quarters and starts punching buttons. A second later, there are piano chords, then Paul McCartney's voice: "Maybe I'm Amazed." Coop approves, and apparently, so does Jake. He gets to his feet and says, "Dance with me."

"No," Mallory says.

"There's no dancing at PJ's," Coop says.

"Just dance with me to this one song," Jake says.

"No," Mallory says, but Jake wins her over and they start slow-dancing in front of the jukebox, which is strange, but whatever, they're all getting drunk and Cooper is distracted anyway because at that moment, his old girlfriend from Goucher, Stacey Patterson, walks into the bar.

Is this a coincidence? No; Cooper did some investigative work and learned that Stacey is VP of marketing for the Baltimore Aquarium and she's still single. He called information, got her number, and invited her to meet them here.

Stacey is wearing a red wool coat and a houndstooth miniskirt with high black boots. She looks every bit as beautiful as she did in college. Coop hurries over to greet her; they hug. He shepherds her over to the bar and says, "Let's get you a drink. What would you like?"

"A glass of merlot, please."

Cooper isn't sure merlot is a wise choice at a place like PJ's, but oh, well. Stacey peers over Coop's shoulder.

"Is that Jake McCloud?" she says. "I haven't thought about him in *years*."

"Yes, it is," Coop says. "He'll be psyched to see you."

"Is that his wife he's dancing with?" Stacey asks.

"No," Coop says. "That's my sister, Mallory."

"Oh," Stacey says. "Well, they would make a cute couple."

Cooper turns to watch Jake and Mallory spinning slowly in front of the jukebox; Mallory's head rests for a second against Jake's chest.

They *would* make a cute couple, Cooper thinks. In another life.

Summer #7: 1999

What are we talking about in 1999? Gun control; Y2K; Kosovo; Napster; John F. Kennedy Jr.; Carrie, Samantha, Charlotte, and Miranda; Egypt Air Flight 990; "I try to say goodbye and I choke"; gun control; Brandi Chastain; The Matrix; Tae Bo; Elián González; Amazon; Jack Kevorkian; Hurricane Floyd; the euro; gun control; violent video games; gun control.

Jake's memories of Mallory and his anticipation of seeing her—in nine months, in nine weeks, in nine days—serve as the emergency reserve of oxygen in his emotional scuba tank.

Jake has had one hell of a year.

Ursula celebrates her seventh anniversary at the SEC by announcing she's leaving. If you stay any longer than seven years, the saying goes, you're there for life. She's courted all over the city and ends up taking an accelerated partner-track position in mergers and acquisitions at Andrews, Hewitt, and Douglas for a mind-blowing salary and the prospect of an even more mind-blowing bonus.

With Ursula making so much money, Jake decides to quit PharmX, a job he has hated in practice and principle since he started. He's tired of meeting with congressmen and local lawmakers in an attempt to ease regulations and raise drug prices for the pharmaceutical industry. He tells Ursula he's quitting, she tells him he's a fool, he tells her he doesn't care, and she's too busy to do battle.

Fine, she says. *Don't come crying to me when you're sitting home in your boxers watching Montel Williams.*

Jake gives his notice, then the next day schedules a root canal; he wants to get it done while he still has full dental. Jake's boss, Warren, swings by his office more than usual, each time dangling some new enticement to get him to stay—a promotion, a raise, two extra weeks of vacation. (Warren can't believe Jake McCloud lasted as long as he did in the glad-handing, soul-destroying world of pharmaceutical lobbying. Jake somehow managed to keep his personal integrity intact, fighting only for the drugs he believed in. He has been a tremendous asset all these years, and while

Warren is sorry to see Jake go, he's also cheering for him. His talents can be put to better use.)

When Jake clears out his office, he starts with his top center desk drawer, where he keeps the photograph of Mallory eating noodles and a number 10 envelope that holds three sand dollars and seven fortune-cookie fortunes. He throws the photograph away, telling himself it's outdated—but it pains him nonetheless. He has looked at the photograph every single day the way other people look at pictures of Caribbean beaches— to remember that there is another world out there, one that provides escape, solace, joy.

He slips the envelope holding the sand dollars and fortunes into a manila envelope stamped INTEROFFICE and secures the metal tabs. He tucks this between drug reports in his briefcase. He nearly laughs at himself for taking this precaution. He could wear the sand dollars on a necklace and Ursula wouldn't notice.

No sooner does Jake leave PharmX than he gets sick. Really sick—a high fever with aches and chills. He sweats, he's freezing. He sleeps during the day and is awake in a dazed stupor all night. Ursula is sympathetic at first. *Poor baby,* she says. She rubs his back and places a bowl of ice cubes on his nightstand. She sleeps on the daybed in the living room because she "can't afford to catch it." She works even longer hours than she did for the SEC but Jake gets it, she's in M and A, it's a twenty-four-hour thing, plus she wants to make partner so that they can eventually have some kind of life. She asks Mrs. Rowley down the hall to do a pharmacy run—Advil, Tylenol—and she finds a deli that delivers soup.

The phone rings and messages pile up—it's Cooper,

it's Jake's mother, it's Ursula's mother, it's Jake's father, it's Warren from PharmX, it's his buddy Cody saying he has a lead for a lobbying job at a "big-time" organization. Jake is too sick to answer. The messages from his parents and Lynette are urging him to go to the doctor. ("Otherwise we'll fly out there," his father says, only half kidding. They lost a child, so no illness is taken lightly. But Jake also knows his parents are too busy to fly to Washington, just like Ursula is too busy to take half a day off to accompany him to the emergency room.)

On day seven, when there has been no improvement and Jake is lying in bed, weak and shaking, with a fever of 103, barely able to get to the bathroom, Ursula appears in her light gray suit and her sharp stiletto heels and says, "Enough is enough. We're going to the hospital."

Turns out he has a staph infection in his bloodstream, probably from the root canal. Did he take all of his antibiotics? He can't remember. Well, it hardly matters now; he's earned himself a two-night stay at Georgetown Hospital on intravenous antibiotics. Jake knows the names of these specific drugs only too well, and he also knows these drugs are a hospital's last line of defense. He is profoundly sick, almost-dying sick. He shudders to think of how close he came to letting the infection rage on. Ursula taking action saved his life.

"You saved my life," he says.

"You're going to be fine," she says, kissing his forehead. "And besides, it wasn't me. Your mother called." Liz McCloud is the one woman in the world who intimidates Ursula; this has been true since they were in middle school, back when Jessica was still alive. Apparently, Liz called Ursula's work and with surgical precision sliced away the layers of paralegals meant to protect her time until she had Ursula herself on the phone, and then Liz McCloud was even more formidable than her usual formidable self. *Get my son to the hospital, Ursula. Now. I don't mean three billable hours from now. I mean* now.

Twenty-four hours later, Jake feels much better. By the middle of the second day, he's sitting up in bed eating a tuna fish sandwich and rice pudding, watching *The Montel Williams Show* with a nurse named Gloria.

Ursula comes to collect Jake at the end of his stay, but she seems quiet—not distracted, not snippy, just quiet. Jake wonders if maybe his unexpected illness has made her introspective. When he asks her what's wrong, she shakes her head and fiddles with the new cell phone that the firm insists she carry so they can get hold of her any hour of the day. She flips it up, then snaps it down. Is she *angry?* He can't tell.

At home, she gets him settled into bed—the sheets, he notices, have been changed—and she brings him a glass of ice water with his pills. He still has two weeks of two different antibiotics, neither of which can be taken on an empty stomach, so she's also brought in the takeout menus from Vapiano's and I-Thai.

"Unfortunately, I have to go back to the office," she says.

"Okay," he says. "Thank you for everything."

"Warren called and said the person who took over your office found something you left behind. Warren stopped by this morning to drop it off."

"Whatever it is, I don't need it," Jake says, and then suddenly, his gut, which feels like glass anyway, goes into free fall. Oh no. Oh no, no, no, no, no, no, no.

"He dropped off an envelope," Ursula says. "Looks like pictures. I didn't open it because…well, because it's not mine. Warren says the guy found them hidden inside the code-of-conduct pamphlet and thought you'd probably want them back."

"Pictures?" Jake says. "Hidden? Honestly, I haven't the foggiest." He's just going to deny they're his, the pictures of Mallory. Mallory driving, Mallory sleeping, Mallory laughing at the TV as Alan Alda bangs on the piano and sings "If I Knew You Were Coming, I'd've Baked a Cake." "I don't know what those would be, and as I'm sure you're aware, I never even picked up the code of conduct. Maybe the pictures were left by the guy before me."

Ursula nods once. "Maybe," she says.

Jake waits for Ursula to leave the apartment and then he waits half an hour longer, just in case. He climbs out of bed, his legs weak, his gut watery, as he approaches the mail table. Lying on top of a ceramic platter that someone gave them as a wedding gift—mistaking them for people who entertained—is the packet of photos. The envelope says QUIK PIC in clownish red letters and just below that is Jake's name and his office phone number in his own handwriting. Ursula obviously knows the pictures don't belong to anyone else.

But did she look at them?

Did she look at them?

Did she?

Jake holds the pictures in one shaking hand. She must have peeked at one or two, right? Just to see what they were? And if she did, she would have seen Mallory. Jake hadn't taken a picture of anything

else—not the beach, not the pond, not the ocean—
which means Ursula might not have realized the
pictures were taken on Nantucket, and she might not
have recognized Mallory.

No, she definitely would've recognized Mallory if
she'd looked. She had noticed Jake dancing with Mallory at Cooper's wedding and she'd commented on it,
which meant it bothered her. She was jealous, and a
jealous woman did not forget. But Mallory had been in
full hair and makeup at the wedding, so maybe…

Ursula didn't look at the photos, he decides. She
would have stormed in and demanded an explanation.
And what would Jake possibly have said?

The truth. He would have told her the truth. *That's
Mallory Blessing, Cooper's sister. She is my Same Time
Next Year.*

It's possible that Ursula didn't look because
she sensed that whatever was inside would be a
relationship-ender. After all, Jake doesn't even own
a camera.

He doesn't look at the pictures himself because it
will only make what he has to do more difficult. He
opens the apartment door and walks to the far end
of the hall, where the incinerator is. He opens the
door; he and Ursula call it the mouth of hell because
it sounds like there's a fire-breathing dragon down
there. He holds the pictures for a moment and tries to
talk himself off the ledge. They're just photographs,
images on paper. It's not like he's throwing Mallory
herself into the fire. Still, he imagines her beauty
curling into itself as it melts, distorting her features,
blackening, then turning to smoke and ash. He can't
do it—but a trip to the street to throw them away is
beyond him.

He lets the envelope go.

When he gets back to the apartment, he's sweating and shaking. He should toss the other envelope as well, the one with the sand dollars and the fortunes.

But no, sorry, he can't do it. He has to hold on to something.

When Jake regains his health, he finds himself at a loss. What has been going on with his job search? Nothing, that's what, because he's been so sick, and there's no denying that quitting his job has left him in no-man's-land. They have plenty of money, so Jake buys himself a new Gateway computer, sets up his own personal e-mail account, and polishes his résumé. He establishes a routine—he goes for a morning run in East Potomac Park, then buys the *Washington Post* on his way home and peruses the classifieds. He toys with going back to school, even medical school, but in his heart, he doesn't want to be a doctor. He thinks again of becoming a teacher, like Mallory. He envisions himself overseeing labs and giving quizzes on the periodic table.

He likes people, he likes talking to people, he likes advocating for the things he believes in. He should go into development, fund-raising. He has no qualms about calling people up and asking for money. He contacts the alumni office at Johns Hopkins. They invite him down for an interview and offer him a job on the spot. They're no dummies; Jake was a popular, well-liked, and successful student at Hopkins, president of the Interfraternity Council and a member of Blue Key, giving tours to prospective students. Who better to represent Johns Hopkins than Jake McCloud?

But the job is in Baltimore; it would be a commute,

and presently he and Ursula have no car. He could take the train up each day, he supposes, but something about the job doesn't feel quite right. It doesn't feel like he's stretching himself enough. He wants to grow.

Ursula is patient and encouraging but the bubble over her head says: *Just figure it out, already!* It also says: *I am too busy to get into the foxhole with you.* (The bubble over her head always says this, no matter which foxhole it is.) Jake can sense her interest in him waning. She is so immersed in work—big companies gobbling up little companies like a corporate game of Pac-Man—that he can tell she has to remind herself to ask about his day. She's careful not to offer too many hard opinions. *You want to work at Hopkins, then work at Hopkins*—although when he turned the job down, he could see she was relieved. Or maybe she was disappointed? Maybe she wanted to be able to tell people that her husband "works at Johns Hopkins" (she wouldn't have to say "in the development office" and she wouldn't have to mention it was his alma mater). Maybe she wanted him to have a long commute so they would never see each other.

In June, Ursula gets assigned to a merger in Las Vegas.

She flies out there for a week. The firm puts her and her team up at the Bellagio; Ursula has a suite. She flies home for the weekend, then flies back, then does the same the following week. But then one Friday she calls to say her meetings ran late, she missed her flight, and she's just going to stay in Vegas for the weekend. "In fact, it doesn't make sense for me to keep going back and forth," she says. "I should just stay out here until the deal is finished."

"Okay?" Jake says. "Is that what Anders is doing?"

"Anders?" Ursula says. "I mean, yeah, that's what the whole team has been doing. I'm the only one going back and forth. Well, except for Silver, but he has kids."

"The team" is only four people—Ursula, Anders Jorgensen, a colleague named Mark something, and Hank Silver, Ursula's boss. Anders is single, Mark is single and gay, Hank is married with five kids, all of whom play squash and have tournaments literally every weekend. Hank goes home because his wife insists on it; it's just not possible to have five kids playing squash and only one parent present. Anders was once a linebacker at USC, which gives him a non-work-related rapport with Ursula because of the famous USC–Notre Dame rivalry. Ursula can talk college football like no other woman Jake or Anders has ever met.

Is Jake jealous of Anders? Well… "Oh, okay," Jake says. He *is* jealous, but he won't succumb to this base emotion, he's hardly innocent himself—and besides, to act jealous of Anders will only make Anders appear bigger and Jake smaller. "Enjoy. Get some sleep."

"Why don't you come here next weekend?" Ursula says. "I think you'd actually like it."

When Jake lands in Vegas, it's 111 degrees. He flew coach because he didn't feel right using Ursula's miles to upgrade to first class when he was contributing exactly zero to their household income. He arrives tired and foul-tempered and therefore finds nothing to appreciate in either the desert landscape or the skyline, which looks, from a distance, like some kid forgot to pick up his toys. Jake's taxi cruises past the iconic WELCOME TO LAS VEGAS sign and within moments they are on the Strip. Jake's taxi driver, Merlin, takes it upon himself to act as Jake's personal tour guide. (Merlin can tell that this particular fellow will be difficult to impress. Merlin concedes that Vegas isn't for everyone, but that doesn't stop him from flexing his powers of persuasion. He points out the Stratosphere with the roller coaster at the top; Circus Circus; the Mirage, where the white tigers live; Treasure Island, with a pirate show out front every hour on the hour; the Venetian, which has canals winding through it and singing gondoliers; Caesars Palace; Paris; New York–New York, with a Krispy Kreme doughnut shop inside; Excalibur; Luxor; and Mandalay Bay, which has a Four Seasons Hotel in one of its towers. Merlin pulls up to the Bellagio. "This is the jewel in the crown," Merlin says, and he believes it. Sometimes he smokes a joint and watches the dancing fountain show out front three, four times in a row.

He hands the fellow a card. "Fifty percent off Cirque du Soleil," Merlin says. "Call me."

"Thanks," the fellow says. His voice is flat but that doesn't mean he won't call, Merlin thinks. It can take time for Vegas to grow on you.)

At check-in, it's discovered that Ursula has forgotten to put Jake's name on the room, so the front-desk clerk, Kwasi, can't give him a key.

"But I'm her husband," Jake says.

"I understand your position," Kwasi says. "And I hope you understand mine." (Kwasi's position is that maybe this guy is Ursula de Gournsey's husband, maybe he's not—but even if he *is* her husband, she might not want him in her room.) Kwasi slides a ten-dollar poker chip across the desk, which Jake accepts before he even realizes what it is.

He says, "What am I supposed to do with this?"

(Kwasi thinks, *If you have to ask* ...) He smiles. "I recommend the roulette wheel."

Jake finds a pay phone and calls Ursula's cell. He gets her voicemail and hangs up. The point of her cell phone, he thought, was so that people could reach her night and day. But likely she's cloistered with her team in meetings—except that it's six o'clock and Ursula told him that morning, which now feels like three days ago, that she would wrap up at four because Silver needed to catch a flight back to his family.

Jake decides to sit on the banquette by the main elevators and wait. He has a book with him—*Plainsong*, by Kent Haruf, which is spare, haunting, and precisely the opposite of what he should be reading when he's already feeling abandoned. To pull it out and read amid the exuberant go-for-broke atmosphere of the lobby, with its lights and sound of raining coins, its smoky haze and smell of rye whiskey, would make him seem hopelessly square. He has a ten-dollar chip. He should use it.

He doesn't know the first thing about gambling and he's worried about making an ass of himself if he sits down to blackjack or tries to throw craps. The slots don't interest him in the slightest. What did Kwasi say? The roulette wheel.

It's as easy as placing the chip on a number, right? He watches the ball drop and wheel spin three times— twenty-three, four, thirty-five. What number should he pick? He thinks about Mallory's birthday, March 11, but he's never been with her on her birthday or, per their arrangement, even called her on it.

He chooses nine for their month, September; he sets his chip down on the red nine and thinks, *All or nothing.* It was free money, anyway.

And guess what.

Nine wins.

It wins.

Jake lets out a whoop as his one chip turns into a pile of chips. That was incredible, right? Ha! His very first try, he won!

"I won!" he says to the woman next to him. She's older, smoking a cigarillo. Her lipstick has bled into the lines around her mouth. "And that was the first time I ever gambled!"

(The woman's name is Glynnis. She wants to tell this kid that beginner's luck isn't just a Santa Claus myth. It's more predictable than death.) "Do yourself a favor," she says. "Cash out."

But Jake doesn't cash out. Instead, he takes half his chips and places them on five, for May, which is the month of Ursula's birth, and twenty, which is the day.

The number that wins is, again, nine.

Jake blinks. Nine again? His money is swept away.

Glynnis exhales a stream of cigarillo smoke and says, "This town runs on fools like you."

It has taken Jake less than five minutes to experience the highs and lows that Vegas has to offer. He returns to the pay phone, tries Ursula's cell again—voicemail. He supposes the natural next step is to go to the bar and wait. The Bellagio is actually quite lovely. There's a Dale Chihuly glass ceiling, *Fiori di Como,* that he could be very happy staring at as he sips a bourbon.

But his present state of mind is one of exasperation.

He came all the way here to see his wife and not only is she not answering her phone but she neglected to add his name to the room. Her consideration for him is nonexistent. It has always *been* nonexistent. Why has he tolerated it for so long?

Well, no matter now. He's leaving. He'll catch the redeye home.

But he can't find the exit. He can't even find the front desk to ask where the exit is. He must have made a wrong turn and now he has been engulfed by the casino proper—rows and rows of slot machines, acres of blackjack and Texas Hold'em and craps and the now-dreaded roulette wheels. There are cocktail waitresses wearing black satin bustiers gliding around like they're on skates. Three of them ask what he's drinking. He says he's looking for the nearest exit and they turn and glide away.

I give up, Jake thinks. How about a bar, then, just a good old-fashioned bar? But in this part of the hotel, those seem to have disappeared as well.

Miraculously, he finds his way back to the main elevator bank and that's it, he's staying put. He pulls out his book, wondering exactly what Ursula thought he would like about this place.

"Jake?"

It's his wife, standing before him, wearing a pale pink suit and nude patent-leather pumps. Her hair is down; it's longer than he remembers, or maybe that's because she blew it out today, and it's parted on the side. She is so stunning that there can't possibly be a man on this earth worthy of her, himself included.

"Hey," he says. He stands to kiss her and tastes tequila on her lips. "Have you been…drinking?"

"Yeah," she says. "Mark, Anders, and I went to

Lily Bar after we finished today. It's our Friday tradition."

"So just now...you were at a *bar?*" Jake says. "Having a drink with Mark and Anders when you knew my flight landed an hour ago? I've been sitting here waiting for you, Ursula, because you forgot to put my name on the room. I tried calling."

"Yes," she says. "I saw that."

"If you saw that, why didn't you answer?"

"I was finishing up my workweek," Ursula says. "And I figured I'd see you in the room. I made us reservations at the Eiffel Tower for tonight."

"I couldn't get into the room," Jake says. "Because you forgot to add my name."

"I heard you, Jake," she says. "I'm sorry but I've been busy. It's not a big deal, is it? You survived, right?"

Her tone is chiding. She knows she was negligent but she wants him to shake it off, just as he's shaken off all her self-absorption the past nineteen years.

"Not a big deal at all," he says. "But, Ursula?"

"What?"

"I'm leaving," he says. He hoists his bag over his shoulder and heads in what he now knows is the opposite direction of the infernal casino. In a few seconds, he sees the unmistakable beacon of natural light beckoning him like the entrance to the afterlife. He steps out the front door into the baking sun.

Back at the Las Vegas airport, Jake hears his name being called. It's a man's voice, not Ursula's. Ursula has undoubtedly gone up to the room, poured herself a glass of wine, and drawn herself a bath, where she will wait for Jake to return.

But this time, Jake isn't running back. Ursula can

stay in Vegas the rest of her life if she wants. He's going home.

"Jake! Jake McCloud!"

There's a man slicing through the crowds of people who are trying to make their redeyes. It's Cody Mattis, an acquaintance from DC, and Jake feels uneasy because he listened to Cody's voice message weeks ago when he was sick but never got back to him.

Jake gives Cody his best effort under the circumstances. *Hey, Cody, how you doing, what brings you to Sin City?* The answer is a bachelor party, the Spearmint Rhino, never seen women like that before in my life, blah-blah-blah. Jake blocks this last part out. He doesn't want to think about women.

"Sorry I never returned your call, man," Jake says. "I've been busy…"

"Oh yeah? Did you find a job?"

"No, not yet, still looking."

Cody hands Jake a business card. "You know I'm working as a lobbyist for the NRA, right? When I mentioned to my boss that you left PharmX, he basically issued me a mandate to bring you in for a meeting."

"He did?" Jake says, taking the card. NRA—the National Rifle Association. "This is Charlton Heston's gig, right?"

"Protecting the good old Second Amendment," Cody says. "We'd love to have you on board."

Jake must be angry, because for the entire six-hour flight back to Washington—out of spite, he upgraded himself to first class—he turns over the possibility of lobbying for the NRA in his mind.

"Protecting the good old Second Amendment": *A*

well regulated Militia, being necessary to the security of a free State, the right of the people to keep and bear Arms, shall not be infringed. The amendment was ratified in 1791, back when a person might have had any number of reasons to own a gun. Now, however, with the new millennium on the horizon, Jake believes there are too many guns, and a lot of them are in the wrong hands.

But then Jake plays devil's advocate. He spent enough time in Michigan growing up to know that a lot of good people, his friends' fathers, for example, hunt, and they shouldn't have a hard time getting rifles or ammunition, should they? And what about keeping a gun around for self-defense? If Jake were the one traveling for work all the time and Ursula were home in the apartment by herself, wouldn't he want her to have a gun, just in case? *Maybe,* he thinks, although if she had a gun, she might be tempted to use it in a situation that didn't warrant it, and if she used it, someone would get hurt or maybe even die.

He's not going to work for the NRA.

Still, it's nice to be wanted and he does need a job and the pay is probably excellent, which would be good for his self-esteem. Something's got to give.

On Monday, Jake calls Cody's boss, a man named Dwayne Peters, and sets up a meeting for the next day. Even over the phone, Dwayne Peters is a good salesman—"The NRA gets a bad rap here in the East, we need a public relations overhaul, Jake, and that's where you come in. We need these mommies and daddies and the intelligentsia who wouldn't know a forty-five from a thirty-aught-six to understand that *we* are the ones keeping America safe. Don't you want to help keep America safe, Jake?"

Jake nearly responds, *Yes, sir, I do*—that's how persuasive Dwayne Peters is. The Second Amendment is as ironclad as the right to free speech or freedom of religion. The nation's forefathers weren't wrong. But they *were* wrong, Ursula would point out. Because back then, only white men had the right to vote.

So instead, Jake says, "I'll see you tomorrow, sir. I look forward to learning more about the NRA."

That night, Jake is sitting at the coffee table eating a bologna sandwich—even with the AC running, it's too hot to cook anything—when Ursula walks in. She's in her travel clothes—linen pants and crisp white shirt.

"Hey," she says. She drops her suitcase and her briefcase and drapes her garment bag over the railing. She looks sad. Or maybe just defeated. The bubble over her head is…empty.

Jake doesn't care. He returns to his sandwich, cracks open the beer that's sweating in front of him. He's sitting around in his boxers just like she predicted he would be. He resents Ursula showing up without warning; if he'd known she was coming home, he would have put on pants.

"I'm not going to apologize for leaving," he says. "And I'm not going to apologize for making you leave Vegas, because that was your choice."

"You didn't make me leave," she says. "The deal is done. We closed."

"Oh," Jake says. He knows he should feel happy about this but he wants to believe that Ursula left Las Vegas because she's putting their marriage first. "Well, you'll be pleased to know I have a job interview tomorrow. With the NRA."

"The NRA?" Ursula says, and she makes a noise that sounds like a cough or a laugh. Her expression is incredulous. "You might want to cancel that. Haven't you seen the news?"

That very afternoon, in the town of Mulligan, Ohio, a seventeen-year-old boy whose name was being withheld walked into his summer-school class with an AK-47 and killed twelve students, his teacher, and himself. It's all over the news. The boy purchased the gun at a Walmart. No one asked him for ID. He paid in cash, walked out of the store with the gun and thirty rounds of ammo, and drove to his high school to show everyone just how much he hated summer school.

"Don't worry," Ursula says. "Something else will turn up."

Jake's only worry is that he even considered working for the NRA. He remembers the long-ago phone conversation he had with Mallory while they were both still in college. *I'm one of the good guys, Mallory.* He's going to make sure that's true.

Ursula gets no downtime. The week following the shooting, she's assigned as the lead attorney—a tremendous honor—on a case in Lubbock, Texas. Lubbock is closer than Las Vegas, but it takes longer to get there because there aren't any direct flights. Commuting home on the weekends won't be feasible, though staying in Lubbock is no treat; they'll have her at a Hyatt Place near the Texas Tech campus. Ursula can't see any reason for Jake to visit. There is nothing to do but work.

"I hope Anders is on your team?" Jake says when she tells him about the assignment, though he doesn't.

"Oh, he is," Ursula says. "We do well together. He

gets me. They assigned Mark to a different case, so it's me, Anders, a first-year associate named AJ, and two paralegals." She pauses. "AJ looks like a supermodel. I bet she and Anders will be engaged by the time we finish."

Jake knows Ursula far too well for him to relax at this statement. She never, ever comments on other women's looks; to Ursula, the value of a woman is how smart she is, how competent, how interesting, so she is saying this simply to put Jake's mind at ease. But why?

"I feel bad leaving you alone for the rest of the summer," she says. "We didn't get a chance to go away."

"It's fine," Jake says. "Your career comes first."

Ursula wraps her arms around him. "Will you go to Nantucket?" she asks. "On Labor Day weekend?"

"Yes," Jake says.

He arrives on Nantucket on Friday and Mallory is there to pick him up at the airport in the Blazer. However, instead of driving down the no-name road toward the cottage, she heads into town.

"Uh-oh," he says. "Are we changing up the program?"

"'Fraid so," she says. She pulls into one of the reserved spots in front of the A and P and Jake feels a heightened sense of concern. Town means people and people means a greater chance of bumping into some-one he knows. The past couple of summers they have frequently seen Mallory's students or former students or parents of students while they were out and about. Mallory always introduces him as "our family friend Jake," which makes their relationship sound platonic and innocent while also being true. But even so, Jake is uncomfortable. He feels like he's wearing a T-shirt that says I'M CHEATING ON MY WIFE.

He lost all his chips in one fell swoop in Vegas, but the real gamble he takes is coming to Nantucket every year like this. He wonders what the odds are that they'll *never* be discovered. A thousand to one?

"Where are we going?" Even across the parking lot, he can hear the end-of-summer revelry over at the Gazebo. He imagines that crowd peppered with people from Hopkins, Notre Dame, Georgetown, all waiting for him like land mines.

"I bought a boat," she says. "We're going to Tuckernuck!"

The back of the Blazer is packed with grocery bags and Mallory's monogrammed duffel. They carry all the supplies down the dock to a slip where a sleek sailboat awaits. It's called *Greta,* and it has one 250-horsepower Yamaha motor hanging off the back. The hull is painted teal blue and there's a small cabin below. Jake can't believe it.

"This is yours?"

"Meet my Contessa Twenty-Six," Mallory says. She goes on to say that she got the sailboat the same way she got her bike and the Blazer—someone wanted to get rid of it. "When I broke up with the Newport guy, I realized that the thing I missed most about him was spending time on the water. So I took sailing lessons. I just finished the advanced course last week."

Yes, Jake remembers her mentioning the sailing lessons the year before. He also recalls being jealous of her instructor, Christopher, until she let it slip that Christopher was nearly eighty years old. "Is this Christopher's boat?" Jake asks. "Did Christopher die?"

"He's still alive," Mallory says. "But he can't sail anymore, his wife made him stop. So he basically *gave* me his boat. All I had to do was hire his friend Sergei to do the overhaul." She climbs aboard in bare feet and Jake sheds his shoes and follows. "And I bought a new motor. Not cheap, but completely worth it."

"Good job, Mal," Jake says. "I'm so proud of you." He pops downstairs to the cabin, which is simple but cozy; there's a galley kitchen, a navigation table, a V-shaped berth, and a head. "So where did you say we were going again?"

They're going to Tuckernuck, which is a completely separate island within spitting distance of the west coast of Nantucket but a world apart. Tuckernuck is private; only the people who own property there and their guests are allowed. There are twenty-two homes serviced by generators and wells. There are no public buildings on Tuckernuck, not even a general store. There is no internet, no cable TV, and limited cell service.

This describes Ursula's idea of hell, Jake thinks. And his own idea of heaven.

Mallory anchors *Greta* off Whale Island and they wade ashore with their luggage and provisions. Mallory sets off alone on foot to the house, which is three-quarters of a mile away. Jake stays behind with the things. He feels like a pioneer. What do you need to create a life, after all? Food, clothing, shelter, a person to love. Jake marvels at the sheer beauty around him. Whale Island isn't an island at all but rather a ribbon of white sand that is the only place boats can anchor. Beyond lie green acres crisscrossed with sandy paths and, here and there, a glimpse of gray-shingled rooftops. Across a narrow channel lies Smith Point and the island of Nantucket, which seems like a metropolis in comparison.

Jake hears someone calling his name and sees Mallory sitting behind the wheel of a battered red Jeep with no top and no doors.

They're off!

The house belongs to the family of Dr. Major's wife and was built in 1922. It's a simple saltbox upside-down house with a great room upstairs that has enormous plate-glass windows all the way around for 360-degree views of the island and the water beyond. Mrs. Major's niece recently redecorated, so the place feels like a graciously appointed Robinson Crusoe hideaway. There's a rattan sofa and papasan chairs with ivory cushions; there are funky rope hammocks in the corners, and the plywood floor is painted with wide lemon-yellow and white stripes. Jake is surprised to see a small TV with a shelf of videos, across which lies a hand-painted sign: *Rainy Day Only*.

Jake whistles. He feels like they've stepped into another world. No one will find them here.

It's their seventh weekend together, lucky seven, maybe, because it's the best yet. On Friday night, Mallory grills burgers, as usual, and although there's a small cookstove, she grills the corn as well. On Saturday, they pull two bikes out of the shed and explore the island. They visit both ponds—North Pond, which they swim in, and smaller and murkier East Pond, which they don't. They lie on three different sections of golden-sand beach. They see other people from afar and simply wave; there's no reason to exchange any words. It would feel like talking in church.

On Sunday, they hike through the middle of the island. Mallory shows Jake the old firehouse and the old school. Most of the other houses are shuttered now that the summer is drawing to a close. Jake is captivated by a small cottage that has clearly seen better days. Its windows are clouded and cracked, the paint on the trim is peeling, and the gutter on the front appears to be hanging on by one rusted screw. It has a deep porch that is oddly reminiscent of *Out of Africa,* Jake thinks, and though he isn't prone to adopting strays, he can't help but imagine what it would be like to buy the place and fix it up. He says as much to Mallory, who scrunches up her eyes behind her sunglasses. "You have crummy taste."

"It's off the grid," he says.

"Put mildly," she says.

"We could grow old together here," he says. It's always on their Sundays that he starts to feel this way—like he won't survive if he leaves her.

"How's Ursula?" Mallory hasn't asked until now, and he knows her timing is no accident. When he talks about growing old together, Mallory gently reminds him that he's already vowed to grow old with someone else.

"Things are tough," he says.

"Good," Mallory says. She squeezes his hand. "I'm kidding. What's going on? Can you tell me?"

"I know the person I married," he says. "But I'm still shocked by the way she is sometimes." He then regales Mallory with the story of his trip to Vegas.

"Ouch," Mallory says. "Have you considered that

maybe what draws you to Ursula is that she makes herself unavailable? And I'm too available."

"You're not available at all," Jake says.

"Too emotionally available," Mallory says. "You know how I feel about you."

"Do I?" Jake says. He turns away from the house to face her. A red-tailed hawk circles overhead, but there's no one else in sight. It feels like they're the last two people on the planet. He realizes that every single year he has been waiting for Mallory to cry uncle and say, *That's it, I give up, please leave Ursula and move to Nantucket, or I'll come to you, or we'll make it work long distance.* But she never says this, and so what can Jake think but that Mallory likes the arrangement the way it is? She prefers it to a bigger commitment. She has him…and she has her freedom, which, in years past, has meant other men. "I'm going to be honest here, Mal. I'm not sure how you feel about me."

"Jake," she says. "I love you."

She said it.

I love you.

Jake has said the words to her thousands of times in his mind, whether Mallory was lying in bed next to him or six hundred miles away.

He doesn't want to mess up this moment. He wants it to be unforgettable. He's going to make this a moment Mallory thinks about not only for the next 362 days, but for the rest of her life.

"I love you too, Mallory Blessing," he says. "I. Love. You. Too."

It works; tears are standing in her eyes. She hears him—and, more important, she believes him.

When he kisses her, however, she pushes him away.

"We have to go," she says. "We have to be at Whale Island by six. I have a surprise."

The surprise is a strapping, incredibly handsome man who pulls up to Whale Island in a thirty-six-foot Contender. Jake squares his shoulders and tries to sit up straighter in the wonky seat of the old Jeep while Mallory runs over to greet their visitor. Jake isn't sure how he feels about this particular surprise.

Mallory and Mr. America talk for what seems like an awfully long time—yes, Jake is jealous—then Mr. America hands Mallory a paper shopping bag and she gives him a kiss on the cheek and waves good-bye. Mr. America revs his engines, expertly sweeps the boat around, and heads back in the direction of Nantucket.

"Who was that?" Jake asks.

"Barrett Lee," Mallory says. "He caretakes all the homes out here, and in the summertime, he brings provisions."

"Did we need provisions?" Jake asks.

Mallory opens the bag. Jake sees familiar white cartons and catches a whiff of fried dumplings.

"He brought our Chinese food," she says. "Now let's go home. We have a movie to watch."

Summer #8: 2000

What are we talking about in 2000? Hanging chads; Broward County; Katherine Harris; the Human Genome Project; Yemen; the Subway Series; Walter Matthau; the International Space Station; getting voted off the island; Charles M. Schulz; Sydney Olympics; Slobodan Miloševič; Pilates; Tony, Carmela, Christopher, Big Pussy, Paulie Walnuts; USS Cole; Microsoft antitrust; Almost Famous; EVOO; "Who Let the Dogs Out."

The new millennium is upon us and guess what: Cooper Blessing is getting married again!

His fiancée's name is Valentina Suarez. She's an administrative assistant at the Brookings Institution. Valentina is from Uruguay, a beach town called Punta Este, which is a renowned resort area with a well-heeled international clientele. Valentina's family owns a beachfront restaurant, and for this reason, they can't get away, even for Valentina's wedding. This sounds fishy, and when Mallory presses her brother, he admits that Valentina's family have no idea she's getting married because Valentina didn't tell them. The reason she didn't tell them is that they wouldn't approve. They would like Valentina to marry a Latino, preferably a fellow Uruguayan, preferably the son of the owners of the casino next door to their restaurant, Pablo, who was Valentina's childhood sweetheart.

Mallory would have guessed that a second wedding—and one where the bride would have no family in attendance—would be a small, modest affair. Maybe even a courthouse ceremony followed by lunch.

But no. Valentina has always dreamed of a big wedding, and Cooper plans to make this dream come true—which pleases no one as much as it does Kitty.

"We get to do the whole thing over," Kitty says. "And in June, which is much better."

Mallory is to serve as Valentina's maid of honor. Fray will be the best man—again. Is Cooper having any other ushers?

"Jake. Jake McCloud," Cooper says, as though Mallory might not remember him. "And Valentina will have her downstairs neighbor, Carlotta, as a bridesmaid."

For Cooper's second wedding, we once again return to Roland Park Presbyterian, which Kitty Blessing decks out in a palette of pinks. The flower of choice is the peony. Everyone loves peonies—but is there such a thing as too many peonies? If so, that's the case at Cooper's second wedding.

Mallory's dress is a standard floor-length sheath in ballet-slipper satin. She gets her hair styled the same way she did for the first wedding, only with tiny pink roses tucked into the chignon rather than baby's breath.

Mallory sees Jake at the rehearsal an hour before the ceremony and her hopes feel like lemmings rushing to the edge of a cliff. Will they be dashed? Has Jake brought Ursula? Jake and Mallory both have cell phones now and they've exchanged numbers, but the rules they established years earlier still apply. Mallory isn't to contact him for any reason other than engagement, marriage, pregnancy, or death. So she didn't call him to ask if he was bringing Ursula to Cooper's wedding. She'll know soon enough.

He's wearing a dove-gray morning jacket with tails. Again: tails. Kitty likes things as formal as possible.

When Jake sees Mallory, he raises his eyebrows. In appreciation—yeah? She looks good? He comes over and kisses her. Chastely. It's torturous.

In her ear, he says, "She's here. I'm sorry."

Mallory will not let this unfortunate piece of information ruin the evening ahead.

"Great," she says. "I look forward to catching up with her."

During the ceremony, which is performed by Reverend Dewbury with as much hopeful optimism as he displayed at Cooper's first wedding, Mallory turns her head to survey the guests. On the groom's side, fourth row back, seated on the aisle, is Ursula de Gournsey in a stunning seafoam-green appliquéd sundress with a sweetheart neckline. Her hair is long and shiny, parted to the side; she's wearing bright red lipstick. Mallory can't stop staring at her until, in one awful moment, Ursula notices her and they lock eyes. Mallory snaps her attention back to her brother, that tall, smiling golden boy, the most quality person Mallory has ever known. Mallory wants to believe that Cooper's love for Valentina will last until the grave, but secretly, she feels that this wedding has *doomed* written all over it.

*   *   *

The reception is, once again, at the country club, only this time the cocktail hour and pictures are held outside with the emerald links of the golf course in the background. Because it's June 24, the daylight is never-ending, and even at seven thirty, there's a foursome—the Deckers and the Whipps—still finishing up at the eighteenth hole. Wedding guests can hear the *thwock* of Paulson Whipp's shot off the tee, but instead of admiring her husband's drive, Carol Whipp squints toward the clubhouse and says, "That's Cooper Blessing's wedding. Oh, and look— isn't that Mallory? I wonder why she hasn't met anyone yet."

This will be a frequently asked question of our girl this evening: *When will it be your turn?*

Mallory greets the question with irritation and embarrassment, but the people who ask are friends of Senior and Kitty; Mallory has known them all forever, and she understands that they only want to see her happy (which apparently means "paired off"). She can't bear to give them false hope, however, so she says, "This might be a case of always a bridesmaid, never a bride."

Fray overhears her. "Amen," he says. "I, for one, am never getting married."

"Cooper is getting married enough for all of us," Mallory says. "Wanna come with me to the bar?"

"I haven't had a drink in six years, nine months, and two weeks," Fray says. "Since my trip to Nantucket."

Six years, nine months, two weeks. This, then, is how long she and Jake have been together. "Just come with me and get a seltzer, then," Mallory says. "I need a bodyguard to protect me."

"From whom?" Fray says.

"Everyone," she says.

There's a seated dinner, salmon or lamb, new potatoes, tiny sweet peas. Mallory sneaks glances at the next table. Ursula isn't eating; she never eats, Jake has confided—though tonight, Mallory isn't eating either. She's too anxious. Jake is talking to Geri Gladstone, who is seated to his right. Does Jake know that Geri is Leland's mother? Leland and Fiella were invited to the wedding, but Fifi is on tour in Europe and Leland went with her. Geri Gladstone has gained weight, most of it in bags under her eyes and a pooch under her chin; Mallory doesn't like to be ungenerous but she wishes things had gone the opposite way when Steve left her for Sloane Dooley—she wishes that Geri had become incredibly slender and started dating Cal Ripken Jr.

Mallory is drinking champagne but she's careful *not* to dive headfirst into glass after glass. She doesn't want to be the drunk girl at the wedding—at least, not yet. She thinks back to the sweet longing she felt for Jake at Cooper's first wedding; it seems so mild and innocent compared to the wild jealous storm brewing within her tonight. She loves Jake now. Their last weekend on Tuckernuck was sublime, and Mallory doubts they'll ever be able to top it. And yet, she says this every year, and isn't every year just a bit better than the last? Their relationship grows like a tree—the roots go deeper and they add a ring around the trunk.

The band starts to play for the first dances. Cooper heads out to the floor with Kitty, Valentina with Senior. Valentina looks beautiful and happy—but *is* she happy without her family? Or is she just pretending, like Mallory?

(She's pretending. Valentina can't believe lightning didn't strike the altar, so blasphemous is this thing she's doing, marrying without her parents' blessing, without her parents' *knowledge*. Her parents are skiing in Las Leñas this weekend, for the elder Suarezes are very well off, very sophisticated, very active, and yet they are of one mind when it comes to the future of their daughter Valentina. They expect her to return to Uruguay for good and marry Pablo Flores. In fact, Señor and Señora Suarez will *see* Pablo in the lodge, and the three of them will discuss Valentina's return as though it's a given, none of them expecting that she's dancing at her own wedding with her brand-new father-in-law.)

Someone taps Mallory on the shoulder. It's Fray. "Wanna sneak a cigarette?" he asks.

"Maybe in a minute," Mallory says. Commiserating with Fray has its appeal but right at this moment, Mallory wants to be alone. She heads for the ladies' room.

The ladies' room at the club hasn't been renovated since 1973, which makes it look hopelessly old-fashioned but also comforting. One enters a lounge with rose-colored wall-to-wall carpeting and a rose-colored Naugahyde divan and three stools with needlepointed covers that are positioned under a long counter. Above the counter is a mirror where, for generations, ladies have applied lipstick, powdered their noses, and stared into their own eyes pondering…what? Well, all kinds of things: *What am I doing with Roger? Do I have a drinking problem? Why didn't I pursue a doctorate? How much should I pay the babysitter? Do I look fat? Do I look old? Why can't Roger stop bashing [Ford/Carter/ Reagan] so loudly in public? Why is Helen giving me the silent treatment? How long until I can go home to bed?*

There's a cut-glass bowl of butter mints, individually wrapped in cream-colored cellophane. Out of habit, Mallory takes a handful and drops them into her clutch. Just as Mallory is feeling a small burst of joy at bumping into her old friend the butter mint, she hears a noise coming from the ladies' room proper. Someone retching.

Mallory quickly enters a stall; the retching continues. Someone has had too much to drink—but who? This wedding reception is decidedly tamer than Cooper's first. Where is Cooper's friend Brian from Brookings? He was oodles of fun, and, if Mallory isn't mistaken, he succeeded in making Jake jealous.

(Brian Novak is married with three children, and because he unwisely invested in a crepe restaurant in the town of Cheverly, Maryland, where he lives, he's three months behind on his mortgage, his wife has had to take a weekend job as a receptionist at a walk-in emergency clinic, and he can't come to Cooper's wedding because he is stuck at home caring for the kids and worrying about foreclosure. At this very moment, Brian is fervently wishing he were in Baltimore, spinning Mallory around on the dance floor. She was cute, with her freckles, ocean-colored eyes, that tiny gap between her lower teeth, and she had a sense of mischievous fun, which is more than Brian can presently say for his wife.)

When Mallory comes out of the stall, she sees Ursula de Gournsey leaning over the sink, rinsing out her mouth. Mallory freezes.

"Are you okay?" Mallory asks. Was it *Ursula* she heard retching? Apparently—they're the only two people in the ladies' room.

Ursula's eyes meet Mallory's in the mirror. Her skin is paste gray.

"I think I'm pregnant," she says.

Pregnant.

It feels like several days pass while Mallory is sucked down into a spiral of agonizing self-pity, jealousy, anger, and spite. In fact, it's amazing that Mallory is still upright. Let's return to the tree analogy: It feels like Ursula has taken a freshly sharpened ax and felled the relationship between Mallory and Jake at its very base. Despite this, Mallory takes a step forward, turns on the water in the sink next to Ursula's, pumps out a dime-size squirt of pearlescent gardenia-scented hand soap (another aspect of this ladies' room that transports Mallory back to her childhood), smiles into the mirror, and says, "Wow! Congratulations!"

"No," Ursula says, tears standing in her eyes. "This is awful. This is a disaster."

Mallory dries her hands on one of the paper hand towels embossed with the country club's logo and then hurls it into the trash. There's a flare of pure fury: Having Jake's baby is *awful*? It's a *disaster*?

Mallory supposes that Ursula is upset about the pregnancy because it will interfere with her trying to make partner at the firm. Jake has made how Ursula feels about work crystal clear.

Just as Mallory is about to shrug and walk away— because Ursula has no right to feel anything other than blessed that she's carrying Jake's baby, in Mallory's opinion—Ursula breaks down into full-blown sobs, and Mallory softens. Maybe Leland was right—Mallory is suggestible, easily swayed. Or maybe our girl is just kind and sympathetic.

"Come here," Mallory says. She leads Ursula to the lounge and sits next to her on the divan. She places a tentative hand on Ursula's back; Ursula is so thin, Mallory can feel the distinct knobs of her spine. She isn't sure what to say, so she nods at the bowl on the counter. "Would you like a butter mint?"

Ursula shakes her head, though the sobbing subsides a bit.

"I'm Mallory Blessing. Cooper's sister."

"I know," Ursula says. "I saw you at the first wedding."

"I'm sorry you're upset about this. Is it the timing or…"

Ursula drops her face into her hands and shakes her head. "No. Well, I mean, *yes,* but that's not the worst part."

Mallory produces a tissue from her clutch and presses it on Ursula. This is crazy, right, that she's here in the bathroom, comforting Ursula?

Yes, it is crazy. But then, a second later, *crazy* is redefined.

"The problem is," Ursula says, "it's not…it's not…jayblibberkiz."

"Wait," Mallory says, because she didn't catch the second part of Ursula's sentence. "What? It's not what?"

The door swings open and the lounge is overtaken by white organza and the sound of Spanish wailing. It's Valentina. Carlotta dutifully follows behind, holding up Valentina's prodigious train.

Valentina is hysterical. She looks around the lounge.

She clearly needs a place to collapse, but the best spots are occupied by Ursula and Mallory.

Ursula stands up, and she and Valentina execute a do-si-do. Should Mallory ask Valentina what's wrong? She probably doesn't want to talk to Mallory, and anyway, she has Carlotta, who can speak her native tongue and who is not her new husband's sister.

Mallory and Ursula aren't finished. Or are they? They have no choice but to step out into the hallway, where they can all too clearly hear the band playing "Two Tickets to Paradise." The moment of confidence between them has been broken, but Mallory gives it one last shot.

"I think I missed part of what you were trying to tell me in there," she says. "You said, 'It's not,' but I didn't hear the rest. It's not…what?" Mallory's nerves are jangling like the zills of a tambourine. Did Ursula say, "It's not fair"? Pregnancy and childbirth aren't particularly fair. Women get the short end of the stick. They have to carry the baby, they endure the pain of delivery, and the time-consuming job of nursing…and that's only the beginning.

Ursula shakes her head. She looks at Mallory warily now, as though Mallory is trying to wrest away something that Ursula isn't willing to relinquish.

It's not…what?

Well, Mallory can guess the unspeakable truth.

It's not Jake's baby.

But Ursula will neither confirm nor deny.

"I should get back," Ursula says. "Thank you for the Kleenex." As if the damp, disintegrating tissue she's holding in her hand is the sum total of what Mallory offered.

Before Mallory can respond, Ursula disappears into the ballroom.

Mallory pulls Fray off the dance floor. He's doing the twist with Geri Gladstone, and how odd is *that,* considering that Geri's ex-husband is now shacking up with Fray's mother, Sloane, in nearby Fells Point? Geri looks to be genuinely enjoying herself and Mallory feels bad about stealing Fray away but…desperate times.

"I need you," she says. "And that cigarette. Outside."

Mallory also needs tequila. Two fingers of Patrón Silver, which she procures from the bar and takes with her as she weaves through the tables toward the back door. Jake and Ursula are seated; Ursula has flipped open her phone, of all things, and Jake cocks an eyebrow at the sight of Mallory and Fray leaving together.

It isn't Jake's baby. Is this *possible?* It's like something out of *All My Children,* but this isn't a soap opera, this is real life. Did Ursula *cheat* on Jake? Mallory feels affronted by the idea—and how hypocritical is *that?* Mallory is Jake's Same Time Next Year! She has no room to judge *anyone.*

If Ursula *is* pregnant by someone else and Mallory knows it, should she tell Jake? The answer is obviously no. So Mallory should keep the secret and let Jake believe it's his baby when it's really not?

Mallory can't think about it. She follows Fray outside.

They sit on the stone retaining wall on the far edge of the patio, the dark end, so people won't see them smoking. The people Mallory is worried about are her parents; in so many ways, she still feels like a teenager.

"Did you always smoke?" Mallory asks. "I can't remember."

"I started when I stopped drinking," Fray says. "I needed a new vice, one that would kill me more slowly."

Mallory is already feeling the tequila three sips in, and the first inhale off the cigarette makes her so heady that she nearly topples off the wall like Humpty Dumpty. She grabs for Fray's hand and ends up clutching his thigh. Which is a little awkward, right? She steadies herself and taps ashes into the manicured grass. "So how are you?" she asks. "You're good, right? A millionaire?"

"Six coffee shops in western Vermont and one opening in Plattsburgh at the end of the summer, all operating at a profit," he says. "Next week I fly to Seattle to see about launching my own brand of coffee. Starbucks did it. Peet's did it. No reason I can't do it."

"You should call it Frayed Edge," Mallory says. She cackles. "Never mind, that's a terrible name for a coffee brand."

(Fray kind of likes the name Frayed Edge. The future of coffee lies with young people, and young people like irreverence. He can see Frayed Edge coffee shops at every major university in the country, girls showing up in their frayed jeans—they buy them intentionally ripped and whiskered now—kids pulling all-nighters during midterms and finals. And, as Fray has learned, what twenty-year-olds want drives business to other demographics, because everyone wants to be twenty.)

"I *am* going to call it Frayed Edge," he says. "Thanks, Mal."

"Give me a commission, please." She throws back what's left of her tequila and *whoa!* It has *You'll pay for this later* written all over it, but it does the trick. She feels nothing but a slow, dirty burn inside. "This wedding is…I don't even know." She longs to tell Fray about the love triangle that has ruled her life for the past six years, nine months, and two weeks and how it has been, maybe, revealed to have another side. But it would be too much for Fray—or anyone—to digest. And Fray might feel like telling Coop in the name of "protecting" Mallory.

Next, Mallory considers telling Fray that she saw Valentina crying in the bathroom, but she doesn't want to stir that pot either. The wise thing is to keep quiet.

"I'm going to keep quiet," she says, because she's drunk and can't keep quiet.

Then an astonishing thing happens: Fray turns Mallory's face toward him and they start kissing. Fray maneuvers himself off the wall and ends up standing to the left of Mallory's legs, which are bound together by the ballet-slipper-silk skirt of her sheath.

Mallory is enjoying herself. Is it weird that she's kissing Fray, a person she has known since she was a little girl? She might feel that way tomorrow, but tonight she's hungry for his attention. Besides, she has always had a thread of sexual curiosity about Fray, deeply sublimated, but come on, he was older, a little dangerous, and off-limits to Mallory because of Cooper and Leland, which only made him that much more intriguing. He's sober, he knows full well what he's doing, so Mallory can only think that either Fray has held a torch for her all this time or Mallory has somehow transformed herself into an object of desire, either of which would be gratifying. In any case, she lets Fray lead her to the woods on the far side of the eighteenth hole and they make love leaning against a tree, which sounds rushed and uncomfortable but is, in fact, the opposite. Fray takes his time and deals with the restrictions of her sheath so expertly that Mallory wonders if he often makes love to bridesmaids at wedding receptions while leaning against trees. What neither of them thinks about until the last possible minute is birth control; Fray promises he'll pull out and then breaks that promise.

When they walk back to the reception, the band is playing "At Last," which is the song Mallory danced to with Jake at Coop's first wedding. She seeks him out—and sees him staring right at her and Fray. His eyes remain on her as she reaches up and pulls a leaf from her hair.

He shakes his head almost imperceptibly, or maybe he doesn't shake his head, maybe Mallory is imagining this gesture of disapproval, of jealousy. Mallory longs to take his hand and pull him onto the dance floor, she longs to whisper in his ear, *Yes, I was just in the woods with Fray, but it's you I love, it has always been you, it will always be you, Jake McCloud.*

But she can't. Ursula is sitting right next to him, shaking the ice in her glass. Ursula has told Mallory she's pregnant and maybe Ursula told her something else as well, or maybe she didn't, but either way, Mallory can't go near Jake for the rest of the night.

"Wanna dance?" Fray asks.

"Sure," Mallory says.

*   *   *

Labor Day is ten weeks later. Mallory is waiting in the Blazer when Jake steps out of the Nantucket airport. He climbs in without a word. Mallory turns the key in the ignition without a word.

Mallory turns down the no-name road, and dust, sand, and dirt billow behind the Blazer in a cloud, just as they always do. Mallory has burger patties waiting under plastic wrap in the fridge, six ears of corn, shucked, four perfectly ripe tomatoes from Bartlett's Farm sliced and drizzled with olive oil and balsamic, and a wedge of Brie softening next to an artful pile of water crackers and a small dish of chutney. There are novels stacked on Jake's side of the bed—this year, *Bee Season,* by Myla Goldberg, and *The Blind Assassin,* by Atwood—just as there always are. But this year, something is different. Maybe more than one thing.

Mallory pulls into the driveway, turns off the car, and looks at Jake.

"Home," she says, trying for cheerful.

"Ursula is pregnant," he says. "I know I should have called, but I wanted to tell you in person. I thought you deserved that."

Mallory can't decide if she should act surprised or not. Not, she decides. She appreciates the effort to get it all out on the table right away so they can talk it through, then enjoy their weekend.

"I understand," she says. "Better than you know."

"What?" he says.

"I'm pregnant too," she says.

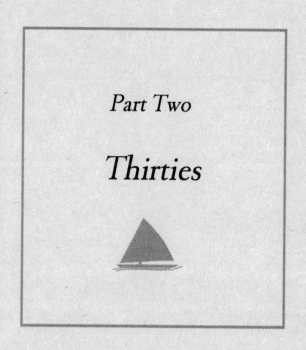

Part Two

Thirties

Summer #9: 2001

What are we talking about in 2001? A Tuesday morning with a crystalline sky. American Airlines Flight 11 from Boston to Los Angeles crashes into the North Tower of the World Trade Center at 8:46 a.m. United Airlines Flight 175, also from Boston to Los Angeles, crashes into the South Tower at 9:03. American Airlines Flight 77 from Washington Dulles to Los Angeles hits the Pentagon at 9:37 a.m. And at 10:03 a.m., United Flight 93 from Newark to San Francisco crashes in a field near Shanksville, Pennsylvania. There are 2,996 fatalities. The country is stunned and grief-stricken. We have been attacked on our own soil for the first time since the Japanese bombed Pearl Harbor in December 1941. A man in a navy-blue summer-weight suit launches himself from a 103rd-floor window. An El Salvadoran line chef running late for his prep shift at Windows on the World watches the sky turn to fire and the top of the building—six floors beneath the kitchen where he works—explode. Cantor Fitzgerald. President Bush in a bunker. The pregnant widow of a brave man who says, "Let's roll." The plane that went down in Pennsylvania was headed for the Capitol Building. The world says, America was attacked. *America says,* New York was attacked. *New York says,* Downtown was attacked.

There's a televised benefit concert, America: A Tribute to Heroes. *The Goo Goo Dolls and Limp Bizkit sing "Wish You Were Here." Voicemail messages from the dead. First responders running up the stairs while civilians run down. Flyers plastered across Manhattan:* MISSING. *The date—chosen by the terrorists because of the bluebird weather—has an eerie significance: 9/11. Though we will all come to call it Nine Eleven.*

If there'd been anything else we cared about that year before this happened, it was now debris. It became part of what we lost.

Ursula loves being a mother.

This surprises no one more than Ursula herself. Her pregnancy was difficult. Everything that could go wrong did: she had aggressive morning sickness, she got carpal tunnel in both hands, she had gestational diabetes, and, finally, in her seventh month, placenta previa, which put her on bed rest until her delivery date.

This last development, the bed rest, was not received well at work. Hank Silver did the predictable thing, showing up at Ursula's apartment and suggesting that maybe her priorities were shifting, maybe instead of relentlessly pursuing partner, she wanted to consider part-time hours, a support role.

"The Mommy Track?" Ursula asked with no small amount of disgust, for that was what everyone called it. "You know me better than that, Hank. I'm going to close this case from bed. And after the baby is born, I'm going to work twice as hard. I will make partner *this year.* That was my goal when I started. That's my goal now."

(Hank knew to tread carefully; the last thing he wanted was a sexual-discrimination suit. But Hank had five children; he understood better than anyone that children changed things. They took priority, as Ursula would soon find out.)

"Okay," Hank said. "I just wanted to let you know that if you feel differently after the baby is born, we will all understand."

They would understand? Sweet of them. Ursula had seen the way her coworkers' attitudes toward her changed with the news of the pregnancy. Ursula had once heard two of the male partners call her a ball-crusher, and privately she was flattered. But gone were her slim tailored suits and her wicked stilettos. She had grown round and soft; her breasts were swollen and heavy, and the only pair of shoes that fit were her Ferragamo flats, and even those were uncomfortable. She took them off under her desk and rubbed her sore insteps.

Once Ursula announced her pregnancy, her decision-making was questioned and people talked over her; even *paralegals* talked over her. Ursula couldn't *believe* the stereotypes that came to life in vivid Technicolor right before her eyes.

Ursula wanted to *cut* Hank Silver. He had five kids of his own and crowed about their accomplishments—the squash!—but there had been no such conversation in the office with Hank when his children were born, because Hank was a man. Hank had a wife at home to handle the kids, and even if he had been a single father, there would have been his mother, his sister, a housekeeper, a legion of nannies or au pairs, and no one would have batted an eye, no one would have said he was "farming the kids out," no one would have called him a bad father or suggested that he go part-time, take on a support role.

Incredibly, however, Ursula had one worry more pressing than her career or discrimination in the workplace.

That worry was the baby's paternity.

Ursula and Jake had had all of the standard prenatal tests done—two ultrasounds, nuchal-fold test to check for Down syndrome, Rh factor and carrier screening— but none of these told Ursula what she really needed to know: Was the baby Jake's or Anders's?

Ursula's emotional affair with Anders Jorgensen started in Las Vegas, but they didn't cross the line until they were assigned the case together in Lubbock, Texas, where there was absolutely nothing to do in their downtime but go to the rinky-dink hotel bar— aptly named Impulse—and drink. During her first visit to Impulse, Ursula ordered a glass of champagne and was given Prosecco that tasted like a green-apple Jolly Rancher. She switched to vodka (they had Stoli, thank goodness) and soda with a quarter lemon. She could drink ten in a row; they were sharp enough to cut through the heat outside the bar and the cheesiness inside it.

The surprising thing wasn't that Ursula slept with Anders; the surprising thing was how long she waited. Anders was tall, broad, blond, a Viking—that's right, descended from *actual Vikings*. His size and strength were surpassed only by how *smart* he was, how savvy in negotiations, how ridiculously good at his job. He pushed Ursula to work harder and better; he inspired her. She was energized when he was in the room. Could she impress him? Yes, she saw that she did impress him. It gave her a jolt. She became an addict for his attention.

But what about Jake?

While Ursula was sucking down bright, citrusy Stoli sodas at Impulse, Jake was at home in Washington playing games on his computer instead of job hunting. He was, Ursula thought, in danger of becoming as interesting and influential as a soft-boiled egg. But Ursula had been raised Catholic and she had personal honor. She was not morally flimsy.

Or was she?

The allure of Anders was stronger than Ursula's innate morality. He broke her code, cracked the safe—whatever metaphor you want to use, the result was Ursula and Anders in bed. A lot.

Ursula reasoned—as she padded barefoot down the hallway of the Hyatt Place back to her own room, her skirt suit hastily donned, hanging crooked, partially unzipped—that the problem was that she and Jake had met too young, and during the times when they had been broken up, Ursula hadn't sowed her wild oats the way she should have.

Excuses: She despised them. She had been led to temptation, she had not been noble enough to resist, and her bad behavior had resulted in this punishment: she didn't know whose baby she was carrying.

When Anders found out Ursula was pregnant, the affair ended abruptly. Anders had only this to say to Ursula: *It's not mine. Do you hear me, Ursula? Even if it's mine, it's not mine.*

He then accepted a transfer to the New York office, and the gorgeous six-foot-tall blond associate Amelia James Renninger, a.k.a. AJ, went with him. They moved into a loft in SoHo together.

Even if it's mine, it's not mine. Ursula was, on the one hand, reassured by this blunt statement; she chose to believe that since Anders had categorically rejected paternity, the baby must be Jake's. Still, she worried the baby would come out blond and oversize when both she and Jake were dark and slender. She feared bringing pictures of the baby to the office and watching everyone at the firm realize that Ursula's baby looked *exactly* like Anders Jorgensen.

On January 23, 2001, Elizabeth Brenneman McCloud was born, weighing six pounds, eleven ounces, and measuring nineteen inches. Dark hair, dark eyes, something in her face that echoed Jake's.

God is good, Ursula thought. Though she knew there would be payback somewhere down the road.

After Bess was born, Ursula hired a baby nurse who slept on a cot in the second bedroom, now the nursery, but Ursula got up for every single feeding. She expressed milk nonstop, labeled the bags, stockpiled them in the freezer. She returned to work after only four weeks. She traveled to Omaha, Nebraska, for a case but flew home every weekend, sleep be damned. She interviewed nannies and found Prue—sixty years old, Irish, the mother of four grown children herself. Prue takes excellent care of Bess, and Ursula watches Prue's every move, hoping to imitate her calm, sure hands, her ability to be present with the baby, never distracted, never rushed.

I can guarantee you one thing, Prue says. *These are days you'll miss.*

Ursula is doing it all, and for months, she's been doing it all well. She has a thousand billable hours by the end of June. After Omaha, she takes a case in Bentonville, Arkansas. Isn't there anything closer? Jake asks. He's helpful, hands-on, every bit as smitten with Bess as Ursula is if not more so—Ursula caught him dancing with her in the nursery to the strains of

Baby Mozart—but he has just started as the VP of development for the Cystic Fibrosis Research Foundation and he travels across the country to meet with donors. Ursula's third case of the year is in Washington proper, so she's able to feed Bess every night and every morning. When summer rolls around and Bess starts eating solids, Ursula goes to the Orchard Country Farm Stand and buys produce to steam, purée, and strain. Jake is impressed; Ursula has never cooked anything in her life.

Bess meets all of her developmental milestones early. She rolls over, sits up, smiles, laughs, coos. She has soft brown hair coming in and large, chocolaty eyes. She has Jake's smile. What a smile. Ursula has never melted at anything in her life—but that smile.

Jake goes to Nantucket over Labor Day and Prue is away visiting her daughter on Lake Lure so Ursula has Bess to herself for the weekend. She is…the perfect mother! The perfect *working* mother! She nurses Bess, feeds her, changes her, takes her to the park and pushes her a hundred and fifty times in the bucket swing, reads to her, puts her down for her nap. While Bess is napping, Ursula works, and when she takes a break, she gets on the treadmill and powers out four miles. At the end of the day, she is too tired to even make a sandwich or call the Indian place a block away so she pours a glass of wine and eats an apple for dinner.

As soon as Jake returns from Nantucket, Ursula goes back to work, but it's harder after such a wonderful weekend than it was even right after Bess was born. Ursula considers Hank Silver's offer anew. What exactly does she want to achieve by making partner? Money? Prestige? An ego boost? Ursula always had some sense that she would change the world, make a difference—but she's the first to admit this isn't happening in the world of mergers and acquisitions.

The following weekend, Bess has a low-grade fever. She's cranky and gnaws on her fist; she sneezes, her nose runs, her cries are ragged with mucus. Ursula gets home from work Monday evening and Prue announces that it's not teething, like they all thought. Bess needs to see the pediatrician. Prue has made an appointment for nine o'clock the next morning.

No problem, Ursula will take her, go into the office late.

"Are you sure?" Jake says. "Prue can take her."

"I am not the kind of mother who makes her nanny take her sick child to the doctor," Ursula says.

Jake squeezes her shoulder. "I know you're not," he says. "I'm proud of you." The words are meant to be kind, she knows—Jake is as kind a person as God ever created—but they also sound vaguely patronizing. He's proud of her for choosing Bess over work because he expected the opposite. He's proud of her, but *he* isn't volunteering to take Bess, even though it was fine for him to take last Friday off so he could go to Nantucket on his boys' weekend.

Ursula could start a fight, but she won't because they will go around and around and say hurtful things they don't mean and Ursula will still end up taking Bess to the doctor. She keeps quiet. She's learning.

She's smart enough to be the first parent at Dr. Wells's office the next morning. Ursula doesn't have a minute to waste—look in her ears, write a scrip, and we're off. It's five minutes to nine. The staff is milling about n the back, getting ready to start a day of caring for he children of Washington's elite. Deena Dick, the eceptionist at Dr. Wells's office, is among the most)owerful women in Washington, and she knows it.

)eena sees Ursula enter the waiting room five minutes :arly and she takes a sustaining breath. These parents. But better early than late, she supposes—her day will :nd with one of the ambassador wives rushing in at :en past five with her kid in tow, pedicure foam still)etween her toes. Priorities.

Deena stands up to call Ursula and baby Bess back; :he doctor is perpetually late and won't be here for another ten minutes at least, but they can get the)aby weighed and check her vitals. Parents are less :mpatient once they cross the threshold to an examin- :ng room.

Then the emergency line rings.

Ugh, Deena thinks. She picks it up.

"Honey?"

It's Deena's husband, Wes.

"What's wrong?" Deena asks. When Deena left the house that morning, Wes was dressed for work, mak- ing Braden and the twins French toast and watching the morning news.

"Something's happened," Wes says. "Turn on the TV."

Deena is confused. A plane hit the World Trade Center? At first, she thinks it's a small plane, an inex- perienced pilot, a rogue gust of wind, maybe. Deena doesn't have time to turn on the TV—okay, maybe she does, there's a small one in their lunchroom. She finds CNN. Sure enough . . . wow, it looks bad. The building

is on fire, and people are dead for certain. Deena says
a prayer and goes to fetch Ursula and baby Bess.

Bess is on the scale; she weighs nearly fifteen pounds,
the nurse, Kim, says. Kim sticks a thermometer in
Bess's ear. Temp is 99.3, so not even a fever. Has
Ursula given her any Tylenol drops this morning?

Ursula is distracted by the buzzing of her cell phone
in her purse. It must be work. The case in Washington is complicated, with lots of red tape and political
ramifications—imagine that. "No," Ursula says.

Kim eyes Ursula's bag distastefully. "The doctor
will be in shortly."

Shortly could be four minutes or forty, Ursula
knows. Kim hands Bess back. Ursula holds Bess in
one arm and rummages through her purse for her
phone with the other.

It's Jake, probably calling to find out how the appointment went. Well, if he was so keen to know, he
could have brought Bess in himself. Ursula ignores it.

Ten minutes later, there is still no doctor and Ursula
is getting antsy. It's 9:15. She hears voices in the hallway, picks up on a sense of urgency—maybe they have
a very sick or injured child? Ursula checks her cell
phone; Jake has left a voicemail. Ursula doesn't have
time to listen to it. She calls her assistant, Marjorie,
at work. Marjorie doesn't answer, which is highly
unusual, as Marjorie is the most reliable and efficient
legal assistant in the District.

Another ten minutes pass. This is ludicrous, right?
Ursula would stick her head out into the hallway
but she suspects that as soon as she complains about
how long this is taking, she'll be bumped back even
further.

Ursula's phone rings again. Marjorie.

"You've heard?"

"Heard what?"

"Two planes hit the World Trade Center in New York," Marjorie says. Her voice sounds funny, like maybe she's about to cry. Marjorie, cry? She's the daughter of a World War II colonel.

Then Ursula gets it. *The World Trade Center.*

"They're saying between floors ninety-three and ninety-nine of the North Tower," Marjorie says. "I'm not sure about the South Tower. We're trying to find out."

"Oh dear God," Ursula says. The New York offices of Andrews, Hewitt, and Douglas are on the eighty-fourth floor of the South Tower of the World Trade Center.

Anders.

Ursula lays Bess on the table and tries to snap her back into her onesie with trembling fingers. She goes out into the hallway. Where *is* everyone? Ursula moves down the corridor, deeper into the office. She finds Deena, Kim, and Dr. Jennifer Wells staring at a boxy little TV. On the screen, a plane flies directly into the top of a skyscraper, leaving fiery destruction in its wake. It looks like a movie.

Ursula gasps. Dr. Wells turns around. "I'll be right in," she says.

"No," she says. "I have to go."

She doesn't bother with a cab. Her apartment is only ten blocks away, and Ursula wants to walk. Fresh air, sunshine. People on the street are either oblivious or on their mobile phones in obvious distress. There's a crowd gathered outside of an electronics store that has a flat-screen TV in the

window. Ursula peers over a gentleman's shoulder
and sees more footage of a plane hitting a building.
Or maybe that was the other building, the South
Tower?

The gentleman turns around and fixes his eyes on
Ursula. He's about sixty, bulbous nose, visible pores,
kind eyes brimming with tears. "People are jumping,"
he says.

Ursula hurries down the street pushing Bess in her
Maclaren stroller; it's the Ferrari of strollers, the ride
is smooth, Bess is quiet, Ursula just has to get home.
The eighty-fourth floor of the South Tower. Was that
hit? Was it below the crash? Above it? Below it would
be better, right? But maybe not. Maybe not.

People are jumping.

Ursula pushes Bess into the lobby of their building.
The doorman, Ernie, sees Ursula. He's spooked, she
can tell.

"A plane just hit the Pentagon," he says.

"What?" she cries. She pulls Bess out of her stroller
and hugs her to her chest. She needs Jake. Where
is Jake?

"Mr. McCloud is upstairs?" she says. "He hasn't
come down?"

"No, ma'am," Ernie says.

Ursula hurries to the elevator. Is it safe to go
up? They live on the eleventh floor. Surely a plane
won't hit a residential building in the middle of town.
Will it?

The next two hours are a blur. The Pentagon, a mere
three miles away, has been hit. Three miles; if she
walked Bess to the river, they would see the smoke. A
plane has crashed somewhere in Pennsylvania; rumor

…as it this plane was headed for the White House or
…he Capitol Building. The White House is less than a
…nile away. They're under attack. Despite this, Ursula
…vants to go into work. She needs to know how the
New York office is faring. Jake tells her she's not going
…nywhere. Ursula calls Marjorie, gets no answer.

Hank calls and says it's likely the law firm lost
…veryone in New York, or everyone who was in the
…ffice by nine that morning. He's trying to get a list of
…ames. Ursula is shaking. "Anders?" she says.

"I'll let you know." But Hank's voice says he al-
…eady knows. Anders, like Ursula, always got to the
…ffice early. He liked to get a jump on the day.

Jake shouts from the other room. The North Tower
…as collapsed. It just…sunk in on itself. And then the
South Tower collapses.

Finally, Ursula cries.

That night, as Ursula sits in front of the television,
…otted like a plant, nursing Bess, she makes a decision.
…t's radical. Maybe even crazy.

But what qualifies as crazy now? Hank confirmed
…ate that afternoon that Andrews, Hewitt, and Doug-
…as lost seventy-one people in the New York office—
…ttorneys, paralegals, secretaries.

Anders is presumed dead.

The managing partner, a Goliath named Cap Ran-
…dle, is presumed dead, and his wife, eight months
pregnant, immediately went into labor when she
heard and delivered their first child, a son.

It's too awful to think about.

Amelia James Renninger, AJ, is alive. She had an
…ppointment to get her eyebrows done in Chinatown
…t eight thirty that morning, and as she was walking

to work, she told Hank, she watched the second plane hit.

Why couldn't it have been Anders with some kind of appointment? Ursula wonders. A haircut for his golden locks, or the dentist? Then she feels monstrous.

Jake stands between Ursula and the TV screen. "I think we should turn it off for tonight," he says.

"But what if something else happens?"

"Nothing else is going to happen."

Ursula turns off the TV and unlatches Bess, who has fallen asleep at the breast. Sweet, innocent baby girl. She deserves a world better than this—and Ursula is going to give it to her. "Sit with me," Ursula says to Jake.

"Do you want me to put the baby in her crib?"

"I want you to sit down," Ursula says. She's suddenly all nerve endings.

Jake perches on the edge of the sofa. "What is it."

"I want to leave Washington," she says. "I want to move back to Indiana."

"What?" Jake says. He laughs. "What are you talking about? I know you're upset, Ursula. I'm upset too. The entire country is upset. But we can't just uproot our lives and move back to the Bend because you think it's safer."

"Sure we can," Ursula says. "My mother is there, and your parents are there. We have family there."

"Right, I know. But your career is here, Ursula. What on earth do you think you're going to do in South Bend?"

Ursula gently kisses Bess's forehead, then smiles down at her. "I'm going to run for office."

Summer #10: 2002

What are we talking about in 2002? The Queen Mother; No Child Left Behind; Daniel Pearl; Homeland Security; the Beltway sniper attacks; Elizabeth Smart; farm-to-table; Chandra Levy; Jed Bartlet, Leo McGarry, Toby Ziegler, Sam Seaborn, Josh Lyman; "My friend the Communist holds meetings in his RV"; The Nanny Diaries; Andrea Yates; American Idol; 8 Mile; Match.com.

On Saturday, April 6, Lincoln Cooper Dooley celebrates his first birthday and Mallory throws a party at the cottage.

Who comes?

Well, Kitty and Senior fly up from Baltimore; they're staying at the Pineapple Inn because the White Elephant and Wauwinet have yet to open for the season. Cooper, now divorced from Valentina, says he can't make it, and Mallory doesn't push for a reason though she suspects it's because he's in a new relationship. In lieu of his presence, he sends presents, including a four-foot-high stuffed giraffe from FAO Schwarz that is such overkill, Mallory rolls her eyes, even though the giraffe is cute and does sort of resemble Cooper.

Fray drives down from Vermont with his girlfriend,

Anna, pronounced "Ah-nah." She's the bassist in an all-female post-grunge band called Drank.

Also coming for Link's birthday are Sloane Dooley and Steve Gladstone. They're staying at a different inn from Kitty and Senior because Kitty has been staunchly aligned with Geri Gladstone since the Gladstones split. Mallory doesn't particularly relish the idea of Sloane and Steve in her cottage, even for a matter of hours, but Sloane is Link's grandmother, so what can Mallory do?

The second Mallory became a mother, she felt like she had finally entered a room where she belonged. Link was delivered by cesarean section at Nantucket Cottage Hospital, and the nurse whisked him off to get cleaned up while the surgeon stitched Mallory up. The operating-room nurse said, "They'll bring your boy back in a few minutes."

"He's mine," Mallory said. "He's mine for the rest of my life."

This was the happy ending to a situation that started out as...*complicated,* to say the very least. Mallory and Fray were not in love, and any lust they felt for each other evaporated the instant they walked off the dance floor at Cooper's second wedding reception.

Six weeks later when Mallory called Fray and told him she was pregnant and that the baby was his, he asked if she was sure. She said yes, she had taken three pregnancy tests, all of them positive, and she hadn't been with anyone else since the previous September. *Okay,* he said, *so what do you want to do?* She said, *I want to have the baby and you can be as involved or uninvolved as you want to be, no pressure, I don't expect you to marry me or move to Nantucket or even kiss me again,*

ut *if you could throw me some money for expenses, I*
ould be grateful.

And guess what—Fray was as amazing as could
e. Yes, he was excited too. They were going to have
baby! It seemed funny and surreal, as though they'd
aken a biology class together and during lab, this
vas what they'd produced: a baby. Fray had always
vanted to be a father, especially since he had never
ad one. He would be present but not omnipresent.
le would travel to the island the first year or two and
hen, once the baby was weaned, Fray would bring
im or her to Vermont for stays. They would figure
t out; they wouldn't argue or quarrel. This was a
niracle they would both cherish.

Sharing the news was thorny. Mallory and Fray de-
ided on the unvarnished truth: They'd hooked up at
Cooper's wedding and Mallory had gotten pregnant.
They were no longer involved but they were going to
o-parent.

Mallory decided the best way to tell her parents was
n a letter. She explained what happened, and at the
nd, she wrote: *Call me when you're ready to discuss.*
This was a genius move on her part because Kitty was
ble to process her emotions offstage and then call
Mallory once she'd sorted her thoughts. She said that
lthough this was "quite unexpected," both she and
senior had always loved Frazier like their own child
nd they were, of course, "simply thrilled" to become
grandparents.

Next up for Mallory was Cooper. She called him
n the evening after work. She said, "Listen, I have
ome crazy news. I hooked up with Fray during your
vedding reception and now I'm pregnant."

Cooper had laughed. Of course he'd laughed.

"I'm serious," Mallory said.

She should have sent a letter to Coop as well because that phone conversation lasted forty-five minutes, with Cooper starting out incredulous, then moving on to angry (Cooper had apparently made Fray promise, way back in high school, that he would never "go after" Mallory), before ending up at loving acceptance. It was going to be great, he said, the two people he loved most in the world were having a baby together.

Two people he loved most? Mallory had thought at the time. What about Valentina?

The final hurdle was Leland. How could Mallory tell Leland that she was pregnant with Fray's baby and expect the friendship to survive? There was no way. Leland was still with Fiella Roget, they were in love, a couple—but no matter, Leland would see this as a betrayal. Fray was *hers*.

Mallory would have gone the letter route but she was afraid Fray would tell Sloane, then Sloane would tell Steve, and then Steve would tell Leland. Mallory couldn't let the news reach her that way.

She called the apartment in New York and left a message for Leland to call her back, she had urgent news. The phone in the cottage rang at quarter past two in the morning, waking Mallory up. She knew who it was and she was glad for the late hour, the velvety dark, and even Leland's inebriation because it made the whole thing slightly easier.

Sit down.

Who's dead?

No one. I'm pregnant.

What?

Lee, let me finish. I hooked up with Fray at Coop's wedding and now I'm pregnant.

Silence. Which Mallory had anticipated. She resisted the urge to fill the space with words. She waited, said nothing.

Finally: *You're telling me you're having Fray's baby?*

That is what I'm telling you.

Oh my God, Leland said. *Fifi won't believe this. I mean, you can't make this stuff up, right?*

Right? Mallory thought. Leland didn't sound angry, only baffled and maybe amused. Was everything going to be okay, then?

Just know this baby will have two godmothers who will make her every wish come true. We're here for you, Mal. She paused. *Good God, Fray's baby. You aren't a...couple, are you?*

No, Mallory said. *It was a one-time thing. Well, I mean, except for this.*

Leland said, *Fifi, get over here and congratulate Mallory. She's going to have Frazier's baby.*

Yes, Mallory thought. *Everything will be okay.*

Now Link is a year old, fat, happy, smiling, babbling, three-toothed, putting everything in his mouth, drooling, crawling, cruising as he holds on to the furniture, cheered on by people who love him. Apple is at the party with her fiancé, Hugo, and Isolde and Oliver come as well. Isolde starts passing appetizers and Oliver is bartending and Mallory tries to stop them from working but it's what they do. After everyone has a drink (this is a party for adults; there isn't a single other kid here. Link has "friends" at his day care, but Mallory wasn't about to throw unsuspecting parents into her bizarre family dynamics), the atmosphere becomes more relaxed. Cooper Senior and Steve Gladstone step out onto the front porch together, though Kitty and Sloane are holding down opposite ends of the living room like they're tent stakes. Kitty is very much the alpha grandmother. Sloane looks like an older and slightly more distinguished version of the person Mallory remembers, though she has shown up wearing black leather leggings and a diaphanous yellow blouse, showing off a black lacy bra beneath. Her hair is still long and tangled, as though she just rolled out of bed. She seems aware that her presence here is controversial, but Sloane never cared much what others thought of her, and why should that change now just because she's a grandmother? She sits with Fray and Anna. Anna is wearing ripped jeans and a Veruca Salt T-shirt and heavy black eyeliner; her left ear is pierced eight times. She is a very sweet person; Mallory likes her a lot, and she's good with Link, and Fray seems happy. He comes to Nantucket once a month and rents a very cool apartment in town across the street from Black-Eyed Susan's and he takes Link all weekend, stopping by only to pick up breast milk and extra clothes if he needs them.

And so—the party! Mallory keeps the music mellow—Simon and Garfunkel and Jim Croce—and she cranks out the hot appetizers: sausage in brioche, cheddar tartlets, Sarah Chase's famous Nantucket bay scallop puffs. In between pulling things out of the oven and loading up platters, she checks on Link, on her mother, on Sloane.

Where is Sloane? Mallory does a quick scan of the cottage—no Sloane; no Steve either, for that matter—and Mallory wonders if they left. Did Kitty say something impolite? Mallory hands her mother the scallop puffs to pass as she does a quick lap. Bathroom?

Empty. Mallory's bedroom? Empty. (Thank goodness.) Link's nursery? Empty. She thinks they might have gone out to the front porch to look at the ocean and get some air, but then Mallory sees the door to the guest room is cracked open and she spies Sloane and Steve inside, clearly having a whisper-fight. Sloane's face is twisted into a furious snarl and Steve is holding his palms up.

Mallory hears him say, "You were the one who insisted we come."

Mallory walks away. She tries to imagine Sloane and Steve in the early passion of their secret affair— the all-consuming obsession, the stolen moments of rendezvous made more heady because it was so forbidden. Had they viewed their love as a rare jewel, something no one else could possibly understand? And if so, how did it feel now that they had devolved into being just like the masses, squabbling because they felt uncomfortable at Sloane's grandson's first-birthday party?

Food for thought. If Mallory and Jake were ever *together*-together, would they wake up one day to find the magic gone? Probably yes.

Fray and Anna have brought Link a pile of gifts, which he's tearing open, and Kitty comes to the kitchen for more wine. "Don't you think everyone should gather if the baby is going to open his gifts?" she asks.

"No," Mallory says. "He's one." She wants to avoid a big to-do about the presents because it will turn into a showdown between grandmothers. Honestly, Mallory would like the party to be over. She's weaning Link slowly but her breasts are still producing milk and right now her breasts are hot and full.

She should go into the bedroom and pump but she's afraid if she does, the party will detonate like a bomb, and innocent people—Apple, Hugo, Isolde, Oliver, Anna—will get hurt. She looks at Link sitting in the center of the floor, banging on a new drum that Anna got him—gee, thanks, Anna—and her eyes well up with tears because she loves him so much and yet she worries about bringing him into such a nontraditional family situation. Someday he will grow up and learn that his father was his uncle's best friend as well as his mother's best friend's boyfriend and he'll learn that his grandmother broke up the marriage of his mother's best friend's (and father's ex-girlfriend's) parents— and what will he think of that?

Never mind Kitty.

There's a knock at the door and whoever walks in is temporarily blocked from view, though Mallory does see a taxi pulling away down the no-name road, and she thinks, *Huh?*

A second later she sees her brother.

Cooper is here. He came. The tears Mallory was holding back start to fall because some people just make everything better, and Cooper is one of them.

"Surprise!" he says. "My sister and my best friend have a baby and you think I'm going to miss the first birthday? You think I'm going to send a giant giraffe in my place?"

Mallory has bought a cake from the Nantucket Bake Shop. They light the single candle and sing. Link couldn't care less, but it's all good because this is the final hurdle before everyone can go home. Apple and Hugo, Isolde and Oliver, are the first to leave; the exodus has begun.

Senior and Kitty have bought Link a fat plastic baseball bat and a squishy baseball, among other things, and Senior is eager to take Link out onto the beach so they can play. It's chilly but bright, Mallory says okay, fine. She and Kitty and Cooper and Steve Gladstone go outside to watch while Sloane, seeming a little calmer, offers to clean up. Senior stands a few feet away from Link and tosses him the ball. Without any instruction, Link swings at the ball and makes contact on the first try and everyone cheers.

"Natural talent here, Mal!" Senior calls out.

After a few more pitches—two hits out of five— they all go inside. Cooper volunteers to run Sloane and Steve Gladstone back into town. Once they're gone, Fray says that he and Anna should probably leave as well; they have a dinner reservation at American Seasons that evening. Fray will be back in the morning to pick Link up for the day.

They leave and Mallory tells Kitty she needs to nurse Link and put him down for a nap. Kitty blinks and Mallory waits for her mother to comment on the fact that she's still breastfeeding one year in, but instead, she shocks the hell out of Mallory by saying, "I'm proud of you, darling."

"What?" Mallory says. "You are?" She doesn't mean to sound woe-is-me or dramatic but Mallory is pretty sure she has never heard these words come out of her mother's mouth. Kitty was proud of Cooper growing up; they were all proud of Cooper. Mallory was certainly loved but not often celebrated.

"The party was lovely," Kitty says. "And the food delicious. I chatted with your friend Apple, and she told me what a good teacher you are and how much your students love you. She says you're getting them *all* to read, which is just marvelous, darling."

"Oh," Mallory says. She's so unused to hearing this kind of praise from Kitty that she feels nearly uncomfortable. "Thanks."

"It couldn't have been easy to have Sloane Dooley and me in the same room. You and Frazier are acting like mature adults, and it's remarkable how warm and generous you are with his girlfriend. And you are a *wonderful* mother. Link is such a sweet, good-natured baby, even-tempered and bright, and that's because of you." Kitty stops. There's something else coming, Mallory thinks. With Kitty, there's always something else coming. "I just wish you would find someone special. I want you to be happy."

"Oh, Mom," Mallory says. "I *am* happy."

Kitty smiles, but it's clear she isn't convinced.

An hour later, Link is napping and Mallory and Cooper are sitting out on the front porch with drinks, braving the chilly wind blowing off the water.

"Mom doesn't think I can be happy without a man," Mallory says.

"It is curious that you haven't met anyone," Cooper says. "You're quite a catch."

Mallory doesn't respond right away. Wine and confessions are the best of friends, so she has to be careful. She wants to tell Cooper about Jake, but she just can't. The reason their relationship works is because absolutely. Nobody. Knows.

There *was* that night at Christmas a few years ago when she and Jake broke protocol and danced at PJ's. Surely Coop picked up on something then? He must be thinking the exact same thing because the next words out of his mouth are "So did I tell you that Jake McCloud moved back to South Bend? And that his wife, Ursula, is running for Congress?"

Mallory nearly drops her wineglass. "What?"

"Yeah," Cooper says. "And it looks like she might win."

On August 30, Jake arrives by ferry, though in his postcard, he said she shouldn't pick him up, that he would take a taxi to the house. Mallory knows this is so no one sees them together.

When he walks in, she hands him a beer. Cat Stevens is on the stereo. The cheese and crackers are ready, burger patties in the fridge, the last hydrangea blossom is in the mason jar next to a single votive candle, and Mallory has placed two novels on Jake's bedside table: *The Lovely Bones,* by Alice Sebold, and *The Little Friend,* by Donna Tartt.

Everything is the same—except for the basket of toys in the corner and the stray Cheerios underfoot. Mallory finally got Link weaned; he's spending the long weekend in Vermont with Fray and Anna.

The first kiss is Mallory's favorite part of the weekend. It's like taking a long cold drink of water after wandering in the desert for 362 days. Every year she worries that the chemistry will be gone—for Jake or for her—and every year the kiss is hotter and more urgent than the year before.

This year, Jake grabs her ass, squeezes, pulls her closer and tighter, and murmurs into her mouth, "You have no idea how much I've missed you."

Mallory wants to make love, but she stops herself and pulls away ever so slightly.

"Tell me what's going on," she says. "South Bend? Running for *Congress*?"

It was 9/11, he says. Ursula lost coworkers—many acquaintances and one close friend. "Maybe he was more than a friend," Jake says. "I always suspected that Ursula and Anders had something going on."

"Oh yeah?" Mallory says. This is the first time Jake has ever hinted that Ursula might have been unfaithful. Mallory hasn't breathed a word about the nature of her conversation with Ursula at Cooper's wedding, or even that they had a conversation.

"Doesn't matter now," Jake says. "Except that it spurred this decision in Ursula. She wants to make a difference. Change the world."

Jake and Ursula have bought a home on LaSalle Street in South Bend, a single-family, flat-roofed stucco house on a half-acre lot. Jake has kept his job with the CFRF; he flies around the country raising awareness about cystic fibrosis and lots and lots of money for research. Ursula is nominally employed by a law firm in downtown South Bend, though most of her time is consumed with learning the issues of Indiana's Second Congressional District and campaigning. The seat has been held for over thirty years by a gentleman named Corson Osbourne, who is now retiring. He was Ursula's professor at Notre Dame and has given her an enthusiastic endorsement. Osbourne is a Republican, but Ursula is running as an independent.

"An independent?" Mallory says. "Isn't that a lonely position to take?"

"With both sides fawning all over her?" Jake says. "Hardly."

*　　*　　*

Mallory won't lie: she's stung that Jake's life has undergone such a major change and she had no idea. She spends the whole weekend grappling with why it bothers her so much, but it's only on Sunday evening, after they finish watching *Same Time, Next Year,* that she can put it into words.

"Do you not think it strange that George and Doris both have entire lives at home that just sort of *disappear* when they get to the inn?"

"Isn't that the point?" Jake says. "What matters to them is what matters to us: they get to live in a happy bubble one weekend per year."

"It's a movie, Jake. The viewer is willing to suspend disbelief. But this is real life."

"What are you trying to say, Mal? You want to know how I feel about the terms of my mortgage? You want to know who I sit with in church?"

"You go to church?"

"We do now. Ursula is running for office."

"Ursula is running for office," Mallory says. "The United States Congress. You're going to be thrust into the public eye. And we both have children now…"

"We both had children last year," Jake says. "Last year was great and this year has been even better."

"Maybe we should stop," Mallory says. As soon as the words are out, she wants to snatch them back. Neither of them has ever said this before. "I noticed you didn't want me to pick you up on the dock."

"Simple precaution."

"I think it would be better for *you* if we stopped," Mallory says. She stares at the two fortune cookies on the coffee table, still wrapped in plastic. It would be helpful if they really *could* predict the future. "It's a miracle we haven't been found out yet."

"I think it would be better if we *didn't* stop," Jake says. "This weekend is important to me. It has become a part of who I am. Do you understand that?"

Mallory climbs into Jake's arms and rests her head on his chest. She loves their Sunday-night routine and she hates it. She would give anything for it to be Friday again. She feels this way every year. "Tell me the truth," she says. "Is there a tiny part of you that hopes she loses?"

"I will tell you the truth," Jake says. "And only you. There's a tiny part of me that hopes she wins."

The midterm elections in November are quiet. Few Americans are paying attention, but Mallory Blessing is. She watches Tim Russert all evening long until he announces winners in the minor congressional races, including Indiana's Second Congressional District, where a young attorney named Ursula de Gournsey—born and raised in Indiana, valedictorian of the University of Notre Dame's class of 1988—has come home and won in a landslide, running as an independent.

Summer #11: 2003

What are we talking about in 2003? Homeland Security; space shuttle Columbia; Mr. Rogers; the Atkins Diet; Saddam Hussein and the Iraq war; pumpkin-spice latte;

Lost in Translation; *P90X; Martha Stewart insider trading; "Shake it like a Polaroid picture"; New York City power outage; Arnold Schwarzenegger; weapons of mass destruction;* Everybody Loves Raymond.

Mallory has lived on Nantucket for ten years and she's learned that the best month here is...September. The days are filled with golden sunshine and mild breezes. All of the shops, galleries, and restaurants are still open but the crowds are gone. It's heaven!

The Saturday after Labor Day, Mallory's heart is still recovering from Jake's departure. The best thing for her is to get outside, and, thankfully, the weather is glorious—it's seventy-four degrees with a cloudless, cerulean-blue sky. God doesn't make days any finer than this one, so Mallory packs a picnic, her beach blanket, a basket of toys. She slathers Link with sunscreen and straps him into his car seat in the back of the Blazer.

They're off to the beach!

This is funny, right, because they live at the beach? However, Link is still so little and the south shore's waves so unpredictable that Mallory prefers to take him to the north shore on Nantucket Sound, where the water is flat and calm.

She can drive the Blazer right onto the sand at Fortieth Pole. Mallory lets some air out of her tires and they sail up over the whoop-de-dos in the dunes to the beach.

They have the golden crescent of sand almost entirely to themselves; it's just them and one guy with a silver pickup who's surf-casting a couple hundred yards away while a chocolate Lab sniffs the seaweed at the waterline.

"This is the life," Mallory says to Link as she frees him from his car seat. "September is still summer, buddy."

"Summer!" Link calls out as he kicks his feet. He can't wait to get into the water.

What does the best beach day ever look like? Well, to Mallory, it looks like hours of warm sunshine, dips into cool clear water, reading on a blanket while Link digs a hole and then throws one rock after another into the ocean because he likes the sound of the splash. They share lunch—a chicken salad sandwich, celery and carrots with hummus, cold slices of watermelon, lime-sugar cookies. Then Mallory sets up a spot for Link under the umbrella and he lies down for his nap. Mallory curls up next to him and closes her eyes.

She jolts awake when she feels something cold and alive touching her foot. It's the chocolate Lab, sniffing her. She tries to gently shoo it off the blanket as the owner comes jogging down the beach. Mallory puts her finger to her lips. It's okay that the dog woke *her* up but if the dog or its owner wakes Link up, she will not be amused.

Mallory stands as the guy grabs the dog by the collar. "Come on, Rox," he whispers. "Sorry about that."

Mallory follows them a few steps toward the water so their conversation doesn't wake up Link. "No problem," she says. The guy is cute—tall, with a crew cut and friendly eyes. "Did you catch anything?"

"Nah," he said. "I've had crappy luck."

"Well," she says, "there's always East Coast Seafood."

"I wanted to come over here anyway," the guy says, "because I sold you that car."

It takes a minute for Mallory to figure out what he's talking about. "The Blazer?"

"It was mine," he says. "I sold it to you. I got your name from Oliver, the bartender at the Summer House—"

"Yes!" Mallory says. She takes another look at the guy. He does seem sort of familiar now that he's told her this, though she never would have recognized him in a million years. "You're…"

"Scott," he says. "Scott Fulton."

"Scotty Fulton, yes, I remember you!" Mallory says. "I have to thank you. I've had her ten years and she's been a total rock star."

"I can see you've taken good care of her," Scott says. "It broke my heart to sell her but I remember how happy you looked behind the wheel and that made it easier. Good home and all that."

"Didn't you leave island?" Mallory says. "Weren't you going to…"

"Business school," he says. "Yep, I moved to Philadelphia, bought a Jetta, got married, got my MBA, went into commercial real estate, got divorced, poured all my time and energy into work, had a health scare at thirty-three, and decided I needed a lifestyle change. So I moved back here this summer, bought the storage center out on Old South Road as well as the six commercial lots right next door, and now I'm building affordable housing units."

"Wow," Mallory says. "Well, I'm Mallory Blessing, I teach English at the high school, I'm a single mom of one, Lincoln—Link—who's two and a half."

"You're single?" Scott says. "Forget what I said about crappy luck."

* * *

It's a meet-cute, and for that reason, Mallory is wary. It feels like a setup—the beautiful day, the empty beach, the dog making the introduction, the beyond-bizarre fact that Scotty Fulton sold her the Blazer and therefore can hardly be considered a random stranger. He's single, he owns a business on the island, and he's committed to living on Nantucket year-round. He's renting a house in town, on Winter Street, across from the inn that's owned by the Quinn family (Ava Quinn is one of Mallory's best students). He sounds too good to be true. *Is* he too good to be true?

Mallory is going to find out.

She can't go on a date during the week—it's too much with school and Link—but she agrees to go to dinner with Scott at the Company of the Cauldron the following weekend.

There is no restaurant on the island more romantic than the Cauldron. It's tiny, rustic, candlelit, tucked away on cobblestoned India Street. The dining room is decorated with copper pots and dried flowers, and there's a harp player. A harp player! This is, to be honest, Mallory's first time eating at the Cauldron, because going there requires a date and who would Mallory have gone with? It was out of JD's comfort zone, and she and Bayer never went anywhere. (Mallory doesn't want to bring JD and Bayer with her on this date, though what were her past relationships *for* if not to teach her a lesson?)

There is one set menu at the Cauldron each night. Tonight, it's a Bartlett's Farm baby greens salad topped with a lemon-thyme poached lobster tail followed by a wood-grilled sirloin followed by an apricot tarte tatin with buttermilk ice cream. Scott picks a white wine to go with the first course and a red wine to go with their steaks. Mallory admires how confident and at ease he is and how down-to-earth when talking to their server. She imagines this is how Jake would act if he were across the table from her right now. She doesn't want to bring Jake with her on this date either, but because Jake was on Nantucket a scant two weeks earlier, he's still fresh in Mallory's mind—everything he said and did, every time he touched her, every time he kissed her, every time he looked at her with smoldering desire. What would he say if he could see her now with Scott? Would he be jealous? Yes, of course. Mallory knows there's no reason for her to feel *guilty*—after all, at that moment, Jake is probably attending some fancy political fund-raiser with Ursula. He will climb into bed with Ursula that night; he might even make love to her. (Mallory tries never to think about this.)

Across the table, Scott is shaking his head. She's been caught loving Jake in her mind.

"I can't believe you're single," he says.

"I can't believe *you're* single," she says. She leans in. They're seated at the best table, by the front window—or at least, it's the best unless one of Mallory's students strolls by. "You *are* single, right? I know you said you're divorced, but are you *officially* divorced?"

"Officially divorced for six years," he says. "Lisa stayed in Philly, married one of my Wharton classmates, and they have a baby now."

Wharton; Kitty would be thrilled to hear this. But no, sorry, Kitty isn't welcome at the table tonight. "But *you* don't have any children? Now is the time to tell me."

"No children," Scott says. He reaches for her hand.

They are holding hands. Does it feel okay? Yes, it feels nice. "But I'd like to have children someday."

"Did you just say that on a first date?" Mallory asks.

"Was that a goof?"

"Um…" Mallory says. She isn't sure how she feels about having more children; she's never had a reason to consider it. "Let's not get ahead of ourselves. Our first course hasn't even arrived."

What does Mallory learn about Scott Fulton on this date?

He's thirty-four years old, turning thirty-five in May. He grew up in Orlando, Florida; his father was an animator for Disney and died of a heart attack when Scott was a sophomore at Florida State. His mother got married again, to a man who works for the State Department and lives in Dubai, so that is where she now lives. No siblings. He met his future ex-wife at FSU; she was in hotel management and brought Scott to Nantucket when she got a job at the White Elephant. He fell in love with Nantucket. He worked at the Lobster Trap six nights a week, which was how he met Oliver (yes, Oliver used to hang out at the Trap; Mallory remembers this), and he drove the Blazer to Nobadeer during the day.

The health scare was a mild heart attack, caused by stress and coffee and cigarettes—and cocaine, he admits. He quit the stress, the cigarettes, and the cocaine. "But not the coffee," he says.

"But you did quit the cocaine?" Mallory asks. She knows she sounds like a federal prosecutor, but that's because suddenly Krystel is at the table.

"Yes," he says.

He likes to surf-cast and walk in the moors with Roxanne, his Lab, who's six years old; he bought her right after the divorce. He plays golf and recently joined the club at Miacomet. He's going to stay in his rental on Winter Street through next spring, though he's looking to buy a house in town.

Houses in town start at a million dollars, Mallory thinks. She banishes Kitty from the table once again.

"This has been incredibly one-sided," he says. "When are we going to talk about you?"

"Next date," Mallory says.

Scott drives Mallory home to the cottage. There's no question about inviting him in because Mallory asked Ava Quinn to babysit for Link. It was almost too convenient—Scott brought Ava over when he picked Mallory up, since Ava lives right across the street from him, and he'll take Ava home.

Mallory lets Scott kiss her good night. The kiss is lovely—warm, sweet. There's chemistry. Mallory tries not to think about kissing Jake goodbye in nearly the exact same spot two weeks earlier before he climbed into his rental Jeep and drove to the airport.

Just go away, she tells Jake in her mind. *Let me see if this works.*

Mallory and Scott go on a second date—to Le Languedoc for their famous cheeseburger with garlic fries—and then to the Club Car to sing at the piano bar. Mallory requests "Tiny Dancer," and Scott throws twenty bucks in the glass jar. It's a fun night. Scott knows people; the bartender greets him by name and they bump into two of his site foremen at the bar and Scott is gracious, introducing Mallory and buying them a round of drinks.

On their third date, they take both Link and Roxanne out to Sconset. They do the bluff walk with its uninterrupted views of the Atlantic Ocean to the right and magnificent homes to the left. For some reason Link wants to hold Scott's hand, so the two of them go up ahead and Mallory takes Roxanne's leash and follows. This switcheroo is immediately unsettling to Mallory. Link and Scott could too easily be mistaken for father and son, and Mallory is talking to Roxanne like she's *her* dog.

They wander around Sconset, peeking into pocket gardens, some of which are still lush with flowers and a second bloom of climbing roses. They peer at the tiny cottages, built in the 1700s, when people were smaller. Scott leads them down New Street toward the Chanticleer with the famous carousel horse out front and then farther down to the quaint, shingled Sconset Chapel.

"Could you ever see getting married here?" Scott asks Mallory.

"Did you just ask that on our third date?" she says. "What's wrong with you?"

He puts his arm around her shoulders and squeezes. She still has Roxanne's leash wrapped around her wrist, and Scott has Link's hand, and they're like a little family unit—except they're not. "I like you, Mallory."

You don't know me, she wants to say. She's told him basically her whole life story—Kitty and Senior, Coop and his two failed marriages, Aunt Greta and Ruthie, Leland and Fifi, Apple and Hugo, Dr. Major; she even told him the story about Jeremiah Freehold. They talked at length about Fray and why Mallory decided on single motherhood. Although Scott has learned all this—he's a very good listener—he still doesn't *know* her.

What does it take to know a person?

Time. It takes time.

Will Scott still think she's so wonderful when she has the stomach flu or he hears her on the phone with the parent of a student who's underperforming? Will he think she's a good mother when she snaps at Link for splashing in the bathtub or when she skips reading stories because she's too tired? Will he find her fun when she informs him that she can never see him on Fridays during the school year because Fridays are for Apple? She doesn't like lima beans or beans of any kind; she has no sense of direction; she doesn't care for the theater and last year went home during the intermission of the high-school musical. She has *so many flaws,* so many areas that need improvement, and yet Mallory lacks the time and energy to work on them. She doesn't make a charitable donation to Link's day care because she pays so much in tuition already, even though she could, technically, afford an extra hundred bucks. She never watches the news and doesn't know who the prime minister of the UK is. Well, yes, she knows it's Tony Blair, but don't ask her anything else about Great Britain. The president of France? She would say Mitterrand, though she suspects that's wrong; Mitterrand might even be dead. She reads the *Inquirer and Mirror* but only to make sure there's no one she knows in the police blotter; she has never once attended town meeting. He couldn't find a less informed person. Well, except she does know about celebrities because she did, this year, get a subscription to *People* magazine,

which was thirty bucks she could have donated to
the day care.

Will any of this bother him once he figures it out?

After their fourth date—they go to see *Love, Actually*
at the Dreamland and then to the Pearl for tuna
martinis and passionfruit cosmos—Mallory agrees to
go back to Scott's house on Winter Street, and they
sleep together. The sex is good—better than good!
Scott is the right balance of gentle and firm. He knows
what he's doing.

Later, as Mallory lies in his bed—which is high
and wide and, because it's now October, made up
with flannel sheets in a navy plaid——he brings her a
glass of ice water and a couple of coconut macaroons
on a plate, and after she devours them he says, "Let's
get you home. And no arguing—I'm paying the
babysitter."

Full steam ahead; they become a couple.

They bundle up to watch the Nantucket–Martha's
Vineyard football game; they pick out pumpkins at
Bartlett's Farm and carve jack-o'-lanterns with Link.
Mallory starts calling Scott at his office when she gets
home from school to tell him about her day. He learns
all the kids' names—Max and Matthew, Katie and
Tiffany and Bridget and the two Michaels—and their
backstories. He memorizes her schedule.

The first week in November is unusually mild and
Scott plays eighteen holes of golf. Mallory and Link
go to meet him at the club when he's finished and
Mallory admires how lean and strong he looks in his
golf clothes. Even his spikes look good on him. He
finds a child-size putter and takes Link over to the
practice green. He bends over and wraps his arms

around Link to show him how to hold the club. They tap the ball into the cup again and again; Link loves pulling the ball out and starting over.

The towel bar in Mallory's bathroom falls off and Scott asks if it's okay if he comes over while Mallory is at school to fix it. She hesitates. She never let JD fix anything in the cottage and she certainly would never have let JD prowl around when she wasn't home. However, she surprises herself by saying, *Sure, that would be great.* The towel bar has been lying on the floor for over a week; she's been too busy to pull out her drill.

The towel bar is fixed the same day he offers and he leaves her a cute little cartoon of the two of them kissing. The cartoon is *good*—he's a real artist, like his father must have been; Mallory tapes the cartoon to the fridge.

Mallory starts taking Roxanne running with her. She lets Roxanne sleep on the green tweed sofa.

As Mallory is teaching her senior creative-writing class at the end of the day—it's the first year for this; Mallory lobbied to make it an elective—there's a knock on the classroom door. Mallory opens it to find Apple holding the most beautiful bouquet of flowers Mallory has ever seen.

"These arrived for you," Apple says. "Guess who sent them."

The card says: *Just because. Love, Scott.*

Mallory decides to do something nice and un-expected for Scott. The next day, she leaves school during her lunch period, picks up a Turkey Terrific sandwich from Provisions, and takes it to the office at the storage center.

Scott has an administrative assistant named Lori

Spaulding; Mallory knows her slightly. She's a single
mom like Mallory and has a daughter a year older
than Link. The two of them used to cross paths
at Small Friends, dropping the kids off and picking
them up. "Hey, Lori," Mallory says. "I brought lunch
for the boss. Is he in?"

Lori takes a beat. "He is. Let me get him."

"Or if he's busy, I can just drop it?" Mallory says.

"I'm sure he'll want to see you," Lori says. There's
an edge to her gravelly voice. "I hear you two are
having quite the whirlwind romance."

That night on the phone, Mallory says, "Were you
and Lori ever involved romantically?"

Scott laughs. "Not at all. Why?"

Mallory isn't sure what to say. She got a vibe.
Lori likes Scott; she's jealous of Mallory. *Why Mallory
and not me?* she probably thinks. Why indeed? Lori
is pretty; she has blond hair that's always in an
impeccable French braid. Mallory admired this long
before Scott was in the picture and wondered how
a single working mother could have such good hair.
Did she get up an hour early to do it? Did she use two
mirrors? And was it just a natural talent? Mallory
would never in a million years acquire the skill because French braiding is one of the many mysteries
of being a woman that has eluded her. She puts her
hair up in an elastic, and even then, her ponytails are
off-center.

"She's attractive. She has that sexy voice. She's
single."

"She does nothing for me," Scott says.

The holidays approach. Mallory goes home to Baltimore for Thanksgiving; Scott stays on Nantucket.
He cooks for all the guys who are working for him,

many of whom are single and don't have anywhere else to go but the bar.

Mallory misses him while she's away. She calls him from behind the closed door of her childhood bedroom because she doesn't want her mother or Coop to overhear her. She loves the sound of his voice. She loves how he's deep-frying a turkey in the backyard for the guys and making cornbread dressing and brussels sprouts that he saw Tyler Florence make on the Food Network. He tells her he's going into town the next night to see the tree lighting—at five o'clock, all the Christmas trees on Main and Centre will light up at once—and Mallory gets jealous, wondering who he's going with, wondering if maybe he's going with Lori and her daughter, wondering if they'll go get a drink at the Brotherhood afterward.

Missing him and feeling jealous are good signs, she thinks. They're on the right track.

Around Christmas, Link goes up to Vermont to spend the holiday with Fray and Anna, and Mallory and Scott become inseparable. They alternate between spending the night in town at his house, which Mallory likes because the Winter Street Inn across the street is all decked out for the holidays, and at Mallory's cottage, which she likes because Scott "planted" a small Christmas tree on the beach and rigged it with white lights and it gives Mallory such joy to look out her kitchen window and see it. They attend the annual Christmas pageant at the Congregational church; they shop in town and get hot chocolate with homemade marshmallows at the Even Keel Café. Two days before Christmas, it snows, and they put on boots and walk Roxanne into town early in the morning to take pictures of Main Street, silent and shrouded in pure white. Then they let Roxanne off her leash and she skids down the street like a kid on skates.

On Christmas Eve, they go to the annual party at the Winter Street Inn and hang out with Kelley and Mitzi and the police chief, Ed Kapenash, and Dabney Kimball Beech from the Chamber of Commerce and Dr. Major and Apple and Hugo. Ava Quinn sits down at the piano and plays carols and Mallory nearly chokes up as they sing "O Come, All Ye Faithful" because she has now lived on this island for ten years and look at the community she has built. It was an act of faith, moving here. Aunt Greta had told Mallory long ago that Nantucket chose people and that it had chosen Mallory, but she feels this with absolute certainty only right in this instant.

Scott must notice her moment of introspection because he squeezes her hand.

They drink Mitzi's mulled cider (it's strong; Mallory can handle only a few sips before she switches to wine) and they eat the pine-cone cheese ball and stuffed dates, and by the time Mallory and Scott stumble across the street, it's after midnight and already Christmas.

On the afternoon of New Year's Eve, they take a long beach walk with Roxanne. The sun is low in the white sky; it's cold. The waves pummel the shore like they're trying to make a point. This is winter on Nantucket, and it's only just beginning.

As they are about to go back up to the cottage to prepare for their New Year's Eve festivities—Apple and Hugo are coming over for fondue and a bottle of Krug that Scott insisted on splurging on—Scott says, "Hey, I want to tell you something."

The tone of his voice sets off an alarm. A confession

s coming: He *is* married after all; he does have a child,
r children, who are living overseas in Dubai. The
project on Old South Road isn't affordable housing
out a front for the Mob. Scott has a gambling problem.
He's a cocaine addict. He's sleeping with Lori.

"What is it?" she says.

"I love you," he says.

Mallory closes her eyes. She is seized by panic. She
sn't sure what to do. Why is she not prepared for
his? Any idiot could have seen this was where things
were headed.

"I love you too," she says, then immediately hates herself. She *is* suggestible and easily
swayed, just like Leland told Fifi so many years
earlier.

She's lying to Scott. She doesn't love him. She
really, really likes him. She thinks he's a wonderful
person. He's smart and kind and sexy and funny and
absolutely wonderful with Link. She's happy every
time he walks in the door; she feels a ping of pleasure
every time he calls. He has filled a void for her
and for Link that she didn't even realize was there.
Her relationship with Scott has been a joyride. It has
been heady infatuation. She loves having a partner in
crime. And it has been luxurious, all the ways big and
small that he's made life on this island easier for her
with his companionship, his ardor for her. She has
spent the past three and a half months being adored.
Flowers delivered to her classroom! A house in town
and one at the beach! The little cartoons he leaves
for her all the time now that he knows how much
she enjoys them. This is the stuff other women dream
of. Mallory and Scott can get married at the Sconset
Chapel; Roxanne will wear a wreath of white roses

around her neck, and Link a tiny tux. There is still plenty of time for Mallory to have another baby.

But...Mallory doesn't love him.

January passes. February passes.

Mallory doesn't understand what's wrong with her. Scott checks all the boxes.

She tries to break it down. She loves the way he smells. He has no annoying habits. He doesn't over stay his welcome; he respects her time with Link, her time by herself. His taste in music is good; there's a lot of overlap with hers, although his favorite band is the Red Hot Chili Peppers, a group Mallory can take or leave.

Her not-loving him has nothing to do with the Chili Peppers.

There's no issue with the sex. The sex is amazing.

March passes.

Shall we use a golf metaphor? Why not, since at the end of March there's a string of days when it's nice enough for Scott to play and he asks Mallory and Link to meet him afterward so he and Link can continue to practice Link's putting. Mallory's feelings for Scott are the ball that glides toward the hole but stops *just* short, resting on the lip of the cup, eliciting a shout of disbelief and frustration. *Drop in already!* she thinks.

Mallory begins to fear that this isn't something that "just needs more time." What did Kitty say? Love is love—or not-love is not-love, as the case may be— and, really, there's no explaining it.

But that feels like a cop-out. Mallory can explain it just fine.

Scott doesn't read fiction, but Mallory once noticed him standing in front of the shelf that held the novels

Jake sent her each Christmas. She's not sure what she would have done if he'd picked one of the books up. Would she have asked him to put it down, like she did with Fifi? Tucked inside the newest book, *The Curious Incident of the Dog in the Night-Time,* is the envelope where Mallory keeps all of her fortunes from their weekends. What would she say if Scott saw them? Sand dollars that she and Jake found at Great Point are lined up in front of the books, and Scott did pick one of those up and Mallory felt anxious and sick during the seconds it took him to replace it.

Her Cat Stevens CDs and World Party's *Bang!* are hidden in her underwear drawer. She can't risk Scott playing them. Back in January, Scott asked if she wanted to drive up to Great Point, since she had the sticker, and she said no, she'd rather not.

Mallory loves Jake. Her heart is not transferrable. It has belonged to Jake since the first time he answered the phone in Coop's room, since the afternoon he stepped off the ferry and onto the dock, since the moment he slid an omelet onto her plate.

What can she do about this? Anything? Is she simply being stubborn? Has she been, effectively, brainwashed? No; Mallory anticipated that she would someday meet a man who would eclipse Jake. She has even *welcomed* this, because although loving Jake is the sweetest kind of agony, it's agony nonetheless.

The end of April brings the Daffodil Festival. This is the first big weekend of the year, the official start of the season on Nantucket. There's a classic-car parade out to Sconset where everyone gathers to tailgate. Scott enters the Blazer in the parade and says he'll decorate the car if Mallory will handle the theme and the picnic. Mallory and Apple come up with *The Official*

Preppy Handbook as the theme—"Look, Muffy, a book for us"—and Mallory pulls out the Baltimore Junior League cookbook that Kitty gave her several Christmases ago to find recipes for their preppy picnic.

Mallory can't believe how great the Blazer looks when Scott is finished with it. It has a blanket of daffodils on the hood and a cute daffodil wreath on the grille. It's a sunny day, though chilly, but they decide to drive out to Sconset with the top down. Scott and Hugo sit up front in their navy blazers and pink oxford shirts and Mallory and Apple and Link and Roxanne sit in the back. Apple is wearing a white turtleneck and a navy cardigan, and Mallory has on a yellow Fair Isle sweater and the Bean Blucher moccasins she's owned since high school. Link is in a polo shirt with the collar popped. They wave at the spectators on the side of Milestone Road, and Roxanne barks; she has on a collar printed with navy whales.

They get to Sconset and set up their picnic: gin and tonics, tea sandwiches, boiled asparagus spears, deviled eggs, tiny weenies in barbecue sauce. The judges come by and spend a long time admiring the fine detail on the sandwiches; they take note of the outfits, Apple's grosgrain watchband, Scott's tortoiseshell Jack Kennedy sunglasses. Mallory catches a glimpse of herself in the side-view mirror. In her sweater and pearl earrings, she looks alarmingly like Kitty. A photographer from the *Inquirer and Mirror* snaps a picture of Mallory and Scott in front of the Blazer. Scott tells the reporter the story about how he sold Mallory the Blazer back in the summer of 1993 and how they met ten years later and are now dating.

They win first prize for their tailgate and an honorable mention for the Blazer.

Mallory and Scott's picture is on the front page of the newspaper the following Thursday, and if Mallory hears it once, she hears it a thousand times: *You guys are so perfect together. You are the perfect couple.*

To which Mallory responds, "The perfect couple? There's no such thing."

May arrives. When Fray takes Link for the weekend, Scott tells Mallory that he's planned a getaway to Boston—a suite at the Four Seasons, luxury box at Fenway, dinner reservations at No. 9 Park. They've been talking about going to Boston all winter, but something always came up. Now that it's happening, Scott sounds...nervous.

"The Japanese cherry blossoms are going to be at their peak in the Boston Public Garden," he says. "We have to ride the Swan Boats; in fact, I may hire one so that we have it all to ourselves."

Mallory knows she has waited too long. He's going to propose. She imagines him pulling out a velvet box, opening it as the Swan Boat glides under the cotton-candy-pink blossoms of the Japanese cherry tree, presenting a ring in a way that he's sure will fulfill her dreams. Mallory wants to shrink to the size of a mouse and scurry under the green tweed sofa. She wants to bury herself in the sand.

"Scott," she says. "We need to talk."

Summer #12: 2004

What are we talking about in 2004? The Boston Red Sox; quinoa; Pat Tillman; Fallujah; Condoleezza Rice; Indian Ocean tsunami; Ronald Reagan; "I'd like to phone a friend"; Julia Child; Janet Jackson's wardrobe malfunction; Michael Bluth, Gob, George, Lucille, Maeby, Lindsay, and George Michael; Ken Jennings; Mean Girls; Momofuku; "It started out with a kiss, how did it end up like this?"

It's the last day of school, and Mallory and Apple head out to celebrate. They decide to go for broke and have a late lunch on the luscious green lawn of the White Elephant Hotel. It's the epitome of waterfront elegance, which is exactly what they both need after a hundred and eighty days of lockers slamming, fluorescent lights buzzing, and Cheetos flying through the air of the cafeteria.

The hostess at the White Elephant, Donna, has three boys who all went through the school system, *naughty* boys—Apple knew them well—so Donna seats Mallory and Apple at the edge of the patio with the best views across the harbor. There's a guitar player named Tony Maroney singing "Fire and Rain." Mallory flashes back to Jake in college.

She wonders if he ever picks up his guitar anymore.

"Your first round is on me," Donna says. "And you get one song request."

"I'll have a cosmo," Mallory says. This is another tradition, drinks right out of *Sex and the City*. "And would you please ask Tony to play 'School's Out,' by Alice Cooper?"

"Just a seltzer for me," Apple says.

When Donna walks away to put in their order, Apple turns to Mallory and whispers, "I'm pregnant."

There is much rejoicing! Mallory is...*Eeeeeeeeeee! So happy!* "When did you find out?" Mallory asks.

"Last weekend," Apple says. "I'm just eight weeks, so we haven't told anyone but family yet."

"And Hugo?" Mallory says. "He's happy?" Mallory has started referring to Hugo as GGW, for "greatest guy in the world." There's no need to explain why; he just is.

"He wants to move the wedding up," Apple says. "His mother, his aunties, his granny Beulah...they're old-fashioned."

Donna drops the drinks off and Mallory takes the first tart, refreshing, and well-deserved sip of her cosmo. Tony Maroney says into his microphone, "Here's some Steely Dan for two beautiful teachers, 'My Old School.'"

"That's *not* what I asked for," Mallory murmurs.

Apple says, "So, anyway, we've decided to get married Labor Day weekend over on the Vineyard."

It's a situation.

Apple is Mallory's best friend on Nantucket. Apple is the reason Mallory has her job at the high school, her identity, her entire island life. Apple is her *person*—when Mallory needs someone to watch Link at the last minute, when she needs a ride down to the ferry or someone to pick her up after a root canal it's Apple. Mallory and Link spend the holidays with Apple and Hugo—the fondue on New Year's Eve, Easter brunch, the fireworks on the Fourth of July.

There can be no missing Apple and Hugo's wedding.

Mallory tells herself it will be fine. But how? How will it be fine? It's not just a Saturday ceremony and reception where Mallory and Jake might fly over for the day and Jake would go to the Navigator for a few beers while Mallory attended the wedding. It's a whole-weekend extravaganza. There's a Friday-night clambake at Lambert's Cove, then the wedding at the Old Whaling Church, then the reception in the garden at Preservation Hall, then a dance party at the Hot Tin Roof. And on Sunday, a brunch at the Art Cliff Diner. Hugo belongs to one of the most prominent African-American families on the Vineyard. His mother, Wanda, has five sisters, one of whom is a longtime selectwoman. There is no messing around when one of their children gets married. They're renting out the Charlotte Inn for their guests.

Mallory has to figure out her options while at the same time remaining not only supportive and helpful but exuberant about Apple's impending nuptials. Apple has two sisters and two sisters-in-law, so Mallory doesn't have to worry about being a bridesmaid. Which means she will be just a regular guest.

Could she skip it? She fabricates excuses and tries each of them on. A nasty stomach bug? Something with Link—he can't go to Fray's like he's supposed to because Fray and Anna switched the schedule at the last minute? Apple would say, *Bring Link, he can be the ring bearer.* So it'd have to be the stomach bug.

Mallory feels like the most despicable human being ever born for even having this thought. She doesn't deserve a friend like Apple.

There's no one Mallory can ask for advice. She has to look inward, and her gut is telling her there's only one answer: Go to the wedding, have fun, cancel Jake.

She thinks about what it would mean to cancel Jake, not to see him for yet another year. She thinks about the phrase *No matter what.* She thinks about Doris, in the movie, saying, "I knew...that no matter what the price, I was willing to pay it," as she stands at the airport in 1956 when George threatens to fly home because his guilt is overwhelming.

They've made it through eleven summers. That in itself is remarkable. Having a conflict like this is a part of life; it happens to everyone. You want to be two places at once but it's impossible.

Maybe they can reschedule for the weekend before or the weekend after. In years past, Jake has spent the last two weeks of August with Bess and Ursula in Michigan, so the weekend before might not work for him. The weekend after, Link will be back home from his time with Fray, so that's no good.

Mallory considers simply informing Jake that they're going to Martha's Vineyard for the weekend. They won't stay at the Charlotte Inn with everyone; they'll get a hotel room somewhere else, maybe in Chilmark or Aquinnah. She'll make a brief appearance at the clambake; she'll skip the brunch. She'll ask Jake to meet her at the Hot Tin Roof. It will be dimly lit and loud; people will be drunk. They'll go back to Nantucket first thing on Sunday.

It's not optimal, nope, not at all. Jake might even refuse to go. But every relationship requires compromise, especially this one.

Jake would never want her to miss Apple's wedding.

Mallory wastes precious hours imagining how Apple and Hugo's wedding weekend *should* go. Mallory should be able to take a date to the clambake who will sit with her in the sand as the sun sets, then spread a blanket out for her in front of the bonfire. She should be with someone who charms Hugo's aunties and brings them whiskey sours from the bar during the garden reception so they don't have to walk across the grass in their heels. She should be with someone she can introduce as her boyfriend, someone she can slow-dance with, someone she can hold hands with as Apple and Hugo say their vows.

Someone like...Scott Fulton.

Yes, let's say it: Scott would be a good date for Apple and Hugo's wedding. But that ship has sailed. Scott and Mallory broke up over six weeks ago, and Scott has vanished from Mallory's life. He's conducting himself in the breakup as nobly as he conducted himself in the relationship. Mallory has to sit on her hands to keep from calling him sometimes. One night, when Link asked for Scott, Mallory decided that she'd made a mistake and that she would drive to his office the next morning to tell him she wanted to get back together. She would have to deal with Lori Spaulding first—Scott might even be dating Lori now—but Mallory would give it a shot.

In the morning, she came to her senses. All it took was imagining organ music spilling out of the Sconset

Chapel, Mallory waiting outside the double doors in a white dress, about to commit to Scott Fulton for the rest of her life.

Nope.

There is no one for Mallory but Jake. She thinks all the way back to her bubblegum-princess days with Leland, listening to the *Grease* album on the record player—he's the one that she wants.

She prays to God for an intervention, a revelation, a solution. For something to happen. Something, anything, please.

The second Saturday in August every year brings the Boston Pops to the island. They perform a benefit concert on Jetties Beach for thousands of people, raising two million dollars for the Nantucket Cottage Hospital. It's one of Mallory's favorite nights of the summer. She and Link go with Apple and Hugo; they always set up camp in the very back by the lapping waves of the sound so that they can enjoy an evening swim and then a gourmet picnic—Mallory plans what she's making all year long and Apple brings the wine—and they listen to the orchestra and wait for the fireworks at the end of the *1812 Overture*.

Mallory checks in with Apple on Friday morning—Picnic prep, see you tomorrow, 5:30?—to which Apple responds, Kk, their faux-high-school-student response, but sends nothing else.

Mallory knows that Apple has been flattened by both exhaustion and nausea and she also knows that Apple will have an ultrasound at Beth Israel in Boston at eleven o'clock on Saturday morning, which has

Apple on edge. She has a feeling that "something is up" with the baby.

At one o'clock on Saturday afternoon, Mallory finishes with the picnic. She has made Sarah Chase's Asian carrot dip, which she's serving with rice crackers; rare roast beef, Boursin, and arugula pinwheel sandwiches; chicken-and-potato salad with celery and chives; a marinated cucumber salad from the trusty Baltimore Junior League cookbook; and lemon bars with a coconut shortbread crust. Does a more perfect picnic exist? Mallory thinks not.

She hasn't heard from Apple yet, which is a little surprising. And by two o'clock, Mallory's mind travels to that forbidden place where "something is up" with the baby becomes "something is wrong" with the baby.

At two thirty, Mallory sends an exploratory but non-prying text: You good?

There's no response, which is very unlike Apple. But they're off-island so maybe her phone died or maybe, in the excitement of the day, she forgot her phone altogether. It's possible.

By four o'clock there has still been no word from either Apple or Hugo, and when Mallory calls Apple, she's banished straight to voicemail. Should Mallory and Link go to the Pops without them, set up camp as usual in the back, and just expect them to show?

Yes, she decides. She puts Link in a pair of star-spangled swim trunks and a white polo shirt and combs his blond hair and kisses each of his cheeks fifty times. She tickles him until he squeals, then sits him on her lap to secure the Velcro straps of his sandals. She is so lucky she has a healthy child.

Apple will have a healthy child too, she thinks. A girl, maybe, who will grow up to marry Link.

Mallory parks on North Beach Street and she and Link join the masses who are marching toward Bathing Beach Road. Mallory is holding the picnic hamper in one hand and Link's hand in the other, so when her phone rings, she has to stop, put the hamper down, and tell Link, "Stay right there," while everyone moving around them grumbles. Sorry, people, Mallory has to take this call. She knows it's Apple.

Probably she's calling to say they missed the boat and they'll be late. "Apple?"

"Mal?"

"Everything okay?" Mallory asks. "Everything good?"

There's a pause. Apple breathing. Apple crying? Mallory plugs her other ear. She locks her eyes on Link; this would be exactly the kind of situation where he would get lost. She feels a heavy dread. She'd prayed for something to happen but she had not wanted anything bad to happen to Apple or the baby.

Please God, no! Mallory thinks. *I take it back!*

"We had the ultrasound," Apple says. "It's twins. Twin boys."

"Oh my God," Mallory says. She's relieved. Right? "That's incredible. That's what was up! Are they healthy?"

"Healthy," Apple says, but something is strange about her voice. It's loaded with something else. "Listen...don't kill me."

"You're going to miss the Pops?" Mallory says. "Don't worry about it. You received monumental news today. I'm sure you're overwhelmed."

"*Overwhelmed* is the word," Apple says. "Hugo is...he's...listen, don't kill me."

"I won't kill you," Mallory says. "What's going on?"

"Hugo is overwhelmed, I'm overwhelmed, we were at each other's throats even before we got this news because of the wedding and his family and, okay, yes, *my* family too. But this changes things."

"What things?" Mallory asks. She's worried again. Are Apple and Hugo going to *split*? "What things does it change, honey?"

"We're at Logan Airport right now," Apple says. "We're flying to Bermuda tonight. We're eloping, Mal. The wedding is off. I'm so sorry."

Mallory wedges the phone between her ear and shoulder and scoops Link up before he wanders away. She bumps into an older gentleman in Nantucket Reds who says, "Watch where you're going, missy."

Mallory dislikes being called missy, but she's so happy, she could kiss the man. Apple is eloping! She's eloping! The wedding is off!

"Don't apologize to me," Mallory says to Apple, her person, her best person. "I'm so happy for you, honey. Go marry the greatest guy in the world. Congratulations!"

Summer #13: 2005

What are we talking about in 2005? Hurricane Katrina; Brad and Jen; YouTube; Terri Schiavo; John Roberts; the White Sox; Scooter Libby and Valerie Plame; Alinea;

Xbox 360; Carrie Underwood; Marilynne Robinson; Russell Crowe; Jude Law; the New Orleans Saints; Avon Barksdale, Stringer Bell, McNulty, and Bunk; "I wish I knew how to quit you."

Leland Gladstone and Fiella Roget have been together for ten years. They're a fixture in the New York literary scene and get invited to twenty events per week: gallery openings, readings, author luncheons, secret high-stakes poker games, and midnight raves at the hottest clubs on Twelfth Avenue. They are their generation's Gertrude Stein and Alice B. Toklas, only biracial and far, far better dressed.

Fifi is a professor in the MFA program at Columbia, a job that requires her to teach one workshop per semester in exchange for a generous salary. This leaves her long stretches to work on her new novel, which she's having a hard time birthing. Her first two novels dealt with her childhood and adolescence in Haiti, and now Fifi is writing a novel set in the United States, but it feels wobbly and predictable. She tries not to let the novel shackle her. The inspiration comes when it comes, and her editor understands this; Fifi just wishes people would stop asking her when they can expect it. Leland knows enough not to mention the novel at all, though Fifi recently overheard Leland telling the cleaning ladies not to bother with Fifi's office. *She hasn't been in there in weeks.*

Fifi is invited to do paid speaking events across the country, and in the spring of 2005, she accepts an offer from the department of women's studies at Harvard. Fifi decides to make a trip of it—maybe two nights, maybe three. She likes Boston. It's charming and old-fashioned with its proper Puritan aesthetic. Boston doesn't have a dirty mind the way New York does.

"I can maybe do two nights," Leland says when Fifi shares her plans. "But I definitely cannot swing three."

"I think I'd like to go alone," Fifi says. "We each could probably use some space."

Fifi can see Leland wavering between a bitter response and an offended one. Fifi finds both tiresome. She believes every relationship needs a little air, but Leland sees things differently. Over the past few years, she has developed the tendency to smother. She likes to travel *everywhere* with Fifi and make connections for *Bard and Scribe,* where she is now editor in chief and which is now failing because everyone is on the internet. Fifi used to be fine with Leland's constant companionship, but now the phrase *riding her coattails* comes to mind.

If Fifi was second-guessing her decision to go alone, she stops doing so the instant she checks into Fifteen Beacon, orders up some room service, and draws herself a bath. Because she grew up with so little, five-star hotel rooms still strike her as an unfathomable luxury—the delicious linens, the fine, heavy pens and creamy stationery, the waffled robes hanging in the closet. Here at Fifteen Beacon, Fifi's room has a gas fireplace and two deep leather chairs. Someone has sent up a fruit and cheese plate—the front-desk clerk, Pamela, it turns out! She's a big fan of *Shimmy Shimmy*.

The greatest luxury of the room is the solitude. Fifi pulls out her manuscript and starts revising. She works until five minutes before she has to leave, at which point she slips her dress over her head and goes down to the lobby. A car is waiting to take her to the Brattle Theatre.

Long relationships have peaks and valleys, and Fifi has every right to some time to herself. What happens next, however, is more difficult to explain.

The day after she speaks at the Brattle is a beautiful spring day. Fifi can shop on Newbury Street, stroll through the Public Garden, even sit on the rooftop at Fifteen Beacon and continue her revisions. But instead, she calls the car service and asks to be delivered to the ferry dock in Hyannis. She's going to Nantucket.

She calls Mallory in advance (she's impulsive but not rude) and catches her between her first and second classes.

Thinking about coming to the island overnight; I can probably make it in time for your last class if you'd like me to stop in?

Are you kidding me? Mallory says. *My last class is my senior creative-writing seminar. We read* Shimmy Shimmy *last month. The kids devoured it. I told them we were friends but I don't think they believed me.*

We'll show them, Fifi says. *I'm on my way.*

Fifi won't tell Leland about her change of plans. She knows she should…but she doesn't want to deal with the inevitable static. *Mallory is* my *friend, not your friend.* (Oh, but who is the person who insists they share everything—the apartment, the parking spot in the Bleecker Street garage, the Peugeot that occupies that parking spot? Yes, that's right, Leland.) Fifi wants to go to Nantucket and see Mallory on her own terms. But why? Is she doing it to piss Leland off?

That may be part of it.

But there's something else as well. Fifi *likes* Mallory. She's smart and fun and…normal. She's Leland minus the drama. She's pleasant to look at, though her beauty is quiet, natural—the golden tan, the sunbleached hair, the ocean-colored eyes. Fifi's writerly instincts tell her that with Mallory, still waters run deep. Something is going on with her, maybe. Or maybe not.

Fifi and Leland visited Mallory the summer before. They stayed at the Wauwinet Inn for the sake of everyone's privacy but they had dinner at Mallory's cottage. The little boy, her son, was spending time with his father in Vermont, so Mallory had the carefree attitude of a teenager whose parents were away. After dinner, Mallory took Fifi and Leland to the piano bar at the Club Car. It was a cramped, narrow, dimly lit space filled with joyful people singing their drunken little hearts out. Mallory knew Brian, the piano player; she sat down next to him on the bench and turned the pages of his sheet music while everyone gathered around to sing "Hotel California" and "Sweet Caroline," then threw money into a glass jar. Leland had the nicest voice of the three of them but she was the one who had wanted to leave. It was as Fifi followed an impatient Leland out of the Club Car that she'd thought, *This would be much more fun without her.*

So, now.

Fifi spends less than twenty-four hours on Nantucket, but her time there is transformative for two reasons. The first is Mallory's creative-writing seminar. Fifi and Mallory arrive at the door of the classroom seconds after the bell has rung; the twelve kids are already seated in a circle and have their notebooks out. Fifi peeks at them through the window.

Mallory swings the door open and says, "You guys, I have a surprise. Fiella Roget has come by to say hello."

The kids' heads snap up. Fifi enters the class with just a wave, and she can see the kids puzzling. *Is it really her?* Then: *It's really her. It's really her!* They start to clap and then one of them stands and then they're all standing and clapping, a twelve-person standing ovation, and Fifi, who has been applauded and feted and praised all across the country, feels her eyes well up with tears.

There are nine girls and three boys. It's funny to Fifi how girls dominate creative-writing classes but men dominate the bestseller lists...but don't get her started. There are five people of color, which surprises Fifi. Nantucket Island; she would have thought that all the kids would be lily-white, privileged, and entitled. But Fifi learns that Nantucket has quite a diverse year-round population; the school's e-mails, Mallory says, come out in six languages. The kids in Mallory's class are growing up on an island, like Fifi did, some of them as eager to escape as Fifi was. It's no wonder they liked *Shimmy Shimmy*.

It's obvious that the kids adore Mallory. They call her Miss Bless and they kid with her and tease her, though respectfully. She is *that* English teacher, the one Fifi wished she'd had in secondary school—the one who listens, the one who reads her students' work carefully and asks questions without prying, the one who presses a novel into a student's hands and says, *I thought of you when I read this. Let me know if you like it.*

Fifi wishes Leland were with her just so she could see this. Fifi and Leland live in a rarefied literary stratosphere where they believe they're creating culture and influencing public opinion, but the person who's actually making a difference is Mallory.

The second thing that blows Fifi away is Mallory's son, Link. He's four years old, a towhead, a beautiful child with sweet, smooth cheeks and Mallory's eyes—are they blue? Are they green? Fifi's experience with children this age is nonexistent; she might as well be meeting a lemur. Link studies Fifi's face, touches the skin on the back of her hand. He likes her name, *Fifi;* it makes him laugh. He says it over and over again in his high, clear little voice.

Mallory says, "Your auntie Fifi is a writer. She writes books."

She tries to write books, Fifi thinks.

Link hears *books* and brings a stack over to the sofa for Fifi to read to him. *How Do Dinosaurs Say Good Night? Bear Snores On. Toot and Puddle.* Link points to the pictures he likes and explains them—Toot isn't wearing pants but that's okay because he's a pig—and in some places, he reads along. He's smart—indeed precocious!

Mallory feeds him small bowls of pasta and edamame, then she gives him a bath; Fifi can hear him splashing and laughing. He comes out to the living room in blue pajamas printed with trains. His blond hair is wet and combed and he smells like toothpaste.

He takes Fifi's hand and tugs. Mallory pokes her head out of the bedroom. "He wants you to tuck him in," she says.

This feels like a greater honor than winning the Pulitzer Prize. "Of course," Fifi says. She hears her cell phone buzzing—Leland—and she thinks about answering it and stepping outside to confess her treachery. *I'm on Nantucket with Mallory*. But instead, she turns her phone off. She has more important things to do.

Link climbs into his little bed. Fifi smooths his hair and kisses his forehead. There's a night-light in the corner, an impressive number of books on the bookshelf, a four-foot giraffe, a photograph of a couple that Fifi guesses is his father and his father's girlfriend. It's Leland's old beau, Frazier. Even a few months ago—hell, even a week ago—Fifi would have studied the picture, interested to see the kind of man who had so enraptured Leland in her youth.

But now, it's irrelevant.

"Good night, sweet prince," Fifi says. "Sleep tight."

Fifi and Mallory settle at the harvest table, which is lit by one votive candle. Mallory pours them each a glass of wine. She has, amazingly, pulled together dinner: pan-roasted chicken in a mustard cream sauce and a green salad with cornbread croutons that she made herself.

Mallory raises her glass. "Honestly, I can't believe you're here. I can't believe Lee let you come alone."

Fifi smiles. They touch glasses, drink.

"I'm leaving Leland," Fifi says.

"What?" Mallory says. "Why?"

Why does anyone leave anyone? The love has run out, or it has changed. It's probably the latter for Fifi. Despite all the pushier emotions Leland inspires—annoyance chief among them—Fifi knows she will always love her. Leland is family; she's a sister. But Fifi doesn't want to live with a sister or make love to a sister.

There's something else too, a secret. Fifi recently bumped into a writer she'd met back in 1995 at Bread Loaf. Her name was Pilar Rosario, she was Dominican, and when they'd met, it was immediately clear that Fifi and Pilar were attracted to each other. But Fifi had been in the first thrill of her relationship with Leland at that time, so her attraction to Pilar went unexplored.

Then a month or so ago, after a reading Fifi gave at the Ninety-Second Street Y, Pilar appeared—conveniently while Leland was sucking up to *The New Yorker*'s fiction editor—and slipped Fifi her card.

"Call me," she said. "I'd love to catch up."

Fifi nearly threw the card away—meeting Pilar would be a betrayal of Leland—but she changed her mind, deciding one glass of wine couldn't hurt.

But, ah…it *had* hurt. Fifi found herself drawn to Pilar for many reasons, not least of which was that Pilar confessed she wanted a baby.

Yes, Fifi had said, shocking herself. *Me too.* This was the real betrayal, because although Fifi hadn't slept with Pilar or even seen her again, she had acknowledged this truth despite the fact that Fifi and Leland had vowed that theirs would be a blissfully childless existence. Leland felt fiercely about this—no children, no pets, not even a houseplant, nothing to care for except themselves.

Talking with Pilar allowed Fifi to recognize the pressure building inside of her, her biology asserting itself to the point that Fifi can no longer ignore or deny it. She wants a baby.

"That's why I came to Nantucket," Fifi tells Mallory. "I wanted you to be the first to know. Leland is going to need you."

Summer #14: 2006

What are we talking about in 2006? TSA; Steve Irwin; "SexyBack"; the Duke lacrosse case; Dick Cheney's shooting accident; Miranda Priestly; AIG and Tyco; the subprime-mortgage crisis; TRX; The Osbournes; Ben Bernanke; "Clear eyes, full hearts, can't lose"; Suri Cruise; Tom DeLay; Eat Pray Love; Meredith Grey and Dr. McDreamy.

The reality of serving in the House of Representatives is as follows: You spend one year getting things done and one year campaigning so you will be reelected so you can get more things done.

Who originally came up with a two-year term? One of the Framers of the Constitution who was terrified of imperial rule, possibly someone with a personal vendetta against King George III. Jake understands protection from the power hungry, but he personally thinks a three-year term in the House would be more productive.

Ursula is thinking more like a six-year term.

After she finds out that she's running unopposed in

her second reelection bid, she tells Jake she wants to run for the Senate in 2008.

"Tom's term is up and he's slipping in the polls," she says. "Now is the time, I think. I know I'm still the new kid on the block, but…"

But…have you seen the news? Ursula de Gournsey is a media *darling*. The Washington correspondent for *Newsweek* noted the monogram on her attaché case as she ascended the steps of the Capitol Building in her four-inch stilettos and started referring to her as UDG, a trend that quickly caught on. UDG has become a very hot commodity in American politics.

First of all, she's a young, beautiful, stylish woman. And how does Ursula handle being described as such? Jake only too vividly recalls their college days. *Tell me I'm smart. Tell me I'm strong.* Is it not insulting to have the press clamoring for the names of her designers, for the shade of her lipstick? (It's Cherries in the Snow by Revlon, which she purchased for the first time at age fifteen from L. S. Ayres with money she made selling programs at Notre Dame games. True to her roots, she has stuck with the lipstick.) Jake would have said all the attention to Ursula's physical traits rather than her intellectual gifts would have caused her to show her fangs, but he's wrong. Ursula is happy to get attention any way she can. If it takes Cherries in the Snow to spotlight the welfare-reform bill that she wrote with Rhode Island senator Vincent Stengel, so be it. Ursula is style plus substance, as many people have pointed out. The complete package.

Ursula was built for politics, but Jake has no stomach for it. He has firm views on the issues— and some of his views differ from Ursula's—but he loathes the wheeling and dealing, the bargaining chips, the side deals. He tries to stay out of it; he appears only at wholesome family-friendly events— Toys for Tots drives at the Grape Street mall, polka dancing on Dyngus Day—and he always has Bess in tow. Bess is in kindergarten at McKinley Elementary. Jake walks her to school every morning and picks her up every afternoon. They still have their nanny, Prue, in Washington, but here in South Bend, Jake handles all things Bess-related, and if he's traveling for work, then Ursula's mother, Lynette, covers. Bess visits with Jake's parents every Sunday. They are surprisingly hands-on, taking Bess to the Potawatomi Zoo or to the ice-skating rink, the same rink where Jake met Ursula so many years ago.

They eat a lot of pizza from Barnaby's.

Jake would like a second child. He would like a third, a fourth, even a fifth. But Ursula barely sees Bess as it is now. She's supposed to handle school pickup on Wednesdays and take Bess to her ballet class, but last Wednesday, Ursula had a meeting with workers from the ethanol plant and the week before she was at a first-responders event and when Jake asked her if she wanted to change "her" day, she snapped at him.

I'm doing all this for her, Ursula said.

She's too young to understand that, Jake said. *She needs her mother.*

You're not too young to understand it, Ursula said. *Bess is fine. I read to her at night. We cuddle. I took her to the library last week. The person who has a problem is you.*

Ursula is right; he *does* have a problem. He isn't happy. Every day he thinks about asking for a divorce. He thinks about Mallory, about taking Bess and moving to Nantucket, about marrying Mallory an having a child of their own.

"Are you sure you want to run for senator Jake says.

"Yes," Ursula says. "Good night."

How are things going for Jake at work? Well, that the good news: He loves his job. Jake is executive vi president of development for the Cystic Fibrosis R search Foundation, which means he asks individua and companies for money. Some people—most peopl in fact—hate the mere idea of asking for money, b it turns out, Jake has a knack for it. It helps that he passionate about the cause, that he can make statisti sound anecdotal, and that he understands the medic advances in CF research. If the medicine of 2006 ha been available back in 1980, Jessica could have live an extra decade, maybe even two.

Jake doesn't say this, however. He has refraine from marching out his dead sister in order to pr donations out of people. The closest he comes mentioning her is this: When people ask why he so passionate about research for cystic fibrosis—ne cancer, not ALS, not heart disease—he says he lo someone close to him to CF and leaves it at that.

Jake doesn't attend every CFRF fund-raiser acro the country—that would be impossible—but he do appear at the major ones, such as the benefit hel in Phoenix in May. The philanthropic set don the tuxes and gowns, drink a few flutes of champagne, ea canapés, find their place cards, admire the tablescape listen to an inspiring speaker, eat some kind of sauce chicken, and raise their paddles.

The Phoenix event, held at the JW Marriott i

Desert Ridge, has one thousand forty-four attractive and well-dressed people attending. The chairwoman's name is Carla Frick. Jake has met a lot of chairpeople and Carla is the best. She organizes everything down to the minute, she's prepared for any one of a hundred snafus, and she has put together a committee of sixteen women who are just as unflappable, detail-oriented, and gracious as Carla is.

When Jake sees these women in action in Phoenix, he wonders how it is that men have historically been in charge of the world. Women should be running everything everywhere—and Jake's not just saying that because he's married to Ursula de Gournsey.

Jake is talking to Dave Van Andel from Grand Rapids, Michigan, who came to Phoenix specifically for this event (and to drive his Porsche 911 on the flat, straight desert roads) when Carla appears at Jake's elbow. They are still in the cocktails-and-canapés portion of the evening. There's a big band with a Frank Sinatra look-alike crooning standards. The affair is elegant; the drinks are strong; the bite-size arepas with hot-pepper jelly are delicious. Phoenix does things right. Why doesn't everyone live in Phoenix?

Carla smiles at Dave. "I need to borrow Jake for a minute."

Carla leads Jake out of the ballroom and into the hallway. She's wearing a black jumpsuit with rhinestone straps and a diamond cross around her neck. When she fingers the cross, Jake sees something new in Carla: a crack in her façade.

"Sydney has been taken to Banner," she says.

"What?" Jake says. Banner is the Phoenix hospital and Sydney Speer is a twenty-nine-year-old local news anchor from Scottsdale who has CF. She's one of the best ambassadors Jake has. The foundation has flown Sydney all over the country—to Dallas, to Miami, to Kansas City—because when people hear the daunting odds Sydney overcame to appear on television each night, they double whatever amount they had planned to donate. "What happened?"

"She has an infection," Carla says. "Her oxygen level dropped dangerously low and Rick didn't want to mess around. Sydney wanted to do her talk first, then go." Carla's eyes brighten with tears. "Because that's the kind of warrior Syd is." A single silver tear rolls through Carla's perfect makeup. "Plus, you know, she loves this party."

Jake pulls his phone out and texts Sydney's husband, Rick. Sending you guys my love. Keep us posted. Then it's on to a much smaller problem but a problem nonetheless. "Who's going to speak?"

Carla says, "I have contingencies for every emergency but I don't have a backup speaker. I didn't think we'd need one. I saw Sydney on Sunday at the PCC playing *golf*." Carla scans the ballroom. "The Gwinnetts lost their son, they have firsthand experience with the disease and I know Joanne is comfortable talking about it, but I'm not going to throw her up in front of a thousand people without any warning."

"Obviously not," Jake says. He sighs. "I'll do it."

"You'll ask Joanne?" Carla says.

"No," Jake says. "I'll be the one to speak." He clears his throat. "I lost my twin sister to CF when we were thirteen."

(Carla Frick feels her mouth drop open in a way she is sure is unattractive. She scrambles for something to say. "Did I *know* this, Jake? I didn't know this." Carla is halfway madly in love with Jake McCloud. He's so handsome, so upright, so *good*…and so unavailable, married to a stylish congresswoman back in Indiana. Carla has recently gotten divorced from a man who, although handsome, is *not* upright and *not* good, and Carla has vowed that the next man she becomes involved with will be like Jake. This news about his sister, while unexpected and out of the blue, explains a lot. Jake is outstanding at his job, vested beyond just showing up to work, and now Carla knows why. She didn't think her feelings for him could get any more intense, but they just have.)

"I don't tell very many people," Jake says. He lays a hand on Carla's forearm, then quickly lifts it. Carla is newly divorced and they've been out in the hallway for too long, probably. He's sure that people in Phoenix gossip just like they do everywhere else. "I'll speak."

Jake is good with people—but his strength is one-on-one or small-group conversations. His strength is *not* public speaking.

He jots down a couple of notes on a cocktail napkin, but they're disjointed, so he throws the napkin away. He's seen enough speakers at enough benefit dinners to know that all he needs to do is tell his story.

Still, his stomach churns and he feels uncomfortably warm and prickly in his tuxedo. He can't eat anything, and he certainly can't *drink* anything; even with half a Jim Beam and Coke in him, he's worried he's going to make a complete idiot of himself. What is he *doing*?

The lights go down and people find their tables, which are now bathed in candlelight with the salad course plated. They pass rolls, then scalloped pats of butter. They pour wine. The lights go up on the stage, the band plays some background music, and Carla strides over to the podium, the pants of her jumpsuit billowing, and takes the microphone. There's cheering. This crowd is friendly, Jake thinks. They'll forgive him if he's awful.

"I've spoken to Rick Speer and told him we are all sending Sydney our prayers tonight," Carla says after explaining the situation. "And I'm happy to tell you that in Sydney's absence, Jake McCloud, executive vice president of the Cystic Fibrosis Research Foundation, has bravely agreed to share his own story publicly for the very first time. So please, ladies and gentlemen, let's give a warm Phoenix welcome to Jake McCloud."

Applause. Jake can't tell if it's half-hearted—these people paid to hear Sydney—because of the blood rushing in his ears. Imagining them in their underwear isn't going to work. Jake is nervous—not about the speaking itself but about what he's about to say. He has told the story of Jessica to so few people. Who? He didn't have to tell Ursula because Ursula lived through it with him. Bess is still too young to understand. He'll tell her when she gets older.

Mallory, Jake thinks.

He told the story to Mallory.

So when Jake replaces Carla at the podium, he isn't looking out at one thousand forty-four people. Instead, he's looking at one person: Mallory. It's 1993; she's twenty-four years old. She's lying on the old blanket on the beach in her T-shirt and her cutoffs; her hair is spread out behind her as she gazes up at the night sky. When Jake starts to tell her about Jessica, she rolls onto her side, props herself up on her elbow. Her eyes are green tonight and they're fastened on him.

She's listening.

"When does memory start?" Jake says. "Age four? Age five? Sometime within that year, a child's synapses connect, creating lasting memory. And it was at around this age that I realized there was something different about my twin sister, Jessica—coughing fits, hospital visits." Jake pauses. "It was probably a year or two later that my parents explained that she had cystic fibrosis." The room is absolutely silent. "And, yes, I did say my *twin* sister. We were—obviously— fraternal twins, though people would ask once in a while if we were identical." There are a few laughs, probably from parents of twins or people who were twins themselves. "Because we were fraternal twins, our DNA was only as similar as any other two siblings'. In our case, Jessica had the CF genes and I didn't." Jake pauses again. "You can probably all imagine how that made me feel. If I had been able, I would have…happily, *gratefully*…taken the burden of the disease from her and carried it myself." Jake's eyes fill; the audience is blurry, but he's in control. "That wasn't possible, of course. But that's why I have worked for the past seven years raising money for the Cystic Fibrosis Research Foundation. I do it so no other children like me have to lose a sibling at the age of thirteen and so no other parents like my parents— who I think felt all the more helpless because they are both doctors—have to lose a child." Jake stops to take a breath. "I'm standing before you asking for your support because my twin sister can't."

Jake McCloud receives a standing ovation. The CFRF dinner in Phoenix raises one and a half million dollars—over four hundred thousand dollars more than the year before.

* * *

Jake is through security at the Phoenix airport the next day when his boss, Starr Andrews, calls. Starr is seventy years old; she has been heading up the CFRF since its inception and shows no sign of stopping anytime soon. She's the best boss Jake could ask for, primarily because she gives him autonomy and lets him do his thing.

"I heard you talked about Jessica last night," she says.

"I did," Jake says. Another person Jake told about Jessica was Starr Andrews—at his initial interview, when he explained why he wanted the job. He'd also told Starr he would prefer to keep his personal history with the disease private. He wonders if Starr is calling to remind him of this.

"I'm proud of you," Starr says. "You stepped out of your comfort zone. You opened up to strangers about something very personal. And you made a *hell* of a lot of money. So here's my question: Would you be willing to do it again?"

Jake speaks in Cleveland and Raleigh in May. He speaks in Minneapolis and Omaha in June. He speaks in La Jolla, Jackson Hole, and Easthampton in July.

Event-based donations to CFRF are up more than 30 percent.

Does Jake brag about this to Ursula? Yes, a little bit. She's the superstar of the couple, no one is disputing that. But Jake has come a long way from watching Montel Williams in his boxer shorts.

Before Congress adjourns for the summer, Ursula and Vincent Stengel get their welfare-reform bill passed in the House *and* in the Senate, a tremendous coup. The bill is a brilliant one. It manages to empower single working mothers while also saving the government a hundred and sixty million dollars.

Ursula is riding high. She and Jake rent a house on Lake Michigan, and Ursula relaxes a little. They grill on the sand; they take Bess on the dune buggies and to the water park; they attend the blueberry festival in South Haven and eat ice cream at Sherman's.

In the middle of August, Ursula gets a phone call from Vincent Stengel. He invites her and Jake to Newport over Labor Day weekend. There's a potential donor, a *major* donor, who would write checks not only to Vincent but to Ursula as well. This guy—Bayer Burkhart is his name—liked what he saw with the welfare-reform bill. He sees potential for an emerging centrist position, a perfect cocktail of the Left and the Right that he wants to foster. He wants to have a conversation, or a series of conversations, over the course of the long weekend. And in addition to all this, he has a 110-foot yacht with three staterooms, a pool, a gym, and a movie theater.

"This could be big for me," Ursula says. "Plus it seems like fun, right? A long weekend away? You like New England."

Jake knows he should only be surprised this hasn't happened earlier. "Sounds great," he says, thinking, *Keep it light! Keep it light!* "But Labor Day weekend doesn't work for me."

"Tell the CFRF to find someone else to speak, Jake, please," Ursula says. She gives him an imploring look. "I know you're good at it and I'm proud of you. But take a pass this once, for me?"

She thinks his conflict is work. He has been going

to Nantucket every year for thirteen years and Ursula never remembers. Jake knows he should be grateful it's not on her emotional calendar. Could he get away with telling Ursula that it *is* a work thing? No—he'll be caught. "It's not work," he says. "It's my trip to Nantucket."

"Nantucket?" Ursula says. "You've got to be kidding me. You can skip Nantucket, Jake, come on."

"Sorry, darling," Jake says. "Any other weekend works, just not that one."

"We were the ones who were *invited,* Jake," Ursula says. "With Vince, who serves on the Senate Judiciary Committee, where I would eventually like to earn a seat. This guy Burkhart has *billions.* I need to cultivate him."

"No one is stopping you from cultivating him," Jake says. "But I can't go."

"You're being unreasonable," Ursula says. "Why don't you ask *Coop* to switch weekends?"

"I don't want to ask Coop," Jake says. "I want to go to Nantucket like I always do."

"What if I call Coop?" Ursula says.

Jake takes a breath. Is she bluffing? "Go ahead," Jake says. "Please be the one to explain that your political career takes precedence over a tradition that I've maintained for thirteen years. You show Coop just how compromise in a marriage works."

"You going to Nantucket a different weekend *is* a compromise," Ursula says. "What you're offering is...nothing."

"I'm sorry, Ursula," Jake says. They lock eyes and he feels certain the truth is there, written on his face: there's another woman.

"I hope you're happy with yourself," Ursula says.

"Robbing me of this opportunity. Robbing me of the money that could launch me to certain victory."

"It might be better if you went alone," Jake says. "Maybe this Bayer Burkhart is single with a penchant for powerful women."

"He's happily married," Ursula says. "To a woman named Dee Dee, whose father was the political mastermind behind Buddy..." Jake tunes her out. He doesn't care how rich and connected these people are. "Anyway," she finishes, "I won't go alone."

But you will, Jake thinks.

And she does.

Summer #15: 2007

What are we talking about in 2007? The iPhone; Nancy Pelosi; Halo 3; Oprah's school for girls in South Africa; Barry Bonds; Juno; *Paris Hilton; the Burj Dubai, Lindsay Lohan; Whoopi on* The View; *Gordon Brown; Virginia Tech; McLovin; acai bowls; Anna Nicole Smith; Don Imus; Serena van der Woodsen and Blair Waldorf; "If you ain't got no money, take yo' broke ass home."*

Cooper is getting married again and this time, he's doing it right. Tish—Letitia Morgan—comes from an old Philadelphia family. She grew up in Radnor on the Main Line, went to Agnes Irwin and then

Vassar, where she majored in art history, and now serves as the director of the Phillips Collection in Dupont Circle. Cooper noticed Tish at the Metro stop—once, then twice. He decided that if their paths crossed again he would ask her out. He had to wait a long time, so long that he feared she'd taken a different job or maybe left DC altogether. But then, one Friday morning, there she was. She was carrying an armful of cut flowers wrapped in brown paper in addition to her leather bucket purse and a tray of something that appeared to be artichoke bruschetta. As she ascended the escalator at the Dupont Circle stop with Cooper in hot pursuit, something shifted in her balance, and when she stepped off the escalator, her purse overturned and everything in it dumped to the ground.

This was bad news for Tish (the station floor was filthy) but good news for Cooper, who was able to come to her rescue and help pick up everything—her wallet, her cell phone, pens, loose change, a packet of tissues, a trial-size bottle of skin lotion, a cherry Chap-Stick, her checkbook, a few loose shopping lists and receipts, and a flat disk that Cooper held in his hands probably a second or two longer than he should have because he was trying to figure out what it was.

"My birth control pills," she said. "Thank you." And, as Tish said later, Cooper looked so mortified that she had burst out laughing.

They'd been inseparable ever since.

The ceremony is held at St. David's in Wayne, Pennsylvania, with a reception following at the General Warren Inne in Malvern. It's Cooper's third big wedding. He wanted something more intimate, but this is Tish's first go-round and her parents are paying, so they have groomsmen and bridesmaids, a twelve-piece orchestra, Jordan almonds. There are one hundred and thirty people in attendance but only two dozen or so from Cooper's side—his parents and sister, obviously, and Fray and his longtime girlfriend, Anna, and Jake and Ursula (who is running for senator, so Cooper figured Jake would come alone, but no, Ursula is here), plus a selection of people from Brookings including Brian Novak, who is now divorced and has asked Coop no fewer than three times if Mallory is still single.

Yes, Cooper said. He's not sure Brian is good enough for Mallory. She deserves a prince, someone like Tish's family friend Fred, though Fred lives in San Francisco and is therefore geographically undesirable.

Cooper's favorite part of his previous two weddings was the cocktail hour that falls after pictures (which he suffers through) and before the whole rigmarole of dinner. His third is no exception. He has a cold gin and tonic and the guests are in the garden behind the inn, which is lush with flowers and shaded from the early August sun by stately two-hundred-year-old oaks. A server comes by with flaky triangles of spanakopita and lemony crab salad on cucumber coins, and Cooper wishes he could just stay in this moment forever instead of dealing with the tricky business of being *married*.

Cooper and Tish are talking to Ursula de Gournsey, and Cooper can tell Tish is a bit starstruck; Tish can't believe Coop *knows* UDG and that the superstar congresswoman is *attending their wedding!* Tish is telling Ursula about their honeymoon to the Italian Riviera—Capri, Sorrento, Positano—which, like the wedding, is being paid for by Tish's parents. She and Cooper are leaving in a few weeks.

"At the end of August?" Ursula turns to Coop. "So does that mean you're canceling on Jake this year?"

"Canceling...what?" Tish says. She smiles at Coop, waiting for an explanation.

Coop has no idea what Ursula is talking about. He and Jake do meet for the occasional beer at the Tombs, but only when Jake is in Washington. They have also subbed on each other's company softball teams, though that was long ago.

"Coop and Jake go to Nantucket every Labor Day weekend," Ursula says. "It's guys only, which is something you'll come to appreciate after a while. Jake is always the nicest right after he gets back from the island. And you two have been doing it for...what? Thirteen, fourteen years?"

Cooper has enough experience with relationships to just smile and nod.

"Huh!" Tish says. "I didn't know anything about this!"

Nantucket every Labor Day weekend for thirteen or fourteen *years*? Exit—he needs an exit!

Cooper chuckles. "We'll talk about it later," he tells his new wife. "Let's get one more cocktail before we're seated."

Nantucket every Labor Day weekend for thirteen or fourteen years? Meaning since...1993? Yes, that was the first time they went to Nantucket, for his bachelor-party weekend, right after Mallory inherited the house. That was the year he married Krystel. Krystel, ugh—Cooper can't think about it, and he shouldn't think about it. Krystel was two wives and five serious girlfriends ago.

That first year, he'd left the same day he arrived, and then they'd returned the following year—was that on Labor Day weekend?—but other than that, Cooper had been to Nantucket only for his nephew's first birthday. He feels guilty about not visiting more often but he's been busy.

Why would Ursula think that Cooper and Jake have been going to Nantucket every Labor Day weekend for the past however many years? Obviously, that's what Jake has told her. Is Jake up to something? Has he fabricated a long-running lie to his wife, the person whom some people hail as "the smartest woman in America"?

There must be another explanation, but Cooper won't worry about it right now. It's time to sit down to the Caesar salad. The General Warren Inne is famous for it, Tish says.

Cooper has all but forgotten the conversation with Ursula but the newly minted Letitia Morgan Blessing has not. She brings it up over the tenderloin with Bordelaise and sweet-corn risotto.

"You're going to Nantucket over Labor Day weekend with Jake McCloud?" she says. "This is a thing you do? You might have thought to mention it. You do realize that's only a couple days after we get back from Italy." (Tish doesn't want to quarrel during her wedding but Cooper has insisted on both of them being completely transparent in this relationship because he was so badly burned by his previous two wives—the first wife was a crack addict; the second was escaping an arranged marriage down in Uruguay. Tish can't believe she is only now hearing about some bromance trip that Cooper takes every year. It's weird, though, because Tish knows that Coop didn't go to Nantucket last Labor Day weekend; they had spent that weekend in Bay Head, New Jersey, with her family. So what's going on?)

"I don't go to Nantucket with Jake every year," Coop says. "I mean, I *have,* but not in over a decade. I think Ursula is just mixed up."

(*Really?* Tish thinks. Ursula de Gournsey doesn't seem like the kind of woman who gets mixed up.)

Coop starts watching Jake. He's sitting at table 4 with Ursula and Tish's family friend Fred-from-San-Francisco and some friends of Tish's from Vassar. Ursula is on her phone, texting, it looks like, which is vaguely insulting—but then again, she is running for the U.S. Senate, so she probably has urgent business, even on a Saturday evening in August. Jake rises from the table and heads to the bar where…Mallory is ordering a drink. The two of them talk; it looks like an intense conversation. Is it intense, or is Cooper just projecting? Jake and Mallory know each other; they've known each other since that first summer and knew *of* each other while Coop and Jake were in college. They're friendly—so what?

Mallory gets her wine. She heads back to table 2, where Brian Novak is waiting with his arm draped over the back of her chair.

Cooper watches Jake's eyes follow Mallory back to the table. Even once she's sitting down, his gaze lingers. Cooper thinks: *Mallory and Jake?* Coop has a vision of the two of them slow-dancing at PJ's however many years ago. That had been…a little strange, even unsettling, but the dance had ended and they'd returned to the table.

Every Labor Day weekend on Nantucket for the past thirteen years.

The next time Jake gets up—he's heading toward the men's room—Cooper follows him.

"Be quick," Tish says. "It's almost time for the toasts."

Tish is very excited for the toasts—because who doesn't like hearing other people say nice things about them?—though Cooper dreads the inevitable "Third time's the charm" joke.

"Nature calls," he says. As he follows Jake to the men's room, Cooper realizes that Jake and Mallory would have been left on Nantucket *alone* that first year because Fray had some crazy accident and Leland bailed, as Leland does. At the time he thought nothing of it. Then the second year, Cooper met Alison the flight attendant and ended up spending the entire weekend in her room at the Nantucket Inn, again leaving Jake and Mallory alone. He didn't wonder about that then because...well, because he was in his twenties and woefully self-absorbed.

Has Jake returned to Nantucket every year to...see *Mallory*? To...*sleep* with her? That must be wrong. Jake has always been with Ursula. They have a child. Furthermore, Mallory has a child, Link, whose father is Fray. *That* development was bizarre enough. There is nothing going on with Jake and Mallory. Coop should go back and sit down. He should check that Fray's best-man toast doesn't make any references to Coop's previous marriages.

But instead, Coop pushes into the men's room.

Jake is at the sink, hands on either side of it, staring into the mirror. He looks...agitated.

"You okay, man?" Coop asks.

Jake straightens. "Yeah, I'm sorry. It's just…a lot."

"What's a lot?" Cooper asks.

"My life," Jake says. "I don't expect you to understand and I'm not going to bore you with the particulars."

"Speaking of particulars—" Cooper stops himself. He can't ask Jake about it. But then again, he can't *not* ask. "Does Mallory let you use her cottage on Labor Day weekend? Do you go every summer? Labor Day weekend?"

"Did *she* tell you that?" Jake asks.

"No," Cooper says. "Ursula said something. You want to tell me what's going on?"

He and Jake stare at each other. Cooper finds he's shaking. Jake is Cooper's *role model* and has been ever since Cooper picked him as a big brother in the fraternity so long ago. And Jake's relationship with Ursula has been a paragon for Cooper; it's what he's been looking for all these years and what he has finally found with Tish. He doesn't want to hear that it's fatally flawed.

"No," Jake says. "I'm sorry, I don't."

Later, after the first dances and all the garter and bouquet nonsense—Mallory doesn't catch the bouquet and Coop overhears Kitty scolding Mallory for not even trying—Cooper corners his sister at the bar. The band is playing "Rock Lobster," and Tish and her bridesmaids are going nuts on the dance floor, so Coop has a minute.

"I want to bring Tish to Nantucket," he says.

"You should," Mallory says.

"What about Labor Day weekend?"

"Won't you be in Italy?" she asks.

"We get back the twenty-eighth."

"Don't you have a job?" Mallory asks. Her voice is light. "You're going on a two-week honeymoon, then you're going to turn right around and come to Nantucket for the long weekend?"

Cooper shrugs. "Why not?"

"Doesn't *Tish* have a job?" Mallory asks.

"Just answer the question, Mal," Cooper says. "Can Tish and I come up to Nantucket for Labor Day weekend?"

Mallory takes a sip of her wine. Does she look guilty? Is she a homewrecker? A longtime serial homewrecker?

"Labor Day isn't great for me," she says.

"Really? How come?"

"Bunch of reasons," she says. "I like to prep for my first week of school. And Link comes back from Fray's on that Monday, so over the weekend I clean his room, wash his sheets, sort through his toys, that kind of thing. Any other weekend would work, though."

"Sort through his *toys?*" Cooper says. "*That's* the excuse you're handing me?"

Mallory bumps him with her shoulder. "Wait until you have kids," she says. "Hey, best wedding so far."

A week before Thanksgiving Jake calls Cooper and asks if he wants to meet for a beer at the Tombs. Cooper wants to meet Jake very badly—because his marriage to Tish is over. The third time was *not* the charm; the third time was shorter than even the ill-fated first and second times. Cooper overheard Tish on the phone with her "family friend" Fred, who is *not* a family friend, it turns out, but an old boyfriend, and actually, not even an *old* boyfriend—when Cooper checked Tish's cell phone, he found sixty-eight calls between the two over a ten-day span. Tish cried and begged for forgiveness when he confronted her. It was only an "emotional affair," she said. She'd never slept with Fred. Well, okay, she'd slept with Fred once, but it wasn't memorable. Actually, a handful of times. She had slept with Fred a bunch of times, but she wasn't in love with him. She was in love with him but he lived in San Francisco. She was moving to San Francisco; she had accepted a position at the de Young Museum.

Yes, Cooper wants to have a beer with his old friend Jake McCloud, but Cooper has a nagging suspicion that Jake and Mallory have some kind of arrangement, and, sorry, Cooper won't collude. He isn't able to cut Mallory out of his life, she's his *sister,* but he can put his friendship with Jake on ice.

"Sorry, man," Cooper says. "I'm all jammed up."

Summer #16: 2008

What are we talking about in 2008? Eliot Spitzer; Wisteria Lane; the New York Giants; Dancing with the Stars; the Beijing Olympics; the Kindle; Slumdog Millionaire; SoulCycle; Fannie Mae and Freddie Mac; Wii; Lehman Brothers; High School Musical; the global financial crisis; the election; "Who Would Ever Want to Be King?"

Everyone is focused on who will be the next president of the United States. But not Mallory. She watches the election coverage—Wolf Blitzer on CNN because her beloved Tim Russert passed away in June—only to find out if Ursula de Gournsey unseats incumbent Indiana senator Thomas Castillo.

Why, yes; yes, she does.

Ursula de Gournsey—UDG—is a United States senator.

Summer #17: 2009

What are we talking about in 2009? Bernie Madoff; US Airways Flight 1549 landing in the Hudson River; Springsteen Super Bowl; Somalian pirates; the Nook; Michael Jackson; Sonia Sotomayor; Twitter; barre class; Ted Kennedy; Dunder Mifflin; Tiger Woods; al-Qaeda; The Hangover; "Boom Boom Pow."

The older Jake gets, the more he realizes that very few situations are purely good or purely bad. Ursula wins her Senate seat, which initially seems purely good. She has launched herself onto an even larger platform, and she secures a coveted spot on the

Judiciary Committee. She's only forty-three years old; her future is bright.

There's a victory party in Washington held at the Willard Hotel, and all of the donors who gave above a certain level have been invited. Bess has been spared—she's back at the condo with Prue—but Jake has to stand by his wife and thank every single person who comes through the line. Only about half of these people are from Indiana. The other half are Washington establishment and political operatives, people who use their money to buy influence.

A big man in a double-breasted blazer comes through the line and Ursula murmurs, "Bayer Burkhart, the guy from Newport, and his wife, Dee Dee, in the pink. They're friends with Vince and Caroline Stengel, remember?"

Jake remembers Newport, the invitation that he declined because it was on Labor Day weekend, yes, but the who-knows-who-from-where has been lost. Obviously Jake knows Vince Stengel, the Rhode Island senator, but has he ever met the wife? He can't remember. His brain has short-circuited when it comes to meeting people. He knows everybody he needs to know, and even that number can be whittled down to double digits. Low double digits.

Still, Jake plays along. "Hello there, Mr. Burkhart." He shakes the guy's huge, powerful hand. "I'm Jake McCloud."

Bayer tilts his head like he has a crick in his neck. "Jake McCloud. I told your wife this already, but I feel like I've met you somewhere. Years ago. Your name is familiar. I'll figure it out at some point."

Jake has never seen this guy before in his life. He

laughs. "All right, Mr. Burkhart. Thank you for your support."

Bayer Burkhart holds on to Jake's hand an instant longer than is socially acceptable—Jake has at least developed an instinct for this much—and he's still looking at Jake strangely. He thinks he knows him from somewhere. Everyone wants a personal connection, Jake gets it, but come on. He extracts his hand.

A little while later, there's a familiar face in the line that Jake hasn't seen in a long time. It's Cody Mattis, the guy who tried to get Jake a lobbying job with the NRA. Cody has risen in the ranks there. Now he's the number-two or number-three guy.

But what is he doing *here?* "What is Cody Mattis doing here?" Jake asks Ursula. His voice is low but she can probably sense his concern. "You didn't…Ursula, you didn't take money from the NRA, did you?" If Cody Mattis is here, then the answer is yes. Even if Ursula didn't accept money directly from the NRA, she took it from a dark-money source in bed with the NRA. For all Jake knows, Bayer Burkhart is the dark money.

"We'll talk about it later," Ursula says.

"Later" is midnight in the condo. Bess is asleep; Prue has gone home after a long day. Jake goes into the dark bedroom, where Ursula is pretending to be asleep.

"Your campaign accepted money from the NRA?" he says.

"Don't sound so self-righteous," she says. "You were the one who lined up an interview to work for them."

"That was ten years ago, Ursula. And I canceled it."

"Because I told you to," Ursula says.

"No, because you told me about the shooting in Mulligan, and, using my own moral compass, I decided I didn't want anything to do with the gun lobby."

"You're sounding pretty sanctimonious," Ursula says.

"How much did you take from them?"

"Seven hundred," she says, then she clears her throat. "Seven fifty."

Seven hundred and fifty thousand dollars. "What did you have to promise them in exchange for that money, Ursula?"

She sighs. "You and I both know that Indiana is a pioneer state. Hoosiers like their rifles. All I promised was that I wouldn't vote to take them away or make them any harder to get."

"Rifles meaning AR-15s."

"Rifles meaning for hunting, Jake," Ursula says. "Turkey, quail, rabbit, deer…"

"Return it. Return the money."

"I can't," Ursula says. "They gave it to me, I spent it, I won. I can't just return it like a sweater I've decided I don't like."

Jake swallows. He has been with Ursula for nearly thirty years and he would have said he knew everything about her. But it turns out he doesn't know her at all.

"That Mulligan shooting," Jake says. "The kid, a *seventeen-year-old,* Ursula, bought the gun at Walmart and no one asked him for ID. Gun laws need to be tightened, not kept the same, and certainly not loosened."

"Can we just go to bed?" she says.

"Return the money," he says. "Or I'm leaving."

Ursula laughs indulgently, like he's a little kid holding his breath. "Okay."

Jake sleeps in his study. He thinks about the media circus that will take place if he leaves Senator Ursula de Gournsey over a policy decision. They made a pact back when Ursula first ran for Congress that they would not bring politics into their home. They weren't going to agree on everything; that was a given. Politics covers such a vast spectrum of issues that it's unlikely any two Americans hold the exact same views; each person's political DNA is unique, like biological DNA. Jake thinks gun control is a big deal that will keep getting bigger until some laws are passed. It's feasible that, ten years from now, there will be mass shootings like the one in Mulligan happening every week.

Ursula disagrees—maybe. Maybe she is siding with her constituents who hunt. Or maybe she is so blindly ambitious that she takes any cash she can get.

Will Jake leave her?

No.

But he wants to.

Summer #18: 2010

What are we talking about in 2010? Haiti earthquake; the Tea Party; SeaWorld; The Hurt Locker; *BP oil spill in the Gulf of Mexico; Elena Kagan; El Bulli; Rahm*

Emanuel; Don't ask, don't tell; Chilean miner rescue; Alexander McQueen; 127 Hours; WikiLeaks; Leslie Knope, Ron Swanson, Chris Traeger, Tom Haverford, April, Andy, and Ann Perkins; "I see you drivin' round town with the girl I love."

Her favorite moments of the year are the moments right before she sees him. He's on the ferry. He has boarded the plane. He's on his way. His rental Jeep is going to be speeding down the no-name road toward her cottage, bringing a cloud of dust and dirt and sand. The anticipation is ecstasy. It's a perfectly ripe strawberry dipped in melted milk chocolate; it's a roaring fire on a snowy night; it's a double rainbow; the green-glass barrel of a wave; the first sip of ice-cold champagne.

And then...he arrives, he's there. They lock eyes; he rushes out of the car—forget the luggage, worry about that later—wraps his arms around her, picks her up off the ground, sets her down, holds her face in his hands, and they kiss.

Stop time, she thinks. *Please, God.*

It's the inverse when he leaves. The most excruciating pain she has ever known is watching him drive away, knowing it will be 362 days until she sees him again (and a day longer in leap years).

What will change in that year?

Will anything happen that will keep him from coming back?

Mallory's fortune: *An acquaintance of the past will affect you in the near future.*

Jake's fortune: *Feeding a cow roses does not get extra appreciation.*

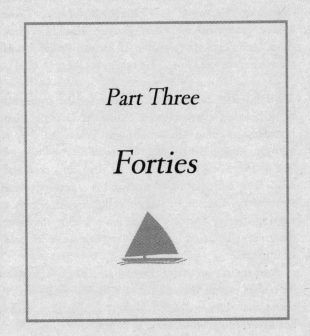

Part Three

Forties

Summer #19: 2011

What are we talking about in 2011? SEAL Team Six; Osama bin Laden; the Affordable Care Act; Nicki Minaj; the Penn State football scandal; the debt ceiling; Gabrielle Giffords; Cam Newton; Occupy Wall Street; Don and Betty Draper, Peggy, Roger, and Joan; cake pops; Rory McIlroy; Eleven Madison Park; Anthony Weiner; Andy Rooney; "Rolling in the Deep"; Steve Jobs; Moneyball.

At the end of the school year, Dr. Major announces that the high school has received a large monetary gift from an anonymous donor that is earmarked to reward excellence in teaching. One teacher will be chosen each September to receive a seventy-five-thousand-dollar cash prize—which, in Mallory's case, is the amount of her current salary. A committee of parents and community members will convene over the summer to evaluate candidates, and the winner will be announced the first week of school.

"You're going to win the first one," Apple says. "I can feel it."

"Thanks for jinxing me," Mallory says. "I know I'm a good teacher. I don't need outside validation."

"But you do need seventy-five large," Apple says.

"Yes," Mallory says. "Yes, I do."

It was a cold, windy, rainy spring on Nantucket, and the roof of Mallory's cottage leaks. She had a roofer named G-Bow come look at it and he found extensive rot and places where the wind had blown off shingles. *It's waterfront, built in the 1940s,* G-Bow said. *Roof was probably replaced sometime in the 1970s. It's time for a new roof.*

Mallory asked how much it would cost.

Not much, he said. *Forty to forty-five grand.*

Mallory has the money that Aunt Greta left her conservatively invested, but she has dipped into it for various home improvements and a new Jeep to replace the K5, which died on Eel Point the summer before.

Technically, Mallory has the money to replace the roof, but it will leave her very depleted.

She could ask Fray for the money, or part of it. He's generous when it comes to Link; the child wants for nothing and Mallory knows that college will be handled. But it's not Fray's job to support Mallory. She's the mother; she has primary custody. The roof over their heads is her responsibility.

Kitty and Senior?

No, never.

Announcing the teaching award was cruel, Mallory decides. It's all she thinks about now. She wonders who's on the committee—any parents of the kids she's taught? Well, she's taught everyone's kids, so the answer is yes and it's true that most parents love her. At Christmas, Mallory always receives the biggest haul of gifts—pumpkin muffins, scented candles, bottles of Sancerre, hand-knit scarves, monogrammed toiletry cases, cookies, cookies, cookies, gift certificates to Mitchell's Book Corner, fancy hand lotion, Christmas ornaments, Whitman's samplers, Bacon of the Month Club. Some of it is bribery—Mallory writes at least two dozen college recommendation letters each year—but most of it is due to genuine gratitude and affection. In teaching, as with everything in life, you get out of it what you put into it.

Mallory susses out her competition for the award. There's Mr. Forsyth, who teaches biology. At nearly seventy years old, he's a legend; everyone adores him. One year, his students made T-shirts that said RESPIRATION IS THE RELEASE OF ENERGY IN THE FORM OF ATP. He's the sentimental favorite. There's Rich Bristol, the music teacher and choral director of the Accidentals and Naturals. He's young and handsome and the theater girls love him; he's their heartthrob, though this might work against him. And then there's Apple, but she's guidance and therefore not eligible, which is unfair, though Mallory is also a bit relieved, which makes her feel like a terrible friend and a bad person. She doesn't deserve the Excellence in Teaching award.

Yes, yes, she does. Positive thinking. One of the leaks in the roof is right over Link's bed.

If she wins, she thinks, she'll pay for the roof and donate the rest to the Boys and Girls Club.

Except she knows she won't. Life has too many surprises for a single working mother to be that magnanimous.

She goes back to Rich Bristol. There were whisperings about him and a student named Danielle Stephens. Too chummy, someone said. Red flag. Mallory thinks back to her second year of teaching and the incident with Jeremiah Freehold. She shudders.

She was so young then, and now, of course, Mallory would no sooner take a student off the property in her car than she would lop off her own hand. But back then she had; she was in the same space then that Rich Bristol is in now, maybe worse. Do people remember about Jeremiah? Is it a stain on Mallory's reputation that will never fully come out?

Apple is asked to be the administrator of the committee. She has no decision-making powers but she will attend all the meetings. She will know the frontrunners. She knows the committee members.

"I can't tell you a thing," Apple says. "I shouldn't even have told you I'm the admin."

"How about one thing?" Mallory says. "Is Mrs. Freehold on the committee?"

Apple inhales and Mallory's heart slips a notch in her chest. "No," Apple says.

Link is ten now, old enough to spend the entire month of August up in Vermont with Fray and Anna. Fray lives on Lake Champlain. He has a motorboat; they water-ski and fish for trout; they mountain-bike; they build fires to cook over. Link loves his Vermont summers, but this will be the last one. Fray is launching his Frayed Edge coffee brand this fall, and he and Anna are moving to Seattle.

Link is a well-adjusted kid. He knows he has to make the most of his trip to Vermont this year and he's also excited about eventually visiting his dad and Anna in Seattle. The Space Needle is there, and Pike Place Market, and the Seahawks!

Mallory supposes Link will get used to flying cross-country. Fray will probably put him in first class—at least, until Fray buys a plane of his own. And here's Mallory, trying to figure out how to replace her roof.

Her obsession with the roof and the award and Link flying to Seattle in a G5 serve one purpose: The summer zips by. Labor Day is on her doorstep and Mallory vows that she will not worry about the roof while Jake is here. She will not worry about anything.

Friday night, September 2, 2011: The burger patties are in the fridge covered with plastic wrap. The corn is shucked, the tomatoes sliced and drizzled with balsamic, the charcoal is a pulsing orange, turning gray at the edges. The hydrangea blossoms—three this year, the bushes were late due to the chilly, wet spring—are in the mason jar next to the one votive candle.

"Can we have extra candles this year?" Jake asks. "My eyesight isn't what it used to be."

There's always a year's worth of catching up. Where do they even start?

"How's Leland doing?" Jake asks.

Not well, Mallory says. After she and Fifi broke up, Leland moved to Brooklyn, a neighborhood called Williamsburg, where property is nearly as expensive as in Manhattan. Mallory has a hard time believing this and she can't quite picture Leland in an *outer borough*. Back in 1993, you couldn't even get a cab to take you to Brooklyn. But now Brooklyn is gentrified; the people are artsy and liberal, and the restaurants are outrageously good. But although Leland has friends and a community, she pines for Fifi. Leland finally left *Bard and Scribe* and started an online journal called *Leland's Letter* whose target audience is "strong, independent women from ages eighteen to ninety-eight." She has fifty-one thousand subscribers and twenty-two advertisers. Even so, it's not enough to make a living on yet, so she is also working as the director of the summer publishing course at NYU.

"Has she got a new girlfriend?" Jake asks. "Or boyfriend?"

"I wish," Mallory says. "Either, both, doesn't matter. I'm worried about her."

Jake says, "I haven't seen your brother since his last wedding. When I call him, he's perfectly civil but he never has time to meet me for a drink."

"He's engaged," Mallory says. She shakes her head. "To a woman he met on Match.com. Tammy. She's divorced with three children."

"Is it going to last?"

"Um...no?" Mallory says. "Though where the wedding is concerned, they're doing the kind thing and eloping. They're getting married in Tortola."

"Kind because I don't have to watch you flirt with Brian from Brookings?"

Mallory can't hide her smile. Poor Brian—he was completely smitten with her but she indulged him only to make Jake jealous. "Kind because I don't have to see you with UDG," Mallory says.

"Arrrgh!" Jake yells. "Why did I not just marry you after that first summer?"

"We aren't going down the road not taken tonight, my friend. Let's watch the sun set."

Jake had taken his usual swim after they first made love and now he's wearing only his board shorts. His muscles are a little softer, she notices, his middle a little thicker; his dark brown hair is shot through with silvery strands. Mallory can easily picture him as he was the summer she met him. She loves him more now for his age, the gray, the lines around his eyes and his mouth when he smiles. They've been doing this nineteen years without interruption. They have been so lucky.

The sun sinks into the ocean. Jake grills their burgers. Cat Stevens is on the stereo, "Hard Headed Woman." Mallory has started playing the CD for Link. He loves Mallory's music—Cat Stevens, R.E.M., World Party—and he loves Nirvana, Pearl Jam, and Soundgarden because of Fray. Musically, he's a forty-year-old trapped in a ten-year-old's body.

Mallory lights the candles—three votives and two tapers in proper candlesticks.

Jake says, "And what about you? How's school?"

She decides not to tell him about the award because talking about the award will lead to talking about the roof. "It's like you and me," she says, and she locks eyes with him. He's here, he's here, it's him, he's across the narrow table, she is going to crawl into bed with him tonight, wake up with him in the morning. It's like a fairy tale. It's like a game of Would You Rather? Would you rather have perfect bliss for only three days or a solid but dull relationship all year long? Mallory would choose Jake every time. "Each year I think there's no way it will be better than the last, but then it is."

Jake blows her a kiss.

"This past year I had a once-in-a-lifetime student," Mallory says. "Abigail Stewart." Mallory rises to get a copy of the short story Abby handed in for her final paper. It's about a seventeen-year-old girl who dates a guy in a garage band. She accidentally gets pregnant at the same time that his career takes off. The story was so well done that Mallory initially worried that Abby had plagiarized it. She scoured the internet but thankfully found nothing. The voice of the story *was* similar to Abby's other work, completely fresh and sassy and irreverent and smart-smart-smart.

"I'm just going to read you the first paragraph," Mallory says. She loves how Jake rests his chin in his hand and gazes at her as she reads, his face glowing with the candlelight.

"Keep going," he says when she's done.

She reads the first three pages, then stops because their food is getting cold. "You can finish the rest tonight in bed," she says.

Jake has been touching Mallory's shin with his foot this whole time. They touch each other whenever they can, however they can. He's here, he's here.

"I'm going to be too busy in bed to do any reading," he says.

"Oh yeah?" she says.

"Yeah," he says, and that's it—they're up, heading for the bedroom, dinner forgotten, Abby's brilliant story forgotten.

They have long since stopped going to the Chicken Box. The risk that Jake will bump into someone he knows is too great. After they make love, they doze off. They have done this in past years, then woken up at two or three in the morning to feast on cold burgers.

Mallory is dreaming about her old ten-speed bicycle. The chain has fallen off and she is trying to put it back on, messy work; she has grease all over her fingers that mixes with the dust and sand of the no-name road.

"Mal." Jake's voice startles her awake. She sometimes dreams that he's in bed with her when he's not and it's a crushing disappointment to wake up alone. When she opens her eyes, Jake is there, his warm body pressed up against hers. She can see the silver in his stubble. But then he curls up, alert, straining. "Do you smell smoke?"

Yes, she thinks. The smell of the grill, maybe, wafting in through the open window. An instant later, the smoke alarms start shrieking and Mallory thinks: *The candles!* Jake yanks on boxer shorts and goes out to the great room with the comforter from the bed. The harvest table is on fire—Abby's pages, the tablecloth, Mallory can't see what else. Jake throws the comforter over the table and Mallory grabs the pot of water she used for the corn and douses the comforter. There's a splash and dripping and hissing and smoke and a smell of melting plastic and charred wood and corn. Mallory is shaking. The smoke detectors are still screaming at them: *How could you let this happen?* She fills the pot again.

"It's out," Jake says. "Mal, it's out."

They both hear the sirens at the same time and all of a sudden it's 1993 again and she and Jake are on the beach, screaming for Fray.

Mallory hears voices, then the slam of a truck door. "Hide in the bedroom," she tells Jake.

Jake says, "Are you kidding me? I'm not going to hide. Go put clothes on." Mallory is naked; she didn't even realize. She grabs a robe off the back of the bathroom door and is just belting it when the door swings open. Three firemen in black uniforms, heavy army-drab jackets, and hats burst in. Mallory knows them: Mick Hanley, Tommy Robinson…and JD.

JD sees Mallory and takes in the sight of the smoking, dripping table. "Thank God you're okay," he says. "Your alarm company automatically calls the station."

Yes, this is something Fray insisted on. The fire department has shown up twice before. Once for burning bacon, once for pine nuts that Mallory was toasting for a salad and then forgot about. After the pine nuts, Mallory invested in a hood for the stove, one with a strong exhaust fan.

Mallory stutters, "C-c-candles. One of the candles must have fallen." She thinks about the tapers, slim and elegant in a pair of silver candlesticks that Cooper gave her for Christmas last year (re-gifted from his most recent wedding, she suspected). One of the tapers was a little loose, maybe, and fell over onto the story pages.

"Is your son here?" JD asks. He looks around and that's when he sees Jake. Mallory wipes the tears and smoke out of her eyes. Mick opens the door to the porch, and a welcome breeze blows through the house.

"Hey," Jake says. He's wearing only the boxer shorts, so there's no real question what was going on.

Please don't introduce yourself, Mallory thinks.

It is *very* bad that JD has shown up, and here's why. At the beginning of July, Mallory attended a graduation party at Corazon del Mar—it was, in fact, a graduation party for Abby Stewart, who was off to Sarah Lawrence—and Mallory saw JD there. JD and Tonya Sohn had long since broken up, and JD was known to be a confirmed bachelor, and although Mallory was still angry at him for spreading the awful rumor about her and Jeremiah Freehold, time (and margaritas) did their trick and Mallory and JD were able to talk, civilly at first, then fondly. He apologized to Mallory for the abhorrent thing he'd said to their driver in Puerto Rico—*Were you a Fresh Air Fund kid?*—something Mallory had tried to forget. The whole fire department had attended sensitivity workshops, he said, and now he had a new attitude. "Evolved, if you will." Mallory won't lie: She wanted to let bygones be bygones and get back in JD's good graces. The island was too small for grudges. As the night progressed, real affection surfaced, and common sense departed. Mallory ended up going back to JD's house and sleeping with him. In the moment, it had seemed harmless, possibly even sweet. Mallory had treated the whole thing as fun, a lark; she had left JD's house at midnight so her babysitter could get home, and only when JD called the next day to see if Mallory wanted to go to Black-Eyed Susan's for breakfast had she seen the error of her ways. In trying to make things better for herself, she had made them much, much worse.

She'd said, *JD, we can't do this.*

He said, *Why not?*

She said, *Because we can't. I'm sorry, I didn't mean to give you the wrong idea.*

JD had hung up abruptly—of course he had. That was what he did, who he was. Mallory hadn't seen him since then.

"Hey," JD says. His voice is friendly, even chummy, and he shakes Jake's hand. It's all an act, Mallory thinks. "I'm JD. I remember you from…jeez, years ago, back when your friend disappeared."

Jake nods slowly. He must realize that this is the guy Mallory dated. She didn't tell Jake too much about him, though she should have—she should have!—so he would realize how dangerous JD is.

"But I don't remember your name," JD says.

"Jake," he says. (Mallory closes her eyes and thinks, *This is where it all falls apart*.) "My name is Jake."

JD nods. He doesn't ask for a last name. He says to Mallory, "The safest thing is if we move the table out onto the beach. Then tomorrow when everything has cooled down, you can figure out how you want to dispose of it."

"Okay," Mallory says.

"The table is probably a goner," JD says. "Which is too bad. I have some fond memories of that table." He chuckles in a way that makes it sound like they had *sex* on the table—if they did, it wasn't memorable—but Mallory doesn't care. Jake disappears to put on shorts and a shirt; Mick, Tommy, and JD maneuver the table out the door, off the porch, and into the sand.

(Despite the fact that there was a fire and every fire is serious, especially in a tinderbox like this cottage, Mick Hanley wants to laugh. When JD saw the address come up in the alarm system, he hauled ass, shouting in Mick's face to *Hurry the hell up*—even though Mick had both legs in his pants and JD had only one. It was *his girl* out in Miacomet, JD said, Mallory Blessing, it was her house that was on fire. Mick thought JD and Mallory had broken up back in the '90s, but then again, what did he know? To come in and find her basically naked with some dude...well, she is *not* JD's girl, that's for damn sure, or not *only* JD's girl, and Mick is planning on giving JD a hard time about it all the way back to the station.)

The Excellence in Teaching award goes to Bill Forsyth. It's announced in assembly the afternoon of the first day of school and the kids go wild. It's a good result for sentimental reasons. Bill will be retiring this year after forty-four years of teaching at Nantucket High School. It was the right choice, the only choice, Mallory tells herself. Bill Forsyth has been teaching longer than Mallory has been alive. Still, her anxiety ratchets up until there's a high-pitched noise in her ears. She tries to calm herself: she is healthy and Link is healthy. He came home on Monday lean and tan, his hair sun-bleached to white blond, wearing a concert T-shirt from Anna's former band, Drank. He has a newfound love of Impressionist painters. Anna was an art history major at Bennington, and this summer she taught Link all about Renoir, Degas, Monet, Manet, and, his favorite, Camille Pissarro. He has flash cards of paintings, which he showed Mallory immediately upon his return.

Mallory *has* the money for the roof *in the bank* and if she's squeamish about blowing the whole nut, she can replace the roof in stages. She can start this fall with the half that has the leaks over Link's bed and do the rest next year. Lots of parents of these very kids work two and three jobs just to make the rent or the mortgage, so Mallory has no right to complain. In the end, the harvest table doesn't even need to be replaced—just sanded and refinished.

She's fine. She's fine. She'll replace the whole roof. She can always make more money. If she gets into a tight spot, she can ask Fray for money. She should be more concerned about the way Link comes home at the end of each summer so *transformed* by Fray and Anna.

Or maybe she should feel grateful for that. She's not sure.

Apple grabs Mallory's arm, hard, after the final bell. "That was bullshit."

"What?" Mallory says.

"Don't repeat this."

"Who am I going to tell?" Mallory asks. She and Apple have successfully escaped most of the politics of the high school because they have chosen to confide only in each other.

"I love Bill Forsyth, you love Bill Forsyth," Apple says. "Bill Forsyth is a good teacher. But he has been using the same lecture notes for forty-four years."

"Well, yeah," Mallory says. "Biology doesn't change."

"It's a science, not an art," Apple says. She frames her forehead with her fingers the way she does when she just can't wrap her mind around something. She lowers her voice and says, "You were supposed to win it. Right up until the last meeting, you were the favorite. Something must have happened. Someone must have had a change of heart."

Mallory is tempted to ask if either JD's cousin Tracey the ER nurse or his sister-in-law, Brenda, who had five kids in the system, was on the committee, but knowing exactly who JD turned against her won't fix anything.

"It's not the end of the world," Mallory says. The end of the world would have been Jake saying, "Jake McCloud," and then JD later Googling the name. "It's fine, really."

Summer #20: 2012

What are we talking about in 2012? The Kardashians; Whitney Houston; Joe Paterno; Uber and Lyft; the Kentucky Wildcats; Trayvon Martin; Lance Armstrong; Walter White, Skyler, Jesse, and Gus; Zumba; the Aurora shooting; Instagram; Sandy Hook; Hurricane Sandy; Noma; Barclays Bank; LeBron James; Silver Linings Playbook; *kale; Jimmy Kimmel; "We are never, ever, ever getting back together."*

Everyone Jake knows is on Facebook. Three times recently he has come back into the CFRF office after lunch and found his assistant, Sara, mesmerized by the screen of her computer—likes, tags, shares. When Jake clears his throat—they have a rule about personal business on the office computers that, clearly, everyone ignores—Sara looks up at him and says, "I can't help myself. It's like I'm in quicksand. I just keep sinking deeper and deeper."

If you can't beat 'em, join 'em.

Jake asks Sara to show him how Facebook works. He brings up the site on his laptop and she helps him create a profile using his official headshot from the foundation.

"This is dull and corporate," she says. "Most people

use pictures of their families on a mountaintop skiing or at Disney."

"Disney?" Jake says.

"Do you want to use one of you and Ursula?" Sara asks.

"Not a good idea."

"Bess, then?"

"I'd rather not," Jake says. What he doesn't tell Sara is that he only wants a Facebook account so he can look people up. That's what it's used for, right? To reconnect with people from the past?

(Sara can barely hide her dismay that Jake is insisting on using his bland headshot as a profile picture and refusing to post a cover photo at all. Why is he even bothering with this? In the About section, he lets her list his job title—what a snooze!—then Johns Hopkins University; John Adams High School; South Bend, Indiana; and the fraternity Phi Gamma Delta. He lets her post his status as "married" but doesn't add his spouse's name, which Sara can, sort of, understand. She shows him how to upload photos, should he ever choose to do that.

"Now, you request friends," Sara says.

"You do realize how pathetic that sounds?" Jake says. "*Requesting* friends? I thought I could just add the people I know."

"You have to make a request and they can either accept or decline," Sara says. Nobody in his or her right mind would decline a friend request from Jake McCloud. For Sara, it's another story. She has one ex-boyfriend who declined her friend request and another who hasn't made a decision one way or the other, so with Brad Bardino, she remains in what she thinks of as Friend Limbo.

"Thank you, Sara," Jake says. "I'll come find you if I have any more questions."

"Good luck," Sara says. She considers Jake getting on Facebook a positive development because now maybe he'll understand why she can't keep off the site on her lunch break. "I'll friend you in a minute."

"*You're* going to friend me?" Jake says. "Why? I see you every day. You work ten yards from me."

"Social media is a parallel universe," Sara says.

Jake gives her a blank look.

Sara goes back to her desk and sends a friend request to Jake McCloud's brand-new account. She will be his first friend.

He accepts. He's not completely hopeless.)

Jake spends the better part of an hour on Facebook. He sees how easy it is to disappear down the rabbit hole. Just clicking on his chapter of Phi Gamma Delta brings up fraternity brothers Jake hasn't thought about in eons. Ditto the Johns Hopkins Facebook page. Ditto John Adams High School. Ditto South Bend. Ha! Jake's mother, Dr. Liz McCloud, is on Facebook. How does *she* of all people have time?

Jake sends his mother a friend request. His own mother! This feels extremely weird.

His father, Dr. Alec McCloud, is not on Facebook.

Jake checks to see if Ursula is on Facebook. She is *definitely* too busy for this nonsense. Yes, correct—but there's a Facebook page for Ursula de Gournsey, U.S. senator from Indiana, that he can "follow," and they'll send him "updates" about Ursula's hard work for all Hoosiers. Would he care to follow?

No, thanks.

Jake friends Cooper Blessing and, while he's at

it, Tammy Pfeiffer Blessing, Coop's new wife. (Is it worth it? Jake wonders. Or will Tammy go the way of Coop's three previous wives?) He figures out how to get into Coop's list of "friends," and he cherry-picks a few more Fiji brothers that way, as well as Stacey Patterson from Goucher—why not?—as well as Frazier Dooley, who has both a personal page and a page for Frayed Edge Coffee. Coffee has its own Facebook page? Jake decides not to follow this page even though he goes to the Frayed Edge Café in Dupont Circle all the time. He sends a friend request to Katherine "Kitty" Duvall Blessing. Coop is friends with his own mother, so maybe this is a thing. (To say something is a thing is now a thing, eleven-year-old Bess has informed Jake.)

Is *Bess* on Facebook?

No, thank goodness, and if Jake has anything to say about it, she won't be allowed to get on Facebook until she's thirty years old. It's such a waste of time!

A waste of time, yes, especially since it's taken Jake this long to get to the real reason he created an account.

Mallory, obviously.

She's a friend of Coop, Kitty, and Fray. He clicks on her name, and, like magic, her face fills his screen. He…he…well, he nearly slams his computer shut because it's so surreal. Her profile picture is a photo taken from the side on the front porch of her cottage. The setting sun makes her glow rose gold. Her hair is in a messy bun and he can see her freckles as well as some lines in her face. In Jake's mind, she's always twenty-four years old, but in this photo, she almost looks her age. She's wearing a navy hooded sweatshirt that looks vaguely masculine and he wonders if she's dating someone. Then of course there's the question of who took this picture in which she's looking so dreamy and pensive. How can he find out?

A notification appears on his screen: *Carla Frick has sent you a friend request.*

Carla Frick, the chairperson from the event in Phoenix, has found him *already?* He's been on Facebook for only sixty seconds.

Jake feels exposed but he accepts the friend request, and at nearly the same moment, Frazier Dooley and Jake's mother accept *his* friend requests.

Jake laughs. Frazier is running a coffee empire and Jake's mother is an ob-gyn. So what's happening here? In between hysterectomies and C-sections, Liz Mc-Cloud is on Facebook? While overseeing a workforce of thousands, Fray is accepting friend requests?

Apparently so.

Stacey Patterson accepts Jake's friend request.

It's eerie. Will Mallory be able to tell that Jake checked out her page like a common stalker? He should click out of it but he can't help himself. He studies her cover photo. It's the view of Miacomet Pond. Because Jake knows what he's looking for, he spies a glimpse of Mallory's kayak overturned on the small beach.

In eleven weeks and three days, he will be paddling in that kayak.

Should he look at the pictures Mallory has posted? He's afraid—because what if there's one of her with the new boyfriend? Jake's day will be ruined—his week, his life. But curiosity gets the best of him and he scrolls down.

There are only two pictures. One is of Link in a catcher's uniform, leaning on a bat. The caption reads:

He made the ten-year-old all-star team! The other picture is of Mallory and Link and an African-American couple with two little boys standing in front of the Old Mill. Jake knows this is Hugo and Apple, Mallory's closest friends, and their twins, Caleb and Lucas.

Jake lets out a relieved breath. Maybe Mallory is new to Facebook as well? He sees that she has ninety-seven friends and he scrolls through them. There are a bunch of names he doesn't recognize, but some he does: Leland Gladstone, Fiella Roget, Dr. Major. Jake sees the name Scott Fulton. That was the guy Mallory dated, the one who almost proposed to her. Jake is about to click on Scott Fulton when his good sense kicks in and he thinks, *Come on, man, enough is enough.*

Katherine "Kitty" Duvall Blessing accepts his friend request. Jake is now Facebook friends with Kitty. What will Mallory think of that?

He wonders if Coop will accept or decline his friend request. If Coop accepts his friend request, does this mean things are okay? If he declines, does that mean things are irreparably damaged?

Jake moves his mouse over to the blue button on Mallory's page that says *Add friend*. Should he add her as a friend? Social media is a parallel universe, as Sara said, and in the parallel universe, it would be perfectly reasonable for Jake and Mallory to be friends.

She would kill him, he thinks. She would most definitely decline the request.

He closes Facebook and tucks his laptop into his briefcase.

Later, when he's leaving the office, he stops by Sara's desk.

"Hey, thanks for your help today. With Facebook."

"Use responsibly," she says. "It's a drug."

On August 31, 2012, Jake takes the direct American Airlines flight from DCA to Nantucket. This is risky, of course—he could easily run into someone he knows on the plane—but it's convenient. The trip is ninety minutes from wheels up to wheels down. Jake rents a Jeep and drives out to the no-name road. It feels like coming home.

Friday night: burgers, corn, tomatoes, Cat Stevens, candles that they extinguish with wetted fingertips and then double-check, triple-check, before they go to the bedroom.

The harvest table, Jake thinks, looks as good as new.

They spend Saturday morning out on the kayak, and the pond is just as Jake has been picturing it; they even see a pair of swans. They paddle all the way inland, then turn around. On their way back, they pass a woman with a little boy standing in the muck, casting lines. Mallory waves and calls out, "Good morning!" Jake gives them the slightest glance and he notices the woman staring at him.

He tilts in the seat and the kayak wobbles. It's Stacey Patterson from Goucher, Coop's old flame.

"Hey?" she says. "Jake? Jake McCloud?"

"Go, go, go," Jake whispers, but Mallory doesn't need any prompting, she's paddling with swift, strong strokes while still managing to appear unconcerned.

Jake hears the boy say, "Who's that, Mommy?"

"No one, I guess," Stacey says. "Let's catch a fish."

Close call. They get back to the cottage and Jake tells Mallory that the fisherwoman was Stacey from

Goucher. *Remember she met us that night at PJ's?* Yes, Mallory remembers, of course. Then they sit in silence for a second, thinking the same two things.

It would have been bad had they not escaped.

It's a miracle something like this hasn't happened before.

Because of the Stacey Patterson near disaster, they decide it's best if Mallory goes to the fish store to pick up the lobsters by herself. Jake misses her the entire time she's gone, though it gives him a chance to poke around the cottage unobserved. He could also do this while she's out running in the morning but usually he just sleeps with his face buried in her pillow, inhaling her scent. The reason he comes to Nantucket every year is to see Mallory, pure and simple, but there are so many other things he loves about this weekend, one of which is three days of unstructured time. There are no meetings, no calls, no agendas, no parties, no lunches, no daughter to drop off or pick up. He and Mallory have the things that they do, but they've adjusted these with age and circumstances. Maybe she feels as bereft about going to the fish store alone as he feels about having to stay behind, but she understands. She doesn't want to be found out any more than he does. He's safe with her.

His "poking around" includes studying the books on her bedside table—*The Paris Wife, State of Wonder*— then opening her closet and looking at her clothes. He pulls out a blouse, then a dress. He imagines her wearing them to school. All of her students, male and female, must be in love with her; he can't imagine they wouldn't be. The night before, he asked her if she was dating anyone, though he didn't admit to seeing her wearing the navy sweatshirt on Facebook and wondering whose it was. Mallory said there was no one special. Jake couldn't help himself; he asked if there was anyone "not special," and Mallory confessed that she and Brian from Brookings had had a bit of a text flirtation that ended when Brian sent her a picture of his penis. She said she burst out laughing, then deleted the entire text thread. He'd sent ten follow-up texts asking if he'd crossed a line or offended her or if maybe it wasn't "big enough," and Mallory finally answered that she was forty-three years old, too old to be sexting, and when he responded that there was "no such thing as too old for sexting," she said she thought they'd better stay friends.

Texting is dangerous, they've both agreed. It's tempting, oh, so tempting, to shoot Mallory a message every time he's thinking of her, but they both know people who have been discovered this way—entire affairs, secret relationships, double lives, et cetera, revealed on a cell phone bill. Jake sends Mallory only two texts a year—one at the end of August to let her know when he's arriving and one when he's in the rental Jeep on his way. She doesn't text him at all.

They eat the lobsters on the beach and wash them down with a bottle of very good champagne—this year, vintage Veuve Clicquot that one of her students gave her as an end-of-year gift. The champagne loosens him; it sends glitter through his veins. They finish their lobsters and fall back on "their" blanket—it's the very same blanket they've used since the first year—holding hands, balancing plastic cups of champagne on their chests.

Are they both still spooked by the proximity of Stacey Patterson? Yes! When Jake opened his laptop before dinner, he heard an unfamiliar *ping!* that turned out to be a Facebook message from Stacey: I could have sworn I saw you kayaking on Nantucket today. Are you here, or am I starting to lose it in my old age? Jake thought about responding with Stacey, you're starting to lose it, but then he decided it was best not to respond at all.

"What if we went away next year?" Mallory asks. "What if, instead of here, we went to Saskatchewan or Altoona? Someplace nobody knows us, someplace we can walk around in public?"

"There's always a risk," he says. "Besides, I like it here. This is the home of our relationship. And Ursula has accepted my trip to Nantucket as a matter of course. She doesn't question it."

"She might someday."

"She might," Jake says. He pours them each more champagne. It's better to acknowledge the possibility of Ursula finding out than dismiss it. At this point, Jake is far more concerned about Bess discovering his secret. She's at the age when she's just becoming aware of boys, and Jake would like her to believe they are trustworthy. A better man might decide to give up the relationship with Mallory out of respect for his daughter. But Jake finds himself unwilling—he would like to say "unable," but he knows better—to do that, and so should Bess ever find out, he will admit to his failure. He conducts himself like a prince the other 362 days of the year in hopes that this will balance out his weekend "away" in some karmic sense.

They finish the champagne, then head to bed, hand in hand. They are living inside a magic bubble, the kind that doesn't pop.

* * *

Sunday, it drizzles, and so Jake feels okay about driving up to Great Point, though he wears a baseball cap. Once they pass the Wauwinet gatehouse, they don't see another soul. The sky is moody, striated "fifty shades of gray," Mallory quips, and the water is a steel-blue plate. The eelgrass sways; the gulls dip and swoop unpredictably in the wind.

On the way home, they stop to get the Chinese food. Mallory goes in alone. Jake sinks in his seat, pulls down his cap, waits for her to pop out of the restaurant holding the hood of her raincoat closed so it doesn't blow down in the wind. She has been inside for only three or four minutes, but she grins at him with so much enthusiasm when she reappears that he starts laughing. If he ever has to explain himself to Bess, he will describe how good it feels to know there is one person on earth who is always happy to see him.

Summer #21: 2013

What are we talking about in 2013? The Boston Marathon bombing; Lean In; the fiscal cliff; North Korea; Roger Ebert; "I've never seen a diamond in the flesh"; Chris Kyle; Snapchat; the Met Ball; One World Trade Center; Danica Patrick; Frank and Claire Underwood; Sandra Bullock; John Kerry; Aaron Hernandez; The Goldfinch; James Gandolfini.

Every day when Ursula wakes up, she checks her work phone (a BlackBerry), then her personal phone (the iPhone 5s), and then she gets on the exercise bike with her iPad and reads four newspapers—the *Washington Post,* the *New York Times,* the *Wall Street Journal,* and the *South Bend Tribune.* She would like to say she reads all four cover to cover, but she doesn't have time. While Congress is in session and she's in Washington, Ursula rises at a quarter after five and her mind is still half asleep, so who can blame her for skimming the headlines first? She normally ignores the Metro section of the *Post* and the *Times* because the murders and house fires of DC and Flushing, Queens, are low on her list of priorities. But on the morning of October 23, 2013, Ursula intentionally checks the Metro section of the *Post* because she has heard the most outrageous rumor. She heard from Hank Silver, her former boss at Andrews, Hewitt, and Douglas, that A. J. Renninger is considering a run for mayor of DC.

Ursula feels this must be bad information. AJ—Amelia James Renninger, the six-foot blonde who transferred to the New York office and managed to escape the fate of nearly everyone else in the firm on September 11 by virtue of her eyebrow appointment—is now back in the District, working as a "freelance consultant," which could mean any number of things. Ursula has heard bits and pieces about AJ over the years, none of it terribly positive. She suffered from PTSD after 9/11 and took a leave of absence from the firm even though they'd moved to midtown, and who could blame her? But then, apparently, she got addicted to something, probably Ativan, and there was a period when she dropped off the grid. She resurfaced back in DC a year or two ago and now she's entering the political fray.

Mayor of DC? Ursula can't think of a more thankless job. She remembers that AJ grew up a military brat, her father a lieutenant commander in the navy, so she doesn't have a hometown, per se, and Washington is good at absorbing people.

Ursula doesn't see any mention of the mayoral race in general or of AJ specifically, though her attention does snag on a headline that reads "Baltimore Couple Killed on Beltway."

…pulled over to change a flat…wife stood beside her husband, presumably to alert oncoming traffic to his presence…both husband and wife hit by tractor-trailer…neighbor confirmed the couple was on their way home from a performance at the Kennedy Center.

It was probably Yo-Yo Ma, Ursula thinks. She had wanted to take Bess but her schedule had been too busy.

And then Ursula sees the names: *Cooper Blessing and Katherine (Kitty) Duvall Blessing.*

Ursula stops pedaling. Cooper Blessing is dead? And who is Kitty? The newest wife? Ursula rereads the article and only then sees the ages—*Cooper Blessing, 73, and Kitty Blessing, 72*—and she realizes it's not Cooper himself but Cooper's parents. Ursula has met the elder Blessings three times; these were people she knew, or sort of (she's not sure she could have picked them out of a crowd). They're dead. Killed on the Beltway.

Survived by a son, a daughter, and a grandson, it says in the last line.

Ursula's hands are ice-cold. The exercise bike is in the basement of their condo unit, and as Ursula climbs the stairs to the second floor, where the bedrooms are, she wonders how to break the news to Jake.

She'll wake him up gently, she decides, then hand him his reading glasses and let him see for himself.

She eases onto his side of the bed and studies his face. His hair is more gray than brown now. When did that happen? She realizes that although she sees him every day, she never really *looks* at him. Long marriages have peaks and valleys, she knows, and while Ursula's career has been one peak after another, their marriage is surviving solely because of Jake's steadfastness and his unflappable demeanor. Anyone else would have left her long ago.

When she touches the side of his face, he startles awake. It's true that she never wakes him this way.

"What is it?" he says.

"I have bad news," she says. "Here." She offers him his glasses and points to the headline on the iPad.

Jake accepts the glasses and takes the iPad; Ursula watches his eyes scan the screen. He sucks in his breath and recoils. He drops the iPad, falls back into his pillows. "Oh God."

"I'm so sorry, honey," Ursula says. "At first, I thought it was Cooper, our Cooper, who died."

"It's Senior," he whispers. "And Kitty."

"Were you…close to them?" It embarrasses Ursula that she doesn't know the answer to this. "I mean, obviously I know they're Coop's parents and we've been to all those weddings. But did you have a relationship with them beyond that?"

Jake shakes his head. "I'm sorry, Ursula," he says. "Can you please give me a minute?"

* * *

He's in shock, he needs to process this; Ursula gets that. Unfortunately, she has a Judiciary Committee hearing at nine so she needs to skedaddle. She goes the extra mile by bringing Jake his coffee while he's in the shower.

"I'll be home around seven, seven thirty," she says. "Maybe in time for us to go to Jaleo tonight?"

Jake says, "Not tonight."

"Oh," Ursula says. "Okay." She knows she shouldn't feel rebuffed, but she does. "I love you."

Jake doesn't respond. Ursula can see him through the steam of the shower just standing there, letting the water pummel the back of his head. "I love you, Jacob."

"Okay," he says. "Thank you. Thanks."

For reasons that Ursula cannot fathom, Jake doesn't want to go to the Blessings' funeral.

"Cooper is your friend," Ursula says. "You go away with him every year. You've known him forever. You've stood up at three of his four weddings. You knew his parents. Why do you not want to go pay your respects?"

"It's going to be a circus," Jake says. "There will be hundreds of people there. You, Ursula, are a major distraction. I don't want to create a...sideshow."

"A *sideshow*?"

"People will hound you, they'll ask to take your picture, they will whisper. You attract attention in line at Starbucks. I don't think it's fair to inflict ourselves on the Blessings in their time of mourning."

"So you would go if it weren't for me," Ursula says. "You go, then, go alone."

"I don't think I can," Jake says. "It would be tough, emotionally, but also I'm supposed to be in Atlanta on Tuesday. Overnight. I'm meeting with the guy from the CDC. That meeting took me three months to get."

"Right," Ursula says. "But this is your best friend's parents. And it's not like just one parent who was sick for a long time. This is both at once, suddenly. This is tragic. This demands your attention."

"I'll call Coop today and set something up for week after next," Jake says. "Once the crowds have thinned. You remember what it was like when your dad passed, Sully." *Sully;* Jake hasn't used that nickname in *decades,* not since they were in high school. He's trying to butter her up. But why? "You wouldn't have noticed if one person was missing."

"Still…" Ursula says. Something about this feels off.

"It will mean more to Coop when it's one-on-one," Jake says. "I know I'm right about this."

Ursula disagrees—so much so that, after Jake leaves for Atlanta, she clears her schedule the afternoon of the funeral and drives to Baltimore.

The parking lot of Roland Park Presbyterian is packed. There are signs directing people to park down the block; church vans will shuttle them to the funeral. When Ursula climbs into one of the vans, she wonders if maybe Jake was right. The other eleven passengers stop talking and gape at her. One surprised-looking older gentleman says, "Senator de Gournsey?"

She gives him a somber smile. Says nothing.

There's a line to get inside the church. Ursula is impressed by the turnout. All these people, the accumulation of two lives—their friends, their coworkers, their neighbors, the mailman, probably, and the woman from the dry cleaner's, fellow country-club members, their children's teachers and coaches, the dog groomer. Ursula works twenty hours a day to ensure that American citizens are free and able to create this kind of community. But she's jealous too. If Ursula died and her mourners were limited to those who felt genuine love and affection for her, the crowd would be three: Jake, Bess, and her mother.

Funerals are sobering for more than one reason. Everyone must ask: *What will people say about me?*

Ursula searches for someone, anyone, she recognizes. She attended three of Cooper's weddings—there was one other, an elopement to the Caribbean somewhere—so surely she will find a familiar face. Cooper's friend Frazier Dooley, the coffee mogul (Ursula remembers him because Jake pointed him out on the cover of *Forbes*), is there with his—girlfriend? wife?—who looks less like the punk-rock queen Ursula remembers and more like a proper trophy wife with sculpted arms and a Stella McCartney bag. Money will iron the kinks out of anyone, Ursula thinks somewhat sadly. Standing with them is a kid about Bess's age, looking handsome but uncomfortable in his suit, blond forelock falling into his face. He must be Frazier's son.

Marriage material for Bess! Ursula thinks, to cheer herself up. She already jokes about Bess marrying money, which Jake finds offensive.

She waits in line to pay her respects because part of the point of coming—the entire point—is so Cooper knows that Ursula cared enough to show up. It's only Cooper and his sister receiving people. Ursula studies the sister; she can't come up with the woman's name.

Maddie is what presents in Ursula's mind, though she knows that's not right. And what's worse is the mortifying memory that seeing Not-Maddie elicits. The bathroom of the country club, Ursula in the throes of morning sickness when she was first pregnant with Bess, back when she thought—no, was *convinced*—that Bess was Anders's child. And hadn't Ursula nearly confessed this to Not-Maddie?

Mallory—that's her name!

Ursula had come very close to confessing that hideous idea to Mallory Blessing, a complete stranger. She had stopped herself just in time because somewhere in her mind's eye, she saw the trajectory of Mallory confiding in her brother and Cooper then feeling he needed to share the news with Jake.

There's a hand on Ursula's back. She turns to see an attractive woman in head-to-toe black Eileen Fisher with a stylish asymmetrical haircut and a chunky statement necklace.

"Senator de Gournsey?" she says. "I'm Leland Gladstone."

The woman's voice is brimming with easy self-confidence; she announces her name as though Ursula might recognize it. Does Ursula *know* Leland Gladstone? The name sounds vaguely familiar. Is she a newscaster? A columnist? Ursula can't think any further because now it's her turn to pay her respects.

Cooper sees her and his eyes widen; he checks behind her. "Jake's not here, is he?" His voice sounds nearly hostile.

Ursula hugs Cooper. "I'm so sorry, Coop. Jake is in Atlanta on business and couldn't get away. He sends his condolences, of course."

Cooper nods. He looks overcome, exhausted and beyond exhausted, weary. "Of course," he says. "Thank you for coming." He looks past Ursula to Leland Gladstone, and his face softens. "Hey, Lee."

That's it, then; Ursula has been dismissed. She feels a tiny bit put out. She is, after all, a United States senator, and she made time for this today. But that, she supposes, was Jake's point; there are so many people here that no one is special, and to be a special person and expect special treatment is just obnoxious.

Ursula moves on to the sister, Mallory. Whereas Cooper looks tired, Mallory appears absolutely devastated. Her eyes are like empty sockets; probably, she has taken a pill. She squints at Ursula hard, like she's looking into the sun, and then she checks behind Ursula—looking for Jake, most likely. Because these are *Jake's* people, not Ursula's.

"Hello?" Mallory says in a way that seems very nonplussed. But then she must remember her manners because she offers her stiff, cold hand. "Thank you for coming, Senator."

"Ursula, please." She shakes Mallory's hand, although she wants to give the poor woman a hug. How awful for her, losing both parents in one fell swoop like that. "Jake wanted to come but he's away on business. He sends his condolences."

Mallory nods, though it's not clear that she's registering who Jake is.

"We're very sorry, Mallory. Sorry for your loss."

"Okay," Mallory whispers. She, too, peers beyond Ursula to see Leland Gladstone, at which point Mallory breaks down and the two women embrace and rock back and forth, wailing. Ursula looks on for a moment and feels nearly jealous. Ursula doesn't have a single girlfriend she could cry with like that. She never has.

An usher leads Ursula to the second row. She protests, whispering, "I should be in the back. I hardly..." But the back of the church is standing room only; the last available seats are up front. Ursula internally cringes. She hardly knew Mr. and Mrs. Blessing but she's getting this prime real estate because she's a senator. Jake was right; she shouldn't have come. He always knows best. He's a social genius; he can read people and situations better than anyone she knows. He should be an ambassador. Why is he not an ambassador? Ursula would like to walk right out of the church, but she's made her bed, so now she has to lie in it; she sits down. The woman who was behind her in line, Mallory's friend Leland Gladstone, takes the seat next to her.

Leland leans in and whispers, "I have tissues if you need them, and licorice drops. Would you like a licorice drop?"

Ursula is grateful for the kindness, however perfunctory. "Yes, please," she says. "I'd love one."

Leland opens a fancy little tin, European maybe, and hands Ursula a frosted hard candy the size of a pea. "I've been Mallory's best friend since childhood," she says. "I knew Kitty and Senior my entire life. I can't remember not knowing them."

"Mallory is lucky to have you," Ursula says.

Leland gives a dry laugh. "I don't know about that," she says. "I'm difficult."

"Well, then," Ursula says. "That makes two of us."

"Can I ask you a question?" Leland says.

"Sure," Ursula says—but then the organ music starts and everyone in the church rises.

"We'll save it for later," Leland says.

At the graveside, Leland links her arm through Mallory's. On Mallory's left are Coop and Fray, Fray's girlfriend, Anna, who looks nothing like the punk rocker Leland was promised, and Link. Leland's mother, Geri, is on the opposite side of the two graves with her new boyfriend, John Smith, whom she met on Match.com. (Leland wants her mother to make sure that John Smith is in fact this guy's name because it sounds like an alias, and John Smith has the bland looks and mild manner of someone who's trying to erase an unsavory past. The last thing Leland wants to see is Geri duped by some scam artist who meets lonely divorcées on Match.com and then takes them for everything they're worth.) Leland's father and Sloane are standing behind Leland somewhere. It should be the other way around—Geri was Kitty's best friend, so she should be standing on the side with the family while Steve and Sloane watch from afar, but Leland won't say anything.

Kitty and Senior are dead. That's all that matters.

The silver lining—and yes, Leland does know how egregious it is that she's managed to find a silver lining at the funeral of her best friend's parents—is that Leland now has Senator Ursula de Gournsey's cell phone number and e-mail address. Ursula has graciously agreed to be interviewed for *Leland's Letter*. Leland can't believe it. It's *such* a coup! She wants to tell Mallory, but naturally, it will have to wait.

*   *   *

After the burial, there's a reception at the country club. It's a reception worthy of Kitty Blessing—passed hors d'oeuvres (Leland recalls how much Kitty loved gooey Brie and chutney on a water cracker) and a buffet for three hundred that includes carving stations of ham and prime rib. There's a chamber quartet and an open bar. It's quite lovely and Leland marvels that Cooper and Mallory managed to arrange all this. She wonders if perhaps Kitty left the staff at the club pages of instructions and a blank check in case of her and Senior's untimely demise. At least twice, Leland scans the room expecting to see Kitty. But that's the thing about death—Kitty is no longer. Kitty and Senior are gone, they're never coming back, and how is that *possible?* The rest of the world continues, the club is exactly the same, the Deckers and the Whipps are here—they're talking with Geri and John Smith; no doubt they want to check out the new guy—plus every single person Leland and Mallory and Cooper and Fray knew growing up. All still alive, drinking white wine or bourbon or crisp martinis, plucking tiny crab cakes off passing trays, smearing Bremner wafers with Brie, willfully ignoring the fact that someday they, too, will die and everyone will cry, then hit the raw bar.

Ursula de Gournsey is not at the reception. She had a four o'clock meeting back at the Capitol, she said. The mere phrase *back at the Capitol* made Leland's nipples harden. She loves powerful women.

Leland had realized, sort of, that Cooper's friend Jake, whom Leland had dinner with decades ago on Nantucket, was married to Ursula de Gournsey, but that still didn't prepare Leland for finding the woman standing in front of her in the receiving line. UDG may not be the most powerful woman in politics—

there's Hillary, Palin, Pelosi, and Feinstein—but she is certainly a media darling. Luckily, Leland has always been good at thinking on her feet. *Leland's Letter, tens of thousands of subscribers, ninety-eight percent women, eighty-five percent college-educated, meaningful content across a wide spectrum, would love to interview you, let my readers get a woman-to-woman understanding of you, wouldn't take much time at all, a concise phone call, I'm not interested in wasting anyone's time, not yours, not mine.*

The no-time-wasted line seemed to secure Ursula's interest. *Sounds good,* she said. *Here's my contact info.* Hand on Leland's arm. *And thank you for being so kind to me.*

"Would you please get me another?" Mallory asks as she hands Leland her empty martini glass. "Dirty. As dirty as Bridger will make it, plisssss."

"And how about some water, Mal?" Leland says. The reception is winding down. Steve and Sloane are—weirdly? miraculously?—driving Geri and John home. The loss of the Blessings has apparently softened her parents' utter disdain of each other and now they're all chummy. Or maybe not. Maybe Geri just wants to smooch with John Smith in the back seat to prove some kind of twisted point.

"I'll drink water later," Mallory says. "Right now, I'm drinking gin."

Leland obliges, asking Mr. Bridger the bartender—he's been at the club for so long that Leland remembers him making her Shirley Temples—for a dirty martini. "Really dirty, Mallory said, whatever that means."

Mr. Bridger shakes his head and says, "Damn shame." He means the Blessings, not Mallory's drink order—she thinks. When Mr. Bridger hands Leland the cloudy drink with three olives speared on a toothpick, he says, "You ever get married?"

"God, no!" Leland says with more gusto than she feels. She must be a little tipsy as well because she adds, "I was a lesbian for a while, you know. Now I don't know what I am." *Lonely* is the answer, Leland thinks. She's lonely. She would be self-conscious about this except for the fact that both Mallory and Cooper are single too. Cooper is four times divorced. Four times! And Mallory just never got married. She had a baby with Fray, but Mallory and Fray weren't a couple for even five minutes. Mallory dates guys on Nantucket, or at least Leland *thinks* she does. It seems odd. Mallory is so pretty and so smart; she would be a catch for any man. Leland thinks back to herself and Mallory playing records in Leland's bedroom, stuffing socks into their bras and singing into their hairbrushes. Is there something wrong with them?

"Is there something wrong with us?" Leland asks later. They are in the Blessing house, in the "library," which Kitty decorated like an English hunting lodge; there's a print of a dead pheasant over the stone fireplace and an antique branding iron with the initials CB on the hearth next to a pair of leather bellows. Mallory and Leland are alone, sitting on the deep suede sofa. There's a wet bar in the room so they can continue drinking at a brisk pace and there's also a closet where Senior kept his stereo, a turntable, and his vinyl collection—Neil Sedaka, the Beach Boys, the Spinners. Mallory has put on the Beatles' *Revolver*. Night has fallen early, as it does in late October.

Mallory lit a fire, and there's a lamp with a rosy shade in the corner. It's cozy; they're alone. Coop took Link to see *Free Birds*. He wanted to think about something else for a while, he said.

"Something wrong with us?" Mallory says.

"We never got married," Leland says. "Fifi and I were together ten years, but…"

"Would you have married her if you could have back then?" Mallory asks. She's down at the end of the sofa, her stocking feet resting on the coffee table. She's drinking Tanqueray and tonic, because that's what's in her father's bar.

"Fifi isn't the marrying type," Leland says. Even saying the woman's name makes her throat ache.

"But she is the maternal type," Mallory says.

Yes, Fifi now has a child, a son named Kilroy—conceived via sperm donor—who's five. Every once in a while, Leland will see Fifi at literary events with Kilroy in tow, and Leland always leaves immediately. She yearns to have a conversation with Fifi but she refuses to be the one to initiate it. She can't believe Fifi hasn't called her or texted her to say congratulations on *Leland's Letter*. Surely, she must know about it? Her friends and colleagues must be reading it? Leland has decided to just wait. Someday, Fifi will realize that she loves Leland and has always loved Leland. "I believe Fifi will be back in my life someday. Everything works out the way it's supposed to, in the end."

"Do you believe that?" Mallory asks. "Do you think my parents were supposed to be mowed down on the side of the road like…like possums or raccoons? Because that's what they ended up as, you know, Lee. Roadkill."

"It's time for you to go to bed," Leland says. "It's

been a long day. Where are the pills Dr. Roche gave you? You're taking one and so am I."

"I'm not ready for bed," Mallory says. She sounds like she used to when she was nine years old and Senior and Kitty were enforcing their strict bedtime—eight o'clock on weeknights and nine o'clock on weekends. Leland started sleeping over here in third grade, though they would more often stay at Leland's house because Leland had the downstairs rec room and the hot tub and the garage fridge filled with soda, plus Steve and Geri let her stay up as late as she wanted. But when Leland and Mallory entered high school, the pendulum swung back the other way and they would more often sleep here at the Blessings so they could see what Cooper and Frazier were doing. Fray had kissed Leland for the first time in the den of this house while they watched *Flashdance*.

Leland had forgotten about that.

"There's something I want to tell you," Mallory says, sitting up straight now. "It's a secret. A real secret, the kind that nobody knows except for me and one other person."

Leland knows she should stop Mallory from divulging a secret while completely blotto on the night of her parents' funeral. What is Mallory about to say? That Kitty was having an affair with Mr. Bridger? That Senior was wanted by the FBI for tax fraud? Something about Cooper and one of his four ex-wives? They could hold an entire symposium on what's up with Cooper.

"What is it?" Leland asks.

"You have to promise not to tell anyone."

"I promise." Leland says this in good faith, but, come on, they're forty-four years old, so by now they realize that no secret in the history of the world has ever been successfully kept. The truth always comes out. Or maybe it doesn't. Maybe there are millions, indeed trillions, of secrets that get buried in dark, rectangular holes like the ones Kitty's and Senior's coffins were lowered into.

"I have a Same Time Next Year," Mallory says.

Leland repeats the sentence in her brain, hoping it will make some sense. Nope. "Excuse me?"

"I have a person in my life," Mallory says. "A man whom I see one weekend per year. Like in the movie *Same Time, Next Year.*"

Same Time, Next Year; Leland vaguely recalls it. Maybe Geri had it on one long-ago Sunday afternoon; maybe it was rainy and there was a chicken roasting in the oven for supper. Maybe Geri asked Leland to come watch with her for a minute and maybe Leland was young enough that she obliged her mother rather than running upstairs to listen to the weekly countdown on 98 Rock as she finished her homework or write notes to pass to her friends the next morning in the hallway. Maybe she came in a third of the way through—the man, Hawkeye from *M*A*S*H,* was wearing a wide-collared jacket and a string of beads to indicate that he was a new-age enlightened man of the 1970s. Maybe Geri had explained the premise—this seemingly normal, suburban-looking couple meet for a fling one weekend per year over the course of decades, and as the times change, so do they.

Maybe Geri had said, *It sounds like a heavenly arrangement, actually.*

"Wait a minute," Leland says. "You do?"

"I do. And I'm in love with him. I've always been

in love with him. But it's contained, like in a hermetically sealed box. It has never leaked out into real life. It's come close. But yeah, me and him, one weekend a year, for a long time now. And nobody knows but me and him. And now you."

"Why are you telling me?" Leland says. She's not sure there's such a thing as a relationship that exists in a hermetically sealed box. "Was he at the funeral?"

"No."

"Does he know about your parents?"

"He must."

"He must?"

"I'm telling you because I need to confess," Mallory says. "I know it's stupid, but a part of me believes…" She scrunches her eyes up and emits a couple of throaty sobs. Poor Mal. They're sitting in the library with their drinks in Senior and Kitty's house but Senior and Kitty are in coffins in the ground. Leland leans over and puts an arm around Mallory's back.

"It's okay, Mal," she says.

Mallory shakes her head. She's all clogged up. Leland hurries to the powder room for tissues. She's been a half-hearted friend to Mallory since the beginning, always believing for some reason that she was superior and therefore didn't have to try as hard, but now she wants to make up for it. If Mallory feels like she has to confess about her Same Time Next Year, then fine. Leland will accept the information without judgment.

Mallory mops her face with a tissue, gets in a couple clear breaths, composes herself somewhat. "Part of me believes that what happened to Kitty and Senior is my fault. Because of this thing I've been doing." She pauses. "The other person, the man…he's married."

"Well, yeah," Leland says. "I figured. Otherwise…I mean, if he weren't married, you two would just be together all the time. Or more frequently. But whatever, Mal. What happened to your parents was a random, stupid, senseless accident. It doesn't have anything to do with this other thing. I can assure you of that."

"But you *can't* assure me."

Leland takes her friend's hand. "Tell me about him. If no one else knows about him, then you must have a bunch of pent-up stuff you've been waiting to share."

"Not really," Mallory says. "In some ways, there isn't enough to share. He comes every year, we do the same things, we have a sort of routine—the things we eat, the songs we listen to—and then he leaves."

"You don't call him?" Leland says. "You don't *text* him?"

Mallory shakes her head.

"I find that hard to believe."

"It's even harder to do than to believe," Mallory says.

"And you see him *every* year? What about Link?"

"He's always with Fray when this person comes," Mallory says. "It's at the end of the summer."

Leland is starting to picture it: A sun-soaked weekend, just Mallory and her mystery dream man in that romantic cottage on the beach. They make love and feed each other fresh figs and sing along to the Carpenters and then he leaves; Mallory stands in the doorway, blowing him kisses. They flip the hourglass over again.

It sounds like a heavenly arrangement, actually.

"Still, it's amazing, right, that you've never missed a year? Does his wife *know*?"

Mallory shakes her head. "His wife…I can't even

get into everything about his wife." She drops her voice. "She came to the funeral. By herself."

"She...*what?*" Leland says. And suddenly, she pulls away from Mallory, just a few inches, nothing dramatic, but she needs space. The wife came to the funeral alone. Every year *for a long time now*. How long? Since the beginning, when Mallory inherited the cottage? Leland hadn't planned on asking the guy's name because she wanted to respect Mallory's privacy and also because she'd assumed it was someone she didn't know.

The end of summer.

Leland racks her brain to remember her visit that first summer. They had surprised Fray, that she remembers, and she and Fray had nearly hooked up. Cooper was there, and his friend from Hopkins, Jake McCloud. What does Leland remember about Jake? Aaaaarrrgh! Very little. If he hadn't ended up marrying Ursula de Gournsey, he would have been erased from Leland's memory forever.

But he *had* ended up marrying Ursula de Gournsey.

Who came to the funeral by herself. Why? Why had she been at the funeral without Jake when Jake was the one who was friends with Coop? "Is it Jake McCloud?" Leland whispers.

Mallory releases a breath.

"Oh my God, Mal."

"I know."

"Mal."

"Believe me, I know."

"In the spirit of full disclosure..." Leland says.

Mallory looks up.

"I sat with Ursula at the service. I was shocked to see her, obviously. And this might sound horrible—

no, it definitely *will* sound horrible—but I got her e-mail and her cell phone number. I asked her if she would do an interview for *Leland's Letter* and she said yes."

"Oh, Lee."

"I'm sorry, I had no idea. But yes, I am that friend who took full advantage of your parents' funeral to further her own career. It's just...I didn't know."

"But you know now," Mallory says. "So, please..."

Please *what*? Leland wonders. Mallory doesn't say anything else. Her head falls back against the sofa and her eyes close. Leland considers trying to get Mallory upstairs to her childhood bedroom but it feels like an impossible task. She covers Mallory with the deep red chenille blanket that has lived in this room for as long as Leland can remember and then she succumbs to the allure of the other half of the sofa.

So, please...what? Leland thinks as she falls asleep.

Leland wants to do an extended interview with Ursula de Gournsey, but because of the situation with Mallory, she decides it's best not to dive too deeply into Ursula's life. Instead, she features Ursula in her Dirty Dozen—twelve questions, some rapid-fire and fun, some provocative. Turns out, this suits Ursula better, anyway. She doesn't have time for Leland to do a detailed profile.

Twelve questions is a lot, Ursula says. She hopes they can blow through them in thirty minutes, forty-five tops.

"Or I could e-mail them to you?" Leland says. "So you have time to mull them over?"

"It'll go straight into the black hole," Ursula says. "This isn't constituent business or legislation, which makes it personal, and my personal business gets triaged last. Let's do this now. Go ahead."

Leland's Letter

Dirty Dozen with Senator Ursula de Gournsey

1. Gadget you can't live without?

There's a pause on the other end of the phone.

"Do people ever say their vibrators?" Ursula asks.

"All the time," Leland says.

"That's not my answer," Ursula says. She sounds nearly offended, as though Leland were the one who suggested it. "I was just wondering."

My BlackBerry.

2. Song you want to hear on your deathbed?

"Let It Be."

3. Five minutes of perfect happiness?

"Cool-down after a good, hard run on the treadmill," Ursula says.

"Do you want to think about that answer a little longer?" Leland says. "Maybe mention your husband or your daughter?"

"Oh," Ursula says.

Sixty-degree day, blue sky, fifty-yard-line seats, cashmere sweater and jeans, sitting between my husband and daughter, Notre Dame versus Boston College.

4. Moment you'd like to do over?
   Accepting money from the NRA.
   Brave answer, Leland thinks. *This interview is looking up.*

5. Bad habit?
   Correcting people's grammar.

6. Last supper?
   "I don't understand the question," Ursula says.
   "What would you like your final meal to be?" Leland says.
   "You mean before I die?"
   "Yes."
   "People are interested in this?"
   "Very. It's a little more in depth than just asking your favorite food. You get to pick a meal."
   "Oh," Ursula says. "Cereal, I guess."
   "Cereal?"
   Rice Krispies with sliced banana and skim milk.

7. Most controversial opinion?
   "Men are not the enemy," Ursula says. "I realize that's going to be *very* controversial for your readership. But what I've found in Congress and in my professional life in general is that men want women to succeed. It's the women who are cloak-and-dagger."
   "Hmmmm," Leland says. She's not overjoyed with this answer. The whole basis of *Leland's Letter* is that women can learn and grow from the experiences of other women.

"I hope that changes by the time my daughter, Bess, is grown," Ursula says. "When my mother was young, she was focused on helping my father succeed. That was her job. And then in my generation, our generation, women became focused on their own success. The logical next step is that women will become not only supportive of one another but *vested* in one another's success." She pauses. "But we aren't there yet."

Women have to support each other, be vested in one another's success. Men are not the enemy.

8. In a box of crayons, what color are you?

"Black," Ursula says.

"Black?"

"My father used to say I was as serious as a heart attack," Ursula says. "Plus, you outline everything in black. It's a hardworking color."

"Right, but—"

"I'm not going to say yellow or pink or purple. My answer is black."

Black.

9. Proudest achievement?

"Being elected to the United States Senate is probably too obvious," Ursula says. "I would bring up the welfare-reform bill, but that would put everyone to sleep." Ursula pauses. "I guess I'll say my marriage."

Leland jumps like she's been poked in the ribs. "Your marriage?"

"Yes. I've been married for sixteen years, but Jake and I have been together for over thirty years. Honestly, I don't know why he stays with me."

Leland waits a beat. *Move on to the next question!* she tells herself. But does she? No. "You're an intelligent, accomplished woman."

"I'm a witch at home. I'm demanding and ungrateful and I have to schedule in family time, though that's the first thing I cancel when things get busy. I'm aware that if I don't start having some fun with my daughter, she'll grow up either hating me or being just like me or both. And yet I have this idea that if I stop working, even for an hour, the country will fall apart. People throw around the word *workaholic* like it's no big deal, like it's maybe even a good thing. But I suffer from the disease. I'm a workaholic. I'm addicted to work. So, yeah, I'm not sure why Jake stays, but I'm grateful."

My sixteen-year marriage to Jake McCloud.

10. Celebrity crush?
   Ted Koppel.

11. Favorite spot in America?

"I should probably pick someplace in the state of Indiana," Ursula says. "But I already mentioned Notre Dame stadium, and where else is there? Fishers? Carmel?"

"Are those places that inspire you?" Leland asks.

"I wish I could pick someplace magical, like Nantucket," Ursula says, and Leland flinches again. "Jake loves Nantucket, but I've never been. He goes every year for a guys' trip. I keep telling him I'm going to crash one of these years."

Oh God, oh God, Leland thinks. *Please stop talking about Nantucket.*

"I love Newport, Rhode Island," Ursula says. "But as bizarre as this sounds, I think I'm going to say Las Vegas is my favorite spot. I worked on a case there when I first went into private practice..." Ursula breaks off and Leland assumes she's just gotten a text or another call but then she realizes, from her wavering tone, that Ursula is overcome. "Those were happy days. Vegas is...crazytown, right? But it's unapologetically *itself,* and I appreciated that. I loved it there, for whatever reason."

Las Vegas.

12. Title of your autobiography?

"Straight up the Fairway," Ursula says. "That's in regard to my politics. I'm centrist. People might not agree with all of my stances, but they won't disagree with all of them either. I believe in common sense and hard work and American capitalism and the Constitution and the equality under the law of every single American."

"Okay." Leland is very liberal, just shy of socialist. She doesn't want to get into a political debate here; however, she thinks that "straight up the fairway" is a compromise and a cop-out. She had wanted Ursula de Gournsey to come across as some kind of Superwoman. But maybe the takeaway for the readers of *Leland's Letter* will be this: A woman with real power in Washington is just as self-critical and beleaguered as the rest of us.

Leland also finds herself hobbled by her secret knowledge. Does Ursula de Gournsey have it all? Anyone who reads the Dirty Dozen will see the answer is *no*. But only Leland knows that Ursula de Gournsey has even less than she realizes.

Straight Up the Fairway.

The Dirty Dozen with Ursula de Gournsey goes live on January 20 in advance of the State of the Union, and Leland waits for Mallory to call in a rage. Mallory didn't explicitly ask Leland *not* to do an interview with Ursula, but her "So, please…" had seemed to indicate that she wanted Leland to exercise some kind of restraint. Which she had, because this *isn't* an in-depth profile.

No angry call comes. Instead, Leland receives texts and e-mails and Facebook messages and hits on Twitter and Instagram that say: Loved the piece with UDG! LL is taking it up a notch!!

It takes a few days but eventually, the Dirty Dozen with Ursula de Gournsey goes viral. The answer everyone is talking about is "Men are not the enemy." That line is the subject of an op-ed in the *New York Times* written by the male governor of Nevada, who agrees that men are not the enemy and that men should not be receiving so much blame for social injustice. (The governor is also thrilled with Ursula's answer of "Las Vegas" as her favorite spot in the country.)

The Dirty Dozen with UDG and the attendant

chatter about it result in a near doubling of Leland's audience—she's up to 125,000 readers (one of whom is Ursula de Gournsey herself!) and lures in seventeen new advertisers. *Leland's Letter* is now making enough money for Leland to quit teaching and focus solely on the blog.

Still, Leland worries that she has cashed in on her longest friendship for this success. A week later, Leland looks down at her phone and sees she's received two successive texts from Mallory. She thinks, *Here it comes.* Mallory will say Leland is opportunistic (she is), selfish (ditto), and ruthless (well, yes).

Leland starts reading the texts with trepidation. The first says, Happy birthday, Lee! I love you!

The second text says, Oops, sorry, I thought today was the 29th not the 27th. I'll text you on Wednesday!

Okay, Leland thinks. So Mallory isn't upset about the Dirty Dozen? This is great news because now that Leland has some momentum, she can take *Leland's Letter* to the next level. She can lay claim to some cultural influence. She just needs to keep her foot on the gas and not get slowed down by sticky issues like best friends with hurt feelings.

It's only as Leland is falling asleep that night that she realizes Mallory might not have *seen* the article. It went viral, but that doesn't mean it reached every person in America. Mallory is a single working mother on an island thirty miles off the coast. She's immersed in her school day, her students, Link, the painful and painstaking work of dismantling her parents' financial and business affairs. She might not spend hours online Googling Ursula de Gournsey the way that Leland Googles Fiella Roget and tracks her every move.

Leland opens her laptop (she sleeps with it; she is that pathetic).

Mallory Blessing isn't a subscriber to *Leland's Letter*. Leland's first instinct is to be offended. Her own best friend!

She snaps her laptop shut. Actually, it's a major relief.

Summer #22: 2014

What are we talking about in 2014? Polar vortex; Jimmy Fallon; Flint, Michigan; The Twelfth Man; Vladimir Putin; Malaysia Airlines Flight 17; Ebola; Janet Yellen; mindfulness; Robin Williams; Ferguson, Missouri; CVS; the Oregon Ducks; Cuba; Tim Lincecum; One World Trade Center; Clooney and Amal; ISIS; Minecraft; Hannah, Jessa, Marnie, and Shosh; conscious uncoupling; Tinder; Greg Popovich; "I'm all about that bass (no treble)."

The summer after Mallory's parents are killed…

Okay, wait. She needs a minute just to process this phrase. Her parents killed. Senior and Kitty dead. All through the first half of 2014, Mallory struggles. She wakes up feeling just fine…until she remembers. Then it's like falling into a black, bottomless hole, wind rushing in her ears, vertigo, nausea, a weightlessness, a loss, not only of Senior and Kitty but of herself. There's an assault of emotions, all of them unpleasant, some of them ugly, and the most hideous is guilt. Was Mallory a good daughter? Or even a decent daughter? She fears not.

She resented all the *rules*. Step one, napkin on lap. No yelling to someone in another room; no stomping up the stairs. Bread and rolls were to be broken in half first, then into pieces that were buttered individually. Salt and pepper were always to be passed *together*. Nail polish could be applied only in the bathroom. Thank-you notes were to be written and mailed within three days. There was a list of forbidden TV shows, among them *Prisoner: Cell Block H, Falcon Crest, Hill Street Blues*. No *Rocky Horror. Good morning. Please may I be excused. Hello, Blessing residence.* And above all: Never refer to a person using a pronoun while the person was present. Kitty was a stickler for that one.

Mallory loathed their expectations of her: good grades, good posture, sparkling conversation, spotless driving record, irreproachable work ethic. She had rebelled mentally even as she complied, and she was certain Senior and Kitty could tell. There was nothing her parents had taught her or asked of her that had not served her well. She should have been grateful instead of surly. She should have taken her mother up on her offers of makeup lessons and ballroom dancing. She should have gone shopping with her at the Mazza Gallery; she shouldn't have called the David Yurman earrings Kitty gave her for her fortieth birthday "matronly." Mallory had rejected all of her mother's efforts to refine her. She had joyfully spent her four years at Gettysburg wearing sweatpants, her hair in a scrunchie. She had gotten a *tattoo* her first winter on

Nantucket, a vine that wrapped around her ankle. If anyone had asked her why, she would have said it was just for decoration, for fun, but the real answer was that she reveled in becoming the anti-Kitty.

Mallory avoided the emotional work of dealing with the loss of her parents by focusing on the practical work. What had to happen? Well, immediately, there was the service, burial, and reception to plan. Somehow, Mallory did this on autopilot; Cooper was less than no help. Then there was the house to put on the market, the furnishings to give away or auction off, and Senior's business to sell. Again, Cooper took a pass, so Mallory worked with the family attorney, Jeffrey Todd, and her own attorney, Eileen Beers. During February break from school, Mallory and Link drove down to Baltimore to sort through each room of the Blessing house. Over April break, Link flew to Seattle to see Fray and Anna, who was pregnant with a baby girl, and Mallory and Cooper met in Baltimore to finalize the sale of the house and the business. Even split between them, the money was considerable. To Mallory, it was a fortune. But money, once her largest concern, now meant nothing.

What does Mallory say to herself to fend off the demons?

They were together.

There was no suffering.

They had lived full, happy lives.

She had given them a grandson, whom they both adored.

It wasn't her fault.

The accident had nothing to do with Mallory. She had spoken to both of her parents on Christmas and thanked them for her gifts: a new Wüsthof chef's knife, Malouf linens for her bed, a hardback copy of *The Goldfinch*. They had thanked her for the black-and-white picture of Link and the gift certificate to Woodberry Kitchen. She had told them she loved them. Link had told them he loved them.

Mallory hadn't known about the Yo-Yo Ma tickets, and frankly, she was surprised Kitty had been successful in convincing Senior to go, though he did love Washington in general and the Kennedy Center in particular. Cooper hadn't known about their plans either, but he hadn't been offended. They were two healthy, happy adults, completely self-sufficient. The car they drove was an Audi A4, which Senior had bought the previous spring. There was no reason for the tire to blow other than raw bad luck.

Cooper is of the opinion that when your number comes up, it comes up. Nothing to be done about it.

Mallory tries to adopt this perspective as well, though she has a difficult time. She keeps thinking something went wrong, that there was a mistake; it wasn't supposed to be this way. She wants to fix it. She wakes up in the middle of the night crying. She wants them back. Please—for just a day or an hour or even a minute so that she can tell them she loves them. So she can thank them.

The summer after Mallory's parents are killed, an unlikely savior arrives, and that savior is baseball. Lincoln Dooley is chosen as the starting catcher for the Nantucket U14 travel team. Mallory spends the month of July in the bleachers and behind the backstop at the Delta fields on Nobadeer Farm Road as well as at a dozen fields across Cape Cod and the south shore. As time-consuming and expensive as it is to attend every single game, it's just the preoccupation Mallory needs. The Nantucket U14s are the best team Nantucket has fielded in the history of their baseball program; they have a winning record, which is impressive given that the island has such a small pool of kids. One reason for their success is that ten of the twelve teammates have played together since T-ball. The other reason is the coach, Charlie Suwyn.

Charlie is in his sixties; his own children are grown, he owns a prosperous caretaking business on the island, and he recently lost his wife, Sue, who was the biggest champion of youth sports that Nantucket had ever seen. Charlie's love of the game is infectious, but more than the game, he loves the kids, who are, frankly, at a challenging age. Charlie has schooled his players in strategic baserunning, which is how they often win; the Nantucket team steals home more than any other team it plays. Off the field, Charlie is warm and nurturing. His motto is three words long: *Kids playing baseball.* The players are developing skills, learning sportsmanship, creating a team atmosphere, and having fun. There are many things that are wrong with the world, but this thing is right.

As catcher, Link is the key to the team; he's not as glorified as the pitchers, but he's involved in every pitch of the game. He has a deadly accurate arm, and at least once in every game, he'll throw out someone trying to steal second. He has been inconsistent at the plate and Mallory is never so tense as when he's up to bat. He strikes out a lot, that's fine, but he strikes out *looking,* which is not fine. He bats seventh in the lineup.

Fray hasn't traveled east to see Link play even

once. Mallory knows this bums Link out, though he doesn't talk about it. Mallory sends endless videos with captions that say, *Look at our son!* And *Number 6 is en fuego!* Fray occasionally calls after a game (at Mallory's prompting—*Call now, before the pizza comes!*), and although Mallory hears only Link's side of the conversation, she can tell it's stilted.

The travel season culminates with a week of tournaments in Cooperstown, New York, at the end of July. Mallory splurges on a room at the Otesaga Hotel. The place is filled with history and old-fashioned charm; this is where all the Hall-of-Famers stay when they're in town. In addition to watching a lot of baseball, Mallory squeezes in some pool time and breakfast every morning on the veranda overlooking Otsego Lake.

The living is good; the baseball not so much. Nantucket plays seven games and loses the first six. Link is brilliant behind the plate but abysmal *at* the plate; he strikes out sixteen times. In the final game, however, his luck changes. He hits the ball at his first at bat and it goes sailing over the fence: home run! Mallory is so excited—and so *shocked*—that she starts to cry. Throughout the season, Mallory has pictured her parents up in the sky, sitting in some heavenly version of lawn chairs (like earthly lawn chairs, but comfortable), cheering Link on.

Did Kitty and Senior see that? Home run! Here in Cooperstown!

At Link's second at bat, he hits another home run. *What?* Mallory blinks, confused, but yes, the ball cleared the fence and there goes Link, trotting around the bases, then jumping into the crowd of his assembled teammates at home plate.

His third time at bat, Nantucket is behind by two runs and the bases are loaded. Dewey, the father sitting next to Mallory, says, "What are the chances he does it again?"

"Zero," Mallory says, though she hopes for something better than a strikeout. A single would, maybe, tie the game. The count gets to two and two, and Mallory imagines Senior up out of his heavenly lawn chair shouting, the way he used to at the Orioles games on TV. Then she hears the crack of the bat and the ball goes all the way over the deepest part of the fence and everyone on base scores and while the other parents are jumping up and down, creating cacophony on the metal bleachers, Mallory has her face in her hands. She's sobbing because she isn't sure what happens when people die but she is sure that her parents are here in Cooperstown somewhere— either that or she and Link are carrying Senior and Kitty around inside of them, because they made this happen. She knows they made this happen.

The next day, they drive home. Despite the triumph of the last game, the trip is melancholy. This baseball season was a sweet spot in their lives; Coach Charlie and the other parents have become a family. The games, although not all exciting, were addictive in their own way. Mallory can now tell a ball from a strike from any spot in the park as well as a curve ball from a slider. She has subsisted on hot dogs and peanuts in the shell; she has lived in cutoffs and a visor. Now that the season's over, Mallory won't deny it— she's sad. Link might play next year or he might get a job instead. But even if Link does play, there's no telling which other kids will return, and in any case, it won't be the same. This season is something that can't be repeated; it will just have to live on in everyone's memories. The Nantucket U14s in '14.

It's on this five-hour drive from Cooperstown to Hyannis that Link tells Mallory that he doesn't want to go to Seattle the following week—or at all.

"But…" Mallory says. "Don't you want to see the baby?"

Link pulls out his left earbud. His buddy Cam, the center fielder, is riding home with them, but he's asleep in the back seat. "No," Link says, softly but firmly. "I don't."

"Honey, she's your *sister* and you've never even met her."

"She's too little to know any better," Link says. "I don't want to go."

"But what about your dad and Anna?"

"Anna, ha," Link says. "She doesn't like me."

"What are you talking about? Anna *loves* you." Only a few summers earlier Mallory had been certain she'd lost Link to Anna's influence.

Link shrugs. "I liked summers when we were in Vermont. In Seattle, Dad is always at work, and the house is cold. Anna is either on her phone or on her laptop, and I spend way too much time playing video games. The only day we do stuff together is Sunday, and now there's a baby, so, yeah…I'm not going."

"You don't have the power to decide that, bud, sorry."

"Mom," Link says. "Please don't make me go. I haven't had my summer yet. We haven't sailed, we haven't kayaked. I've barely been in the *ocean*."

"We all make choices," Mallory says. "Your choice was to play baseball."

"What if Dad says it's okay if I don't go?" Link asks. "Then can I stay home?"

Mallory isn't sure how to answer. She has sensed the relationship between Link and Fray deteriorating for a while. Fray used to come to Nantucket all the time, every month. But since he moved to Seattle, he hasn't come once. Not once! Mallory hasn't called him on it because she knows he's busy. He's a wonderful provider for Link, and Mallory figured Fray and Link would reconnect over the month of August like they always did.

She can't stop herself from thinking that if Link doesn't go to Seattle, he will be on Nantucket over Labor Day weekend. Which is not okay. Mallory is sorry, but that is *not okay*.

Is she going to condemn her only child to a month of misery in a house with a newborn just so she can continue her love affair?

Link needs to meet his baby sister, Cassiopeia. Baby Cassie. He needs to spend time with Fray. Link is thirteen years old; it's a crucial time to have a male role model, a *father*.

Surely Fray will agree with this. Fray will never allow Link to skip a summer. Fray will sweeten the deal with Mariners tickets or a father-son camping trip in the San Juan Islands. Anna and the baby will stay home with the cadre of baby nurses. Mallory paints an irresistible picture in her mind: Fray will take his fifty-foot Grady-White over to Friday Harbor to use the luxe cabin of one of the Microsoft execs for a few days. They'll fish for steel-headed trout; they'll see killer whales. They'll build campfires and talk about girls.

"If Dad says it's okay for you to stay on Nantucket,

I'm not going to argue," Mallory says, and this placates Link. He puts his earbud back in.

But Fray will never okay it, Mallory thinks. She has nothing to worry about. Her time with Jake is safe.

Fray okays it.

"What?" Mallory says. She and Link are home now, home sweet home; it's August on Nantucket, the weather is glorious, the water is cool but not cold, and Mallory swims enough to make up for her lost month. She goes to Bartlett's Farm for corn, tomatoes, blueberry pie, broccoli slaw, a bouquet of peach lilies. Baseball has already become a distant memory.

"He said I don't have to if I don't want to," Link says. "He thinks maybe Christmas will be better. We're all going to Hawaii, I guess."

Mallory says, "It's my first Christmas without my parents, but yeah, Hawaii sounds great. Have fun."

"Mom," Link says, and he grabs Mallory around the middle and squeezes her the way he does when the subject of Senior and Kitty comes up. "You can join us."

Mallory laughs through her tears. Yes, she's crying again, for the umpteenth time. Her parents each had their idiosyncrasies. But now she sees that they were her anchors. They were *there*—Kitty with her tennis and her dreams of British royalty, Senior with his pragmatic worldview. Both of them were perplexed about Mallory's partnerless lifestyle not because they disapproved of it but because they loved her and wanted her to find someone.

Mallory calls Fray. In the fourteen years that they have been co-parents, she has never spoken to Fray in anger. But today, yes. Today, she is loaded for bear, as the saying goes.

"You told Link he didn't have to come?" she says by way of greeting. Fray didn't answer his cell so she has ambushed him on his office phone. She sends his secretary, Mrs. Ellison, a large bag of vanilla caramels from Sweet Inspirations every year at Christmas specifically to ensure this kind of emergency access. "What the hell?"

"He doesn't want to come," Fray says. "He was away all summer playing baseball and now he wants to see his friends. I was thirteen once. I get it."

"Don't you want to see *him?*" Mallory asks. "You're his *father*. Don't you want to put your eyes on him, have the birds-and-the-bees talk, introduce him to his sister?"

"His sister has turned the household upside down," Fray says. "Anna has postpartum depression. She's a mess, so she's getting help, and I've hired someone to be with the baby full-time. This isn't a great summer for me, Mal. Frankly, I was relieved."

"Relieved," Mallory says. Postpartum depression is serious; she can't argue with that. Poor Anna. Mallory shouldn't send Link out to that kind of fraught situation.

"It's not forever," Fray says. "I told Link we'd take him at Christmas."

"That's very nice, but that plan leaves me alone at Christmas, and I just can't handle that this year," Mallory says.

There's silence. Fray clears his throat. "That hadn't occurred to me. And I'm sure Thanksgiving will be difficult for you too."

"I need Link at the holidays," Mallory says. "The

holidays are mine, August is yours. That's how we do it. That's what works."

"But not this year," Fray says. "I'm so sorry."

Link isn't going to Seattle for a month, but what about for two weeks? Or a week? Or just over the long weekend before school, Labor Day weekend? By Labor Day, Anna might be feeling better.

"It's too far for a weekend trip," Link says. He sounds seventy years old, Mallory thinks. He sounds like Senior. "Besides, I want to go stay with Uncle Coop over Labor Day weekend."

"Uncle Coop?" Mallory finally gets a clear breath.

"The Black Keys are playing at Merriweather Post Pavilion," Link says. "I was hoping maybe Uncle Coop would take me."

Mallory goes online and buys two seats, row C center, for the Black Keys at Merriweather Post on Saturday, August 30. Link texts all his friends to brag. Mallory steps out onto the deck and sits in her spot in the sun; the boards have two worn-down ovals where her butt cheeks have rested so often for the past twenty-one years. She runs through the reasons this is a good development—Link gets to see his favorite band live in concert, he'll get some quality time with another male role model…and he will not be here on Nantucket.

Mallory calls Cooper. She has a momentary panic that he already has plans that weekend.

"Hey, are you free Saturday, August thirtieth?" she asks.

"Hey, Mal," Cooper says. His voice is flat. His natural pep and charm have diminished since Kitty and Senior died. So another benefit of sending Link is that it will cheer Cooper up—win-win-win! "Yeah, I am. Why?"

Mallory uses a measured, concerned-mom voice rather than a snake-oil-salesman voice. Link doesn't want to see Fray, so he's staying on Nantucket instead; Mallory wanted to surprise him with something special after his incredible performance in Cooperstown and so she was hoping Coop would be willing to host Link over Labor Day. He wants to see the Black Keys at Merriweather Post. Mallory already bought two tickets, row three.

"I probably put the cart before the horse on the tickets," Mallory says. "I'm sorry."

"I'm psyched about the concert," Coop says. "The concert's not the problem."

"Okay?" Mallory says. "What *is* the problem?"

"The problem is, I know what you're doing," Coop says. "I *know* what you're *doing,* Mal."

Mallory focuses on the sparkling surface of the ocean, the waves turning, turning, turning. "What am I doing?"

"You want me to say it? You want me to *say* it? Fine, I'll say it. You're getting rid of Link." He pauses. "So you can be alone over Labor Day weekend. I know about you and Jake, Mal."

Is Mallory surprised to hear this? Yes. Yes, she is. She wants to throw her phone into the water.

Jake told Mallory years ago that Cooper seemed off—maybe sour, maybe indifferent. They didn't get together anymore. Mallory wasn't concerned by this. People grew apart. Adults had busy lives. Hell, Mallory now sees Apple only at school and maybe once or twice over the summer because Apple is married with nine-year-old twins; she's *busy*. Cooper has such a tumultuous personal life that he might not have evenings to spare, especially with Jake back and forth to Indiana.

But now.

"Coop," she says.

"I don't want to be a party to your deception," he says. "It's the adultery I object to, yes. But also, Mal, he's *using* you."

"No," she says.

"He has Ursula," Coop says. "You have…nobody. It kills me thinking about you spending most of the year by yourself, waiting for him to return. You're like one of the sea captain's wives, standing on your widow's walk. It's heartbreaking."

"It's not like that," Mallory says. Mallory had relationships with JD, with Bayer, with Scott Fulton—and she had relations with Fray. She has hardly been alone all these years, but she never found anyone she loved or even liked as much as Jake and she didn't see the point in settling.

She has always felt she has agency in her relationship with Jake. She was the one who decided, that first summer, not to turn it into something bigger. If she had, she's sure the relationship would have ended, maybe even ended badly, and Jake would be nothing but a name from her past. As unconventional as their romance has been, Mallory believes she made the right choice.

She isn't famous like Ursula; she isn't a scene-stealer. She's just a person—a good person, she has always believed. To Coop, it must seem like she has zero integrity, but where her relationship with Jake is concerned, Mallory would argue she has nothing but integrity. She has never taken more than her share. Their weekends together have a certain purity; they aren't dirty or mean-spirited. She's not trying to fool herself; she knows it's wrong. But it's also right.

If Mallory tells Coop this, will he understand? He may; he may not. She isn't sure what kind of warped rulebook he uses when it comes to love. Or maybe she's the one with the warped rulebook. Or maybe there is no rulebook.

Mallory has a ripcord. Will she pull it?

"I've lost a lot already this year," she says. "I can't give him up too."

Yes, she is using the bald, gaping, awful fact of their parents' death.

She might also say: *If you hadn't left your own bachelor party, this would never have happened.*

"Okay," Cooper says. "Send him down."

Mallory breathes out a "Thank you."

"Oh, and by the way, I'm dating someone new," Cooper says. "Her name is Amy. She's a psychologist. I can have her talk to Link, see if he's okay."

"He's okay," Mallory says. "Maybe you should have Amy see if *you're* okay." She cringes, wondering if it's wise to crack a joke at Coop's expense.

He laughs. "Amen," he says.

Summer #23: 2015

What are we talking about in 2015? "Hotline Bling"; Stuart Scott; the Affordable Care Act; Paul Ryan; American Sniper; James Corden; the California drought; Hamilton; FIFA; Subway Jared; American Pharoah; Fitbit; Syria; Bill Cosby; San Bernardino; Ashley Madison; dabbing; Brian Williams; Selina, Amy, Gary, Dan, Jonah, and Mike; "Love Wins."

Ursula still reads four newspapers every morning, though she has added the *Skimm*—and, on Fridays, *Leland's Letter*. The Dirty Dozen feature on her has been viewed over two million times, but it's not the number of people who have seen it that matters. It's the *kind* of people.

On the negative side, it turns out that A. J. Renninger reads *Leland's Letter*. She publicly criticized Ursula for her comment about women supporting each other and becoming vested in one another's success.

"The senator, whom I counted as a dear friend, didn't offer any help while I was running for mayor," she said in a statement to *Politico*. "And I believe that's because she didn't want to view me as the most powerful woman in this city."

Ursula had nearly called AJ then and there to

set the record straight: She hadn't supported or endorsed AJ because she didn't believe AJ would be the best mayor. That AJ had won anyway came as no surprise; her fund-raising efforts were so impressive that Ursula was sure that she promised kickbacks and favors to special interests. Ursula didn't attend the inaugural party because she had "other plans"—she'd worked late, gotten on the treadmill, and had cereal for dinner.

On the positive side, it turns out that the features editor of *Vogue* reads *Leland's Letter,* and she offers Ursula a profile, which is published in the 2015 spring fashion issue. Ursula models power suits by Carolina Herrera, Stella McCartney, and Tracy Reese. The photographs are probably more enticing than the article, though it's a substantive piece, and at the end the writer, Rachel Weisberg, asks Ursula if she's planning on running for president.

Ursula says, "I'm not ready yet, but I wouldn't rule it out for the future."

This statement sets off a string of firecrackers. In a moment of extreme hubris, Ursula showed the article to her daughter, Bess. Bess is fourteen, a freshman at Sidwell Friends, and she has very much come into her own. She plays volleyball and the flute; she reads incessantly about social injustice. The novels she likes best feature marginalized adolescents from third-world countries. Are you walking across Africa with only one red pencil? Then Bess McCloud wants to read your story. Ursula secretly loves how passionate and devoted Bess is to inclusivity and diversity, even though Bess has started going to the mat against some of Ursula's own policies. Bess, like so many young people, is a bleeding-heart liberal.

Ursula thought Bess might like to see the *Vogue* article because Ursula makes her position on certain sensitive issues clear. Ursula wants to pass legislation requiring universal background checks for gun purchases; this simple measure will do wonders, she believes, in keeping assault rifles and bump stocks out of the hands of maniacs, especially underage maniacs. She thinks health care should remain privatized, and she's determined to tackle prescription-drug costs. She has a healthy LGBTQA agenda that protects rights for civilians and military personnel. Ursula is an "independent," a "centrist," a "political Switzerland," but she wants Bess to see what that means, detailed in glossy-paged black-and-white.

However, the next morning when Bess comes into the kitchen, where Jake is making her omelet as usual and Ursula is on her laptop, skimming the *South Bend Tribune*—stormwater drainage issues are on the front page, *again*—she says, "So. You're running for president?"

Jake spins around, spatula in hand. "What?"

Later that day, Ursula's mother, Lynette, calls. Whereas Bess and Jake were both visibly upset about the idea of Ursula running for president, Lynette is elated. "You know your father predicted this when you were seven years old, glued to the Watergate trial. You knew what impeachment was before you knew how to ride a bicycle. I told the girls over lunch at the University Club today and they're all going to vote for you."

Great, Ursula thinks. *That's five people.*

"I didn't announce that I was running for president," Ursula says to her mother, the same thing she said to Bess, to Jake. "I said I wouldn't rule it out. And

I promise that when I do announce, you will not find out from *Vogue* magazine. We will have discussed it thoroughly first."

Jake and Bess had seemed skeptical about this answer; Lynette, disappointed.

Ursula reads *Leland's Letter* now because she's grateful—the overwhelming response to the Dirty Dozen column flipped a switch and Ursula has become intriguing (and maybe even inspiring) to people outside the Beltway—but also because Ursula enjoys it. *Leland's Letter* is smart. There are articles about sex and relationships, books, art, music, sports, movies and TV, food and wine, travel. It's one-stop shopping aimed at American women who want to read about more than just fashion, beauty, and home decorating. Ursula reads a terrific interview with the eighty-year-old poet Mary Oliver; she reads about the French entrepreneurs who rehabilitated the reputation of rosé; she reads about Berthe Morisot's place among the other (all-male) Impressionist painters in 1890s Paris.

Every single article is fascinating, exhaustively researched, and brilliantly written. Frankly, Ursula enjoys *Leland's Letter* more than the *Washington Post* and the *Times* put together.

Ursula spends the first two weeks of August in South Haven, Michigan, visiting her mother. Lynette de Gournsey sold the big house in South Bend and bought a condo on St. Joe's River and this beautiful vacation home on Lake Michigan. Ursula is sitting in an Adirondack chair on her mother's expansive, shady lawn on a bluff overlooking the lake as she opens

Leland's Letter on her laptop. Jake has taken Bess to the Golden Brown bakery for "breakfast" (meaning cookies) and her mother has a "committee meeting" (meaning mimosas with her best friends, Sue and Melissa). The lead article in *Leland's Letter* this week is titled "Same Time Next Year: Can It Save Modern Marriage?"

Ursula clicks on it eagerly. She would love to know how to save modern marriage. If marriage is an "ebb and flow," then she and Jake are in a long ebb, or possibly a permanent, stagnant swamp. This article was written by Leland Gladstone herself. Leland curates and edits the blog, but she doesn't do any writing herself. Except, now, this.

…late-night conversation with an intimate friend revealed a shocking secret…this friend, let's call her "Violet," has been conducting a clandestine relationship over the course of two decades that she calls her "Same Time Next Year." She and her lover meet for one long weekend each year, then they part and do not communicate—no calls, no texts, no e-mails—until the following year rolls around.

At first, I was scandalized. ("Violet" is single, but her lover is very, very married.) However, the more I ruminated upon her confession, the more I think it sounds kind of…heavenly.

It *does* sound heavenly, Ursula thinks. She could only too easily see conducting such an affair with Anders, were he still alive. He might have married AJ, and Ursula would still be with Jake, but she would meet Anders in Las Vegas every spring and they would go to that bar that they went to during the Umbrecht Tool and Die case and sing karaoke. They'd have dinner at the Golden Steer and go dancing at

Hyde as they had that one memorable night, then they'd make love in a suite overlooking the Bellagio fountains.

If Anders were still alive and Ursula could pull this off, she would come back to Jake and Bess feeling so...refreshed, so energized, so grateful.

This, too, is a point Leland explores in the article. Is monogamy in long marriages an unrealistic expectation? So many people fail at marriage. What if it's not the participants but the rules that are to blame? Is it possible that a short, tidy affair like the one "Violet" enjoys is the answer? Violet and her lover meet at the beach somewhere. They sail; they take walks and collect sand dollars; they watch movies; they eat Chinese food and read each other the fortunes from their fortune cookies.

Ursula pulls back like she's been stung. Reads that again.

Sand dollars? Fortune-cookie fortunes?

Leland's intimate friend. "Violet" is a made-up name.

Ursula sets down her iPad. She feels like she's going to vomit. But wait, wait. This is a classic case of Ursula getting ahead of herself—and hasn't her newly hired life coach, Jeannie, provided Ursula with strategies for coping, and isn't one strategy with stressful situations to take things slowly and methodically rather than running around like her hair is on fire?

Sand dollars. Fortune-cookie fortunes.

Years and years ago, after Jake left PharmX and contracted that staph infection, Ursula had been hunting through his desk looking for his COBRA information so she could pay the bill for his hospital stay, and she had come across an interoffice envelope that just looked...strange. When she felt it, it was bumpy. She had opened it and found three sand dollars and a handful of fortune-cookie fortunes. Those two things. Only those two things.

Coincidence?

One long weekend per year—Labor Day weekend. For over two decades—yes, at least.

On the beach—the cottage on Nantucket.

Leland's intimate friend "Violet"—Mallory Blessing.

Ursula combs through the years methodically, or as methodically as she can under the circumstances. Without even realizing it, she has walked to the edge of the bluff. She needs to catch the breeze. Her arms feel numb, like a doll's arms. There was the year Ursula went to Newport alone because Jake refused to cancel his trip to Nantucket. There was the year they pushed up Bess's christening. His own daughter's christening! He never missed his weekend on Nantucket. It was sacred, he said, his time with Cooper, with the guys. And yet, Jake hasn't seen Cooper in Washington recently as far as Ursula knows. And then he'd refused to go to the funeral—the funeral where Ursula met Leland and learned that Leland and Mallory had been best friends growing up.

Intimate friends.

Ursula needs to call someone, but who?

Leland? she thinks. No; Leland would, as a journalist, protect her source.

Ursula dials Cooper at work. He's the current administration's new director of domestic policy, a huge, demanding job, and Ursula has meant to congratulate him, though the lines between the legislative and executive branches are blurry. But she's reaching out now on a personal matter, so there will be no ethics breach.

Even so, it's hard for her to get past his secretary, Marnie; Marnie obviously knows that Ursula is a United States senator and any discussion of business has to be scheduled, which this hasn't been. Ursula says she's calling about a personal matter. Her husband, Jake McCloud, went to Johns Hopkins with Cooper; they were fraternity brothers.

"They were?" Marnie says. "Mr. Blessing has never mentioned that."

"Well, I wouldn't lie," Ursula says. Her tone is peevish, which will only reinforce her reputation as being somewhat bitchy (maybe more than *somewhat;* maybe she's a bona fide insufferable bitch, which is why her husband has been cheating on her for more than twenty years). "They were in Phi Gamma Delta, Fiji. Jake was Cooper's big brother."

Marnie sighs. "He does talk about Fiji," she says. "But I still can't help you. Mr. Blessing is on his honeymoon this week."

"Honeymoon?" Ursula says. *Another* honeymoon? "Well, good for him. I hope they went someplace nice."

"St. Mike's," Marnie says. "Should I tell him you called? Or—"

"Might you give me his cell number?" Ursula asks. "It's a rather urgent personal matter."

"I'm sorry," Marnie says. "I can't do that."

Ursula appreciates Marnie's discretion even though she's desperate to talk to Coop. "Yes, please, then," she says. "Tell him I called." Ursula hangs up. What next? Somewhere she used to have the number of the cottage on Nantucket. She could call and see who answers. If Mallory answers, Ursula will...what? Ask her if she's been conducting an affair with Jake for the past twenty years?

Ursula decides to give it a shot. What choice does she have? The number isn't in either of her phones so she Googles the white pages and punches in *Mallory Blessing, Nantucket, Massachusetts*—but there's no listing.

Of course there's no listing. It's 2015. Everyone got rid of landlines ten years ago.

Another honeymoon. On St. Mike's—St. Michael's, on the eastern shore of Maryland. There's only one place that anyone would honeymoon on St. Mike's, right? The Inn at Perry Cabin.

The woman who answers at the reception desk sounds young and bubbly, which is a good sign. "Good morning, the Inn at Perry Cabin, how may I direct your call?"

"Yes, good morning, this is Senator Ursula de Gournsey." Ursula pauses. *Please let this young woman follow politics.* "I'm trying to reach Cooper Blessing. I believe he's there on his honeymoon?"

"Good morning, Senator! Yes, he is. I'll just need you to provide his room number so I can connect you."

"I don't have the room number," Ursula says. "I didn't anticipate having to call him this week but something urgent has come up. If I leave a message, will you please make sure he sees it right away?"

The desk clerk says, "Ohhhhmmmmm." She pauses. "I suppose I can just put you through. Please hold, Senator."

The phone starts to ring and Ursula wonders how she became a woman who would interrupt someone's honeymoon to ask about her own husband's possible infidelity. She should hang up! But she can't. She needs to know.

A groggy Cooper answers the phone. "Hello?"

She's woken him. Of course she's woken him; it's just after nine in the morning. She tries not to picture Cooper naked and hungover beneath the inn's featherlight comforter, lying next to whatever poor woman has just become the fourth—fifth?—Mrs. Cooper Blessing.

"Cooper?" Ursula says. She sounds unhinged. She *is* unhinged. "It's Ursula de Gournsey, good morning."

She hears a rustling noise that she can only imagine is Cooper sitting up in bed, wondering what the hell is going on. "Good morning?" Cooper says. "Ursula...is everything okay? It's not Jake, is it?" His voice breaks a little. He must think Jake is dead or injured or terminally ill, and now Ursula feels even worse. The last time she saw Cooper was at his parents' funeral.

"Jake is fine," she says quickly. "He and Bess are out to breakfast. They're both just fine." She inhales the breeze blowing in off the lake. The lake is so big, it creates its own horizon; she's pretty sure that people who grew up on the coasts have no idea just how vast the Great Lakes are. "I'm calling to ask about your weekends with Jake on Nantucket."

A beat passes. Cooper clears his throat. "Ursula," he says.

"You and Jake go to Nantucket every year over Labor Day," Ursula says. "Right?"

Another beat passes. Ursula hears a voice, female, the new wife, justifiably wanting to know who is calling their hotel room at nine in the morning during their honeymoon and making Cooper squirm.

Ursula may end up being the reason for Cooper's next divorce.

"Ursula de Gournsey," Cooper whispers. "I'll just be a minute." And then he clears his throat and says, "Sorry about that, Ursula."

"I'm the one who's sorry," Ursula says. "Sorry for inserting myself into your life at what I'm sure is the least convenient moment. But something came to my attention just now. I was reading this…*blog*…and it dawned on me that maybe you and Jake *haven't* been going to Nantucket together all these years. Maybe he's…been going alone? Or with someone else? I don't need any proof from you; you don't need to send me pictures or share any stories. I'll take you at your word." Ursula feels her coffee about to repeat on her. If Cooper says he *hasn't* been going to Nantucket, then an awful, stinking possibility will be exposed and they'll both have to acknowledge it. "Has it been you that Jake spends Labor Day weekend with up on Nantucket?"

Half a beat, maybe not even. "Yes," Cooper says. "Yes, of course, Ursula."

Of course. Ursula closes her eyes. Would Coop lie to her? The answer, she can only assume, is yes. Cooper has a questionable track record with women; that much is irrefutable. Maybe he lies to his wives. Maybe he's pathological. The other person he might be covering for is…his sister, Mallory. Mallory Blessing is pretty, yes. She's a simple, clean kind of pretty. Girl-next-door pretty. She isn't glamorous, isn't powerful, isn't a siren. She isn't anything like Ursula. There is no way Mallory Blessing has enough allure to reel Jake all the way back to Nantucket year after year after year. Ursula is paranoid; deranged, even—and she has just shown her hand to Cooper.

"Great, Coop, thank you so much!" Ursula says. She makes her voice as bright and cheerful as she can so there's no doubt in Cooper's mind that she's a complete sociopath.

"Ursula?"

"Yes?"

"Thanks for checking in," Cooper says. "See you on the Hill."

Ursula hangs up. She walks back to her Adirondack chair. Her iPad is lying in the grass, *Leland's Letter* still glowing on the screen. Everything about the morning has lost its appeal. She did not assess the situation slowly or methodically. She acted on impulse and now she feels like a fool.

The sand dollars and fortune cookies, though. It bothers her.

Mallory drops Link off at Nobadeer Beach to meet his friends. Nobadeer is on the same coastline as the beach they live on and Mallory can't quite understand why Link doesn't just invite his friends to the house like he did when he was younger. Mallory even offered to make everyone fajitas with her homemade guacamole. But Link said that Nobadeer was "more fun."

Plus, he said, *nobody wants to go to the beach when there are parents watching.*

Watching what? Mallory asked, but she received no answer.

"There had better not be any beer in that backpack," she says. "If the police call me, I'm not answering. You'll molder in jail."

"No beer," Link says.

"Prove it," Mallory says.

Link hesitates, then unzips the backpack: two bottles of water and a Gatorade.

"Lucky you," Mallory says.

"Where's the trust?" Link says. His tone is good-natured but when he gets out, he slams the door of the Jeep a little harder than he needs to.

"Hey," she calls through the open window. "I love you."

He raises a hand.

"I love you, Lincoln," she says a bit louder.

He turns around scowling, but he can't hold on to it. He grins. "Love you, Mama."

Mallory's phone rings. It's Cooper. Cooper? He just got married six days earlier on the eastern shore of Maryland. Mallory flew down for the wedding. It had been a simple affair—just her, Amy and Coop, and Amy's sister and mother. While Mallory was away she's pretty sure Link had people over, even though he was supposed to be staying at his friend Bodie's house. When she got home, the floor in the kitchen was sticky, she was out of Windex, paper towels, hot dogs, and ketchup, and she'd found an empty Coke can on the windowsill in the bathroom. She was relieved it was Coke, but Link is fourteen and she has taught high school way too long to be naive; beer is probably not far behind.

Mallory pulls over to the side of the sandy road. She has a million-dollar view of the dunes and the ocean beyond. The waves are good today; there are dozens of people out surfing.

"Coop?" she says. She wonders if the marriage has broken up already. On the honeymoon; that would be a new record (though not by much). "Everything okay?"

"Guess who called me this morning?" Coop says. "Well, you're not going to guess so I'll tell you. Ursula de Gournsey, that's who."

Mallory puts up the Jeep's windows, turns on the air conditioning and aims the vents at her heart. She's sweating. "Really?"

"Really."

"What did she want?" Mallory asks.

"She wanted my assurance that I'm the one Jake goes to Nantucket with every summer," Coop says. "She told me she didn't need *proof;* she said she would take me at my word."

Mallory feels like she's the one riding a wave, but in a nauseated way, not a fun, beachy way. She pinches the skin of her bare thigh. She always thought that if and when she and Jake were discovered, she would have time to come up with a defense. But now she's just…blindsided, a solid, stinging smack to the cheek. "What did you tell her?"

"I said yes. I said it was me that Jake goes to Nantucket with every summer. I lied, Mal. To a United States senator."

"Thank you," Mallory says. "Thank…Coop. Thank you."

"I feel sick," Cooper says. "I'm on my goddamned honeymoon, Mallory, trying to start a life with Amy. Trying to start *fresh.* And yet there I am, lying to protect my sister who has been conducting an affair with my best friend for…how long? How many summers?"

"A lot," Mallory says. "A lot of summers."

"A lot of summers," Cooper says.

"Did she say *why* she was asking? Was it just out of the blue, or did something happen?"

"She said she read some blog post that put an idea in her head."

"Blog post?" Mallory has a hard time picturing Ursula de Gournsey reading a blog post.

"That's what she said. I didn't ask for details. I said as little as possible. But what I did say was a complete lie." Coop stops talking and Mallory hears irregular breathing. Is Coop *crying*? "I stopped speaking to Jake after I figured out what was going on...back when I married Tish. When was that, 2007? I haven't had a meaningful conversation with him in eight years. My best friend. My big brother, the brother I never had, that was Jake. And if I ever have to lie again...I'm not saying I'm going to abandon you, I'm saying, *Don't make me lie again!*" He screams this last bit—and can she blame him?

"I won't," she whispers.

"But you won't stop seeing him. I know you won't."

Mallory doesn't answer.

Cooper says, "Do you know why I lied, Mal? Other than because you're the only family I have left?"

"Why?"

"Because I think you and Jake are probably really good together. You're both...easygoing. And smart as hell. And you're both kind. You're good people. I can see why you like him, I can see why he likes you. But the two of you are doing something that, at base, just isn't right. Which proves something I've suspected all along."

"What's that?" Mallory whispers.

"Everyone is human," Coop says. "Every single one of us."

That does it; tears drip down Mallory's face. She moves her sunglasses to the top of her head and squints at the sparkling surface of the Atlantic until it blurs.

Blog post. Blog post?

When Mallory gets home from the beach, she Googles *Most popular blogs, women.*

Number one is *Leland's Letter.*

Leland's Letter is a blog? Mallory had thought it was…well, she wasn't sure. It was Leland's project, her *platform.* Mallory always felt bad that she hadn't paid closer attention. She had looked at it right when it came out and read articles on self-defense on the subway and the true-life story of a woman in Utah held against her wishes by a polygamist, back when that was a thing everyone was talking about. The website had seemed angry and strident and edgy and urban, just like Leland herself, and Mallory simply wasn't interested.

Mallory clicks on *Leland's Letter.*

The lead article, right there on the front page under the masthead, is titled "Same Time Next Year: Can It Save Modern Marriage?"

"Gah!" Mallory shouts. "She didn't!"

…late-night conversation with an intimate friend revealed a shocking secret…this friend, let's call her "Violet," has been conducting a clandestine relationship over the course of two decades that she calls her "Same Time Next Year."

Mallory keeps reading. Leland did it. Right down to the sand dollars and the fortunes.

Mallory stands up, looks around her cottage as though there's a crowd assembled, an indignant studio audience waiting to see just how Mallory is going to handle this.

She goes to the kitchen for iced tea, cuts a wedge of lemon, takes a sip. It's cold, refreshing, minty because Mallory steeps her tea with fresh mint from the pot of herbs on her porch. She knows she lives a blessed life; she has never denied that. She was given this property when she had nothing else and it's extraordinary by anyone's standards. She has a healthy, strong, intelligent son. Fray's son. Maybe Leland's...*betrayal*—there's no other word for it—has been long planned as revenge because Mallory slept with Frazier Dooley and bore his child. But Leland handled the news of Link's sire with great equanimity. Was that all an *act*? Has Leland been patiently waiting all these years to stick a pin through the heart of Mallory's voodoo doll?

Maybe Leland is angry that Fifi came to visit Mallory alone so many years earlier. Maybe Fifi told Leland that Mallory knew about their breakup before Leland did. That would have hurt. Leland cares about Fifi more than she ever cared about Fray.

Right?

Mallory realizes she has no idea who Leland loves—or has loved—other than herself. And hasn't that always been the case? Mallory thinks back to childhood, adolescence, high school—although, to be fair, everyone was self-absorbed in high school. In young adulthood, there were those loathsome months they lived together in the city. Leland had snatched up the job that Mallory wanted, and even if Leland was better suited for that job, she had treated Mallory like her inferior. She hadn't shared the duck or the lamb shank from the French restaurant on the ground floor of their building; she had eaten those meals ostentatiously, dipping pieces of golden baguette into the pan sauces, holding a forkful of potato purée in front of her mouth before she luridly licked it off and then groaned at how *sublime* it was. All this while Mallory ate her bologna sandwiches, her ramen, her dry scrambled eggs.

There was Leland's disastrous first visit to Nantucket when she vanished with her New York friends, abandoning Mallory, abandoning Fray. And then the catastrophic second visit with Fifi. Leland had said such cruel things: *Mallory is particularly suggestible…She's a follower.* Mallory understood that Leland had been angry at Fifi and jealous of Mallory, but she had meant those words; if she hadn't, she would have chosen other derogatory things to say.

It was a wonder Mallory and Leland had remained friends. They had done so only because Mallory had chosen to overlook Leland's faults. Their friendship had history—not only the moments Mallory readily recalls but also the times she knows she's forgotten. Driving in Steve Gladstone's Saab to the Owings Mills Mall, pooling their money to buy Chick-Fil-A, stopping to put two dollars' worth of gas in the car so they didn't return it to Steve bone-dry, listening to *Songs in the Attic* by Billy Joel. "Captain Jack" was their favorite song; Mallory knew the lyrics a little better than Leland did, and she had been proud of that. Going back even further, there were countless summer days at the country club, handstands in the pool, backflips off the diving board, hitting a tennis ball against the concrete practice wall, both of them wearing only their one-piece bathing suits and their Tretorns, before the age of body-consciousness. They rode their bikes all over Roland Park, one time venturing a block farther than they should have when a carful of older boys stopped to ask their names. Leland, thinking fast on her feet, had given the name Laura Templeton, and Mallory, following suit, had said, Jackie Templeton. These were characters from *General Hospital*. One of the older boys had said, "Are you two sisters? You don't look alike. Who's older?" Leland had opened her mouth to answer—she was most certainly going to say that *she* was older—but at the last minute she had pushed off the sidewalk and started pedaling furiously down the block, and Mallory had followed. They didn't stop until they safely coasted into Leland's driveway, and only then did they let themselves acknowledge that they might have been in real danger, like girls in an after-school special.

They used to have shifting crushes on Mel Gibson, Kevin Costner, Mickey Rourke. They had both been madly in love with Mickey Rourke, but it was a rule that they couldn't have a crush on the same person, so Leland got Mickey Rourke because she was the one who had the poster of him from *9½ Weeks* on her wall. Mallory remembers harboring bitterness about that because there has never been a more desirable photograph of a man than Mickey Rourke in *9½ Weeks*.

Leland had been the alpha, Mallory the beta—there was no way to argue that point. Mallory hadn't cared. In later years, she came to realize that the only person's approval she needed was her own. She didn't need to move the needle on American culture. All she needed to do was be a good teacher and a better mother and the best person she could be.

She has one weak spot, one fault line: Jake. And now the world knows it. Leland has exposed her.

Mallory wants to be the kind of person who lets this go. Cooper reached deep and covered for her. Ursula, hopefully, bought it, and the article that hundreds of thousands of American women will read will be forgotten by next week.

Mallory isn't that person.

Her second choice is to be the kind of person who quietly erases Leland from her life. She will block Leland from her phone and her e-mail. Her parents' house has been sold; there's no longer any reason to return to Baltimore for the holidays. Link can see Sloane, his grandmother, and Steve Gladstone, his grandmother's boyfriend, on Fray's watch.

But she isn't this person either.

She is a person who has been manipulated and pushed around and treated poorly by her best friend for over thirty years, but this is the last time. Mallory is angry. The anger, she knows, will fade, but before that happens, she's going to make Leland feel the searing burn, the acrid bitterness.

She calls Leland.

"Mal?"

Mallory stares into the bedroom mirror as she talks. "I saw the article. 'Same Time Next Year.'" Mallory is proud of herself. Her voice is steady and clear. She holds her own gaze.

Silence.

"Ursula called Cooper."

"Oh God."

"That's not what bothers me about this," Mallory says. "That's an outcome, which is separate from the betrayal itself."

"It wasn't a *betrayal,* Mal—"

"I told you that in confidence. Extremely sensitive top-secret confidence. I was drunk, I own that, and I was sad. It was the night of my parents' funeral. I shared something with you, my best friend since for-ever, and you turned right around and laid it out in your *blog*"—Mallory says this like it's a dirty word—"for all to see. You used my secret as clickbait."

"I didn't give your name—"

"You might as well have," Mallory says. "Ursula called Cooper!" Her face is blotching; she feels her good sense unspooling like the string of a kite snatched by the wind. *There it goes!* Mallory sets the phone down on her dresser. She can hear Leland's voice, though not her actual words. Her excuses. Her obsequious apologies. Mallory takes a deep breath. *Hang up,* she thinks. Except she's not finished. She brings the phone back to her ear.

Silence. Then: "Mal? Are you still there?"

"It doesn't matter if you gave my name. It doesn't matter about Ursula. What matters is that you broke your promise to me. That was an ugly, disingenuous thing to do, Lee. It was precisely the same thoughtless, self-serving behavior you've demonstrated all your life, except exponentially worse. You dealt this friendship a death blow. I will feel sad without you, but my guess is that you'll feel worse than I do because you have to live with the guilt of knowing that you are such an empty, morally bankrupt person that you would cash in on your best friend's deepest secret for…what? Some likes? Some follows? Some *advertisers?* The admiration of strangers?" Mallory takes a breath. "I hope you find what you're looking for. Maybe it's Fifi's approval, maybe it's your father's love—I have no idea. And I don't care. Goodbye, Lee."

"Mal—"

Mallory hangs up. Leland calls back four times and leaves three messages, which Mallory deletes without listening to. She blocks Leland's cell number, she blocks her e-mail, and she blocks the *Leland's Letter* website, marking it *inappropriate*. When all that is done, it's time to go back to the beach to pick up Link.

When Link gets into the car, hair wet and sculpted into crazy waves and spiky peaks, smelling of salt and sweat and sunblock, feet and legs covered with sand, he says, "Have you been crying, Mom?"

It must be crystal clear the answer is yes, but Mallory shakes her head.

Link says, "Tomorrow I'll have the guys over to the house and you can cook for us, okay, Mama?"

She feels the corners of her mouth lift, like they have a mind of their own. "Okay," she says.

It's a week before Christmas and Link is taking out the kitchen trash after dinner, a chore he enjoys this time of year because the air is cold and smells of wood smoke, and the ocean mist glitters like tinsel. On the horizon, he can just pick out the lights of a giant wreath that their closest neighbor hangs on the side of his house.

As he's tying up the bag outside on the back porch, he sees a soft package in a brown UPS bag that has been stuffed halfway down. Further inspection reveals Link's name on the front.

What?

Link pulls the bag out from underneath a chicken carcass and potato peelings and junk mail. It's a package addressed to him from L. Gladstone, Brooklyn, NY 11211. Auntie Leland. What is it doing in the trash?

He tears open the brown mailer to find a wrapped gift, clothing of some sort, it feels like. He unwraps the present. Why not? It's his. It's a Patriots jersey, number 87, GRONKOWSKI. Yes! Link has been dying for one of these and it's an adult medium, roomy enough for him to wear over a hoodie.

He inspects the rest of the contents of the trash bag from the outside in case Mallory has accidentally thrown away any other presents. Then he takes the trash to the cans on the side of the house, admires the neighbor's wreath, and heads back inside with the Gronk jersey. Thank God he saved it!

"Mom?" he says, holding the jersey up. "This came for me from Auntie Leland and you accidentally threw it away."

Mallory is on the sofa in front of the fire, grading essays. She smiles mildly. "Not an accident," she says. "Leland is dead to me."

Summer #24: 2016

What are we talking about in 2016? Prince; the presidential election; Muhammad Ali; Villanova Wildcats; Harriet Tubman; Antonin Scalia; Brexit; Colin Kaepernick; the North Carolina restroom debate; Pulse nightclub in Orlando; Sidney Crosby; Blue Apron; Pat Summitt; Black Lives Matter; goat yoga; Gene Wilder; the Cubs; Brangelina; Standing Rock; Carrie Fisher; preferred gender pronouns; Piper, Crazy Eyes, Alex, Red, and Healy; "Always stay gracious, best revenge is your paper."

Burgers, shucked corn, sliced tomatoes, Cat Stevens's "Hard Headed Woman," hydrangea blossoms in the mason jar, the same mason jar from year number one, which Jake finds comforting; the jar sits on top of the black burn scar on the harvest table. The meal, the music, the mason jar, and the narrow harvest table are the same, but so much else has changed.

Mallory took some of the money she inherited from her parents and completely transformed the inside of the cottage. She…gutted it. Gone is the rustic paneling and the dusty brick fireplace with the slate hearth. Gone is the screen door that slammed with a spine-tingling snap every time someone came in or went out. Gone are the Formica countertops—so outdated they were back in—and the particleboard cabinets and the fudge-brown fridge and the stainless-steel drop-in sink.

By anyone's standards, Mallory's cottage is now dazzling, swoon-worthy. The walls are shiplap, painted white; the old, sagging bookshelves are now floor-to-ceiling white built-ins with accent lighting and cool copper rails and a sliding ladder to help access the upper shelves. The floors are pickled oak. There's a new deep white sofa and two comfy club chairs sheathed in cream linen and underneath is a rug striped in every shade of white from French vanilla to polar icecap. The kitchen cabinets are white with tasteful brass hardware, and the Formica has been replaced with Pegasus marble. Mallory's bedroom is like a middle-aged woman who took a vacation to the Bahamas and returned with a new attitude and a hibiscus behind her ear. The room now has a cathedral ceiling; the walls are painted the faintest peach, and there is a sumptuous king-size bed complete with gauzy white canopies floating down the sides. She has annexed the bathroom as her own, and it's now tiled in jungle green; the old tub was finally removed and replaced with a freestanding stone tub that resembles one of the slipper shells they used to find on their beach walks. The guest room has been extravagantly wallpapered—an azure blue background printed with frolicking zebras.

The only room that has been left untouched is Link's. Entering Link's room is like stepping back in time: There's the familiar paneling, the creaky floors covered by assorted braided rugs, the dresser thick with gray paint. If Jake isn't mistaken, Mallory harvested that dresser from the Take It or Leave It at the Nantucket dump.

Jake runs his hands over the walls of Link's room. "My old friend the paneling," he says. Link's room is the only place that retains the old-fashioned, cottagey smell—salt water and mildew.

"He wouldn't let me change a thing," Mallory says. "Except I turned his closet into the world's smallest bathroom. He says he likes the cottage better the way it was before. Can you imagine?"

"Well…"

"Not you too," Mallory says. "Do you hate it? Do you think I bleached out the character?"

Jake steps back into the great room. "You kept the desk!" he says. He hadn't noticed before, but Mallory's kidney-shaped desk is still in the same place in the far corner of the pond side of the room, nearly hidden by the master bedroom's new six-panel door. The desk appears out of place in this new version of the cottage, like a dowdy maiden aunt at a party of supermodels, and yet Jake would choose the maiden aunt to talk to every time.

"I couldn't bring myself to get rid of it," Mallory says. "I remember Aunt Greta writing letters at this desk. I wonder now if she was writing to Ruthie."

The song changes to "At Last." The music comes from Sonos, a playlist imported from Mallory's phone. The five-CD changer is long gone.

"I'm sorry you don't like it," Mallory says, and she throws back what's left of her wine. Even the wine is fancier—gone is the twelve-dollar bottle of Cypress chardonnay, replaced by a Sancerre from the Chavignol region. "But I'm the one who has to live here. Link will be leaving for college in a couple of years and you'll leave on Monday."

"Hey, hey," he says, gathering her up in his arms. "It's gorgeous, Mal. It's like a magazine spread. It just feels different, and I have to get used to it."

"I didn't want to live in a charming, rustic box anymore," she says. "Fray has a goddamned castle out in Seattle and he and Anna just bought a place in Deer Valley, a *chalet,* Link calls it—"

"You didn't do all this to keep up with Fray, did you?" Jake asks.

"I wanted it to be nice," Mallory says. "Nicer."

"How could anything be nicer than having the Atlantic Ocean as your front yard?"

"I know, but…" Mallory pulls away a few inches and Jake gets his first good look at her. The cottage has had a complete makeover, but Mallory Blessing is exactly the same. There's some gray in the part of her hair, which he's glad she hasn't "bleached out." Her face is suntanned and when she raises her eyebrows, her forehead becomes an accordion of wrinkles, and

Jake loves it. He loves seeing her get a little older, a little more seasoned. She still has the girlish freckles across her nose and tonight, her eyes are bluish, more blue than he's ever seen them.

"Are you okay?" he asks. "Mal?"

She rests her head on his chest and he closes his eyes. Three hundred and sixty-two days he has waited to hold her in his arms.

"I've been tired lately," she says. "Link and I had a tough year. I want him to study and play baseball and be a good kid and he wants to make out with his girlfriend and go to bonfires and get high with his buddies."

"I feel your pain," Jake says.

"Is Bess giving you a hard time?"

"Not me."

"Ursula?"

Jake nods. Bess doesn't have a boyfriend, go to bonfires, or smoke dope. She stays home with her friend Pageant, and the two of them make incendiary posters for the rallies and marches and protests they attend on the weekends to fight for climate change, reproductive rights, transgender rights, immigration rights, gun control, Amnesty International. It's hard to keep up, and whereas Jake tries to be supportive— he loves that Bess is using her voice—Ursula's attitude is one of amusement, which comes across as patronizing.

Off to defend the lesbian cheetahs? Ursula asked recently. *Or is today Ugandan dwarves?*

You're offensive, Bess said. *If anyone knew what you were really like, no one would vote for you.*

Bess! Jake said, but she had already slammed out of the condo.

Ursula tossed it off with a laugh. *Let her go,* she said. *I hated my mother at that age too. It's natural.*

"What if we went out tonight after dinner?" Jake says. "What if we went to the Chicken Box for old times' sake?"

"I'd love to," Mallory says. "But we can't. We dodged a bullet, Jake. I thought for sure Ursula would put you on lockdown and I'd be alone this weekend."

"She seemed unconcerned," Jake says. Mallory told him about the whole situation with *Leland's Letter* and Ursula calling Cooper. Mallory found it strange that Ursula hadn't simply confronted Jake, but that's because Mallory doesn't understand the architecture of his marriage. Ursula doesn't deal with the issue head-on partly because she can't summon the emotional energy and partly because she's afraid if she pulls the wrong block, the whole Jenga tower will fall. A failing marriage is a death knell in politics; Ursula will maintain at any cost.

Jake isn't thrilled that Cooper knows what's going on, although Cooper covering for them has bought them some freedom. Why not enjoy it? "We're so old now," he says. "We won't know anyone at the Box."

"We might, though."

"Let's do something different, then," he says. "How about if after dinner we take a bottle of wine down to the docks and drink it onboard the *Greta*? It'll be nice to be out on the water. We can sit on the bow. No one will see us."

Mallory purses her lips. "Mmm, I don't know about changing up our routine. We do things the way we do them because they work."

"No one is going to see us on the bow of your boat, Mal."

She huffs. "Fine. But when we're walking, stay six paces behind me with your hands in your pockets and wear a hat."

Jake laughs. "Deal."

They park Mallory's Jeep downtown and walk— Mallory first, Jake following—past the Gazebo, Straight Wharf, and Cru and onto the docks. It's fun to be out at night among people enjoying the last weekend of summer. Jake is nervous, which only heightens his pleasure; he's drunk too much wine, probably, and Mallory has a second bottle in her bag. They may have to sleep on the boat and sneak off at the crack of dawn.

They come to the gatekeeper. Beyond a certain point, it's boat owners and guests only. There's a teenager with strawberry-blond hair curling out from beneath his University of Miami hat like lettuce peeking out of a hamburger bun. Jake nearly turns back. Mallory knows every teenager on this island. She's *the* English teacher—the best, the most popular. Any one of her students could whip his phone out of his pocket to snap a pic of the dude Miss Blessing is hanging out with and then post it on Snapchat. Someone else would then do face-recognition. First the high school and then the entire island would know that Miss Blessing was seen at the docks at nine o'clock at night with Jake McCloud, husband of Ursula de Gournsey.

Is he being paranoid? Probably.

"I'm on the *Greta,*" Mallory says to the kid. "Slip one oh six."

"'Kay," the teenager says.

They walk on. Jake feels so relieved that he reaches for Mallory's hand, and she swats it away, as she should. He grabs her by the shoulders and she elbows him in the ribs. They're at slip 100. The *Greta* is three boats ahead on the right. They're almost in the clear.

A man and a woman step off one of the huge yachts on the left. The man is big and burly. Mallory and Jake have to move aside so the couple can pass.

"Evening," Jake says.

The man stops. His weight makes the deck boards creak.

"Mallory?" he says.

Mallory turns. "Oh!" she cries as though someone goosed her. "Bayer?" She moves tentatively in the man's direction but then seems to think better of it and offers half a wave. "Hello there. Good to see you." She has clearly decided against a big reunion with Bayer—talk about an appropriate name; the guy is huge and hairy—and Jake is relieved.

Onward, he thinks. But he's aware that the moment hasn't quite ended. Bayer is staring at them—at Jake now—while the woman, a slim brunette with an armful of gold bangles, is focused on her phone.

"You," Bayer says to Jake. "Do I know you?"

Jake isn't going to risk looking this guy in the eye, so he checks out the boat the two just came off of: *Dee Dee*. "No, I don't think so."

"Are you *sure*?" Bayer's voice presses.

"He always thinks he knows people," the brunette says. She slips her phone into her bag. When she reaches for Bayer's hand, her bracelets jingle. "Let's go, honey. Reservation at nine thirty."

Jake says, "Have a good night."

"Yes," Bayer says. "You too."

Mallory shoots forward like a nervous three-year-old filly out of the gates at the Derby. She practically runs down the dock to slip 106 and leaps onto the boat like it's about to sail away. Jake can't help himself; he laughs.

Clearly, she's spooked. She takes a key out of the back pocket of her white capris, unlocks the padlock, and pulls open the door to the cabin. She descends into the dark.

Jake hears her setting the wine bottle down, then rummaging through a drawer. By the time he's beside her, she has yanked out the cork.

"Who was that?"

"Bayer," she says. "Bayer Burkhart." She takes a deep drink straight from the bottle.

Bayer Burkhart; the name rings a bell. Or is he imagining this? "Who is he?"

"Somebody that I used to know," Mallory says. "Wow, that was weird. Freaky, even. I haven't seen him in twenty years."

"Do you know who the woman was?"

"No, but I have a guess." Mallory goes to the little cabinet for glasses. "When I knew him, he lived in Newport."

Newport. Something is definitely familiar about the name and Newport, but Jake can't quite grasp it.

"Were you and Bayer Burkhart involved?" Jake asks. He's suddenly aflame with jealousy.

"I suppose," Mallory says. "Briefly. One summer. Though it's funny—when I was looking at him just now, I couldn't dredge up one pleasant memory."

"Good," Jake says, and Mallory hands him a glass of wine.

* * *

It's Sunday night, post–Chinese food, post-movie, post–fortune cookies, post-lovemaking. These are bittersweet hours—the last eight or ten before he heads back to the airport. It feels worse this year, but why?

Mallory has fallen asleep and Jake resents her for it, though over the years, he knows, he's usually the one who falls asleep first while she lies awake contemplating the torturous nature of their relationship.

Mallory is breathing into the soft down of her pillow. The new mattress is yielding but firm; it feels like it's made of fondant icing. Jake runs his hands down Mallory's back. She has such soft skin that he makes it a point to touch her any chance he gets. This time tomorrow he'll be back in Washington. Bess and Ursula won't return to DC for another couple of days so he'll have some time to decompress, shake the sand out of his shoes, get his head back where it needs to be—family, work, raising money for the CFRF. This all sounds fine and it will be fine. The goring pain he feels right now at the thought of leaving Mallory will subside, bit by bit, until at last it's bearable—and then, in April or May, the dull melancholy that settles like a blanket of dust over his heart will turn, almost instantly, into anticipation.

There's moonlight flooding through the window from the pond side, so when Jake's finger runs across a rough spot on Mallory's lower back, he squints at it in the ghostly light. A bite, a scrape? A spot of some sort, he sees. He reaches for his reading glasses and his phone and shines a light on it. An irregularly shaped black mark on her back. It looks nefarious, but is it? Jake snaps a picture of it. Is he overstepping his bounds?

Maybe—but in the morning, he's going to show her the picture and insist that she get it checked out.

Summer #25: 2017

What are we talking about in 2017? What aren't *we talking about? The New England Patriots over the Atlanta Falcons;* Moonlight *over* La La Land; *Floyd Mayweather Jr. over Conor McGregor; North Korea; Justin Verlander; Becky with the good hair; Charlottesville; Jeff Bezos; the Tappan Zee Bridge; the Paris Agreement; Steph Curry; avocado toast; CrossFit; Meryl Streep; the eclipse; the Las Vegas shootings; the Women's March; Hurricanes Harvey, Irma, Jose, Maria; #metoo: Harvey Weinstein, Matt Lauer, Mario Batali, Louis C.K.; "I want something just like this."*

Mallory has melanoma. Skin cancer. The words are scary, but she refuses to panic. She has to maintain for Link.

He has grown six inches in the past year, he has his learner's permit, and he's been dating a girl named Nicole DaPra, and by *dating,* Mallory means that they are Siamese twins. She suspects they're having sex so she buys a large box of condoms from Amazon (no point having someone see her doing so at the Stop and Shop and starting gossip) and puts them on his dresser while he's lying in bed, watching some YouTube video on his phone.

He looks up, sees the box, and says, "I don't need those, Mom. Nicole is on the pill."

Suspicions confirmed, then. Mallory feels herself tearing up even though Link's comfort in telling Mallory this indicates that she has done a good job parenting. They have an open line of communication on even the most sensitive of topics. It's a beautiful thing, so why is Mallory crying?

She slips out of his room without his noticing and stands on the front porch where she can watch the ocean. The ocean has been her counsel for all these years, she realizes. The ocean has been her spouse.

She says to the ocean: *I'm crying because he's growing up. He and Nicole—a girl I like very much, a girl I love, I couldn't have picked a sweeter, smarter girl—are sleeping together, which means his childhood is over. I am not his best girl anymore and I never will be again.*

Or maybe she's wrong. Maybe a mother is always her son's best girl. She can hope.

She tells Link about the spot and the diagnosis. She tells him not to worry; they caught it early. Her surgeon, Dr. McCoy, excises the spot and does a sentinel-lymph-node biopsy. The margins are clear; her lymph nodes come back clean. She has a medical oncologist, Dr. Symon, who orders thirty days of radiation at Cape Cod Hospital. *That will take care of it,* Dr. Symon says.

The devastating news is that Mallory can't go back in the sun. She has to cover up; SPF 70 won't do. She buys four beach umbrellas. She buys wide-brimmed hats, Jackie O. sunglasses. Her skin remains winter pale. She can swim if she wears a surf shirt but even so, she has to hurry back to the shade. The sun is a sniper, it's the Grim Reaper, and yet she longs for it. She has lived a life free of vices except for Jake, white wine, and…the sun. The sun has been her drug of choice. She is now in rehab, headed for recovery.

Link and Nicole go to prom together. They are the best-dressed couple; Nicole wears pink satin, a gown that reminds Mallory of the bridesmaid dress she wore to Coop's second wedding, the night she conceived Link, and Link wears pink seersucker pants and a navy blazer. Mallory takes ten thousand pictures. She stands with Nicole's mother, Terri, who is a nutritionist at the hospital and a single mother like Mallory; they would probably be friends if Mallory had the energy to start a friendship from scratch.

She should call Apple and see if she can be lured away from Hugo and the boys to have dinner at Fifty-Six Union—martinis and truffle fries.

No, Apple is not good at last-minute plans. Mallory should have scheduled this last week, last month.

She misses Leland.

Maybe she'll see if Terri wants to go to dinner. Would that be weird, the two of them out while their kids are at prom?

Yes, weird.

Terri turns to Mallory and says, "I have news."

Mallory smiles. *Nicole's pregnant?* she nearly jokes. But that wouldn't be funny.

"Nicole is spending next year abroad, in Ravenna, Italy."

Mallory blinks. "She's in high school."

"This is the new thing," Terri says. "Kids do immersion programs in high school. She'll live with a family that has other kids—an older daughter, a younger son, a daughter Nicole's age—and she'll go to school there. September to June."

"Wow," Mallory says. "That sounds…expanding. I didn't realize this was happening."

"She kept it under wraps in case she didn't get accepted," Terri says. "It's very competitive."

"Does Link know?" Mallory asks.

"Not yet," Terri says. "She wants to enjoy prom. She thinks he's going to be upset."

"Oh," Mallory says, thinking, *They're sixteen and dating, not engaged.* "I'm sure he'll be fine."

Link is not fine. Link is a soggy mess. Nicole didn't say a word to him about her plans to spend an entire school year in Italy, and Mallory has to admit, she's impressed. She thought it was impossible for a modern teenager to keep a secret.

"She's not leaving until September," Mallory says. "That's over three months away. Things may change between the two of you by then."

"Yeah," Link says. "I'll love her more."

It's a rare night that he's home alone. Normally, he and Nicole do all their studying together at either the cottage or Nicole's house. But tonight, Nicole is at the information session for her program. Mallory made Link's favorite meal—grilled Greek chicken and pasta with lemon-garlic cream sauce—but he just stares at it.

"Please eat," Mallory says.

"I can't," Link says, and then tears drop down the cheeks of her big, strong, handsome son's face. "I'm going to miss her so much."

"Come here," Mallory says. She abandons dinner and pulls him over to the new sofa, which is so fluffy and comforting, they call it Big Hugs. Mallory remembers all the times they sat on the old sofa, the sturdy, unforgiving green tweed, in front of the fire in the fall, winter, and early spring or in the summertime when all the doors and windows were thrown open and the cross breeze kept them from melting. They read, they watched TV, they talked; when Link was a baby, she nursed him on that sofa, and it was where he liked to sleep when he was home sick from school.

Mallory sighs. She's a certified expert in the field of missing the person you love. She can't let Link know this specifically, but maybe she can impart some wisdom. "I know you're afraid that Nicole is going to meet a cute Italian boy or that she's going to learn a language, see art, sit in magnificent churches, and eat incredible meals without you and the fact that she has had those experiences and you haven't will put distance between you. She's not only your girlfriend, she's your best friend. You two have found the purest kind of romantic love, which is young love." Mallory's eyes blur with tears. What an emotional year it has been already, and here it is, getting worse. "It will hurt for a while, a few weeks or a month, but in the best-case scenario—and we can only hope for the best—the two of you will find a way of coping with the distance. Or…you'll decide that the year might pass more easily if you break up. Nicole may want to be free to dive headfirst into her new Italian life, and if that happens, you need to let her go graciously. You have school and sports and me. I'll be at your disposal if you want to vent your sadness or your anger or your frustration. I'll also be the first one to understand if, with Nicole gone, you want to date Lauren or Elsa or Asha."

"Ew," Link says. "No."

"You're young," Mallory says. "And the worst thing about being young is not being able to appreciate that you're young because you aren't old enough to know any better."

"Mom," Link says. "I'm going to marry Nicole. Mark my words. We are getting married as soon as we graduate from college."

"That's a solid plan," Mallory says because she realizes these are the words he needs to hear right now. "But don't wish your life away. What if you start by enjoying every second of your time with Nicole between now and the day she leaves? Be present. Don't worry about the what-ifs."

Link's phone starts to buzz. It's Nicole; she must be finished with her meeting. Link jumps to his feet.

"Okay, Mom, thanks." He bends down to kiss Mallory, then answers the phone.

"Come on over," he says. "My mom made dinner. Greek chicken. She said she thinks us getting married after college is a solid plan."

At the end of July, Mallory realizes she's going to have the same problem that she had during the summer of baseball: Link doesn't want to go to Seattle. Not for the month, not even for a ten-day visit, which is what he's done the past two years. He won't go to Washington, DC, to see Coop; he won't go anywhere. He wants to stay on Nantucket and work at Millie's general store alongside Nicole until she leaves for Italy.

Mallory isn't sure what to do about Jake. She can't cancel his visit. If her cancer treatment taught her anything, it's that life is too short.

Link might be old enough for Mallory to simply say, *Listen, I have a friend coming, a male friend, and*

I need privacy for the weekend. Can you hang out at Nicole's house, maybe help get her packed?

But ugh. Ew. No.

Then Mallory thinks of Tuckernuck. She and Jake could sail over like they did back in whatever year and use Dr. Major's house for the weekend. It will be tricky with the sun—there isn't a single shade tree on all of Tuckernuck—but Mallory will be careful. She'll be so careful, if only…please!

She sends Dr. Major an exploratory e-mail. He retired five years ago but Mallory sees him around the island—at the Stop and Shop, in line at the bank and post office—so this won't come completely out of the blue.

Huge favor to ask…is there any way…Labor Day weekend…such joyful memories of the last time and after my parents' death and my recent health scare…please let me know when you can.

The good news is Mallory doesn't have to wait long for a response. The bad news is that Dr. Major tells Mallory that they sold the house the year before. It was just too expensive to keep up and no one ever used it.

Mallory's spirits flag. She could always suggest that Jake stay on the *Greta*. They can take long sails during the day and Mallory can run into town for burgers on Friday night, lobsters on Saturday night, Chinese food on Sunday night. They can stream *Same Time, Next Year* on her laptop. It might be fun?

It won't be fun. It'll feel like they're on the lam. It'll feel shady and cheap and claustrophobic and second rate.

Mallory could throw money at the problem. She could get a room at an inn—no, an inn would be too small. A hotel. The Nantucket Hotel, the White Elephant, Cliffside. She'll put the room in her name and Jake can slip in and out. But a hotel means staff—front desk, bellhops, chambermaids—and other guests. It's too risky.

Could she rent a house, someone else's house? That's weird and seems extreme, but is it?

Nantucket is an island with hundreds, maybe even thousands, of homes for rent, and yet Mallory can't find a home on the water available over Labor Day weekend except for a seven-bedroom out in Wauwinet that rents for twenty-five thousand dollars a week. Although, make no mistake, the house is the highest quality real estate porn imaginable, with jaw-dropping views across Polpis Harbor, a pool, a hot tub, a pool house with a wet bar and an exercise room, a tennis court, an outdoor kitchen and entertaining space, and a home theater.

The house is named Desdemona, which Mallory finds intriguing. Desdemona is the tragic heroine in *Othello;* Othello kills her for adultery that she didn't commit. It seems like an odd name for a summer mansion, and yet it's the perfect name for a house Mallory would rent so that her son doesn't meet her married lover.

Twenty-five thousand dollars. Before Kitty and Senior died, this wouldn't even be an option. Now Mallory has the money—but can she in good conscience spend it on one weekend for a house that is so big, she and Jake won't even set foot in half the rooms?

Definitely not. She can't believe she's even considering it. She'll have him stay on the boat. They'll sail to Chatham on Saturday, Cuttyhunk on Sunday. If it rains…well, she's not sure what they'll do if it rains. The *Greta* is miserable in the rain. It had better not rain.

Mallory revisits the idea of renting Desdemona. Other people take vacations; they go to the isle of Capri, they go on safari. Those trips must cost twenty-five thousand dollars, or nearly. Fray took Link and Anna and the baby and the baby's nanny to the Four Seasons in Maui for ten days this past Christmas. *That* must have cost twenty-five grand. Of course, Fray is in a different category of wealthy from Mallory, but what does money even *mean* if you can't spend it on the things that make you happy?

Mallory and Jake don't need seven bedrooms or a tennis court; they don't need to watch *Same Time, Next Year* in a home theater. But they do need to be together in a safe, private environment and if it takes twenty-five thousand dollars to make sure this happens, then Mallory will do it.

What does Doris say in *Same Time, Next Year*?

I knew…that no matter what the price, I was willing to pay it.

Mallory picks up her phone and calls Grey Lady Real Estate.

"Good afternoon, this is Grey Lady, Jeremiah speaking, may I help you?"

Mallory hesitates. *Jeremiah?* "Hello," she says, praying this isn't who she thinks it is. "My name is Mallory Bless—"

"Oh, hey, Miss Blessing, it's Jeremiah Freehold."

Mallory would like to hang up. "Jeremiah, hey there. This is a surprise. Are you—"

"A licensed broker? Yes, I am, have been for years," he says.

"That's wonderful," Mallory says. She knew that

Jeremiah had supervised a historically sensitive reno-
vation of his parents' home on Orange Street and she
maybe knew that he'd then gone into real estate, but
she is nonetheless surprised—and dismayed—to have
Jeremiah on the phone right now. Even all these years
later, she still feels mortified about that ride out to
Gibbs Pond.

She loves living on an island and being part of a
small community, and she also hates it.

"Is there something I can help you with?" Jeremiah asks.

What should she say? She can't ask about Desdemona. It's twenty-five thousand dollars a week and
she's a schoolteacher. And what possible excuse would
she give for renting it? A family reunion? She has
exactly one family member left aside from her child
and that's Cooper. She should never have called. Why
did she call? How is she going to get off the phone
with Jeremiah?

"I'm calling for a friend," Mallory says, then she
cringes because this sounds *so* fishy. "They're looking for a one- or two-bedroom rental over Labor
Day weekend. Preferably on the water. And not too
expensive. Do you have anything available?"

Jeremiah laughs. "I don't have a single thing."

"Right," Mallory says. She had held out a tiny
hope that maybe there was a separate listing sheet
for locals and that Jeremiah, recalling Mallory's kindness toward him so long ago—because it *had* been
kindness—would share it with her. "Okay, I'll tell
them they're out of luck, then. Thanks, Jeremiah."

"You're welcome," Jeremiah says. "Take care."

(Jeremiah hangs up, then stares at the phone. He
actually *does* have something out in Madaket, right on

the beach at the entrance to Smith Point, that would be perfect for two people. He considers calling Miss Blessing back and offering it to her, but he stops himself. He loved her so much once upon a time. When she invited him to spend lunch at Gibbs Pond during the darkest days of his senior year, he thought his prayers had been answered. The whole drive out to the pond, he'd thought about kissing her. But when they'd gotten stuck in the mud, she'd been flustered and short-tempered with him. She had treated him poorly, sending him out to the road for help like she was the queen and he her footman, and then, once they got back to school and everyone was talking about them—Jeremiah's not going to lie, he found this exhilarating—she became frosty. She stopped reading his poetry; she stopped recommending books. She'd been extra-critical on his final assignments and he'd ended the class with an A minus instead of the A he deserved. No, he will not tell her about the cottage on the beach in Madaket, sorry.)

The conversation with Jeremiah Freehold seems to be a sign from above that renting Desdemona is a rotten idea. Even if Mallory were okay with spending twenty-five grand on a weekend rental, Jake would be aghast. If given the choice, he would pick the *Greta*.

Okay, she'll put him on the *Greta*. He won't be able to shower, he'll return to Washington with a salt crust, but oh well.

The night after all this deliberating takes place, Link comes home just before his midnight curfew and Mallory is, embarrassingly, scrolling through real estate listings—at everywhere *but* Grey Lady Real

Estate—on her laptop, looking for something available over Labor Day weekend that is less expensive than Desdemona.

Why is everything booked? Why is Nantucket so popular? Well, she knows why.

"Mom," Link says, sitting down across from her at the harvest table. "Don't say no."

"To what?"

"Just promise me you'll hear me out before saying no."

"You're not going to Italy," Mallory says.

"That's not what I was going to ask," Link says.

"Okay." Mallory closes out her tabs and shuts her laptop. "Shoot."

"Nicole leaves on Monday, September fourth," Link says. "Her flight is out of JFK and she and her mom are spending the weekend, Labor Day weekend, in New York City so they can shop for clothes and stuff for Nicole's trip and they asked me to go with them."

Mallory's heart is on a trampoline doing flips. "*They* asked? Terri is okay with this? She doesn't want a weekend of mother-daughter time?"

"She's the one who suggested it," Link says. "I guess she has some friend, a guy she visits in New York every year, who she wants to see, and so she's even giving Nicole and me money so we can have a real date night."

"*I'll* give you money for date night," Mallory says. Her thoughts are whizzing around like moths at a porch light. Terri has a friend in New York she sees every year. She has a Same Time Next Year too, maybe? And her Same Time Next Year is saving Mallory's? Is that possible?

"So I can go?" Link says.

"Yes, you can go," Mallory says. "Tell Terri I'm paying for all your expenses. She shouldn't have to spend a dime."

Link collapses back in his chair. "Thank you, Mama."

"You're welcome, my sweet prince."

Link's eyes fill. "I don't want her to go."

"I know," Mallory says. "Believe me, I know just how you feel."

Summer #26: 2018

What are we obsessing over in 2018? The Parkland shooting; Kim Jong-un; tariffs; Justify; the Philadelphia Eagles; the opioid epidemic; Mark Zuckerberg; Waffle House; Bill Cosby; Anthony Bourdain; the Tham Luang cave rescue; Banksy; Larry Nassar; the Colorado baker; Peloton; Kate Spade; family separation at the border; the Boss on Broadway; duck boats; Cardi B.; Annapolis; Barbara Bush; Tree of Life synagogue; Stephen Colbert; Chris Pratt and Anna Faris; Daenerys, Jon Snow, Arya, Cersei, Tyrion, Sansa, and Bran; Bohemian Rhapsody; Jerome Powell; "Kiki, do you love me?"; California wildfires; Jamal Khashoggi; George H. W. Bush.

Ursula wakes up to twenty-four text messages, twice as many e-mails, and fifteen voicemails, three of which are from Lansdell Irwin, chairman of the Senate Judiciary Committee.

Eighty-four-year-old Supreme Court justice Cecil Anne Barton, known as Justice Cece, has died in her sleep. It's not exactly a tragedy at her age, but she was loved by one and all.

The three voicemails from Lansdell Irwin are variations on *Wake up, Ursula. We have work to do.*

The selection of a Supreme Court nominee is delicate and Ursula de Gournsey happens to believe it's the most important thing a president will do during an administration. The current president, eighty-three-year-old John Shields, is a kindly gentleman who comes across like a fun grandpa, the one who takes the kids out to Carvel for dinner. It's understood that because of his advanced age, he's a one-term president, a placeholder until the Future steps forward. Shields gamely admits that he doesn't understand "the social media"—he can't figure out Facebook, never mind Twitter—so he leaves that to "the youngsters." Ursula doesn't have high hopes for any Supreme Court candidate Shields nominates; she's heard whisperings of some of the names on the short list and they're all uninspiring.

When his nominee is announced, Ursula is pleasantly surprised. It's Kevin Blackstone Cavendish; he goes by "Stone" or, to his closest friends, "Stonesy." The only sticky issue with Stone Cavendish is that he's yet another white male, and aggressively WASPy: St. Paul's, Dartmouth, Yale. But overall, he's a solid choice, one that is notably nonpartisan. He's married; he has three kids in public schools; he's personable (for a judge), charming, even. If Ursula herself were president, he might be her nominee. She predicts he'll be confirmed by both the House and the Senate with very little drama.

Ursula is wrong.

A woman steps forward, a well-respected superintendent of schools in Richmond, Virginia, who claims that Stone Cavendish physically and sexually abused her in the summer of 1983, which was the summer before both she and Stone left for college. They met at a bonfire in Point Pleasant, New Jersey. Stone was working as a lifeguard there and the woman, Eve Quist, was visiting her friend's summer home for the weekend. Stone and Eve talked at the bonfire; Stone brought Eve a can of Coors Light. Eve claims that when she went into the dunes to relieve herself, Stone Cavendish sneaked up behind her, tackled her in the sand, hiked up her skirt, and started to unbutton his shorts. When Eve started screaming, he threw a handful of sand into her face, and some of it went into her eyes and some of it into her mouth. She felt like she was choking, she says.

He said, *Just be quiet, please, and give me what I want.*

He tried to slip his hand into Eve's panties and she bit his shoulder, hard; she broke the skin, tasted blood. He loosened his grip enough that Eve Quist was able to struggle free and run back to the bonfire to get her friend. The two girls left the party.

Eve told that friend, Lydia Hager, about the incident and said she wanted to call the police. But the two girls had sneaked out of Lydia's house in order to attend the party and Lydia was afraid of getting in trouble. She begged Eve to forget about it. Lydia knew

Stone Cavendish, knew he was off to Dartmouth. Eve, meanwhile, was headed to UVA.

You'll never have to see him again, Lydia said.

Stone Cavendish categorically denies the accusations; he says he doesn't remember Eve Quist, but there is something in his eyes, Ursula thinks, that says otherwise. Or maybe what she and everyone else in America are seeing is his incredulity that anyone can just come out of the woodwork, say whatever she wants, and threaten his chance at a seat on the Supreme Court.

The FBI investigates the accusations. The media has a field day.

Eve Quist is attractive, poised, articulate, intelligent, and has nothing to gain from coming forward. In fact, she has everything to lose. She stays resolute and consistent with her story. Not a single detail changes over the dozens of times she tells it. Her husband, William Quist, is an orthopedic surgeon; he tells investigators that Eve related this story to him on their third date. He says he knows the incident has probably haunted Eve in a way that bad things from your past haunt you and although she would never have tracked the guy down, she couldn't stand by and let him ascend to the highest court in the nation without letting people know that he is—or was—abusive. They aren't looking to *ruin* anyone. Eve would like an admission of guilt and an apology from him.

Stone Cavendish provides neither.

Lydia Hager would have been an excellent corroborating witness but she died of breast cancer in 2011. Eve didn't know anyone else at the party.

The FBI does its due diligence and contacts all the people who were lifeguards in Point Pleasant during the summer of 1983. They find three men and one woman who remember working with Stone, and all four people say they regularly attended bonfires on the beach at which Stone Cavendish was present. The men say they have no idea which night Dr. Quist is referring to. There were so many parties and it was so long ago. The woman, Cindy Piccolo, does claim to remember the evening in question. Cindy Piccolo had been dating Stone Cavendish for most of the summer of 1983 but they had broken up in the middle of August, she said, because Stone wanted to go off to Dartmouth without any lingering attachments. Cindy had still been hung up on him. It was impossible not to be, she said in her statement. He was good-looking, smart, confident, a preppy boarding-school kid who was going to an Ivy League college. Cindy had seen Stone that night talking to a redhead who someone said was a friend of Lydia Hager's. Cindy had watched them closely. She saw when Stone brought Eve a beer; she watched Stone follow Eve into the dunes. She also claims she saw Eve come out of the dunes alone— Cindy registered relief—and she herself had gone to find Stone. They had ended up making love in the dunes that night.

Does Cindy remember if Eve seemed upset coming out of the dunes?

No, she says. *I don't remember.*

Does Cindy remember if Stone had been bitten on the shoulder? Eve Quist says Stone Cavendish was wearing a tank top, so a bite might have been visible.

No, she says. *I don't remember.*

Did Cindy hear anybody talking that night or the next day about what happened while Eve and Stone were in the dunes together?

No, she says.

Did Cindy ever see Lydia or Eve again?

No, Cindy says. *But I remember the red hair. Eve's hair. That's definitely the person he went into the dunes with.*

The country is divided: Team Stone and Team Eve.

Jake is Team Eve.

"The guy definitely did it," he says.

They're in the kitchen, breakfast time. Jake is making Bess an omelet that she will devour without hesitation. She is wonderfully unselfconscious around food, which Ursula is happy about but also jealous of.

"Agreeing with Dad," Bess says.

Ursula says nothing. She supposes families all over the country are discussing this very same issue and picking sides, but most of those families do not include a U.S. senator who will be voting on whether or not to confirm the accused to the Supreme Court.

"I have to stay neutral," she says.

"Oh, come on, Ursula," Jake says. "You can't tell me you think he's innocent?"

"He's a good judge," Ursula says. "Smart. His decisions are thoughtful and nuanced. He would be a wonderful addition to the bench."

"He attacked a girl," Bess says. "He tried to rape her. You can't just overlook that because you happen to like the way he adjudicates, Mom, sorry."

"*Allegedly* attacked her," Ursula says. "I don't think we have enough proof to convict." She smiles at her daughter. "Sorry."

Three days later, a second woman comes forward. This woman, Meghan Royce, is a public defender in Broward County, Florida. She says she met Stone Cavendish at a New Year's Eve party in Miami in 1991. The party was held in a condo in a luxury waterfront building. Royce and Stone struck up a conversation on the balcony, then moved inside to one of the sofas amid the crowd of noisy revelers. Both of them were drinking. Stone eventually suggested they go "somewhere quieter," so he led Royce back into one of the bedrooms. They started kissing. Royce says that after a little while, Stone worried someone else would come into the room so he suggested they go into the closet. Royce says she agreed, but that once she was in the closet with Cavendish, she started to feel "claustrophobic and uncomfortable." She tried to leave; she explicitly told Stone she wanted to "get out," but he laughed and pushed her farther into the closet, back into the hanging clothes. Royce raised her voice, and Stone clapped a hand over her mouth, saying, *Just be quiet, we both know why we're here.* Royce says she finally kicked him in the crotch hard enough that he called her a psycho and spit in her face, but he let her go. She left the party almost immediately, but before she left, she told her girlfriend what happened; she says she categorized it as "some guy just tried to date-rape me in the closet," to which her friend responded, "Thank God you got out, though it's too bad you're going to miss midnight."

That's the way things were in the early '90's, Royce says. *I didn't realize how bad it was until years later.*

Stone Cavendish claims he has no memory of meeting Royce. He admits to being in Miami over New Year's of 1991 with his friend Doug Stiles, but according to Cavendish, they had dinner at a restaurant, then went to a few clubs. He doesn't remember a party. The girlfriend Royce spoke to about it, Justine Hwang, is an expat living in Mongolia and can't immediately be reached for comment. No one knows where to find Doug Stiles.

The media does a hit job on Meghan Royce. She's twice divorced and lost custody of her only son to her ex-husband, who lives in Tampa. The ex-husband, when questioned, said that Meghan has a drinking problem.

Meghan Royce hires an attorney, and she points out Royce's impeccable record as a public defender; she's never missed a day of work and routinely goes to the mat for defendants who have no other champion. She adds that Royce's personal life has no bearing on her memories of what happened between her and Stone Cavendish on New Year's Eve 1991. He pushed her farther into the closet when she asked to get out. He clapped his hand over her mouth. She had to kick him to escape.

The FBI investigates this second claim and manages to reach Justine Hwang in Mongolia, who makes a statement that she does recall the night in question and she does remember Meghan Royce saying that someone forced her into a closet and that she fought her way out. Justine Hwang can't say for certain that this person was Stone Cavendish. She never met the guy that Meghan was talking to, that party was crowded, and she has no recollection at this point of the address of the party or how they ended up there. Word of mouth, she assumes.

Stone Cavendish's spokesperson says that clearly Meghan Royce had been drinking and while something might very well have happened to her at the party she went to, she is mistaken about the identity of the man because it was not Stone Cavendish.

"She probably heard the other accuser's story and decided to try for her fifteen minutes of fame."

Bess is outraged. "I hope you see what's happening here, Mom. They're shaming these women and they're trying to say that just because a woman has lost custody of her son, she's not credible. It's disgusting. The two stories are pretty similar, and the first story has a corroborating witness who remembers seeing Stone Cavendish follow Eve into the dunes and seeing Eve emerge alone. What other proof do you need? People are saying, 'Oh, Cindy is bitter because Stone ditched her for another girl and now she's getting back at him.' Getting back at him thirty-five years later? What's so hard to believe about a woman just remembering what happened and speaking up?" Bess pauses to catch her breath. "You know he did it, Mom."

"There wouldn't be enough to convict him in a court of law," Ursula says.

"Mom."

Ursula sighs. Frankly, she would like to see Cavendish own up to the allegations—or at least admit the possibility that these women *might* be right even if it's so long ago he doesn't remember—and apologize. How refreshing would it be for someone in power to just *admit* to wrongdoing instead of unequivocally denying it? Stone could say he was forceful with women, that he was—just say it—*abusive,* that he was intoxicated and thoughtless, and that he felt invincible and entitled, like so many privileged white males do. And then he could say that he's sorry now. He wishes he could go back to his younger self and give him a thrashing. He has learned so much in the past thirty years. He has grown up.

Ursula could write the statement for him. *This will work!* she wants to say. But Kevin Blackstone Cavendish remains in deny-deny-deny mode. He digs in. His team collects statements from eighty-four female attorneys that he's worked with over the past three decades vouching for his integrity, his character, his manners. They get letters from his priests, from his neighbors, from his teachers and classmates.

The FBI concludes its investigation.

The night before the confirmation hearing, Ursula receives a phone call from Bayer Burkhart.

"Take it easy on him in the hearing, please," Bayer says. "This is the guy we want. He's centrist, speaks for the majority of normal working Americans. Throw him some softballs, please, Ursula. You'll be rewarded."

You'll be rewarded. What Bayer means is that he and his billionaire friends will back Ursula for president in 2020. Until recently, there was talk of running Vincent Stengel for president with Ursula as VP. But the country is ready for a female president; hungry for one, even.

Isn't that what Ursula wants? Isn't that what she has always wanted?

And isn't it true that Kevin Blackstone Cavendish would make an excellent Supreme Court justice? Doesn't America deserve an end to partisan politics? Can't they compromise on issues while preserving the central tenets of freedom, equality, and justice for all? Isn't it time to usher in an era of reason and enlightenment?

"Do you think he did it?" Ursula asks.

"Whether he did it or not isn't relevant," Bayer says. "It was relevant in 1983 and 1991 but it's not relevant now. Do you know who the president was in 1983, Ursula? Ronald Reagan. Do you know who was president in 1991? Bush the father. What these women are digging up is ancient history. And I'm old enough to remember *someone* saying, 'Men are not the enemy.' Do you know who that someone was, Ursula? It was you."

"What's *relevant,*" Ursula says, "is that Cavendish is *lying* about it. Right, Bayer? If he did these things, and I'm inclined to believe that he did, then why doesn't he just admit it?"

"Have you ever lied about anything, Ursula?" Bayer asks.

"Of course."

"Of course," Bayer says.

"But not about something major like this!" Ursula says. "This is denying some egregious behavior."

"What about egregious behavior like sleeping with Anders Jorgensen while the two of you were working on a case in Lubbock, Texas?" Bayer says. "You were married, were you not?"

Ursula nearly drops her phone. She's behind her partners' desk in her home study, sitting in the dark. Jake is somewhere else in the condo. Watching the news, maybe, the pundits' endless speculation.

Anders. Somehow, Bayer Burkhart knows about Anders.

"Bayer," she says, because she's afraid to say anything else.

"A. J. Renninger told me," Bayer says. "She knows because Anders told her. She thought I would be interested. And I am, Ursula, I am—because you seem so squeaky clean, so...irreproachable. But we all mess up. Believe me, I know. I've done what you did, and worse—and that's why I'm not running for office myself."

"Bayer," she says again.

"Tempted to deny it, aren't you?" he says.

Yes, actually, she *is* tempted to deny it.

"Throw him softballs," Bayer says. "And above all, vote to confirm."

Ursula skulks out to the living room. She's giddy with panic.

AJ knows about Anders, and she told Bayer. Who else might she tell? She hates Ursula. Maybe she's always hated her. Yes, okay, let's be realistic, there wasn't a single woman at Andrews, Hewitt, and Douglas who *hadn't* hated Ursula, but it wasn't Ursula's job to be liked, it was Ursula's job to be the best damn M and A attorney she could be. She was a better attorney than AJ; she was a better attorney than Anders. When AJ ran for mayor and called on Ursula for an endorsement, Ursula said she couldn't get involved, but behind the scenes, she'd supported AJ's opponent, and since nothing in Washington stayed a secret for more than five minutes, AJ must have found out.

And you know what? AJ has been a fine mayor. The city has improved under her stewardship. Ursula was a fool not to endorse her. Why did she not guess that Anders had confided in AJ? Why did Ursula assume that Anders would keep their secret? He had probably told AJ in a moment of tender soul-sharing early in their relationship, when it seems wise to disclose details about your past lovers. He'd probably thought it wouldn't matter. Jake and Ursula were in Washington. Anders and AJ were in New York. Nobody was running for office.

Jake is sitting on the edge of the sofa, nearly doubled over, leaning all the way in to the TV, like he might take a bite of it.

"Where are your glasses?" Ursula asks, and Jake startles, then falls back against the leather cushions.

"You've heard?" he says. "They've found that guy Doug Stiles. He's talking."

Doug Stiles turned up in Sonoma County, California. He lives in the hills amid vineyards, some of which were burned out in the fires. He's a hermit, a survivalist. A woman who works at the Healdsburg post office figured out that this was the Doug Stiles the country was waiting to hear from.

Yes, Doug Stiles remembers New Year's Eve 1991, Miami, with Stone Cavendish, a person he hasn't seen or even thought of in eons. He recalls the night. They went to dinner at Joe's Stone Crab and then to a party in a penthouse apartment overlooking Biscayne Bay. They were at the party all night. Doug Stiles doesn't remember any girl in particular. There were a lot of girls, he says. And he and Stone were drunk and high, and there might have been some cocaine involved as well, he can't say for sure, but it's definitely not out of the question. It was the early nineties.

Despite this bombshell at the last minute, the confirmation hearing goes much as Ursula thought it would. Stone Cavendish is a darling for nearly every senator on the Judiciary Committee. They handle him with kid gloves and no one mentions the new information from Doug Stiles—yes, Stone Cavendish did apparently attend a party in a waterfront condo as Meghan Royce said. He and Doug Stiles did not "go to the clubs." But does this lie—or misremembering—on his part mean that the entirety of Meghan Royce's accusation is true?

When it's Ursula's turn to question Stone Cavendish, she says, "Is there any statement you've made over the past two weeks that you'd like to retract or change, even just a little, so that we have the record straight?"

Stone Cavendish leans into the microphone, eyes down. "No."

"So you are flat-out denying that you ever followed a girl into the sand dunes, tackled her, threw sand in her face—either intentionally or unintentionally—clapped your hand over her mouth, and tried to lift her skirt against her wishes? And you're flat-out denying that you met a woman on New Year's Eve 1991 and asked her to join you in a closet and pushed her farther into that closet when she said she wanted to get out, and clapped a hand over *her* mouth? And furthermore, you're flat-out denying that you were even *at* a party that night, despite the friend you were with recently saying otherwise?"

Stone Cavendish meets her eyes this time. He's defiant—angry, even; she can see that. His expression says, *How dare you hold my feet to the fire like this?* Ursula worries for a second that AJ or Bayer told Stone about Ursula's own indiscretion and that Stone Cavendish is going to turn the questioning back on her in a nationally televised hearing.

"That's right, Senator," he says.

Ursula can feel dirty looks from her fellow committee members. She is not usually a disrupter. She's neutral, a political Switzerland. She is straight up the fairway.

"So you would like us to believe that four American citizens—Dr. Eve Quist, Ms. Cynthia Piccolo, Ms. Meghan Royce, and your own friend Mr. Douglas Stiles—are lying and that you are telling the truth."

"Yes, Senator."

Ursula doesn't ask any further questions, but news anchors and political pundits across the spectrum later comment about the expression on Ursula's face.

Rachel Maddow says, *The senator looks skeptical.*

Shepard Smith says, *Senator Ursula de Gournsey clearly doesn't believe him.*

Luke Russert says, *It's obvious the senator thinks Stone Cavendish is full of…baloney.*

The Senate votes on the confirmation of Kevin Blackstone Cavendish three days later. Before Ursula leaves the house that morning, Jake says, "Just think if one of those young women were Bess."

"Bess is too smart to get herself in that position," Ursula says.

"Is she, though?" Jake asks.

Kevin Blackstone Cavendish is confirmed to the Supreme Court by a vote of 61 to 39, which is not surprising. What is surprising is that one of the dissenting votes is cast by Ursula de Gournsey.

Frankly, she surprised herself.

People will talk about her vote for an entire news cycle—five days—but no one will know exactly what moved her near-certain yes to a resounding no.

Jake might think it was his last-minute insertion of Bess into the conversation, and Bess might think it was because of her own final teary plea to her mother—she'd called Ursula during her car ride to the Capitol Building and said, *Mom, please stand up for womankind!*

No one will know that in the hour before Ursula cast her vote, she was visited by a memory that she'd relegated to the delete-from-deleted file of her brain.

She's a first-semester sophomore at Notre Dame and she and Jake have just broken up. Ursula is upset about this. Jake was the one who wanted to split; he thought they should date other people. *This doesn't mean we won't get married,* he said. *But I think it's a good idea to see what other people have to offer.* Ursula doesn't philosophically disagree but hearing the words come from Jake, who has been so ardent since the age of thirteen, is hurtful. Ursula feels she has lost her magic.

She turns to religion, which is a comfort. She joins the campus ministry and attends every meeting, and in a few short months she is spearheading outreach for the undergraduates as well as service projects in the community. She organizes trips to shelters and soup kitchens in Gary, Indiana. At the start of the spring semester, she's a shoo-in for president of the group. But when she approaches Father Gillis, he suggests she run for vice president instead. Father Gillis supports a junior named Nathan Bowers for president. Nathan, after all, is a year ahead of Ursula and has been in the group a year longer.

Right, Ursula thinks, *but Nathan Bowers doesn't do anything.* He's a heavy-lidded dope smoker, good-looking, and with a certain lazy charm; he's too cool for the campus ministry. He lies around, and makes wisecracks. He's not exactly a model Christian.

In November, when the group goes downtown to fill Thanksgiving boxes—frozen turkey, Stove Top stuffing, cranberry sauce—Nathan keeps calling them *handouts*.

It takes a while for Ursula to realize that Father Gillis wants Nathan to be president because he's male.

Nathan becomes president of the Notre Dame campus ministry and Ursula, VP.

Fast-forward to the end of the spring semester, mid-May. Nathan Bowers and his three roommates are throwing a party at the house they've rented for the summer on Chapin Street and Nathan is eager for Ursula to attend. Ursula doesn't go to parties very often; she's too busy studying. But it's a mild spring evening, it's a Friday, and Ursula thinks it sounds like fun.

She drinks way too much—two cups of the grain alcohol–and–Ocean Spray punch they're pouring out of plastic pitchers. After that, there's a game of Mexican, a bunch of warm beers, maybe a shot of Jägermeister. At some point, Nathan asks Ursula if she wants to go upstairs. Ursula isn't sure if she says yes or no. The next thing she remembers is waking up to find Nathan grinding on top of her. They aren't having sex, but she wants him to stop whatever it is he's doing. However, she's too tired and too drunk to push him away. She closes her eyes.

She wakes up in the middle of the night to find Nathan sitting in a papasan chair in the corner, smoking a joint and staring at her so intensely it feels like a violation.

Ursula looks down. She's lying on Nathan's comforter, fully clothed, thank God. He was on top of her before, yes? Or did she dream that? "What did you do to me?" she asks.

He exhales a plume of smoke. "Don't you remember? You seemed pretty into it."

"I wasn't conscious," Ursula says, and the nascent lawyer in her surfaces. "Did you rape me?"

Nathan laughs. "No, Ursula."

"You did something. I remember"—she's not sure how to describe it—"you were on top of me."

"That was what you wanted."

Ursula swings her feet to the floor. She feels like she's operating a piece of heavy machinery trying to get herself upright. Her head is splitting. "You're disgusting."

"You asked me for it."

"I was too drunk to know what I was doing, Nathan," Ursula says. "What did you guys put in that punch?"

"Oh, sure," Nathan says. "Blame the punch." He sets the roach in an ashtray. "If you report me, no one will believe you. They'll think it's because Gillis made me president when you thought it should have been you."

"It *should* have been me," Ursula says. "But that has nothing to do with what happened tonight. I'm going to call a taxi to take me home, and in the morning, I'm calling the police."

"You're bluffing," Nathan says. But he looks worried.

It turns out, Ursula *was* bluffing. She doesn't go to the dean or her parents, nor does she tell a single one of her friends what happened, mostly because she doesn't know what happened. She knows only that she drank too much and that Nathan took advantage of her drunken state to satisfy his own desires. He shouldn't have touched her. And yet she knows that she's the one who will be blamed.

The bravery of the two women who came out against Stone Cavendish is remarkable.

Ursula imagined how she would have felt if Nathan Bowers were about to be confirmed to the Supreme Court and he flat-out denied having Ursula in his room and grinding himself on top of her when she was too drunk to give consent.

Not on my watch, Ursula thought. And she voted no.

The morning after Cavendish is confirmed, Bayer Burkhart calls. Ursula nearly lets it go to voicemail. She doesn't need to hear what she already knows: Because she voted no instead of yes, he's putting his support behind a different candidate in 2020.

Ignoring his call, however, is cowardly. What was the point of voting her heart, her conscience, if she's too timid to defend it? "Hello, Bayer."

"Ursula." Bayer is eating something—a bagel, probably, slathered with cream cheese, piled with lox. He has quite the impressive appetite. "I can't believe I'm about to say this, but you did good."

"What?"

"Listen, I got the outcome I wanted. Cavendish is on the bench. And you, my friend, are a national hero."

"I am?"

"You've got a seventy-two percent approval rate among women from both parties," Bayer says. "You were the only senator on the committee willing to stand by your principles and not vote for a guy who was lying." Bayer swallows. "You were impressive. Calm but commanding. I would have been mad as hell at you if he'd lost the vote, but he didn't. If I were you, I'd wait no more than a week before you announce."

"Announce?"

"That you're running for president," Bayer says. "My money is on you. You're going to win."

Summer #27: 2019

What are we talking about in 2019? The death of Bernard Slade, playwright; Nancy Pelosi; college admission cheating scandal; Miley and Liam; tamago sando; Lizzo; check your Uber; Jeffrey Epstein; Logan, Kendall, Roman, Shiv, Tom, Gerri, and Greg; Old Town Road; Rob Gronkowski; al-Baghdadi; Notre-Dame; John Legend and Chrissy Teigen; Where the Crawdads Sing; El Paso; Lady Gaga and Bradley Cooper.

On the fifteenth of April, Link gets acceptance letters from the University of Alabama, the University of Georgia, Auburn, Ole Miss, and the University of South Carolina, and Mallory can't help herself: she bursts into tears.

She's so proud of him.

She's gutted by the thought of him leaving. And yet she knows it's natural. If he weren't leaving, he'd be staying, and neither of them wants that.

Link decides on the University of South Carolina. Frazier is excited because U of SC is home to the Darla Moore School of Business, but Link tells Mallory that he has no interest in business. He wants to follow in his uncle's footsteps—major in political science and shape domestic policy that will make life better, easier, more prosperous for American citizens. This all sounds very lofty to Mallory, but then Link admits that he also wants a school with big football, big school spirit, fraternities, pretty girls, and warm weather. Any school in the Southeastern Conference fits the bill. The University of South Carolina is his favorite, and it also happens to be the closest to home. From Boston, Mallory can fly to Charlotte, then it's straight down Route 77 to Columbia.

Once Link makes this decision, things move quickly. All of a sudden, Mallory finds herself sitting in the bleachers of his last home baseball game. How is that possible? When Mallory closes her eyes, she's back in Cooperstown. She's at the Delta fields, watching him wallop a Wiffle ball off a tee. It's his first birthday and Senior is tossing Link the squishy ball that he hits with the oversize plastic bat on his first try.

Natural talent here, Mal! Senior cries out.

Link takes Elsa Judd to the prom—Link and Nicole broke up six days into Nicole's year in Italy—and then he asks Lauren Prestifilipo to the senior ball. He's casual friends with both girls—friends or friends-with-whatever—because he knows he's leaving for college and he learned his lesson with Nicole: he doesn't want to leave with any romantic entanglements.

The last week of class arrives for the seniors, and then the triumvirate of senior ball, baccalaureate, and graduation.

Parents are invited to come to the senior ball after the seniors-only dinner. Mallory goes to R. J. Miller to get her hair blown out and then puts on a new dress, just as she always does the night of the senior ball. Tonight—she has to repeat this to herself several times—she isn't going just as a teacher; she's going as a parent. The mother of a senior.

During the reading of the senior-class prophecy, Mallory's vision starts to get blotchy. At first she thinks it's just her tears, but she can't seem to blink or wipe away the amorphous pink blob in the upper left corner of her field of vision.

The senior-class prophecy involves a fictional tale about Gibbs Pond—*Oh, boy, good old Gibbs,* Mallory thinks—being bought by an evil developer who wants to drain the pond and build a Nantucket-themed amusement park. All the members of the senior class twenty-five years in the future are called on to contribute their particular talents or personality quirks in order to save the pond—but in the end, it's billionaire Lincoln Dooley who is the hero.

The times that Mallory has asked God to stop time for her and Jake seem quaint compared to how badly Mallory wants to stop time now. Just let these high-school days go on forever, please—the gatherings of boys eating chips and guacamole around the harvest table or playing Fortnite while sitting on Big Hugs; the baseball games in thirty-seven-degree weather; the pep rallies and Spanish-club dinners; the Homecoming floats and SAT prep; even the Bud Light cans stuffed deep in the trash and the empty nip bottles of McGillicuddy's scattered across the front porch; even the heartbreak of day six of Nicole-in-Italy when she texted to say she needed *la libertà,* and Link screamed profanities across the ocean, then went into his bedroom and cried.

She'll take it all on a loop, forever and ever.

Baccalaureate is held at the Congregational church. Lauren Prestifillipo sings "Brave," by Sara Bareilles, and that's all it takes—Mallory dissolves. Her vision still isn't clear and all this emotion is giving her a headache. This is probably some kind of karmic payback for the many years when Mallory sat in this church watching other parents cry and scoffed, *Oh, come on, it's not like they're going off to war, they're graduating, be happy!*

Graduation, strangely, is the least emotional day of the week, probably because Mallory has the distraction of guests. Fray, Anna, and Cassie fly in on Fray's plane late Friday night (they're staying at the White Elephant), and Cooper and Amy fly to Boston from DC but get stuck at Logan because of early-morning fog on Nantucket.

Amy calls Mallory in a panic. "I'm not sure what's up with Cape Air," she says. "The woman at the desk says they're waiting for the ceiling to lift. What if we miss the ceremony?" Amy is high-strung for a psychologist, Mallory thinks. She and Cooper have been married for just a few years, and yet Amy has donned the role of Auntie Amy like it's a thirty-thousand-dollar sable coat. It's sweet, if a bit unsettling. Amy has been reposting all of Mallory's photos from this week on her personal Facebook page with the tags *#nephewLink* and *#proudauntie.*

"The fog usually burns off midmorning," Mallory says. "It'll be fine. Deep breath."

And it is fine. Cooper and Amy arrive in plenty of time to clap and cheer as Link walks across the stage in his white cap and gown to accept his diploma.

That's it, Mallory thinks. *It's over. Link is a high-school graduate.* Her field of vision still has that bright spot in the corner like an incoming alien spaceship, though her headache has subsided somewhat. Or maybe she's just used to it.

The worst is yet to come, of course. The summer of 2019 might as well be called the Summer Link Pushes the Envelope. He has given up his job at Millie's general store in favor of a job landscaping. He's out in the sun all day, mowing, weeding, laying sod, trimming hedges. He's deeply tan and his hair is bleached platinum blond; he has real muscles, and he grows another two inches. He looks so much like Fray that Mallory sometimes does a double take when she sees him.

Link goes out with his friends every single night. Mallory knows he's drinking and also probably smoking and sleeping with beautiful, rich summer girls from New Canaan and the Upper East Side. Mallory keeps her rules to a minimum, although the rules she does lay down are ironclad—midnight curfew during the week, no driving at night at all, and no shenanigans at the house. She tries to set up one evening a week when Link eats with her at home and one night when the two of them go out together, but Link cancels and no-shows so much that Mallory gives up.

Apple's twins are spending a month and a half at sleepaway camp in Maine, so Mallory and Apple resume their nights out once a week. They return to

the Summer House. The restaurant has changed—
the days of the Hokey Pokey are long gone—but the
view is still magnificent.

"It's like he's already off to college," Mallory says.
"That's how little I see him."

"Kids do this the summer before they leave for
college," Apple says in her guidance-counselor voice.
"They separate so that it's less painful for them when
you say goodbye. It's completely normal."

"Just wait until it happens to you," Mallory says.
"Then you'll wish you'd been more sensitive."

"You're lucky," Apple says. "You can reclaim your
personhood, become more involved in the outside
world. It's exciting out there, I hear. And it's an
empowering time to be female. I know you don't pay
attention to politics, but there's this incredible woman
running for president." Apple raises her glass of wine.
"Here's to Ursula de Gournsey. May she save us all."

Mallory obviously knows that Ursula is running for
president; the only good thing about Link leaving is
that Mallory is too self-absorbed to think about it.

Southern universities start early, so Mallory throws a
goodbye beach bash for Link and all his friends on
August 14. The kids have a great time—the music is
so loud, it feels like Post Malone is there at the party—
but Mallory can't seem to relax and enjoy the moment.
Her thoughts are heavy, maudlin. When the golden
hour arrives, making everything look like it's been
dipped in honey, Mallory thinks about how her front
porch has served as her church, the ocean as her daily
proof that God exists. She has done all her praying
out here—she has expressed gratitude and wonder,

asked for forgiveness, petitioned for those in need. But today, as Link and his friends dig a hole for the bonfire, Mallory prays for herself. She needs more of everything: strength, clarity, hope, patience, peace.

Please, she thinks. *Send it to me. Or let me discover it within myself.*

Mallory and Link leave for Columbia two days later. The blob in Mallory's vision seems to be getting bigger. She's planning on seeing a doctor the second she gets back to Nantucket.

But first, there's a trip from the suffocating ninety-nine-degree heat to the delicious air-conditioned universe of Target for twin XL sheets, comforter, pillows, a rug, underwear, socks, a case of Gatorade, two cartons of Pepperidge Farm cheddar goldfish, spiral notebooks, pens, phone chargers, ramen, a poster of Dominic West and Idris Elba in *The Wire* (this is Link's idea of an homage to his Baltimore roots, just wonderful), shampoo, deodorant, towels, condoms, Band-Aids, a two-hundred-count bottle of Advil, sunscreen.

"What else?" Mallory asks. As long as there's something more to buy, she can stave off the inevitable.

They move their haul into East Quad. Link meets his suitemates: Eric, Will, Declan. The boys seem nice; the other mothers are busy decorating their sons' rooms and stocking the cabinets in the communal kitchen as though they're expecting a nuclear winter. Mallory helps Link get his room set up, and girls keep poking their heads into the suite to introduce themselves. They all have long beautiful hair and syrupy Southern accents and first names like Shelby and Baker. There's rap music playing, then that song by Lizzo that Mallory loves. This is college, it's fun, Link's going to have the time of his life. His RA introduces himself, nice kid; his name is Jake, so Mallory automatically loves him. Jake asks if Mallory has any questions. Well, yes, she does: How is anyone expected to devote eighteen years to raising a child and then, one day, just leave him in an unfamiliar place among strangers twelve hundred miles from home? And also: What is wrong with her eyesight? She made an appointment with her ophthalmologist for the following week.

"Nope," Mallory says. "No questions."

"All freshmen in this dorm have a mandatory meeting at three o'clock and then there's Convocation, where the university president will speak, and after that are First Night activities." Jake pauses. There's a vintage turntable in the common room playing Fleetwood Mac's *Rumours,* which is a reason to love Jake beyond his name. But despite this, Mallory wants him to stop talking. It feels like the next words out of his mouth are going to be *So now is probably a good time to say your goodbyes*.

Mallory has learned from twenty-six years with Jake that a fast goodbye is better than a long, drawn-out goodbye. She finds Link in his room, putting shirts on hangers.

"I've been given my marching orders," Mallory says. "You have a full docket, so I'm going to go."

"Okay," Link says. He shuts the closet door and then takes Mallory by the shoulders and looks at her with his ocean-colored eyes, eyes she knows better than anyone else's. "I want to thank you for getting me this far, Mama. I'm going to study and exercise good judgment and check my Ubers and be kind to everyone I meet, just like you taught me." He hugs her tight. It very much feels at that moment like he is the adult and she the child. "I love you. You did a good job."

A week later, Mallory is out on her beach under an umbrella reading Dani Shapiro's new memoir when she hears someone knocking on the door of her cottage.

She wants this to be a figment of her imagination—maybe she's hearing things now as well as seeing things—but there's no mistaking the *rap-rap-rap*ping. Mallory considers not moving an inch. FedEx and UPS drop packages. Apple doesn't stop by unannounced, but if she did, she'd just come down to the beach. It's still two weeks until Jake's arrival, and he never knocks anyway. There's no one else Mallory wants to see.

There's a reprieve, then more rapping.

Mallory heads up to the house. On the front porch, she stops to rinse off her sandy feet with the hose. She's wearing linen drawstring pants over her bikini and a long-sleeved Gamecocks T-shirt. Ponytail, hat. She looks like a dirt sandwich.

Through the screen of the pond-side door, she sees the form of a woman and, beyond the woman, a black sedan, a car-service car, dusty after a ride down the no-name road. At the same time that Mallory wonders, *Who is this?* she gets a jolt of incredulous shock because she knows who it is.

The spot in her vision starts to expand and contract like it's a living, breathing thing.

Mallory wants to go into her bedroom, close and

lock the door, and shutter the house as if preparing for a hurricane. But the woman has seen her.

Mallory stops to look around. Without Link here, her house is spotless. Which is a good thing, because she fears the woman she's about to invite inside is Ursula de Gournsey.

Yes; when Mallory reaches the door, she can see it's Ursula. "Hello?" Mallory says. Her voice sounds bright, chipper, wholly unconcerned. She couldn't have done any better if she'd been practicing how to nonchalantly greet Ursula de Gournsey surprising her at the door daily for the past twenty-six years. Meanwhile, inside of Mallory, a woman is releasing a high-pitched horror-film scream.

Mallory checks the car. Is Jake inside? No, it's a driver. The screaming ratchets down one notch.

"Mallory?" Ursula says. "Hello. I'm Ursula de Gournsey."

"Ursula?" Mallory says, still maintaining her cool. "Hello."

"Do you mind if I come in?" Ursula says. "I was hoping we could talk."

Now's not a good time, Mallory thinks. *I'm having a psychotic episode.*

This is it, then—the reckoning. Mallory has long wondered if this day would ever come or if that was the kind of thing that happened only in movies. It notably does *not* happen in *Same Time, Next Year.* George and Doris roll merrily along right into their old age—and their respective spouses, Helen and Harry, remain none the wiser.

"Of course," Mallory says. She pushes the screen door open and Ursula de Gournsey steps inside. She's wearing a blue chambray linen sheath with matching pumps (also now dusty). Her hair is long and thick and luxuriously dark. There are lines around her eyes and mouth that don't show up on television. "Would you like some iced tea? And I made chicken salad this morning if you'd like a sandwich."

"Iced tea would be lovely, thank you," Ursula says.

It gives Mallory something to do. She pours iced tea into two of her brand-new tumblers—to cheer herself up, she went on a nice-things-I-couldn't-have-while-Link-was-around spending spree—puts some pita chips into a bowl, and gets out her silken, luscious homemade baba ghanouj. The other thing she has done to boost her spirits is cook.

"Baba ghanouj," she says to Ursula as she brings everything into the living room on a wicker tray. "The eggplants from Bartlett's Farm are like nothing you've ever tasted."

Ursula murmurs something. She won't touch the food, Mallory knows, because she doesn't eat. She doesn't read fiction either, and yet she's drawing one finger across the spines of the books that Jake has sent Mallory over the years, from *The English Patient* to *Less*. Does she know they're from Jake? Then Ursula picks up one of the sand dollars on that shelf, and Mallory has to suppress the hysterical laugh that's gathering at the back of her throat.

"Let's sit," Mallory says. She places the tray on the coffee table and settles into Big Hugs while Ursula perches on the edge of one of the club chairs.

Ursula de Gournsey is here. In the cottage. In that chair.

Mallory hands Ursula an iced tea garnished with a wheel of lemon and a wheel of lime side by side on the rim, a hundred percent Instagram-able.

Ursula doesn't seem inclined to speak, so Mallory says, "I didn't realize you were on Nantucket."

"I have a fund-raising dinner tonight," Ursula says. "Private." She takes a tiny sip of tea. "I'm running for president."

"Yes, I know," Mallory says. "Your vote on Judge Cavendish—I was proud of you. Every woman in America was proud of you."

Ursula's perfectly shaped eyebrows shoot up; maybe she's surprised at the compliment. "Well, the election is still a long way off," she says. "Anything can happen. Issues arise unexpectedly. Parts of your past come up, incidents you thought were long forgotten—hell, things you don't remember...or even know about. When you're running for president of the United States"—she sets her tea down—"your life has to be transparent. A clean window."

And you've come with the squeegee, Mallory thinks.

"You and Jake see each other?" Ursula says. "Every year?"

She's asking Mallory rather than telling her. She seems uncertain, which Mallory didn't expect. Ursula has a hunch but not proof, maybe? Jake hasn't told her. Jake doesn't know Ursula is here. This whole thing, Mallory understands suddenly, has very little to do with Jake.

"What makes you think that?" Mallory asks. The spot in her vision has quieted, but it's still there, watchful.

Ursula smiles. "I guess if I'm being honest, I would say I've always had a suspicion. Since Cooper's first wedding, when I saw the two of you dancing together."

"During Coop's second wedding, I saw you in the

ladies' room," Mallory says. "You told me you were pregnant. And I got the feeling you were going to confess the baby wasn't Jake's." It's Mallory's turn to use her tea as a prop. She takes a sip. And what the hell, she's hungry; she drags a pita chip through the baba ghanouj. She's not afraid of food.

"At Cooper's third wedding, when I asked Cooper if he and Jake were planning on continuing their Nantucket weekends, it was quite obvious Cooper had no idea what I was talking about. Tish *certainly* had no idea. Which I found odd."

"Tish," Mallory says. "I can't believe you remember her name."

"Then I read the article in *Leland's Letter*," Ursula says. "And I called your brother again, only he was ready for me, or at least readier. He told me that, yes, he and Jake went to Nantucket every summer."

Mallory's breathing is so shallow, she feels like she's playing a dead person on television.

"I thought, *Okay, maybe he's lying, protecting his little sister.* You two had just lost your parents—"

"Please," Mallory says, and she shakes her head.

"And *then* . . . then, then, then." Ursula spins first her watch and then a gold Cartier love bracelet around her wrist, and Mallory can't help but imagine the birthday or Christmas when Jake gave it to her; Ursula's joy, their kiss. "I have an adviser, a donor, a . . . friend of sorts named Bayer Burkhart. From Newport, Rhode Island. You know him."

The *You know him* is pointedly *not* a question. *Bayer,* Mallory thinks. *Bayer, of all people, is the one who told Ursula?* "I knew him a long time ago," Mallory says. "In my twenties."

Ursula nods. "He told me. He was quite taken by

you, apparently, during a time when he and Dee Dee were having trouble. He said he considered divorcing her and marrying you."

"Ha!" Mallory says. The spot in her vision twinkles; it seems to be laughing along. "That's ridiculous. We were…it was…a summer romance. And he was married, but I didn't know that until the night we broke up."

"Which was also the night you told him you had a Same Time Next Year. Whose name was Jake McCloud."

"That was all so long ago—"

"Bayer forgot about it," Ursula says. "He met Jake at a donor party years ago and said he thought something rang a bell, but he couldn't figure out what it was." Ursula slaps her hands on her knees. "Then, a couple of years ago, he saw the two of you on the docks. Friday of Labor Day weekend."

Mallory isn't sure what to say, so she has another pita chip. Her crunching is very loud in her own ears.

"Bayer didn't tell me then because—well, because I think it took him a while to put it all together. And also, I wasn't running for president."

Mallory realizes she doesn't have to say a word. She hasn't broken the law. Ursula isn't the police. Mallory stands up. "I hope your dinner goes well. Thanks for stopping by."

"Mallory."

Mallory won't look at her. She carries the tray back to the kitchen. "Did I tell you my son just left for college? He's at the University of South Carolina. The house is so quiet without him."

"Yes, I have a daughter at college as well. Bess. She's a freshman at Johns Hopkins. As you must know."

Yes, Mallory knows. "I'm from Baltimore," Mallory says. "Cooper and I were raised there." She puts the baba ghanouj back in the fridge without any covering. She is distracted by the pressing need to sweep Ursula out the door. Her driver is waiting. What must he think? What did she tell him? She probably said she was visiting an old friend. The cottage isn't grand enough to belong to a major donor.

"I need you to stop seeing Jake," Ursula says. "He can't come this Labor Day or next Labor Day or—if I win—any of the Labor Days while I'm in office."

Mallory's reaction to this statement must give it all away. She recoils like this is a duel and Ursula has drawn first and shot Mallory between the eyes. Or like it's a swordfight and Ursula has just plunged a saber through Mallory's ribs. Jake won't come in two weeks? He won't come the following year? Or, if Ursula wins, for four—or eight—years? Mallory is fifty years old. She realizes she may be sixty before she feels Jake's arms around her again.

"Why are you talking to *me*?" Mallory asks, turning away. "Jake is your husband. If you don't want him to come to Nantucket, tell him."

"If I tell him that I know—" Ursula stops suddenly. When Mallory looks over, she sees Ursula's head is bowed. "If I ask him not to come here, I'm afraid he'll leave me."

So keep things the way they are! Mallory wants to say. She's tempted to beg. Mallory has lost her parents and dropped her only child off at college. She's alone here. Except for Jake three magical days per year, Mallory is alone.

"But...I can't have the press or my opponent's

camp finding out about this. And trust me, Mallory, you don't want that either. They'll drag your name through the mud. You'll be vilified. You're a teacher, right? Pretty beloved, from what I understand."

"You don't *understand* the first thing about me."

"I do, though," Ursula says. "You love Jake. I understand that better than anyone else. But please, it stops now. He's my husband."

Husband.

The bright spot encroaches a little farther into Mallory's visual field. It's white-hot, insistent. It is, she realizes, her *conscience,* inserting itself into the conversation after all these many years.

Jake and Mallory's relationship is unusual, whimsical, even, like a fairy tale. It has always seemed to exist outside of reality, or so Mallory chose to believe. They weren't breaking any rules if there were no rules. They weren't hurting anyone's feelings if no one knew.

But now.

Now, Mallory has to make a decision. Own up to what she's been doing and stop. Or deny what she's been doing and continue.

The spot in her eye is as bright as a flare.

"Okay," Mallory says.

"Okay what?"

"Okay, I'll stop," Mallory says. "I'll stop."

"You will?" Ursula says. She narrows her eyes. Her irises are so dark, they're nearly black, two chips of obsidian.

"Yes. You have my word."

"Ah."

"Ursula," Mallory says. "You have my word."

Ursula nods. "Thank you." She inhales and seems to take in her surroundings for the first time, moving her eyes around the cottage. Does she approve? And why does Mallory care? She should feel nothing but disdain, or maybe hatred, toward this woman, her longtime rival, but she doesn't, not quite. Ursula stands and clicks in her dusty stilettos over to the screen door, and Mallory feels almost sad that she's leaving. In losing Jake, she loses Ursula too, her shadow opponent, the woman who has been hovering over Mallory's shoulder, motivating her to be her best self. If Mallory were honest, she would admit that the competition with Ursula was inspiring to her.

At the door Ursula turns around. "You make him happy, you know."

Tears, a flood of them, press—but Mallory won't cry in front of Ursula.

"Yes," Mallory says. "I know."

Two weeks later, the text comes to Mallory's phone: I'm here.

She locks up the cottage—the day before, she went hunting for the keys and found them deep in the junk drawer—and heads to the hiding place she's chosen, forty or fifty yards away, behind a dip in the dunes. It's childish to play games like this, she knows, but this was the best option among a host of terrible ones. Jake can't know that Ursula knows. This has to seem like it's coming from Mallory. If Mallory calls him, she'll end up confessing about Ursula's visit. Mallory considered texting Something came up, I have to cancel. Or even I've met someone, please don't come. But she can't be cruel. And, selfishly, she wants to set eyes on him.

She doesn't respond to his text and another text follows: You there? Hello?

It's amazing how seamlessly this relationship has worked on just a simple routine and trust. Nothing has ever trumped their time together—things almost had, several times, but they prevailed.

Until now.

She waits. Will he come or will he sense something is wrong and abort? His radar must be on amber alert anyway, with Ursula running for president. His every move must be monitored.

A little while later, Mallory hears a car. She peers up over the dune to see a Jeep enveloped in the usual cloud of dust. He's here. Mallory's heart leaps exactly as it has for the past twenty-six years.

Who cares *about Ursula?* she thinks.

Except…Mallory gave her word. She knows Ursula was hesitant to trust her, probably figuring that a woman who'd slept with her husband for so long would have no problem lying to her face about stopping.

The car door slams and Mallory shudders. From her hiding spot, she sees Jake get out. She moans softly. Jake! She can tell just from the way he's carrying himself that he's agitated—confused, maybe even angry. He strides up to the pond-side door and tries to open it, but it's locked. She hears him murmur something, and then he goes around the house. She can't see him but she imagines him standing on the porch, checking out the beach in each direction. She hears the creak of the door to the outdoor shower and she breathes a sigh of relief; she had considered hiding in there.

"Mallory!" he yells.

She closes her eyes. His voice.

"Mallory! Where are you?" He's shouting; he must not care who hears him. There's a messy edge to his voice, not tears, exactly, but maybe some panic. Has something happened to her? Is she okay?

Mallory travels back to the first summer when they yelled for Fray on the beach. Mallory had been so terrified, she remembers, or as terrified as a twenty-four-year-old girl who had never had anything bad happen to her could be. She has often scared herself by imagining how awful it would have been if Fray had drowned. Without Fray, there would be no Link. Mallory wonders if she would have gotten married to someone else and had different children—presumably she would have. She and Jake wouldn't have bonded, except in crushing guilt.

It's astonishing how the events of one evening can influence so much. Mallory thinks about her parents. Why did Senior not just stay in the Audi and call AAA? Well, because he was Cooper Blessing Sr. and would have deduced that he could change the tire himself in half the time it would take for AAA to arrive. Kitty had gotten out of the car—well, because she was Kitty and liked to supervise, always.

"Mallory!" Jake yells again. "Mal! Mal, please! Where are you?"

Mallory is forced to face her own disingenuousness. If she'd really wanted this to work, she would have gone away. But she'd wanted to see Jake's reaction. Watching and hearing him without his knowledge is like reading his mind: he loves her.

She gets another text. The buzzing of her phone is louder than she anticipates.

Where are you? Your cottage is locked but your Jeep is here. Just please, for the love of God, tell me where you are. It's not fair for you to just leave me hanging like this, you know it's not.

He's right; it's not fair.

"Mallory!"

She imagines this from his point of view. He waits all year, anticipating. Then he makes the necessary arrangements, lies to Ursula and the forty staff members who are now watching his every move, and shows up here, expecting to step through the door of the cottage and find burgers, shucked corn, sliced tomatoes; Cat Stevens, World Party, Lenny Kravitz on the stereo; a new pile of books on "his" side of the bed—and Mallory.

The door is locked. He's had no warning of this. He's blindsided.

Mallory wants to run over the dune calling out his name and jump into his arms. She wants to kiss him. It will be like the ending of the movie where Doris and George think it's over, but then George comes bursting back in and they reunite—to continue, year after year, *until our bones are too brittle to risk contact.*

But this isn't a movie—that movie, or any other. It's their lives, and she's a human being and can take only so much.

She sends him a text: We can't do this, Jake. It's too dangerous now.

I don't care if it's dangerous.

Not only for you, Mallory writes. For me as well. And for Link. And for Bess.

Are you here somewhere? he writes. Can you see me?

No, she types. But before she can hit Send, her phone rings. The buzzer is loud, and it's a still afternoon, the air heavy with mist; she's certain he can hear the sound floating over the dunes. She declines the call.

You are here, he says.

No, I'm not.

He calls again. She declines the call immediately. She should turn her phone off, she knows, but she doesn't want to end their communication. She and Jake have spent the past twenty-odd years not using cell phones because that's how other people get discovered. Now that they have been discovered, she supposes it doesn't matter.

I want to see you for sixty seconds, he texts. Please. Then I'll leave.

Jake, no. That won't work.

One kiss, he texts. Please. Just one kiss, then I promise, I'll leave.

There might be some among us who would say no to that request, but our girl Mallory isn't one of them.

Close your eyes, she texts.

She climbs out of the dunes and doesn't see him, which means he's moved around to the front porch. And that is indeed where Mallory finds him.

They kiss. It's just one kiss, the deepest, sweetest, most heartbreaking, stomach-flipping kiss of Mallory's life. With only the Atlantic Ocean as their witness, they swear that kiss will hold them through the next two or six or ten years.

"I love you, Mal," Jake says.

Mallory closes her eyes, too overcome to say anything back.

When she opens her eyes, he's gone.

Summer #28: 2020

Ursula de Gournsey has a weeklong campaign stop in St. Louis. Every speech is followed by a reception where they serve fried ravioli, Imo's Pizza, gooey butter cake, and Ted Drewes frozen custard.

Jake is with the campaign in a suite at the Hyatt Regency when he receives the call from Lincoln Dooley.

He hangs up the phone and sits down on the bed that he and Ursula are supposed to be sleeping in, although sleep these days is done mostly on airplanes and in the car. He feels like he's falling. He's been pushed off a building. He's a coin flipped carelessly into a bottomless well. There's air rushing in his ears. Vertigo. He deals daily with the loss of Mallory, but he reminds himself that it's only temporary. They may see each other as soon as next September if Ursula loses.

Ursula, he knows, isn't going to lose.

But now, suddenly, that has no bearing on his life—win, lose, elected, reelected; it doesn't matter. The melanoma came back, metastasized to her brain. Link has called hospice. Mallory is dying.

Jake tries to remember how she looked when he saw her the summer before.

Beautiful. She looked beautiful. She looked like Mallory.

Her eyes had been blue.

Jake enters the suite's sitting room, St. Louis command central, where Ursula is meeting with her young staffers—one of whom is Avery Silver, Hank Silver's oldest daughter, the squash champion—and the UDG campaign manager, Kasie Smith. Ursula met Kasie at a charity event sponsored by *Western Michigan Woman* magazine and hired her on the spot.

We do well together, Ursula said. *She gets me.* Jake remembers that these were the exact phrases Ursula used to describe her relationship with Anders; it's her highest praise. Jake likes Kasie very much. She's smart and focused like Ursula, direct and poised like Ursula—and warm and empathetic, qualities that she's trying to teach Ursula. Kasie is now the most important person in Ursula's life, in all of their lives.

Around Kasie and the staff, Jake works hard to come across as the consummate supportive spouse, but now, his voice is sharp. "Ursula, I need to talk to you."

Ursula is reading something. She doesn't look up.

"Ursula," Jake says.

"Ursula," Kasie prompts, and Ursula puts a finger down to mark her place. Kasie's voice is the only one that can penetrate Ursula's concentration these days.

"What is it?" Ursula asks.

Jake nods toward the bedroom.

The bubble over her head says, *This had better be important.* She follows Jake into the other room. He closes the door.

"I got a phone call just now," he says. "From Mallory

Blessing's son. Mallory has cancer, it's metastasized to her brain, and they've called hospice."

"Oh no," Ursula says. "Jake, I'm so—"

"I'm going to Nantucket tomorrow."

"You can't leave tomorrow."

"St. Louis isn't going anywhere."

"We have three events plus the health-care symposium that *you're* moderating. It's a can't-miss thing."

"Nothing is a can't-miss thing," he says. "Get some perspective, Ursula."

"Jake."

"Fine," he says. "I'll go Saturday."

Later that afternoon, Jake goes into his hotel room and puts the DO NOT DISTURB sign up. He sits at the desk and tries to work on talking points for the symposium, but he has a difficult time concentrating. There's a tentative knock at the door. Jake is sure it's Avery Silver. He's assigned her a top-secret task.

But the person Jake finds is his daughter, Bess. She's wearing a dress, heels, pearls, looking so much like a younger version of Ursula, it's spooky. Bess is working on the campaign this summer, reaching out to Generation Z voters. "Hi, honey," Jake says.

"Please take me with you to Nantucket," Bess says.

Jake flinches. "What? Did your mom—"

"She told me you're going to say goodbye to a sick friend."

Jake closes his eyes. Ursula can't keep her fingerprints off anything he does. She just *has* to be in control.

"Yes," Jake says. "It's delicate stuff and not anything you want to be a part of, trust me."

"Please, Dad," Bess says. "I have to get out of here, even if it's only for a couple days."

"I understand. But, honey, this isn't a vacation…"

"I'll let you do your thing, I promise," Bess says. "I just need a break from the meetings and the strategizing and the canvassing. It's a brain-squeeze. I want to get outside. If I could see the ocean, even for a couple of minutes—" She breaks off and gives him an assessing look. "Besides, Mom says you're going to be sad. And I don't want you to be alone."

After his phone conversation with Jake McCloud— Jake McCloud!—Link has questions. He sits at his mother's bedside Googling Jake McCloud. In every single photograph, Jake is with Ursula de Gournsey. And then Link reads about him on Wikipedia.

…*graduated from Johns Hopkins University*…

Aha! Link thinks. Maybe he knows Uncle Coop? But that still doesn't quite explain it. Why would *his* be the number in an envelope in the sticky drawer?

"Mom?" Link says when Mallory's eyelids flutter. He doesn't like forcing her awake but he needs answers while she's still somewhat cogent. "Listen, I called that number and Jake McCloud answered."

Mallory's eyes open.

"He said for you to hold on," Link says. "He told me he's coming."

A single tear drips from the corner of Mallory's eye. Link wipes it with his thumb.

"Mom?" Link says, but her eyes have closed.

Apple stops by the next day. She reads to Mallory from *The English Patient* for a while; it's not a cheerful book by any means, but it's Mallory's favorite. Then Apple starts talking about their old Summer House– waitressing days—*Hokey Pokeys, Ollie's dollies*—and

Link hears his mother laughing. She seems better. Is she getting better?

Uncle Cooper flies in from DC and he and Link both talk with Sabina, RN case manager. Sabina tells them that watching a loved one "transition" can be painful and draining.

"Make sure you take care of yourselves," Sabina says. "Fill your cup. Do things that comfort you and sustain you so that you can be whole and present for Mallory." She pauses. "She probably has several more days."

Several more days means five or six, maybe even a week. Which means this time next week...what? Mallory will be dead? How is Link supposed to process that?

After talking to Sabina, Cooper and Link take a walk down the beach. It's warm and sunny, one of the first beautiful days of the summer. Link can see people gathering down at Fat Ladies with their brightly colored umbrellas and their coolers, so they walk in the other direction.

Coop says, "You will never be alone. For the rest of your life, I've got you, man. And your dad will be there too, of course. But even together, we aren't going to be able to replace your mom." Coop clears his throat. "Have you contacted Leland?"

"I wasn't sure I should. Mom hasn't spoken to Leland since I was in ninth grade."

"I'll get ahold of her," Coop says.

"Mom asked me to call the number in this envelope that was tucked away in her desk drawer and I did, and you're never going to guess who answered."

Coop kicks at the sand. "Oh, I bet I can guess," he says.

*   *   *

The door opens and Link, her beautiful, sweet, strong boy, says, "Mama, are you up for visitors?"

He doesn't wait for an answer. He just lets them in, one by one.

Cooper.

Fray.

Leland.

Jake.

Everything is okay, she thinks. They're around the harvest table, their faces glowing from the flame of one votive candle. Cat Stevens is on the stereo: *I'm looking for a hard headed woman.*

Everything is still okay.

Cooper is overcome; she can see that. She feels guilty about leaving him like this; first their parents, now her. She hopes he finds someone new, someone who will stay. He kisses her forehead.

She says, "In my next life, I'm going to be cool like you."

"I hate to tell you this, sis," he says, his voice breaking, "but you're already cool."

"Now you're lying."

"I love you, Mal," he says, and then he disappears out the bedroom door.

Fray is next. He roams the room, hands stuffed into the pockets of his very expensive jeans. He's jittery; too much caffeine, probably. All that coffee.

"Mal," he says. "Come on, Mal." His voice is pleading, as though she has the power to change what's happening here.

"Thank you," she says. It's funny, right? Peculiar funny and *funny*-funny that they got drunk at Cooper's second wedding and Fray eased up her ballet-slipper-silk sheath and in that impulsive moment, a lark for both of them, she ended up with the greatest treasure of her life. Their son.

He kisses her cheek and then he too goes out the door.

Leland takes Mallory's hand. Mallory is furious with Leland; she wants to scream. She still has one last fight in her. What she says is "Hi, Lee."

She doesn't say: *You are my best friend, the best friend of my life.*

She doesn't say: *I need you to keep an eye on Link. Please, Lee, fill my shoes. You, Apple, Anna. He's going to need all three of you.*

She doesn't say: *Go win Fifi back. You can do it. You deserve to be happy.*

"Are you angry?" Leland asks.

There are so many reasons to be angry: the duck confit and lamb shank, brunch at the Elephant and Castle, the rooftop thing at Harrison's, "suggestible...a follower," *Leland's Letter*.

"Disappointed," Mallory says, and after a beat, Mallory and Leland grin like the crazy girls they were on Deepdene Road.

Leland bends down and squeezes Mallory so tight that it hurts and then she, too, leaves the room.

How had Jake described it so long ago? *The dog that chased the cat that chased the rat.*

Everything is still okay.

Jake is there. He's there! Mallory can smell the browned butter sizzling in the pan before he makes the omelets. She can see him standing on Tuckernuck, their provisions at his feet, wondering if Mallory is ever going to pick him up or if he's supposed to know where to walk, how to find her. She can hear him reading his fortune aloud: *Practice makes perfect.*

Between the sheets, she says.

"Are you going to leave too?" Mallory asks.

"No," Jake says, and he pulls the chair right up next to her. "If it's okay with you, I think I'll stay."

Let's go back a few days to St. Louis and the top-secret task Jake assigned to Avery Silver.

An acoustic guitar? Avery thought. *Where am I going to find an acoustic guitar?* But St. Louis was a Mississippi River town and therefore a music town. Avery used her personal assistant, Google, and in less than five minutes she had rented a Yamaha Dreadnought-whatever-whatever-whatever for a hundred and five bucks for the week and guess what—the place delivered.

Now Jake pulls the guitar out of its case and slides the strap over his head and shoulder. Mallory makes a noise. He looks over. She's laughing.

"No," she says. "Are you..."

"Yes," he says, sounding way more confident than he feels. He had to double-check the chord progression, but once he saw it, everything came flooding back. Jake closes his eyes, and suddenly, he's a college senior again, sitting on the end of Cooper Blessing's bed with the phone next to him and Mallory on the other end of the line, waiting to hear if he's any good.

He's far more nervous now than he was then.

He strums the D-minor chord, then G, then C. It sounds okay.

He whispers, "This is for you, Mal. My hardheaded woman."

And he begins to sing.

While all the adults are with his mother, Link steps out back to get some air. He takes in the vista: the pond, the rugosa rose, the flash of amethyst irises through the reeds, the swans paddling side by side like a long-married couple. Nantucket Island in June.

Mallory wants her ashes scattered on the pond. The ocean, she fears, will carry her away, and she wants to stay right here.

Suddenly, Link startles; he's just seen, sitting in the passenger side of one of the rental Jeeps in the driveway, a girl with dark hair and deep brown eyes. She has the car window down and is unabashedly staring at him. Link stands up a little straighter. He strides over. "Sorry, I just saw you there. I'm Lincoln Dooley."

"Bess McCloud," she says. "I'm Jake's daughter. It's nice to meet you."

"Okay," Link says. "Wow."

Bess eyes his T-shirt. "Do you go to South Carolina?"

"I just finished my sophomore year," he says.

"I just finished mine too," she says. "I go to Johns Hopkins. What's your major?"

He's afraid to tell her it's political science. That would be weird, right? When her mother is running for president?

He shrugs. "Political science."

"Hey!" she says. "Mine too!" She gazes past him, at the ocean. "I've been stuck with my parents in hotels and conference centers for weeks. Do you think it would be okay if I walked down to the beach? Is there a path?"

Link opens the Jeep door and offers Bess McCloud his hand. What did Sabina tell him? *Fill your cup.*

"There is," he says. "Come on, I'll show you."

Acknowledgments

Let me start with a story. As many of you know, I write two novels a year and I'm the mother of three. I also do over forty speaking engagements and book signings per year. Back in October 2019, I was on tour promoting *What Happens in Paradise*. It was a "short tour"—nine events in eight days. I had two events to do in Houston on the same day, the first of which was an eight a.m. talk to a book group in a private home. I arrived in Houston from St. Louis at one in the morning, and I'm not going to lie: I considered canceling, not only because I wanted to sleep but because, while I was on that tour, I was also finishing this book. I texted the organizer of the book group and she told me that there were two women who were driving to Houston from Rockport, Texas—nearly four hours away—just to see me. Now, listen, I'm neither a saint nor a hero, but on hearing this, I decided I couldn't cancel.

The women's names were Sabina Diebel and Gloria Rodriguez. Sabina Diebel was an RN hospice case manager. When I spoke to her, she told me that she'd had to take time off work to come to the book group but that her supervisor had been excited for her to "fill her cup." Hospice care is so emotionally draining that it's important for caregivers to do the things in their free time that bring them joy. All of this went immediately into the book, as you know. Thank you, Sabina, and thank you, Gloria, for making the drive. The book is better because of you.

To all of my readers who have made sacrifices to meet me in person—driving long distances (one man in St. Louis drove his mother five hours to see me!) and getting babysitters and missing other commitments—thank you. I'm humbled and honored. Meeting you is what fills *my* cup.

I'll do things a little backward for this book and thank my children next. So much of this novel is about parenting, and I used my sons, Maxx and Dawson Cunningham, as models for Link, and my daughter, Shelby Cunningham, as the inspiration for Bess. Years ago, Maxx actually did hit three consecutive home runs in Cooperstown after a mediocre Little League career at the plate. I remember saying at the time, "This is such a great story. I should put it in a book, but no one would ever believe it." Maxx, Dawson, and Shelby are now old—two of them adults—and they are my best friends (or two of the three of them are on any given day!). You guys: I love you. Thank you for being patient with the demands of my career—I'm trying to make you as proud of me as I am of the three of you.

This novel owes an enormous debt to the playwright Bernard Slade, who died on the day I completed the first draft. His play *Same Time, Next Year,* beloved by so many, is this book's emotional touchstone.

Thank you to West Riggs who, as ever, served as my sailing consultant, and also to Donna Kelly from the Newport Ladies Book Group for the racer-cruiser!

A shout-out to the truly inspirational cookbook author Sarah Leah Chase, whose dishes appear throughout this novel. She has been my culinary guiding light since I took a cooking class with her in 1995. Her *Nantucket Open-House Cookbook* is everything I love about my island on a hand-painted platter.

This is the last novel I'll be doing with my brilliant editor Reagan Arthur. (She recently became the publisher at Alfred A. Knopf.) Although I will miss Reagan beyond anyone's comprehension, I know I will be fine, because over the course of the twenty books I did with her, Reagan taught me to believe in myself. She always said, "You make it look easy." Ha! No, it was never easy, but it was *easier*—and fulfilling and meaningful—because I had Reagan Arthur's sensibility and clear-eyed intelligence to guide me.

To my agents, Michael Carlisle and David Forrer of InkWell Management: Thank you for taking such good care of me. You are the finest in the business and I love you forever.

To all of my beloveds at Little, Brown: Mario Pulice, Ashley Marudas, Craig Young, Karen Torres, Terry Adams, Michael Pietsch, Brandon Kelley, and my remarkable publicist, Katharine Myers—thank you for all the hours you dedicate to my novels and for making the ride so much fun. Copyediting is not a glamorous job but it is a vital one, and a big, gooey thank-you with hugs and rainbows goes to Jayne Yaffe Kemp and Tracy Roe (they may edit this out later, who knows).

And to my home team. What would life be without you? Thank you to Rebecca Bartlett, Wendy Rouillard, Wendy Hudson, Debbie Briggs (who named nearly every character in this book; it's her superpower), Chuck and Margie Marino, Liz and Beau

Almodobar, "the Beehive"—Linda Holliday, Sue De-coste, Melissa Long, Jeannie Esti (who gave me the Triscuit line and didn't ask for a commission), Deb Ramsdell, Deb Gfeller, and my darling Katie Norton, who defied Dunbar's number—Manda Riggs, David Rattner and Andrew Law, Evelyn and Matthew MacEachern, Holly and Marty McGowan, Helaina Jones, Heidi Holdgate, Kristen Holdgate, Shelly and Roy Weedon, John and Martha Sargent, Jodi Picoult, Curtis Sittenfeld, Meg Mitchell Moore, and Sarah Dessen. And thank you to Michelle Birmingham, Ali Barone, and Christina Schwefel for giving me the best part of my day.

Thank you to my family: Sally Hilderbrand, Eric and Lisa Hilderbrand, Randy and Steph Osteen, Douglas and Jennifer Hilderbrand, Todd Thorpe, and the one person I would never want to live this life without—you guessed it, my sister and very best friend, Heather Osteen Thorpe. Everyone should have a Heather.

My family lost a special woman this year in Judith Hilderbrand Thurman, my stepmother, who intro-duced me to the beaches of Cape Cod over forty years ago. Like Kitty Blessing, Judy had a lot of rules, as my siblings will confirm, and all of them have served us well. The loss is immeasurable; her legacy will last for generations.

Thank you, Timothy Field. There's too much to say here; just please know I'm grateful for you every day.

Like Mallory, I moved to Nantucket in the summer of 1993, and I too came from New York City, although under vastly different circumstances. As I enter my twenty-eighth summer here, I would like to thank

Nantucket for being such a consistently alluring muse. I am at peace only when I'm home.

In closing, I would like to say a few words about the novelist Dorothea Benton Frank, whom the world lost in September 2019. Writing is, by its nature, a solitary job, and it took me a long time to become friends with other authors. I now enjoy friendships with Nancy Thayer, Adriana Trigiani, Jennifer Weiner, Jane Green, Jamie Brenner, and Beatriz Williams, among others. Dottie and I were the best of friends. I loved her instantly and completely. She was not only a charming and brilliant novelist but also the craziest, funniest, most delightful human being—generous and kind and wickedly irreverent. Losing her was a stunning blow and I feel it every single day. If you haven't read a Dorothea Benton Frank novel, I implore you to do it now. Her last novel, *Queen Bee,* was my favorite among a host of favorites. I send my love and my eternal devotion to her family—Peter, Will, Victoria. Dottie's voice will live on forever, and it is with the humblest broken heart that I offer you this book in her memory. XO

About the Author

Elin Hilderbrand spent her first summer on Nantucket Island in 1993 and has lived there year-round for twenty-seven years. She's the mother of three, an enthusiastic home cook, and a seven-year breast cancer survivor. *28 Summers* is her twenty-fifth novel.

Keep reading for an excerpt from Hilderbrand's next novel, *Golden Girl*.

Martha

She receives a message from the front office: A new soul is about to join them, and this soul has been assigned to Martha.

Martha puts on her reading glasses and finds her clipboard. The soul is arriving from…Nantucket Island.

Martha is both surprised and delighted. Surprised because Nantucket Harbor is where Martha met her own fateful end two summers ago. She thought the front office was intentionally keeping her away from coastal areas so she didn't become (as Gen Z said) "triggered."

And Martha is delighted because…well, who doesn't love Nantucket?

Martha swoops down from the northeast, so her first glimpse of the island is the lighthouse that stands sentry at the end of the slender golden arm of Great Point. Martha spies seals frolicking just off the coast (and sharks stalking a little farther out). She continues over Polpis Harbor, where the twelve-year-old class of Nantucket Community Sailing is taking lessons in Optis. One boat keels *way* over and comes dangerously close to capsizing. Martha blows a little puff of air—and the boat rights itself.

Martha dips over the moors, dotted with ponds and crisscrossed by sandy roads. She sees deer hiding deep in the woods. A Jeep is stuck in the soft sand by Jewel Pond. Next to the Jeep, a young man lets fly a stream of swears (*My, oh, my,* Martha thinks) while his girlfriend tries to get a cell signal. She's sorry, she says, she just really wanted the early morning light for her Instagram photos.

Martha chooses the scenic coastal route along the uninterrupted stretch of the south shore. Despite the early hour, there are plenty of people out and about. A woman of a certain age throws a tennis ball into the rolling waves for a chocolate Lab of a certain age. (Martha misses dogs! She's far too busy to ever make it over to the Pet Division.) A white-haired gentleman charges into the water for his morning swim. There are a handful of fishermen out on Smith's Point, a cadre of young (and *very* attractive) surfers at Cisco, and a foursome—*thwack!*—teeing off from the first hole at the Miacomet Golf Club.

As Martha floats over Nobadeer Beach, she sees the town lifeguards gathering in the parking lot. Their conditioning session starts at quarter past seven, and it's nearly that time now. Martha has to hurry.

She has one more minute to appreciate the island on this clear blue morning of Saturday, June 19. The sun glints off the gold cupola atop the Unitarian church, and a line chef at Black-Eyed Susan's runs full speed down India Street, late for his shift. Across the island, irrigation systems switch on, sprinkling lawns and flower boxes, except for out in Sconset, where residents like to do things the old-fashioned way: They don gardening clogs and grab a watering can. People are pouring their first cup of coffee, reading the front page of the *Nantucket Standard*. The thirty-five women who will be getting married today open their eyes and experience varying degrees of anticipation and anxiety. Contractors pull into Marine Home Center because they have punch lists that need to be completed *yesterday;* the summer people are arriving, they want their homes up and running. Charter fishing boats motor out of the harbor; the first batch of sugar doughnuts is pulled from the oven at the Downyflake—and oh, the aroma!

Martha sighs. Nantucket isn't heaven, but it is heaven on earth.

However, she isn't here to sightsee. She's here to collect her soul. The pinned location on Martha's map is Kingsley Road, almost at the intersection of Madaket, but not quite.

Martha arrives with a full thirty seconds to spare, which gives her a chance to inhale the heady fragrance of the lilacs that are in full bloom below. There's a dark-haired woman with fantastic legs jogging down the road, singing along to her music, but the rest of Kingsley is quite sleepy.

Fifteen seconds, ten seconds, five seconds. Martha double-checks her coordinates; it says she's in the right place…

In the time that Martha takes her gaze off the road, tragedy strikes. It happens quickly, the literal blink of an eye. Martha winces. *What a pity!*

All right, Martha thinks. *It's time to get to work.*

Vivi

It's a beautiful June day, the kind that Vivi writes about. In fact, all thirteen of Vivian Howe's novels—beach reads set on Nantucket—start in June. Vivi has never considered changing this habit, because June on Nantucket is when things *begin*. The summer is a newborn; it's still innocent, pristine, a blank page.

At a few minutes past seven, Vivi is ready for her run. Since her divorce ten years earlier, when she moved into Money Pit, she has taken the same route: down her dirt road, Kingsley, to the Madaket Road bike path. The path goes all the way to the beach, though Vivi hasn't made it that far in years. Her hips. And also, she doesn't have time.

Vivi is agitated (!!!) despite the sunshine, the bluebird sky, and the luscious bloom of the peonies in her cutting garden. The night before, Vivi's daughter Willa had called to say that she's pregnant again. This marked Willa's fourth pregnancy since last June, which was when she and Rip got married.

"Oh, Willie!" Vivi said. "Yay, hurray, good, good news! How far along are you?"

"Six weeks," Willa said.

Still very, very early, Vivi thinks. Willa basically *just* missed her period.

"You took a test?"

"Yes, Mother."

"More than one?"

"Two," Willa said. "The first was indecisive. The second had two lines."

What Vivi did *not* say was *Don't get your hopes up.* Willa had miscarried three times. The first pregnancy had progressed to fifteen weeks. Willa started bleeding while she was giving a tour of the Hadwen House to a group of VIPs from the governor's office. She ran out on the tour and drove herself to the hospital. It was a horrible day, the most physically painful and difficult of the three miscarriages. After the third, Willa became convinced there was a problem.

A thorough examination at the Brigham and Women's fertility clinic in Boston, however, showed nothing wrong. Willa was a healthy twenty-four-year-old. She had no problem getting pregnant. When Rip looked at her, they conceived.

Privately, Vivi suspected the miscarriages had something to do with Willa's type A personality, which Vivi and her ex-husband, JP, used to call her "type A-plus personality" because regular As were never good enough for Willa.

"If this doesn't work out, why don't you and Rip take a break? You're so young. You have years and years, decades, even, to conceive. What's the *rush?*"

Predictably, Willa had become defensive. "What makes you think this won't work out? Do you think I'm a failure?"

"You succeed at everything you do," Vivi said. "I just think your body might benefit from a reset…"

"I'm *pregnant,* Mama," Willa said. "I will give birth

to a perfectly healthy baby." (She sounded like she was trying to convince herself.)

"You *will* give birth to a perfectly healthy baby, Willie. I can't wait to hold her." Though Vivi didn't feel quite old enough to be a grandmother. She was only fifty-one, and in terrific shape, if she did say so. Her dark hair, which she wore in a pixie cut, didn't have one strand of gray. (Vivi checked every morning.) She might be occasionally mistaken for the child's mother. (Well, she could hope.)

The conversation had ended there, but for Vivi, an unsettled feeling lingered through the night. *Are children ever punished for the mistakes of their parents?* she wondered, *or was that just her novelist's mind at work?*

Vivi had woken up at five thirty, not only because it was June and sunlight streamed in through the windows like it was high noon, but also because she heard a noise. When she crept out into the hallway, she saw her daughter Carson stumbling up the stairs, smelling distinctly of marijuana.

Vivi had last seen Carson the afternoon before, dressed for work in cutoff jeans and her marigold-yellow Oystercatcher T-shirt, her dark hair still a little damp, neat in two French braids. Carson was the most attractive of Vivi's three children, though of course Vivi wasn't supposed to think that. Carson alone favored JP—the dark hair, the clear glass-green eyes, the fine pointed nose, and teeth that came in white, straight, and even. She was a Quinboro through and through, whereas both Willa and Leo favored the Howes. They'd inherited Vivi's overbite and crowded lowers and had spent years in braces.

Carson was still in her cutoffs, but she had down-graded her T-shirt to something that looked like a silver-mesh handkerchief that just barely covered her breasts and left her midriff and back bare except for one slender chain. She was barefoot; her hair was out of its braids but held kinky waves. When she saw her mother standing at the top of the stairs, her eyebrows shot up.

"Madre," she said. "What's good."

"Are you just getting home?" Vivi asked, though the answer was obvious. Carson was walking in at five thirty in the morning, when her work shift had ended at eleven. She was twenty-one, fine, so she'd had a drink at work, and she probably went to the Chicken Box to catch the band's last set, then either to the beach with friends or she hooked up with a random stranger.

"Yes, ma'am." Carson sounded sober, but that only served to make Vivi angrier.

"The summer isn't going to be like this, Carson," Vivi said.

"I hope you're right," Carson said. "Work was slow, my tips were trash, the guys at the Box all looked like they were on the junior high school fencing team."

"You can't stay out all night, then come home reeking of marijuana…"

"*Reeking of marijuana…,*" Carson mimicked.

Vivi searched for extra patience, which was like trying to find a lost shoe in the depths of her maternal closet. *This is Carson.* Ten years earlier, when Vivi learned that her husband had fallen in love with his employee Amy, Vivi moved out. The three kids took it hard—but especially Carson. Carson had been eleven years old and was unusually attached to Vivi. Vivian's novel that year, *Along the South Shore,* had been something of a breakout book, and Vivi, wanting to escape the inevitable divorce fallout—people asking "what happened," people asking "was she okay," people telling her she was "brave"—had gone on a twenty-nine-stop book tour that kept her away for seven weeks (and she'd missed the first day of school and Carson's birthday). By the time Vivi got back, Carson had changed from the funny little spitfire of the family to a "troubled child" who threw tantrums, swore, picked fistfights with her siblings, and generally did everything in her power to get attention. Vivi blamed the transformation on JP's affair (which their couples therapist insisted they not disclose to the children), and JP blamed it on what he called Vivi's "abandonment."

Ten years had passed. Carson was no longer a little girl, but she still had her challenging moments.

"This is my house," Vivi said. "I pay the mortgage, the taxes, the insurance, the electric bill, the heating bill, the cable bill. I do the shopping and make the meals. While you're sleeping under this roof, I don't want you out all night, drinking, smoking, and having sex with complete strangers. Do you know how that *looks*?" Vivi stopped just short of reminding Carson that they'd already battled chlamydia once, the previous summer. "You're setting a rotten example for your brother."

"He doesn't need me to set an example," Carson said. "He has Willa. I'm the screwup. It's my job to be a hideous disappointment."

"No one said you were a hideous disappointment, sweetheart."

"I'm twenty-one," Carson said. "I can drink legally, I can smoke pot legally."

"Since you're so grown up," Vivi said, "you can move out on your own."

"That's the plan," Carson said. "I'm saving."

You're not *saving,* Vivi wanted to say. Carson made good tips at the Oystercatcher, but she spent them—on drinks, on weed, on clothes from Erica Wilson, Milly & Grace, and the Lovely. Carson had finally dropped out of UVM after struggling through five semesters— her cumulative GPA was a 1.6—and whereas Vivi was initially aghast (an education makes you good company for yourself!), she knew college wasn't for everyone.

"I'm not giving you a curfew," Vivi said. "But this behavior won't be tolerated."

"This behavior won't be tolerated," Carson mimicked. It was the response of a seven-year-old, and yet it brought the reaction Carson wanted. Vivi took a step toward her, arm tensed.

"Are you going to spank me?"

"Of course not," Vivi said, though she kind of wanted to. "But you have to clean up your act, babe, or I'll ask you to leave."

"Fine," Carson said. "I'll go to Dad's."

"I'm sure Amy would take *very kindly* to you coming home like this."

"She's not as bad as you think," Carson said. "When you demonize her, you show how insecure you are."

Vivi stared at her child, but before she could come up with a response, she smelled something.

"Did you…cook?" Vivi asked.

Carson stepped into the bedroom, slamming the door behind her.

Vivi flew down the stairs to the kitchen, which was filling with black smoke. Vivi's brand new All-Clad three-quart sauté pan was on a lit burner. The sausage-and-basil pasta from last night's dinner. Vivi turned the burner off, grabbed a towel, and carried the smoldering pan outside, where she set it on the flagstone path. The bottom of the pan was charred black. It was so hot, it would have scorched the deck or the lawn.

Brand-new pan, ruined.

The sausage-and-basil pasta in a luscious mustard-cream sauce, which Vivi had been thinking of taking over to Willa's as a peace offering, ruined.

And what if Vivi hadn't gotten out of bed? What if the kitchen had caught on fire, what if flames had engulfed Money Pit while Vivi—and Leo—were sleeping? They could all be dead!

Back in the kitchen, Vivi caught sight of her bottle of Casa Dragones tequila on the side counter, along with a shot glass. She felt a formidable strain of fury brewing inside her. That tequila was *hers;* she wouldn't even let her (almost ex-) boyfriend, Dennis, make margaritas with it. Carson had come home, put the pasta on over a burner, done two—or three?—shots of *Vivi's* tequila, which Carson knew was *not for public consumption,* and then she left the pasta to burn on the stove.

Vivi marched back up the stairs and pounded on Carson's locked door.

"You left the pan on an open flame!" Vivi said. Leo would definitely be awake now, which Vivi felt bad about on a Saturday morning, but oh, well. "What is *wrong* with you, Carson? Do you honestly not think about *anyone* but yourself? Do you not think, period?" There was no response. Vivi kicked the door.

"Please go away" came the response from inside. "I'm trying to sleep."

"And you drank my tequila!" Vivi said. "Which you know is off-limits. You did that just to infuriate me."

"I didn't drink the tequila," Carson said. "I haven't

had a drink since I left the Chicken Box, and that was hours ago."

Vivi blinked. Carson sounded like she was telling the truth, and she had seemed sober. "Who drank it, then?"

There was a pause before Carson said, "Well, who else lives here?"

Leo? Vivi thought. She looked at Leo's bedroom door, which was shut tight. Leo had been going to high school parties since he was a sophomore, but a run-in with Jägermeister had propelled him away from the hard stuff. He drank Bud Light, and the occasional White Claw.

Vivi turned back to Carson's door. "You are scrubbing that pot, young lady," she said. "Or buying me a new one."

After Vivi poured herself some coffee, opened all the windows, turned both sailcloth ceiling fans to high, washed the shot glass, and hid what remained of the Casa Dragones in the laundry room (her kids would never find it there), she calmed down a bit. She was the mother of three *very young adults,* and parenting very young adults required just as much patience as parenting very young children. No one ever talked about this; it felt like a dirty little secret. Vivi had always imagined that by the time her kids were twenty-four, twenty-one, and eighteen, they'd all be drinking wine together around the outdoor table by the pool, and the kids would be cooking, clearing, and giving Vivi sage investment advice. *Ha.*

Vivi ties up her running shoes and stretches her hamstrings, using the bumper of her Jeep—then she clicks on her iTunes and takes off.